THE BELLAMY

BY FRANCES NOYES HART

FRONT PAGE MYSTERY SERIES

First Published 1927

Republished 2023

TO
MY FAVOURITE LAWYER
EDWARD HENRY HART

THE BELLAMY TRIAL

The Judge
Anthony Bristed Carver

The Prosecutor   *Counsel for the Defense*
Daniel Farr   Dudley Lambert

The Defendants
Susan Ives
Stephen Bellamy

FIRST DAY

Opening speech for the prosecution

SECOND DAY

Mr. Herbert Conroy, *real estate agent*Dr. Paul Stanley, *physician*Miss Kathleen Page, *governess*

THIRD DAY

Mr. Douglas Thorne, *Susan Ives's brother*Miss Flora Biggs, *Mimi Bellamy's schoolmate*Mrs. Daniel Ives, *Susan Ives's mother-in-law*Mr. Elliot Farwell, *Mimi Bellamy's ex-fiancé*Mr. George Dallas, *Mr. Farwell's friend*

FOURTH DAY

Miss Melanie Cordier, *waitress*Miss Laura Roberts, *lady's maid*Mr. Luigi Orsini, *handy man*Mr. Joseph Turner, *bus driver*Sergeant Hendrick Johnson, *state trooper*

FIFTH DAY

Opening speech for defenceMrs. Adolph Platz, *wife of chauffeur*Mrs. Timothy Shea, *landlady*Mr. Stephen BellamyDr. Gabriel Barretti, *finger-print expert*

SIXTH DAY

Mr. Leo Fox, *mechanician*Mr. Patrick Ives, *Susan Ives's husband*Susan Ives

SEVENTH DAY

THE BELLAMY TRIAL

CHAPTER I

The red-headed girl sank into the seat in the middle of the first row with a gasp of relief. Sixth seat from the aisle—yes, that was right; the label on the arm of the golden-oak chair stared up at her reassuringly. Row A, seat 15, Philadelphia *Planet*. The ones on either side of her were empty. Well, it was a relief to know that there were four feet of space left unoccupied in Redfield, even if only temporarily. She was still shaken into breathless stupor by the pandemonium in the corridors outside—the rattling of regiments of typewriters, of armies of tickers, the shouts of infuriated denizens of telephone booths, the hurrying, frantic faces of officials, the scurrying and scampering of dozens of rusty-haired freckled-faced insubordinate small boys, whose olive-drab messenger uniforms alone saved them from extermination; the newspaper men—you could spot them at once, looking exhausted and alert and elaborately bored; the newspaper women, keen and purposeful and diverted; and above and around and below all these licensed inhabitants, the crowd—a vast, jostling, lunging beast, with one supreme motive galvanizing it to action—an immense, a devouring curiosity that sent it surging time and time again against the closed glass doors with their blue-coated guardians, fragile barriers between it and the consummation of its desire. For just beyond those doors lay the arena where the beast might slake its hunger at will, and it was not taking its frustration of that privilege amiably.

The red-headed girl set her little black-feathered hat straight with unsteady fingers. She wasn't going to forget that crowd in a hurry. It had growled at her— actually growled—when she'd fought her way through it, armed with the magic of the little blue ticket that spelled open sesame as well as press section. Who could have believed that even curiosity would turn nice old gray-headed ladies and mild-looking gentlemen with brown moustaches and fat matrons with leather bags and thin flappers with batik scarfs into one huge ravenous beast? She panted again, reminiscently, at the thought of the way they'd shoved and squashed and kneaded—and then settled down to gratified inspection.

So this was a courtroom!

Not a very large or very impressive room, looked at from any angle. It might hold three hundred people at a pinch, and there were, conservatively, about three thousand crowding the corridors and walking the streets of Redfield in their efforts to expand its limits. Fan-shaped, with nine rows of the golden-oak seats packed with grimly triumphant humanity, the first three neatly tagged with the little white labels that metamorphosed them into the press section. Golden-oak

4

panelling half-way up the walls, and then whitewashed plaster—rather dingy, smoky plaster, its defects relentlessly revealed by the pale autumnal sunshine flooding in through the great windows and the dome of many-coloured glass, lavish and heartening enough to compensate for much of the grimness and the grime.

Near enough for the red-headed girl to touch was a low rail, and beyond that rail a little empty space, like a stage—empty of actors, but cluttered with chairs and tables. At the back was a small platform with a great high-backed black leather chair, and a still smaller platform on a slightly lower level, with a rail about it and a much more uncomfortable-looking chair. The judge's seat, the witness box— she gave a little sigh of pure uncontrollable excitement, and a voice next to her said affably:

"Hi! Greetings, stranger, or hail, friend, as the case may be. Can I get by you into the next seat without damaging you and those feet of yours materially?"

The red-headed girl scrambled guiltily to the offending feet unobtrusive enough in themselves, but most obtrusively extended across the narrow passage, and turned a flushed and anxious countenance on her cheerful critic, now engaged in folding himself competently into the exiguous space provided by the golden-oak chair. A tall lanky young man, with a straight nose, mouse-coloured hair, shrewd gray eyes, and an expression that was intended to be that of a hard-boiled cynic, and that worked all right unless he grinned. He wore a shabby tweed suit, a polka-dotted tie, had three very sharp pencils, and a good-sized stack of telegraph blanks clasped to his heart. Obviously a reporter—a real reporter. The red-headed girl attempted to conceal her gold pencil and leather-bound notebook, smiling tentatively and ingratiatingly.

"Covering it for a New York paper?" inquired the Olympian one graciously.

"No," said the red-headed girl humbly; "a Philadelphia one—the Philadelphia *Planet*. Is yours New York?"

"M'm—h'm—*Sphere*. Doing colour stuff?"

"Oh, I hope so," replied the red-headed girl so fervently that the reporter looked somewhat startled. "You see, I don't know whether it will have colour or not. I'm not exactly a regular reporter."

"Oh, you aren't, aren't you? Well, if it's no secret, just exactly what are you? A finger-print expert?"

"I'm a—a writer," said the red-headed girl, looking unusually small and dignified. "This is my first as—assignment." It was frightful to stammer just when you particularly wanted not to.

The real reporter eyed her severely. "A writer, hey? A real, honest-to-goodness, walking-around writer, with a fountain pen and a great big vocabulary and a world of promise and everything? Well, I'll bet you a hot dog to a soup plate of fresh caviar that about four days from now you'll be parading through these marble halls telling the cockeyed world that you're a journalist."

"Oh, I wouldn't dare. Do all of you call yourselves journalists?"

The reporter looked as though he were about to suffocate. "Get this," he said impressively: "The day that you hear me call myself a journalist you have my full and free permission to call me a ———. Well, no, on second thought, a lady couldn't. But if you ever call me a journalist, smile. And if you solemnly swear never to call yourself one I'll show you the ropes a bit, because you're a poor ignorant little writing critter that doesn't know any better than to come to a murder trial—and besides that you have red hair. Want to know anything?"

"Oh," cried the red-headed girl, "I didn't know that anyone so horrid could be so nice. I want to know everything. Let's begin at the beginning."

"Well, in case you don't know where you are, this is the courtroom of Redfield, county seat of Bellechester, twenty-five miles from the great metropolis of New York. And in case you'd like to know what it's all about, it's the greatest murder trial of the century—about every two years another one of 'em comes along. This particular one is the trial of the People versus Susan Ives and Stephen Bellamy for the wilful, deliberate, and malicious murder of Madeleine Bellamy."

"A murder trial," said the red-headed girl softly. "Well, I should think that ought to be about the most tremendous thing in the world."

"Oh, you do, do you?" remarked the reporter, and for a moment it was no effort at all for him to look cynical. "Well, I'll have you called at about seven to-morrow morning, though it's a pity ever to wake anyone up that can have such beautiful dreams as that. The most tremendous thing in the world, says she. Well, well, well!"

The red-headed girl eyed him belligerently. "Well, yourself! Perhaps you'll be good enough to tell me what's more tremendous than murder."

"Oh, you tell me!" urged the reporter persuasively.

"All right, I'll tell you that the only story that you're going to be able to interest every human being in, from the President of the United States to the gentleman who takes away the ashes, is a good murder story. It's the one universal solvent. The old lady from Dubuque will be at it the first thing in the morning, and the young lady from Park Avenue will be at it the last thing at night. And if it's a love story too, you're lucky, because then you've got the combination that every really great writer that ever lived has picked out to wring hearts and freeze the marrow in posterity's bones."

"Oh, come! Aren't you getting just a dash overwrought? Every great writer? What about Wordsworth?"

"Oh, pooh!" said the red-headed girl fiercely. "Wordsworth! What about Sophocles and Euripides and Shakespeare and Browning? Do you know what 'The Ring and the Book' is? It's a murder trial! What's 'Othello' but a murder story? What's 'Hamlet' but five murder stories? What's 'Macbeth'? Or 'The Cenci'? Or 'Lamia'? Or 'Crime and Punishment'? Or 'Carmen'? Or——"

"I give up," said the reporter firmly—"or, no, wait a moment—can it be that they are murder stories? Quite a little reader in your quiet way, aren't you?"

The red-headed girl ignored him sternly. "And do you want me to tell you why it's the most enthralling and absorbing theme in the world? Do you?"

"No," replied the reporter hastily. "Yes—or how shall I put it? Yes and no, let's say."

"It's because it's real," said the red-headed girl, with a sudden startling gravity. "It's the only thing that's absolutely real in the world, I think. Something that makes you reckless enough not to care a tinker's dam for your own life or another's—that's something to think about, isn't it?"

"Well, yes," said the reporter slowly. "Now that you put it that way, that's something to think about."

"It's good for us, too," said the girl, "We're all so everlastingly canny and competent and sophisticated these days, going mechanically through a mechanical world, sharpening up our little emotions, tuning up our little sensations—and suddenly there's a cry of 'Murder!' in the streets, and we stop and look back, shuddering, over our shoulder—and across us falls the shadow of a savage with a bloodstained club, and we know that it's good and dangerous and beautiful to be alive."

"I rather get you," said the reporter thoughtfully. "And, strangely enough, there's just a dash in what you say. It's the same nice, creepy, luxurious feeling that you get when you pull up closer to a good roaring fire with carpet slippers on your feet and a glass of something hot and sweet in your hand and listen to the wind yowling outside and see the rain on the black windowpanes. Nothing in the world to make you feel warm and safe and sheltered and cozy like a good storm or a good murder—what?"

"Nothing in the world," agreed the red-headed girl; and she added pensively, "It's always interested me more than anything else."

"Has it indeed? Well, don't let it get you. I'd just keep it as a hobby if I were you. At your present gait you're going to make some fellow an awfully happy widow one of these days. Are you a good marksman?"

"You think that murder's frightfully amusing, don't you?" The red-headed girl's soft voice had a sudden edge to it.

The real reporter's face changed abruptly. "No, I don't," he said shortly. "I think it's rotten—a dirty, bloody, beastly business that used to keep me awake nights until I grew a shell over my skin and acquired a fairly workable sense of humour to use on all these clowns called human beings. Of course, I'm one of them myself, but I don't boast about it. And if you're suffering from the illusion that nothing shocks me, I'll tell you right now that it shocks me any amount that a scrap of a thing like you, with all that perfectly good red hair and a rather nice arrangement in dimples, should be practically climbing over that rail in your frenzy to find out what it's all about."

"I think that men are the most amusing race in the world," murmured the red-headed girl. "And I think that it's awfully appealing of you to be shocked. But, you see, my grandfather—who was as stern and Scotch and hidebound as anyone that ever breathed—told me when I was fourteen years old that a great murder trial was the most superbly dramatic spectacle that the world afforded. And he ought to have known what he was talking about—he was one of the greatest judges that ever lived."

"Well, maybe they were in his day. And you said Scotch, didn't you? Oh, well, they do it better over there. England, too—bunches of flowers on the clerks' tables and wigs on the judges' heads, and plenty of scarlet and gold, and all the great lawyers in the land taking a whack at it, and never a cross word out of one of them———"

"He used to say that is was like a hunt," interrupted the red-headed girl firmly, "with the judge as master of the hounds and the lawyers as the hounds, baying as they ran hot on the scent, and all the rest of us galloping hard at their heels—jury, spectators, public."

"Sure," said the reporter grimly. "With the quarry waiting, bound and shackled and gagged till they catch up with him and tear him to pieces—it's a great hunt all right, all right!"

"It's not a human being that they're hunting, idiot—it's truth."

"Truth!" The reporter's laugh was loud and long and free enough to cause a dozen heads to turn. "Oh, what you're going to learn before you get out of here! A hunt for truth, is it? Well, now, you get this straight: If that's what you're expecting to find here, you'll save yourself a whole lot of bad minutes by taking the next train back to Philadelphia. Truth! I'm not running down murder trials from the point of view of interest, you understand. A really good one furnishes all the best points of a first-class dog fight and a highly superior cross-word puzzle, and that ought to be enough excitement for anyone. But if you think that the opposing counsel are honestly in pursuit of enlightenment———"

A clear high voice cut through the rustle and clatter like a knife.

"His Honour! His Honour the Court!" There was a mighty rustle of upheaval.

"Who's that?" inquired a breathless voice at the reporter's shoulder.

"That's the tallest and nicest court crier in the United States of America. Name's Ben Potts. Best falsetto voice outside the Russian Orthodox Church. Kindly notice the central hair part and spit curls. And here we have none other than His Honour himself, Judge Anthony Bristed Carver."

"Hear ye! Hear ye! Hear ye!" chanted the court crier. "All those having business before this honourable court draw near, give your attention and you shall be heard!"

The tall figure in flowing black moved deliberately toward the chair on the dais, which immediately assumed the aspect of a throne. Judge Carver's sleek iron-gray head and aquiline face were an adornment to any courtroom. He swept a pair of brilliant deep-set eyes over the room, seated himself, and reached for the gavel in one motion.

"And he'll use it, too, believe you me," murmured the reporter with conviction. "Sternest old guy on the bench."

"Where are the prisoners—where do they come from?"

"The defendants, as they whimsically prefer to be called for the time being, come through that little door to the left of the judge's room; that enormous red-faced, sandy-haired old duffer talking to the thin young man in the tortoise-shell glasses is Mrs. Ives's counsel, Mr. Dudley Lambert; the begoggled one is Mr. Bellamy's counsel, Harrison Clark."

"Where's the prosecutor?"

"Oh, well, Mr. Farr is liable to appear almost anywhere, like Mephistopheles in *Faust* or that baby that so obligingly came out of the everywhere into the here. He's all for the unexpected—Ah, what did I tell you? There he is now, conferring with the judge and the defense counsel."

The red-headed girl leaned forward eagerly. The slender individual, leaning with rather studied ease against the railing that hedged in the majesty of the law, suggested a curious cross between a promising light of Tammany Hall and the youngest and handsomest of the Spanish Inquisitioners. Black hair that deserved the qualification of raven, a pale regular face that missed distinction by a destructive quarter of an inch, narrow blue eyes back of which stirred some restless fire, long slim hands—what was there about him that wasn't just right? Perhaps that dark coat fitted him just a shade too well, or that heavily brocaded tie in peacock blue—Well, at any rate, his slim elegance certainly made Lambert look like an awkward, cross, red-faced baby, for all his thatch of graying hair.

"Here they come!" Even the reporter's level, mocking voice was a trifle tense.

The little door to the left of the judge opened and two people came in, as leisurely and tranquilly as though they were advancing toward easy chairs and a tea table before an open fire. A slight figure in a tan tweed suit, with a soft copper silk handkerchief at her throat and a little felt hat of the same colour pulled down over two wings of pale gold hair, level hazel eyes under level dark brows, and a beautiful mouth, steady-lipped, generous, sensitive—the most beautiful mouth, thought the red-headed girl, that she had ever seen. She crossed the short distance between the door and the chair beside which stood Mr. Lambert with a light, boyish swing. She looked rather like a boy—a gallant, proud little boy, striding forward to receive the victor's laurels. Did murderesses walk like that?

Behind her came Stephen Bellamy, the crape band on his dark coat appallingly conspicuous; only a few inches taller than Sue Ives, with dark hair lightly silvered, and a charming, sensitive, olive-skinned face. As they seated themselves, he flashed the briefest of smiles at his companion—a grave, consoling smile, singularly sweet—then turned an attentive countenance to the judge. Did a murderer smile like that?

The red-headed girl sat staring at them blankly.

"Oh, Lord!" moaned the reporter at her side. "Why did that old jackass Lambert let her come in here in that rig? If he had the sense that God gives a dead duck he'd know that she ought to be wearing something black and frilly and pitiful instead of stamping around in brown leather Oxfords as though she were headed straight for the first tee instead of the electric chair."

"Oh, don't!" The red-headed girl's voice was passionate in its protest. "You don't know what you're talking about. Look, what are they doing now? What's that wheel?"

"That's for choosing the jury; it looks as though they were going to start right now. Yes, they're off; that's the sheriff spinning the wheel. He calls the names——"

"Timothy Forbes!"

A stocky man with a small shrewd eye and a reddish moustache wormed his way forward.

"Number 1! Take your seat in the box."

"Will it take long?" asked the red-headed girl.

"Alexander Petty!"

"Not at this rate," replied the reporter, watching the progress toward the jury box of a tow-headed little man with steel-bowed spectacles and a suit a little shiny at the elbows.

"This is going to be just as rapid as the law allows, I understand. Both sides are rarin' to go, and they're not liable to touch their peremptory challenges; and they're not likely to challenge for cause, either, unless it's a darned good cause."

"Eliphalet Slocum!"

A keen-faced elderly man with a mouth like a steel trap joined the men in the box.

"It's a special panel that they're choosing from," explained the reporter, lowering his voice cautiously as Judge Carver glanced ominously in his direction. "Redfield's pretty up and coming for a place of its size. All the obviously undesirables are weeded out, so it saves an enormous amount of time."

"Cæsar Smith!"

Mr. Smith advanced at a trot, his round, amiable countenance beamingly exposing three gold teeth to the pleased spectators.

"Robert Angostini."

A dark and dapper individual with a silky black moustache slipped quietly by Mr. Smith.

"Number 5, take your place in the box.... George Hobart."

An amiable-looking youth in a brown Norfolk jacket advanced briskly.

"Who's that coming in now?" inquired the red-headed girl in a stealthy whisper.

"Where?"

"In the witnesses' seats—over in the corner by the window. The tall man with the darling little old lady."

The reporter turned his head, his boredom lit by a transient gleam of interest. "That? That's Pat Ives and his mother. She's been subpœnaed by the state as a witness—God knows what for."

"I love them when they wear bonnets," said the red-headed girl. "What's he like?"

"Pat? Well, take a good look at him; that's what he's like."

The red-headed girl obediently took a good look. Black hair, blue eyes, black with pain, set in a haggard, beautiful young face that looked white to the bone, a reckless mouth set in a line of desperation.

"He doesn't look very contented," she commented mildly.

"And his looks don't belie him," the reporter assured her drily. "Young Mr. Ives belongs to the romantic school—you know—the guardsman, the troubadour, the rover, and the lover; the duel by candlelight, the rose in the moonlight, the dice, the devil and boots, saddle, to horse and away. The type that muffs it when he's thrown into a show that deals in the crude realism of spilled kerosene and bloody rags and an Italian labourer's stuffy little front parlour. Mix him up with that and he gets shadows under his eyes and three degrees of fever and bad dreams. Also, he gets a little irritable with reporters."

"Did you interview him?" inquired the red-headed girl in awe-stricken tones.

"Well, that's a nice way of putting it," said the reporter thoughtfully. "I went around to the Ives' house with one or two other scientific spirits on the night after Sue Ives and Bellamy were arrested—June twenty-first, if my memory serves me. We rang the doorbell none too optimistically, and the door opened so suddenly that we practically fell flat on our faces in the front hall. There stood the debonair Mr. Ives, in his shirt sleeves, with as unattractive a look on his face as I've ever seen in my life.

"'Come right in, gentlemen,' says he, and he made that sound unattractive too. 'I'm not mistaken, am I? It's the gentlemen of the press that I'm addressing?' We allowed without too much enthusiasm that such was indeed the case, and in we came. 'Let's get right down to business,' he said. 'None of this absurd delicacy that uses up all your energy,' says he. 'What you gentlemen want to know, I'm sure, is whether I was Madeleine Bellamy's lover and whether my wife was her murderess. That's about it, isn't it?'"

"It was just about it, but somehow, the way he put it, it sounded not so good. 'Well,' said Ives, I'll give you a good straight answer to a good straight question. Get to hell out of here!' says he, and he yanks the front door open so wide that it would have let out an army.

"Just as I was thinking of something really bright to come back with, a nice soft little voice in the back of the hall said, 'Oh, Pat darling, do be careful. You'll wake up the babies. I'm sure that these gentlemen will come back another time,' And Mrs. Daniel Ives trotted up and put one hand on his arm and smiled a nice, worried, polite little smile at us.

"And Pat darling smiled, too, not so everlastingly politely, and said, 'I'm sure they will—I'm sure of it. Four o'clock in the morning's a good time too.' And we decided that was as good a time as any and we went away from there. And here we are. And if you don't look sharp they'll have a jury before you understand why I know that Mr. Ives is the romantic type that lets realism get on his nerves. What number is that heading for the box now?"

"Otto Schultz!"

A cozy white-headed cherub trotted energetically up.

"Number 10, take your place in the box!"

"Josiah Morgan!"

"Gosh, they'll get the whole panel in under an hour!" exulted the reporter. "Look at the fine hatchet face on Morgan, will you? I bet the fellow that tries to sell Josh a lame horse will live to rue the day."

"Charles Stuyvesant!"

Charles Stuyvesant smiled pleasantly at the sheriff, his fine iron-gray head and trim shoulders standing out sharply against his overgroomed and undergroomed comrades in the box.

"Number 12, take your place in the box! You and each of you do solemnly swear that you will well and truly try Stephen Bellamy and Susan Ives, and a true verdict give according to the law and evidence, so help you God?"

Above the grave answering murmur the red-headed girl begged nervously, "What happens now?"

"I don't know—recess, maybe—wait, the judge is addressing the jury."

Judge Carver's deep voice rang out impressively in the still courtroom:

"Gentlemen of the jury, you will now be given the usual admonition—that you are not to discuss this case amongst yourselves, or allow anybody else to discuss it with you, outside your own body. You are not to form or express any opinion about the merits of the controversy. You are to refrain from speaking of it to anybody, or from allowing anybody to speak to you with respect to any aspect of this case. If this occurs you will communicate it to the Court at once. You are to keep your judgment open until the defendants have had their side of the case heard, and, lastly, you are to make up your judgment solely on the law, which is the last thing that you will hear from the Court in its charge. Until then, you will not be able to render a verdict in accordance with the law, and therefore you must suspend judgment until that time. The Court is dismissed for the noon recess. We will reconvene at one o'clock."

The red-headed girl turned eyes round as saucers on the reporter. "Don't they come back till one?"

"They do not."

"What do we do until then?"

"We eat. There's a fair place on the next corner."

The red-headed girl waved it away. "Oh, I couldn't possibly eat—not possibly. It's like the first time I went to the theatre; I was only seven, but I remember it perfectly. I sat spang in the middle of the front row, just like this, and I made my governess take me three quarters of an hour too early, and I sat there getting sicker and sicker from pure excitement, wondering what kind of a new world was behind that curtain—what kind of a strange, beautiful, terrible world. I sat there feeling more frightful every second, and all of a sudden the curtain went up with a jerk and I let out a shriek that made everyone in the theatre and on the stage jump three feet in the air. I feel exactly like that now."

"Well, get hold of yourself. Shrieking isn't popular around here. If you sit right there like a good quiet child I may bring you back an apple. I don't promise anything, but I may."

She was still sitting there when he came back with the apple, crunched up in her chair, staring at the jury box with eyes rounder than ever.

"Isn't it nearly time?" She eyed the apple ungratefully.

"It is. Come on now, eat it, and I'll show you what I've got in my pocket."

"Show?"

"The jury list—names, addresses, ages, professions and all. Two of them are under thirty, three under forty, four under fifty, two under sixty, one sixty-two. Three merchants, two clerks, two farmers, an insurance man, an accountant, a radio expert, a jeweller and a banker. Not a bad list at all, if you ask me. Charles Stuyvesant's the only one that won't have a good clubby time of it. He's one of the richest bankers in New York."

"He looked it," said the red-headed girl. "What will they do when they come back?"

"Well, if they're good, the prosecutor's going to make them a nice little speech."

"Who is the prosecutor? Is he well known?"

"Mr. Daniel Farr is a promising young lad of about forty who is extremely well known in these parts, and if you asked him his own unbiassed opinion of his abilities, he would undoubtedly tell you that with a bit of luck he ought to be President of these United States in the next ten years."

"And what do you think of him?"

"Well, I think that he may be, at that, and I add in passing that I consider that no tribute to the judgment of these United States. He's about as shrewd as they make 'em, but I'm not convinced that he's a very good lawyer. He goes in too much for purple patches and hitting about three inches below the belt for my simple tastes. And he works on the theory that the jury is not quite all there, which may be amply justified but is a little trying for the innocent bystander. He goes in for poetry, too—oh, not Amy Lowell or Ezra Pound, but something along the lines of 'I could not love thee, dear, so much, loved I not honour more,' and 'How dear to my heart are the scenes of my childhood'—you know the kind of thing—deep stuff."

14

"Is he successful?"

"Oh, by all manner of means. Twenty years ago he was caddie master at the Rosemont Country Club; five years before that he was a caddie there. America, my child, is the land of opportunity. He's magnificent when he gets started on the idle rich; it's all right to be rich if you're not idle—or well born. If you're one of those well born society devils, you might just as well go and jump in the lake, if you ask Mr. Farr."

"Does he still live in Rosemont?"

"No, hasn't lived there for nineteen years; but I don't believe that he's forgotten one single snub or tip that he got in the good old days. Every now and then you can see him stop and turn them over in his mind."

"What's Mr. Lambert like?"

"Ah, there is a horse of a different colour—a cart horse of a different colour, if I may go so far. Mr. Dudley Lambert is a lawyer who knows everything that there is to know about wills and trusts and estates, and not another blessed thing in the world. If he's as good now as he was when I heard him in a case two years ago, he's terrible. I can't wait to hear him."

The red-headed girl looked pale. "Oh, then, why did she get him?"

"Ah, thereby hangs a tale. Mr. Lambert was a side kick of old Curtiss Thorne—handled his estate and everything—and being a crusty old bachelor from the age of thirty on, he idolized the Thorne children. Sue was his pet. She still calls him Uncle Dudley, and when the split came between Sue and her father he stuck to Sue. So I suppose that it was fairly natural that she turned to him when this thing burst; he's always handled all her affairs, and he's probably told her that he's the best lawyer this side of the Rocky Mountains. He believes it."

"How old is he?"

"Sixty-three—plenty old enough to know better. You might take everything that I say about these guys with a handful of salt; it's only fair to inform you that they are anything but popular with the Fourth Estate. The only person that talks less in this world than Dudley Lambert is Daniel Farr; either of them would make a closed steel trap seem like a chatterbox. Stephen Bellamy's counsel is Lambert's junior partner and under both his thumbs; he'd be a nice chap if he didn't have lockjaw."

"Don't they tell you anything at all?" inquired the red-headed girl sympathetically.

"They tell us that there's been a murder," replied the reporter gloomily. "And I'm telling you that it's the only murder that ever took place in the United States of America where the press has been treated like an orphan child by everyone that knows one earthly thing about it. Not one word of the hearing before the grand

15

jury has leaked out to anyone; we haven't been given the name of one witness, and whatever the state's case against Stephen Bellamy and Susan Ives may be, it's a carefully guarded secret between Mr. Daniel Farr and Mr. Daniel Farr. The defense is just as expansive. So don't believe all you hear from me. I'd boil the lot of 'em in oil. Here comes Ben Potts. To be continued in our next."

The red-headed girl wasn't listening to him; she was watching the dark figure of the prosecutor, moving leisurely forward toward the little space where twelve men were seating themselves quietly and unostentatiously in their stiff, uncomfortable chairs. Twelve men—twelve everyday, ordinary, average men——She drew a sharp breath and turned her face away for a minute. The curtain was going up.

"May it please Your Honour"—the prosecutor's voice was very low, but as penetrating as though he were a hand-breadth away—"may it please Your Honour and gentlemen of the jury: On the night of the nineteenth of June, 1926, a little less than four months ago, a singularly cruel and ruthless murder took place not ten miles from the spot in which we have met to try the two who are accused of perpetrating it. On that summer night, which was made for youth and love and beauty, a girl who was young and beautiful and most desperately in love came out through the starlight to meet her lover. She had no right to meet him. She was another man's wife, he was another woman's husband. But love had made her reckless, and she came, with a black cloak flung over her white lace dress, and silver slippers that were made for dancing on feet that were made to dance—and that had danced for the last time. She was bound for the gardener's cottage on one of the largest and oldest estates in the neighbourhood, known as Orchards. At the time of the murder, it was not occupied, and the house was for sale. She was hurrying, because she feared that she was late and that her lover might be waiting. But it was not love that waited for her in the little sitting room of the gardener's cottage.

"If you men who sit here in judgment of her murderers think harshly of that pretty, flushed, enchanted girl hurrying through the night to her tryst, remember that that tryst was with death, not with love, and be gentle with her, even in your thoughts. She has paid more dearly for the crime of loving not wisely but too well than many of her righteous sisters.

"Next morning, at about nine o'clock, Mr. Herbert Conroy, a real-estate agent, arrived at the gardener's cottage with a prospective client for the estate who wished to inspect the property. As he came up on the little porch he was surprised to see that the front door was slightly ajar, and thinking that sneak thieves might have broken in, he pushed it farther open and went in.

"The first floor at the right of the narrow hall was the sitting room—what was known by the people who had formerly used it as the front parlour. Mr. Conroy stepped across its threshold, and his eyes fell on a truly appalling sight. Stretched out on the floor before him was a young woman in a white lace evening gown. A table was overturned beside her. Either there had been a struggle or the table

16

had been upset as she fell. At her feet were the fragments of a shattered lamp chimney and china shade and a brass lamp.

"The girl's white frock was stained with blood from throat to hem; her silk stockings were clotted with it; even her silver slippers were ruinously stained. She was known to have been wearing a string of pearls, her wedding ring, and three sapphire-and-diamond rings when she left home. These jewels were missing. The girl on the floor—the girl who had been wilfully and cruelly stabbed to death—the girl whose pretty frock had been turned into a ghastly mockery, was Madeleine Bellamy, of whose murder the two defendants before you are jointly accused.

"The man on trial is Stephen Bellamy the husband of the murdered girl. The woman who sits beside him is Susan Ives, the wife of Patrick Ives, who was the lover of Madeleine Bellamy and to whom she was going on that ill-starred night in June.

"Murder, gentlemen, is an ugly and repellent thing; but this murder, I think that you will agree, is a peculiarly ugly and repellent one. It is repellent because it is the State's contention that it was committed by a woman of birth, breeding, and refinement, to whose every instinct the very thought should have been abhorrent—because this lady was driven to this crime by a motive singularly sordid—because at her side stood a devoted husband, changed by jealousy to a beast to whom the death of his wife had become more precious than her life. It is peculiarly repellent because we propose to show that these two, with her blood still on their hands, were cool, collected, and deliberate enough to remove the jewels that she wore from her dead body in order to make this murder seem to involve robbery as a motive.

"In order to be able fully to grasp the significance of the evidence that we propose to present to you, it is necessary that you should know something of the background against which these actors played their tragic parts. As briefly as possible, then, I will sketch it for you.

"Bellechester County—your county, gentlemen, and thank God, my county—contains as many beautiful homes and delightful communities as any county in this state—or in any other state, for that matter—and no more delightful one exists than that of Rosemont, a small village about ten miles south of this courthouse. The village itself is a flourishing little place, but the real centre of attraction is the country club, about two miles from the village limits. About this centre cluster some charming homes, and in one of the most charming of them, a low, rambling, remodelled farmhouse, lived Patrick Ives and his wife. Patrick Ives is a man of about thirty-two who has made a surprising place for himself as a partner in one of the most conservative and successful investment banking houses in New York. I say surprising advisedly, for everyone was greatly surprised when about seven years ago he married Susan Thorne and settled down to serious work for the first time in his life. Up till that time, with the exception of two years at the front establishing a brilliant war record, he seems to have spent most of his time perfecting his golf game and his fox-trotting abilities and devoting the small portion of time that remained at his disposal to an anæmic real-estate business. According to all reports, he was—and is—likable, charming and immensely popular."

"Just one moment, Mr. Farr," Judge Carver's deep tones cut abruptly across the prosecutor's clear, urgent voice. "Do you propose to prove all these statements?"

"Certainly, Your Honour."

"I do not wish in any way to hamper you, but some of this seems a little far afield."

"I can assure Your Honour that the State proposes to connect all these facts with its case."

"Very well, you may proceed."

"At the time of the murder Mr. Ives's household consisted of his wife, Susan Thorne Ives; his two children, Peter and Polly, aged five and six; his mother, Mrs. Daniel Ives, to whom he has always been an unusually devoted son; a nursery governess, Miss Kathleen Page; and some six or seven servants. The only member of the household who concerns us immediately is Susan, or, as she is known to her friends, Sue Ives.

"Mrs. Ives is a most unusual woman. The youngest child and only daughter of the immensely wealthy Curtiss Thorne, she grew up on the old Thorne estate, Orchards, the idol of her father and her two brothers. Her mother died shortly after she was born. There was no luxury, no indulgence to which she was not accustomed from her earliest childhood. She was brilliantly intellectual and excelled at every type of athletics. Society, apparently, interested her very little; but there was not a trophy that she did not promptly capture at either golf or tennis. She was not particularly attractive to men, according to local gossip, in spite of being witty, accomplished, and charming—perhaps she was too witty and too accomplished for their peace of mind. At any rate, she set the entire community by the ears about seven years ago by running off with the handsome and impecunious Patrick Ives, just back from the war.

"Old Curtiss Thorne, who detested Patrick Ives and had other plans for her, cut her off without a cent—and died two years later without a cent himself, ruined by the collapse of his business during the deflation of 1921. Just what happened to Patrick and Susan Ives during the three years after the elopement, no one knows. They disappeared into the maelstrom of New York. Mrs. Daniel Ives joined them, and somehow they must have managed to keep from starving to death. Two children were born to Susan Ives, and finally Patrick persuaded this investment house to try him out as a bond salesman. It developed that he had a positive genius for the business, and his rise has been spectacular in the extreme. He is considered to-day one of the most promising young men in the Street.

"At the end of four years, the Iveses and their babies returned to Rosemont. They bought an old farmhouse with some seven or eight acres about a mile from the club, remodelled it, landscaped it, put in a tennis court, and became the most sought-after young couple in Rosemont. On the surface, they seemed ideally happy. Two charming children, a charming home, plenty of money, congenial enough tastes—such things should go far to create a paradise, shouldn't they? Well, down this smooth, easy, flower-strewn, and garlanded path Patrick and Susan Ives were hurrying straight toward hell. In order to understand why this was true, you must know something of two other people and their lives.

"About a mile and a half from the Ives house was another farmhouse, on the outskirts of the village, but this one had not been remodelled. It was small, shabby, in poor repair—no tennis court, no gardens, a cheap portable garage, a meagre half acre of land inadequately surrounded by a rickety fence. Everything is comparative in this world. To the dwellers in tenements and slums, that house would have been a little palace. To the dweller in the stone palaces that line the Hudson, it would be a slum. To Madeleine Bellamy, whose home it was, it was undoubtedly a constant humiliation and irritation.

"Mimi Bellamy—in all likelihood no one in Rosemont had heard her called Madeleine since the day that she was christened—Mimi Bellamy was an amazingly beautiful creature. 'Beauty' is a much cheapened and battered word; in murder trials it is loosely applied to either the victim or the murderess if either of them happened to be under fifty and not actually deformed. I am not referring to that type of beauty. Mimi Bellamy's beauty was of the type that in Trojan days launched a thousand ships and in these days launches a musical comedy. Hers was beauty that is a disastrous gift—not the common-place prettiness of a small-town belle, though such, it seems, was the rôle in which fate had cast her.

"I am showing you her picture, cut from the local paper—crudely taken, crudely printed, many times enlarged, yet even all these factors cannot dim her radiance. It was taken shortly before she died—not two months before, as a matter of fact. It cannot give the flowerlike beauty of her colouring, the red-gold hair, the sea-blue eyes, the exquisite flush of exultant youth that played about her like an enchantment; but perhaps even this cold, black-and-white shadow of a laughing girl in a flowered frock will give you enough of a suggestion of her warm enchantment to make the incredible disaster that resulted from that enchantment more credible. It is for that purpose that I am showing it to you now, and to remind you, if you feel pity for another woman, that never more again in all this world will that girl's laughter be heard, young and careless and joyous. I ask you most solemnly to remember that.

"Mimi Dawson Bellamy was the daughter of the village dressmaker, who had married Frederick Dawson, a man considerably above her socially, as he was a moderately successful real-estate broker in the village of Rosemont. He was by no manner of means a member of the local smart set, however, and was not even a member of the country club. They lived in a comfortable, unpretentious house a little off the main street, and in the boarding house next to them lived Mrs. Daniel Ives and her son Patrick.

"Mrs. Ives, a widow, was very highly regarded in the village, to which she had come many years previously, and was extremely industrious in her efforts to supplement their meagre income. She gave music lessons, did mending, looked after small children whose mothers were at the movies, and did everything in her power to assist her son, whose principal contribution to their welfare up to the time that he was twenty-one seemed to be a genuine devotion to his mother. At that age Mr. Dawson took him in to work with him in the real-estate business, hoping that his charm and engaging manners would make up for his lack of experience and industry. To a certain extent they did, but they created considerably more havoc with Mr. Dawson's beautiful daughter than they did with his clients. A boy-and-girl affair immediately sprang up between these two— the exquisite, precocious child of seventeen and the handsome boy of twenty-two were seen everywhere together, and it was a thoroughly understood thing that Mimi Dawson and Pat Ives were going together, and that one of these days they would go as far as the altar.

"A year later war was declared. Patrick Ives enlisted at once, and was among the first to reach France. The whole village believed that if he came back alive he would marry Mimi. But they were counting without Mimi.

"War, gentlemen, changed more things than the map of Europe. It changed the entire social map in many an American community; it changed, drastically and surprisingly, the social map of the community of Rosemont in the county of Bellechester. For the first time since the country club was built and many of the residents of New York discovered that it was possible to live in the country and work in the city, the barrier between the villagers and the country club members was lowered, and over this lowered barrier stepped Mimi Dawson, straight into the charmed sewing circles, knitting circles, Red Cross circles, bandage-making circles that had sprung up over-night—straight, moreover, into the charmed circle of society, about whose edges she had wistfully hovered—and straight, moreover, into the life of Elliot Farwell.

"Elliot Farwell was the younger brother of Mrs. George Dallas, at whose house met the Red Cross Circle of which Mrs. Dallas was president. Many of the village girls were asked to join her class in bandage making—after all, we were fighting this war to make the world safe for democracy, so why not be democratic? A pair of hands from the village was just as good as a pair of hands from the club— possibly better. So little Mimi Dawson found herself sitting next to the great Miss Thorne, wrapping wisps of cotton about bits of wood and going home to the village with rapidly increasing regularity in Mr. Elliot Farwell's new automobile, quite without the knowledge or sanction of Mr. Farwell's sister, whose democracy might not have stood the strain.

"Elliot Farwell was one of the two or three young men left in Rosemont. His eyes made it impossible for him to get into any branch of the service, so he

20

remained peaceably at home, attending to a somewhat perfunctory business in the city as a promoter. He would have had to be blind enough to require the services of a dog and a tin cup not to have noted Mimi Dawson's beauty, however; as a matter of fact, he noted it so intently that three months after peace was declared and three weeks before Patrick Ives returned from the war, Mr. and Mrs. Frederick Dawson announced the engagement of their daughter Madeleine to Mr. Elliot Farwell—and a startled world. Not the least startled member of this world, possibly, was Susan Thorne, to whom young Farwell had been moderately attentive for several years.

"Such was the state of affairs when the tide of exodus to Europe turned, and back on the very crest of the incoming waves rode Major Patrick Ives, booted, spurred, belted, and decorated—straight over the still-lowered barrier into the very heart of the country-club set. He was, not unnaturally, charmed with his surroundings, and apparently the fact that he found Mimi Dawson already installed there with a fiancé did not dampen his spirits in the slightest. From the day that he first went around the golf course with Susan Thorne, he was as invariably at her side as her shadow. Mr. Curtiss Thorne's open and violent disapproval left them unchastened and inseparable. Apparently they found the world well lost, as did Farwell and his fiancée. And into the midst of this idyllic scene, a month or so later, wanders the last of our actors, Stephen Bellamy.

"Stephen Bellamy was older than these others—seven years older than Susan Thorne or Patrick Ives, twelve years older than the radiant Mimi. He was the best friend of Susan's elder brother Douglas, and a junior partner of Curtiss Thorne. He had done well in the war, as he had in his business, and he was generally supposed to be the best masculine catch in Rosemont—intelligent, distinguished, and thoroughly substantial. It was everybody's secret that Curtiss Thorne wanted him for his son-in-law, and he and Elliot Farwell were the nearest approaches to beaus that Susan Thorne had had before the war.

"Within a week of their respective returns, she had lost both of them. The sober, reserved, conservative Stephen Bellamy fell even more violently and abjectly a victim to Mimi Dawson's charms than had Elliot Farwell. The fact that she was engaged to another man who had been at least a pleasant acquaintance of his did not seem to deter Mr. Bellamy for a second. At any rate, the third week in June in 1919 brought three shocks to the conservative community of Rosemont that left it rocking for many moons to come. On Monday, after a violent and public quarrel with Farwell, Mimi Dawson broke her engagement to him; on Wednesday Sue Thorne eloped with Patrick Ives, and on Thursday Miss Dawson and Mr. Bellamy were married by the justice of the peace in this very courthouse.

"It is a long stride from that amazing week in June to another June, but I ask you to make it with me. In the seven years that have passed, the seeds that were sown in those far-off days—seeds of discord, of heartbreak, of envy and malice—have waxed and grown into a mighty vine, heavy with bitter fruit; and the day of harvest is at hand—and the hands of the harvesters shall be red. But on this peaceful sunny summer afternoon of the nineteenth of June, 1926, those who are sitting in the vine's shadow seem to find it a tranquil and a pleasant place.

"It is five o'clock at the Rosemont Country Club, and the people that I have brought before you in the brief time at my disposal are gathered on the lawn in front of the club; the golfers are just coming in; it is the prettiest and gayest hour of the day. Mimi Bellamy is there, waiting for her husband. She has driven over in their little car to take him home for supper; it is parked just now beside Sue Ives's sleek and shining car with its sleek and shining chauffeur, and possibly Mimi Bellamy is wondering what strange fate makes one man a failure in the world of business and another a success. For the industrious and intelligent Stephen Bellamy has never recovered from the setback that he received when Curtiss Thorne's business crashed; he is still struggling valiantly to keep a roof over his wife's enchanting head—he can do little more. True, they have a maid of all work and a man of all work; but Sue Ives, who married the village ne'er-do-well, has eight servants and three cars and the prettiest gardens in Rosemont. So does fate make fools of the shrewdest of us!

"Gathered about in little groups are the George Dallases, Elliot Farwell, and Richard Burgoyne, the man with whom he keeps bachelor hall in a small bungalow near the village; the Ned Conroys and Sue Ives, whose husband has been cheated out of golf by a business engagement in the city, in spite of the fact that it is Saturday afternoon. She has, however, found another cavalier. Seated on the club steps, a little apart from the others, she is deep in conversation with Elliot Farwell, who is consuming his third highball in rapid succession. Gentlemen, if I could let you eavesdrop on the seemingly casual and actually momentous discussion that is going on behind those amiable masks, much that is dark to you now would be clear as day. I ask your patient and intelligent interest until that moment arrives. It will arrive, I promise you.

"For here, on this sunlit lawn, I propose to leave them for the present. Others will tell you what happened from that sunlit moment until the dark and dreadful one in the gardener's little cottage, when a knife rose and fell. I have not gone thus exhaustively into the shadowy past from which these figures sprang in order to retail to you the careless chatter of a country club and a country village. I have gone into it because I have felt it entirely imperative that you should know the essential facts in the light of which you will be able to read more clearly the evidence that I am about to submit to you. It is inevitable that each one of you must say to himself as you sit there: 'How is it possible that this young woman seated before our eyes, charming, well bred, sheltered, controlled, intelligent—how is it possible that this woman can have wilfully, brutally, and deliberately murdered another woman? How is it possible that the man seated beside her, a gentleman born and bred, irreproachable in every phase of his past life, can have aided and abetted her in her project?'

"How are these things possible, you ask? Gentleman, I say to you that we expect to prove that these things are not possible—we expect to prove that these things are certain. I am speaking neither rashly nor lightly when I assure you that the state believes that it can demonstrate their certainty beyond the shadow of a possible doubt. I am not seeking a conviction; I am no bloodhound baying for a victim. If you can find it in your hearts when I have done with this case to hold these two guiltless, you will, indeed, be fortunate—and I can find in my heart no desire to deprive you of that good fortune. It is my most painful duty, however, to place the facts before you and to let them speak for themselves.

"I ask you, gentlemen, to bear these things in mind. Susan Ives is a woman accustomed to luxury and security; she has once before been roughly deprived of it. What dreadful scars those three years in New York left on the gallant and spirited girl who went so recklessly to face them we can only surmise. But perhaps it is sufficient to say that the scars seared so deep that they sealed her lips forever. I have not been able to discover that she has mentioned them to one solitary soul, and I have questioned many. She was threatened with a hideous repetition of this nightmare. Her religious principles, as you will learn, prevented her from ever accepting or seeking a divorce, and she was too intelligent not to be fully aware that if Patrick Ives ran away with Mimi Bellamy, he would inevitably have lost his position in the ultra-conservative house in which he was partner, and thus be absolutely precluded from providing for her or her children, even if he had so desired.

"The position of a young woman thrown entirely on her own resources, with two small children on her hands, is a desperate one, and it is our contention that Susan Ives turned to desperate remedies. Added to this terror was what must have been a truly appalling hatred for the girl who was about to turn her sunny and sheltered existence into a nightmare. Cupidity, love, revenge—every murder in this world that is not the result of a drunken blow springs from one of these motives. Gentlemen, the state contends that Susan Ives was moved by all three.

"As for Stephen Bellamy, his idolatry of his young and beautiful wife was his life—a drab and colourless life save for the light and colour that she brought to it. When he discovered that she had turned that idolatry to mockery, madness descended on him—the madness that sent Othello staggering to his wife's bed with death in his hands; the madness that has caused that wretched catch phrase 'the unwritten law' to become almost as potent as our written code—to our shame, be it said. Do not be deceived by the memory of that phrase, gentlemen. There was another law, written centuries ago in letters of flame on the peaks of a mountain—'Thou shalt not kill.' Remember that law written in flame and forget the one that has been traced only in the blood of its victims. These two before you stand accused of breaking that law, written on Sinai—that sacred law on which hangs all the security of the society that we have so laboriously wrought out of chaos and horror—and we are now about to show you why they are thus accused.

"From the first step that each took toward the dark way that was to lead them to the room in the gardener's cottage, we will trace them—to its very threshold—

across its threshold. There I will leave them, my duty will have been done. Yours, gentlemen, will be yet to do, and I am entirely convinced that, however painful, however hateful, however dreadful, it may seem to you, you will not shrink from performing that duty."

The compelling voice with its curious ring fell abruptly to silence—a silence that lingered, deepened, and then abruptly broke into irrepressible and incautious clamour.

"Silence! Silence!"

Ben Potts's voice and Judge Carver's gavel thundered down the voices.

"Once and for all, this courtroom is not a place for conversation. Kindly remain silent while you are in it. Court is dismissed for the day. It will convene again at ten to-morrow."

The red-headed girl dragged stiffly to her feet. The first day of the Bellamy trial was over.

CHAPTER II

The red-headed girl was late. The clock over the courtroom door said three minutes past ten. She flung herself, breathless, into the seat next to the lanky young man and inquired in a tragic whisper, "Have they started?"

"Nope," replied that imperturbable individual. "Calm yourself. You haven't missed a single hear ye. Your hat's a good deal over one eye."

"I ran all the way from the station," gasped the red-headed girl. "Every step. There's not a taxi in this whole abominable place. And you were gone last night before I had a chance to ask you what you thought of the prosecutor's speech."

"Perhaps that's why I went."

"No, truly, what did you think of it?"

"Well, I think that boys being boys, jurors being jurors, prosecutors being prosecutors, and Mrs. Patrick Ives being Mrs. Patrick Ives, he did about as well as could be expected—better than I expected."

"He can't prove all those things, can he?" asked the red-headed girl, looking a little pale.

"Ah, that's it! When you get right down to it, the only things of any importance that he claimed he was going to prove were in one last sentence: That Bellamy and Sue Ives met and went to the front parlour of the gardener's cottage, to confront Mimi Bellamy—that's his case. And a pretty good case, too, if you ask me. The rest of it was just a lot of good fancy, expansive words strung together in order to create pity, horror, prejudice, and suspicion in the eyes of the jury. And granted that purpose, they weren't bad words, though there were a few bits that absolutely yelled for 'Hearts and Flowers' on muted strings somewhere in the background—that little piece about going through the starlight to her lover...."

"I thought the idea was that the prosecutor was after truth, not a conviction," said the red-headed girl gravely.

"The ideal, not the idea, my child. You didn't precisely get the notion that he was urging the jury to consider that, though there was a pretty strong case against Mrs. Ives and Stephen Bellamy, there were a whole lot of other people who might have done it too—or did you?"

"He certainly said most distinctly that he wasn't any bloodhound baying for a victim."

"Well, if he isn't, I'll bet that he gives such a good imitation of one that if Eliza should happen to hear him while she was crossing the ice she'd take two cakes at one jump. What did I tell you about Mr. Farr and the classics? Did you get 'she loved not wisely but too well'? That beats 'I could not not love thee, dear, so much.'"

Ben Potts's high, clear voice pulled them abruptly to their feet. "The Court!"

Through the little door behind the dais came the tall figure of Judge Carver, his spacious silks folding him in dignity—rather a splendid figure. The jury, the counsel, the defendants—Mrs. Ives was wearing the same hat ...

"Hear ye! Hear ye! Hear ye! All those having business before this honourable court draw near, give your attention, and you shall be heard!"

The clear singsong was drowned in the rustle of those in the courtroom sinking back into their seats.

"Is Mr. Conroy in court?"

"Mr. Herbert Conroy!" intoned the crier.

All heads turned to watch the small spare figure hurrying down the aisle toward the witness box.

"You do solemnly swear that the testimony that you shall give to the court and jury in this case now on trial shall be truth, the whole truth, and nothing but the truth, so help you God?"

"I do."

Mr. Conroy's faded blue eyes darted about him quietly as he mounted the stand, as though he were looking for a way out.

"Mr. Conroy, what is your profession?"

"I am a real-estate broker."

"Is your office in Rosemont?"

"No, sir; my office is in New York. My home, however, is in Brierdale, about three miles north of Rosemont."

"Have you the agency of the Thorne property, Orchards?"

"I have."

"To whom does that property belong?"

"It was left by Mr. Curtiss Thorne's will to his two sons, Charles and Douglas. Charles was killed in the war, and it therefore reverted to the elder son, Douglas. He is now the sole owner."

"And he placed it with you to sell?"

"To sell or to rent—preferably to sell."

"Have you had offers for it?"

"None that we regarded as satisfactory; it was too large a property to appeal to the average man in the market for a country home, as it consisted of more than eighty acres and a house of twenty-four rooms. On the afternoon of the nineteenth of June, 1926, however, I showed the photographs of the house to a gentleman from Cleveland who was about to transfer his business to the East. He was delighted with them and made no quibble about the price if the property proved to be all that it seemed."

"You were in New York at this time?"

"Yes; and a dinner engagement there prevented me from taking him out to Rosemont that afternoon. He was extremely anxious, however, to see it as soon as possible, as he was leaving for the West the following afternoon. So I arranged to take him next morning at nine o'clock."

"And did so?"

"And did so."

"Now will you be good enough to tell us, Mr. Conroy, just what happened when you arrived with this gentleman at Orchards on the morning of the twentieth?"

"We drove out from New York in my roadster, arriving at the lodge gates of the property shortly after nine o'clock, I should say. I was to collect the keys under the doormat at the gardener's cottage, which was half-way between the lodge and the main house——"

"Just a moment, Mr. Conroy. Was the lodge occupied?"

"No; at this particular time no building on the place was occupied. In Mr. Curtiss Thorne's day, the lodge was occupied by the chauffeur and his family, the gardener's cottage by the gardener and his family, and there was another cottage used by a farmer on the extreme western boundary. None of these had been occupied for some time, with the exception of the gardener's cottage, whose occupants had been given a vacation of two months in order to visit their aged parents in Italy. Shall I go on?"

"Please."

"The gardener's cottage is a low five-room building at a bend of the road, and is practically concealed as you approach it from the main driveway by the very high shrubbery that surrounds it—lilacs, syringa, and the like. There is a little drive that shoots off from the main driveway and circles the cottage, and we drove in there, to the front of the house, and mounted the steps to the front porch, as my client wished to see the interior. Just as I bent down to secure the keys, I was surprised to see that the door was slightly ajar. I picked up the keys, pushed it farther open, and went in, rather expecting that sneak thieves might have preceded me."

Mr. Conroy paused for a moment in his steady, precise narrative, his pale face a little paler. "Shall I continue?"

"Certainly."

"On my left was the dining room, with the door closed; on my right, the room known as the parlour. The door was open, but only a small section of the room was visible from the corridor, and it was not until I had crossed the threshold that I realized that something frightful had occurred. In the corner of the room farthest from the door——"

"Just a minute, please. Was your client with you when you entered the room?"

"He was a step or so behind me, I believe. In the corner of the room was the— the body of a young woman in a white frock. A small table was overturned beside her, and at her feet was a lamp, the chimney and shade shattered and some oil spilled on the floor. The smell of the kerosene was very strong—very strong indeed."

Mr. Conroy looked a little ill, as though the odour of that spilled kerosene were still about him.

27

"Was the girl's head toward you, or her feet, Mr. Conroy?"

"Her feet. Her head was resting on the corner of a low fender—a species of steel railing—that circled the base of a Franklin stove."

"Did you notice anything else?"

"Yes; I noticed that there was blood." He glanced about him swiftly, as though he were startled by the sound of the word, and lowered his voice. "A great deal of blood."

"On the dress?"

"Principally on the dress. I believe that there was also a little on the carpet, though I could not be sure of that. But principally it was on the dress."

"Can you tell us about the dress?"

Again Mr. Conroy's haunted eyes went wandering. "The dress? It was soaked in blood, sir—I think I may say that it was soaked in blood."

"No, no—I mean what kind of a dress was it? An evening dress?"

"Well, I hardly know. I suppose you might call it that. Not a ball gown, you understand—just a thin lacy dress, with the neck cut out a little and short sleeves. I remember that quite well—the lady's arms were bare."

The prosecutor, who had been carelessly fingering some papers and pamphlets on the top of a small square box, brushed them impatiently aside and scooped something else out of its depths.

"Was this the dress, Mr. Conroy?"

The long screech of Mr. Conroy's chair as he shoved it violently back tore through the courtroom like something human, echoing through every heart. The prosecutor was nonchalantly dangling before the broker's staring eyes a crumpled object—a white dress, streaked and splotched and dotted with that most ominous colour known to the eyes of man—the curious rusted sinister red of dried blood.

"Yes," said Mr. Conroy, his voice barely above a whisper—"yes, yes; that is it—that is the dress."

The fascinated eyes of the spectators wrenched themselves from the dress to the two defendants. Susan Ives was not looking at it. Her head was as high as ever, her lips as steady, but her eyes were bent intently on a scrap of paper that she held in her gloved fingers. Apparently Mrs. Ives was deeply interested in the contents.

Stephen Bellamy was not reading. He sat watching that handful of lace and blood as though it were Medusa's head, his blank, unswerving eyes riveted to it by something inexorable and intolerable. His face was as quiet as Susan Ives's, save for a dreadful little ripple of muscles about the set mouth—the ripple that comes from clenched teeth, clenched harder, harder—harder still, lest there escape through them some sound not meant for decent human ears. Save for that ripple, he did not move a hairbreadth.

"Was the blood on this dress dry when you first saw it, Mr. Conroy?"

"No, it was not dry."

"You ascertained that by touching it?"

Mr. Conroy's small neat body seemed to contract farther into itself.

"No, I did not touch it. It was not necessary to touch it to see that. It—it was quite apparent."

"I see. Your Honour, I ask to have this dress marked for identification."

"It may be marked," said Judge Carver quietly, eyeing it steadily and gravely for a moment before he returned to his notes.

"Got that?" inquired Mr. Farr briskly, handing it over to the clerk of the court. "I offer it in evidence."

"Are there any objections?" inquired Judge Carver.

"Your Honour, I fail to see what necessity there is for——"

The judge cut sharply across Lambert's voice: "You are not required to be the arbiter of that, Mr. Lambert. The state is conducting its case without your assistance, to the best of my knowledge. Do you object, and if so, on what grounds?"

Mr. Lambert's ruddy countenance became a shade more ruddy. He opened his mouth, thought better of it, and closed it with an audible snap. "No objection."

"Mr. Conroy, did you notice whether the slippers were stained?"

"Yes—yes, they were considerably stained."

"What type of slippers were they?"

"They were shiny slippers, with very high heels and some kind of bright, sparkling little buckles, I believe."

"Like these?" Once more the resourceful Mr. Farr had delved into the square box, and he placed the result of his research deftly on the edge of the witness box. A pair of silver slippers with rhinestone buckles, exquisite and inadequate

29

enough for the most foolish of women, small enough for a man to hold in one outstretched hand—sparkling, absurd, and coquettish, they perched on that dark rim, the buckles gleaming valiantly above the dark and sinister splotches that turned them from gay and charming toys to tokens of horror.

"Those are the slippers," said Mr. Conroy, his shaken voice barely audible.

"I offer them in evidence."

"No objections." Mr. Lambert's voice was an objection in itself.

"Now, Mr. Conroy, will you be good enough to tell us what you did as soon as you made this discovery?"

"I said to my client, 'There has been foul play here. We must get the police.'"

"No, not what you said, Mr. Conroy—what you did."

"I returned to my roadster with my client, locking the front door behind me with a key from the ring that I had found under the doormat, and drove as rapidly as possible to police headquarters in Rosemont, reporting what I had discovered."

"Just what did you report?"

"I reported that I had found the body of Mrs. Stephen Bellamy in the gardener's cottage of the old Thorne place, and that it looked as though she had been murdered."

"Oh, you recognized Mrs. Bellamy?"

"Yes. She was a friend of my sister-in-law, who lives in Rosemont. I had met her on two occasions."

"And what did you do then?"

"I considered that the matter was then out of my hands, but I endeavoured to reach Mr. Douglas Thorne by telephone, to tell him what had occurred. I was not successful, however, and returned immediately to New York with my client."

"He decided not to inspect the place farther?"

For the first time Mr. Conroy permitted himself a small, pallid, apologetic ghost of a smile. "Exactly. He decided that under the circumstances he did not desire to go farther with the transaction. It did not seem to him, if I may so express it, a particularly auspicious omen."

"Well, that's quite comprehensible. Did you notice when you were in this parlour whether Mrs. Bellamy was wearing any jewellery, Mr. Conroy?"

"To the best of my recollection, she was not, sir."

"You are quite sure of that?"

"I am not able to swear to it, but it is my distinct impression that she was not. I was only in the room a minute or so, you understand, but I still retain a most vivid picture of it—a most vivid picture, I may say."

Mr. Conroy passed a weary hand over his high brow, and that vivid picture seemed suddenly to float before the eyes of every occupant of the court.

"You did not see a weapon?"

"No. I could not swear that one was not there, but certainly I did not see one."

"I understood you to say that you locked the front door of the gardener's cottage with one of the keys that you found on the ring under the mat. How many keys were on that ring?"

"Seven or eight, I think—a key to the lodge, to the garage opposite the lodge, to the gardener's cottage, to the farmer's house, to the front and back doors of the main house, and to the cellar—possibly others."

"Didn't it ever strike you as a trifle imprudent to keep these keys in such an unprotected spot, Mr. Conroy?"

"We did not consider it an unprotected spot, sir. The gardener's cottage was a long way from the road, and it did not seem at all likely that they would be discovered."

"Whom do you mean by 'we,' Mr. Conroy?"

Mr. Conroy made a small restless movement. "I was referring to Mr. Douglas Thorne and myself."

"Oh, Mr. Thorne knew that the keys were kept there, did he?"

"Oh, quite so—naturally."

"Why 'naturally,' Mr. Conroy?"

"I said naturally—I said naturally because Mr. Thorne had placed them there himself."

"Oh, I see. And when had Mr. Thorne placed them there?"

"He had placed them there on the previous evening."

"On the previous evening?" Even the prosecutor's voice sounded startled.

"Yes."

"At what time?"

"I am not sure of the exact time."

"Well, can you tell us approximately?"

"I am not able to state positively even the approximate time."

"Was it before seven in the evening?"

"I do not believe so."

"How did you acquire the knowledge that Mr. Thorne was to leave those keys at the cottage, Mr. Conroy?"

"By telephone."

"Mr. Thorne telephoned you?"

"No, I telephoned Mr. Thorne."

"At what time?"

"At about half-past six on the evening of the nineteenth."

"I see. Will you be good enough to give us the gist of what you said to him over the telephone?"

"I had been trying to reach Mr. Thorne for some time, both at his home in Lakedale and in town."

"Mr. Thorne does not live in Rosemont?"

"No; he lives the other side of Lakedale, which is about twelve miles nearer New York. When I finally reached him, after his return from a golf match, I explained to him the urgency of getting into the house as early as possible the following morning and suggested that he might drive over after dinner and leave the keys under the mat of the cottage. I apologized to Mr. Thorne for causing him so much trouble, and he remarked that it was no trouble at all, as——"

"No, not what he remarked, Mr. Conroy—only what you said."

"I do not remember that I said anything further of any importance."

"Do you know at what time Mr. Thorne is in the habit of dining, Mr. Conroy?"

"I do not, sir."

"How long should you say that it would take to drive from Mr. Thorne's home to Orchards?"

"It is, roughly, about fourteen miles. I should imagine that it would depend entirely on the rate at which you drove."

"Driving at an ordinary rate, some thirty-five to forty minutes, should you say?"

"Possibly."

"So that if Mr. Thorne had finished his dinner at about eight, he would have arrived at Orchards shortly before nine?"

"I really couldn't tell you, Mr. Farr. You know quite as much about that as I do."

Mr. Conroy's small, harassed, unhappy face looked almost defiant for a moment, and then wavered under the geniality of the prosecutor's infrequent smile.

"I believe that you are right, Mr. Conroy." He turned abruptly toward the court crier. "Is Mr. Douglas Thorne in court?"

"Mr. Douglas Thorne!" intoned the crier in his high, pleasant falsetto.

A tall lean man, bronzed and distinguished, rose promptly to his feet from his seat in the fourth row. "Here, sir."

"Mr. Thorne, will you be good enough to speak to me after court is over?... Thanks. That will be all, Mr. Conroy. Cross-examine."

Mr. Lambert approached the witness box with a curious air of caution.

"It was entirely at your suggestion that Mr. Thorne brought the keys, was it not, Mr. Conroy?"

"Oh, certainly—entirely."

"He might have left them there at eight o'clock or at even eleven o'clock, as far as you know?"

"Exactly."

"That is all, Mr. Conroy."

"No further questions," said the prosecutor curtly. "Call Dr. Paul Stanley."

"Dr. Paul Stanley!"

The man who took Herbert Conroy's place in the witness box was a comfortable-looking individual with a fine thatch of gray hair and an amiable and intelligent countenance, which he turned benignly on the prosecutor.

"What is your profession, Dr. Stanley?"

"I am a surgeon. In my early youth I was that now fabulous creature, a general practitioner."

He smiled engagingly at the prosecutor, and the crowded courtroom relaxed. A nice, restful individual, after the haunted little real-estate broker.

"You have performed autopsies before, Dr. Stanley?"

"Frequently."

"And in this case you performed the autopsy on the body of Madeleine Bellamy?"

"I did."

"Where did you first see the body?"

"In the front room of the gardener's cottage on the Thorne estate."

"Did you hear Mr. Conroy's testimony?"

"Yes."

"Was the body in the position in which he described it at the time that he saw it?"

"In exactly that position. Later, for purposes of the autopsy, it was removed to the room opposite—the dining room."

"Please tell us under what circumstances you first saw the body."

"Certainly." Dr. Stanley settled himself a trifle more comfortably in his chair and turned a trifle toward the jury, who stared back gratefully into his friendly countenance. If Dr. Stanley had been explaining just how he reeled in the biggest trout of the season, he could not have looked more affably at ease. "I went out to the cottage with my friend Elias Dutton, the coroner, and two or three state troopers. Mr. Conroy had turned over the key to the cottage to us, and we found everything as he had described it to us."

"Were there signs of a struggle?"

"You mean on the body?"

"Yes—scratches, bruises, torn or disarranged clothing?"

"No, there were no signs of any description of a struggle, save for the overturned table and the lamp."

"Might that have happened when Mrs. Bellamy fell?"

"The table might very readily have been overturned at that time; it was toward Mrs. Bellamy's head and almost on top of the body. The lamp, on the other hand, was practically at her feet."

"Could it have rolled there as the table crashed?"

"Possibly, but it's doubtful. The fragments of lamp chimney and shade were there, too, you see, some six feet away from the table."

"I see. Will you tell us now, Dr. Stanley, just what caused the death of Mrs. Bellamy?"

"Mrs. Bellamy's heart was punctured by some sharp instrument—a knife, I should say."

"There was only one wound?"

"Yes."

"Will you please describe it to us?"

"There was a clean incision about three quarters of an inch long in the skin just over the heart. The instrument had penetrated to a depth of approximately three inches, and had passed between the ribs over the heart."

"Was it necessary that the blow should have been delivered with great force?"

"Not necessarily. If the knife had struck a rib, it would have taken considerable force to deflect it, but in this case it encountered no obstacle whatever."

"So that a woman with a strong wrist could have struck the blow?"

"Oh, certainly—or a woman with a weak wrist—or a child—or a strong man, as far as that goes. There is no evidence at all from the wound as to the force with which the blow was delivered."

"I see." Mr. Farr reached casually over to the clerk's desk and handed Dr. Stanley the dreadful rag that had been Madeleine Bellamy's white lace dress. "Do you recognize this dress, Doctor?"

"Perfectly."

"Will you be good enough to indicate to us just where the knife penetrated the fabric?"

Dr. Stanley turned it deftly in his long-fingered, capable hands. Something in that skilful scientific touch seemed to purge it of horror—averted eyes travelled back to it warily.

"The knife went through it right here. If you look closely, you can see the severed threads—just here, where the stain is darkest."

"Exactly. Would such a wound have caused instantaneous death, Doctor, in your opinion?"

"Not instantaneous—no. Death would follow very rapidly, however."

"A minute or so?"

"A few minutes—the loss of blood would be tremendous."

"Would the victim be likely to make much outcry—screaming, moaning, or the like?"

"Well, it's a little difficult to generalize about that. In this particular case, there is reason to doubt whether there was any outcry after the blow was struck."

"What reason have you to suppose that?"

"I think that Mr. Conroy has already testified that Mrs. Bellamy's head was resting on the corner of a steel fire guard—a pierced railing about six inches high. It is my belief that, when she received the blow, she staggered, clutched at the table, and fell, striking the back of her head against the railing with sufficient force to render her totally unconscious. There was a serious abrasion at the back of the head that leads me to draw that conclusion."

"I see. Was Mrs. Bellamy wearing any jewellery when you saw her, Doctor—a necklace, rings, brooches?"

"I saw no jewellery of any kind on the body."

"What type of knife should you say was used to commit this murder, Doctor?"

"Well, that's a little difficult to say. There were no marked peculiarities about the wound. It might have been caused by almost any knife with a sharp blade about three quarters of an inch wide and from three to four inches long—a sheath knife, a small kitchen knife, a large jackknife or clasp knife—various types, as I say."

"Could it have been made with this?"

The prosecutor dropped a small dark object into the doctor's outstretched hand and stood aside so that the jury, galvanized to goggle-eyed attention, could see it better. It was a knife—a large jackknife, with a rough, corrugated bone handle.

Mr. Lambert bore down on the scene at a subdued gallop. "Are you offering this knife in evidence?"

"I am not."

Judge Carver leaned forward, his black silk robes rustling ominously. "What is this knife, Mr. Farr?"

"This is a knife, Your Honour, that I propose to connect up with the case at a somewhat later stage. At present I ask to have it marked for identification merely for purposes of the record."

"You say that you will be able to connect it?"

"Absolutely."

"Very well, you may answer the question, Dr. Stanley."

36

The doctor was inspecting it gravely, his eyes bright with interest.

"I may open it?"

"Please do."

In the breathless stillness the little click as the large blade sprang back was clearly audible. Dr. Stanley bent over it attentively, passed a forefinger reflectively along its shining surface, raised his head. "Yes, it could quite easily have been done with this."

The prosecutor snapped the blade to with an enigmatic smile. "Thank you. That will be all."

"Miss Kathleen Page!"

Before the ring of that high imperious summons had died in the air, she was there—a demure and dainty wraith, all in gray from the close feathered hat to the little buckled shoes. A pale oval face that might have belonged to the youngest and smallest of Botticelli's Madonnas; cloudy eyes to match her frock, extravagantly fringed with heavy lashes; a forlorn, coaxing little mouth; sleek coils of dark hair. A murmur of interest rose, swelled, and died under Judge Carver's eagle eye.

"Miss Page, what is your present occupation?"

"I am a librarian at a branch public library in New York."

"Is that your regular occupation?"

"It has been for the past six months."

"Was it previous to that time?"

"Do you mean immediately previous?"

"At any time previous."

"I was assistant librarian in White Plains from 1921 to 1925."

"And after that?"

"During February of 1925 I had a serious attack of flu. It left me in rather bad shape, and the doctor recommended that I try to get some work in the country that would keep me outdoors a good deal and give me plenty of sleep."

"And did you decide on any occupation that would fit those requirements?"

"Yes. Dr. Leonard suggested that I might try for a position as governess. One of his patients was looking for a temporary governess for her children, and he suggested that I might try that."

"And did you?"

"Yes."

"You were successful?"

"Yes."

"Who was the patient suggested by Dr. Leonard?"

"Mrs. Ives."

As though the name were a magnet, the faces in the courtroom swung in a brief half circle toward its owner. There she sat in her brief tweed skirt and loose jacket, the bright little felt hat pulled severely down over the shining wings of her hair, her hidden eyes riveted on her clasped hands in their fawn-coloured gauntlets. At the sound of her name she lifted her head, glanced briefly and levelly at the greedy, curious faces pressing toward her, less briefly and more levelly at the seraphic countenance under the drooping feather on the witness stand, and returned to the gloves. Only the curve of her lips remained for the benefit of those prying eyes—a lovely curve, ironic and inscrutable. The half circle swung back to the demure occupant of the witness box.

"And how long were you in Mrs. Ives's employment?"

"Until June, 1926."

"What day of the month?"

"The twenty-first."

"Then on the night of the nineteenth of June you were still in the employment of Mrs. Ives?"

"Yes."

"Will you be good enough to tell us just what you were doing at eight o'clock that evening?"

"I had finished supper at a little before eight and was just settling down to read in the day nursery when I remembered that I had left my book down by the sand pile at the end of the garden, where I had been playing with the children before supper. So I went down to get it."

"Had you any way of fixing the time?"

"Yes. I heard the dining room clock strike eight as I went by. I noticed it especially, as I thought, 'That's eight o'clock and it's still broad daylight.'"

"Did you see anyone on your way out of the house?"

"I met Mr. Ives just outside the nursery door. He had come in late to dinner and hadn't come up to say good-night to the children before. He asked if they had gone to bed.... Shall I go on?"

"Certainly."

"I said that they were in bed but not asleep, and asked him please not to get them too excited. He had a boat for little Peter in his hand and I was afraid that he would get him in such a state that I wouldn't be able to do anything with him at all."

"A boat? What kind of a boat?"

"A little sailboat—a model of a schooner. Mr. Ives had been working on it for some time."

"Made it himself, had he?"

"Yes. He was very clever at that kind of thing. He'd made Polly a wonderful doll house."

"Your Honour——"

"Try to confine yourself directly to the question, Miss Page."

"Yes, Your Honour." The meek contrition of the velvet-voiced Miss Page was a model for all future witnesses.

"Was Mr. Ives fond of the children?"

"Oh, yes, he adored——"

"I object to that question, Your Honour." The preliminary tossings had resolved themselves into an actual upheaval this time and all of the two hundred and fifty pounds of Mr. Lambert were on his feet.

"Very well, Mr. Lambert, you may be heard. You object on what grounds?"

"I object to this entire line of questioning as absolutely immaterial, incompetent and irrelevant. How is Miss Page qualified to judge as to Mr. Ives's affection for his children? And even if her opinion had the slightest weight, what has his affection for his children got to do with the murder of this girl? For reasons which I don't pretend to grasp, the learned counsel for the prosecution is simply wasting the time of this court."

"You might permit the Court to be the judge of that." Judge Carver's fine dark eyes rested somewhat critically on the protestant bulk before him. "Mr. Farr, you may be heard."

"Of course, Your Honour, with all due deference to my brilliant opponent's fireworks, he's talking pure nonsense. Miss Page is perfectly——"

Judge Carver's gavel fell with a crash. "Mr. Farr, the Court must ask you once and for all to keep to the matter in hand. Can you connect your question with this case?"

"Most certainly. It is the contention of the state that Mrs. Ives realized perfectly that if Mr. Ives decided that he wanted a divorce he would fight vigorously for at least partial custody of his children, whom, as Miss Page was about to tell us, he adored. Moreover, Mrs. Ives had strong religious objections to divorce. It was therefore essential to her to get rid of anyone who threatened her security if she wanted to keep the children. In order to prove this, it is necessary to establish Mr. Ives's affection. And it ought to be perfectly obvious to anyone that Miss Page is in an excellent position to tell us what that affection was. I maintain that this question is absolutely relevant and material, and that Miss Page is perfectly competent to reply to it."

"The question may be answered."

"Exception."

"Mr. Ives adored the children and they adored him. He was with them constantly."

"Was Mrs. Ives fond of them?"

"Objection on the same grounds, Your Honour."

"The question is allowed."

"Exception."

"Oh, yes, she was devoted to them."

"As devoted to them as Mr. Ives?"

"Now, Your Honour——"

Judge Carver eyed the impassioned Lambert with temperate interest. "That seems a fairly broad question, Mr. Farr, calling for a conclusion."

"Very well, Your Honour, I'll reframe it. Did she seem as fond of them as Mr. Ives?"

"Oh, quite, I should think—though, of course, Mrs. Ives is not demonstrative."

"I see—not demonstrative. Cold and reserved, eh?"

Judge Carver's stern voice cut sharply across Miss Page's pretty, distressed, appealing murmur: "Mr. Farr, the Court is anxious to give you as much latitude as possible, but we believe that you have gone quite far enough along this particular line."

"I defer entirely to Your Honour's judgment.... Miss Page, was Mrs. Ives with Mr. Ives when you met him coming into the nursery with the boat in his hand?"

"No, Mrs. Ives had already said good-night to the children before her dinner."

"Did Mr. Ives go into the nursery before you went downstairs?"

"He went past me into the day nursery, and I have no doubt that he then went into the night nursery."

"Never mind that. I only want the facts that are in your actual knowledge. There were two nurseries, you say?"

"Yes."

"Will you be good enough to tell us how they were arranged?"

"The day and night nurseries are in the right wing of the house, on the third floor."

"What other rooms are on that floor?"

"My room, a bathroom, and a small sewing room."

"Please tell us what the arrangement would be as you enter the front door."

"Let me see—when you come in through the door you come into a very large hall that takes up almost all the central portion of the house. The central portion was an old farmhouse, and the wings, that contain all the rooms really, were added by Mrs. Ives. She knocked out the inside structure of the farmhouse and left it just a shell that she made into a big hall three stories high, with galleries around it on the second and third floors leading to the bedroom wings. There were two staircases at the back of the hall, leading to the right and left of the galleries. I'm afraid that I'm not being very clear, but it's a little confusing."

"You are being quite clear. Tell us just how the rooms open out as you come through the door."

"Well, to the right is a small cloakroom and the big living room. It's very large— it forms the whole ground floor of the right wing in fact. Over it are Mr. and Mrs. Ives's rooms."

"Did Mr. and Mrs. Ives occupy separate rooms?"

"Oh, no, there was a large bedroom, and on one side of it was Mrs. Ives's dressing room and bath, and to the left Mr. Ives's dressing room and bath. On the third floor were the nurseries and my room. On the left downstairs as you came in was a little flower room."

"A flower room?"

"A room that was used for arranging flowers, you know. Mrs. Daniel Ives used it a great deal. It had shelves of vases and a sink and a big porcelain-topped table. The downstairs telephone was in there, too, and——"

"Your Honour, may we ask where all this is leading?" Mr. Lambert's tone was tremulous with impatience.

"You may. The Court was about to make the same inquiry. Is this exhaustive questioning necessary, Mr. Farr?"

"Absolutely necessary, Your Honour. I can assure Mr. Lambert that it is leading to a very interesting conclusion, however distasteful he may find both the path and the goal. I will be as brief as possible, I promise."

"Very well, you may continue, Miss Page."

Miss Page raised limpid eyes in appealing deprecation. "I'm so frightfully sorry. I've absolutely forgotten where I was."

"You were telling us that there was a telephone in the flower room."

"Oh, yes—that is in the first room to the left as you come in. It's really part of the hall."

"You mean that it has no door?"

"No, no, it has a door. I simply meant that you came to it before you entered the left wing. It balances the cloakroom on the right-hand side. They're rather like very large closets, you know, except that they both have windows."

"What do the windows open on to?"

"The front porch.... Shall I go on with the rooms?"

"Please, and as briefly as possible."

"The first room in the left wing is Mr. Ives's study. It opens into the dining room. They form the ground floor of the left wing. Above them are Mrs. Daniel Ives's room and bath and two guest rooms and another bath. Above these on the third floor are the servants' quarters."

"How many servants were there?"

"Let me see—there were six, I think, but only the four maids lived in the house."

"Please tell us who they were."

"There was the cook, Anna Baker; the waitress, Melanie Cordier; the chambermaid, Katie Brien; and Laura Roberts, Mrs. Ives's personal maid and seamstress. They had four small rooms in the left wing, third floor. James and Robert MacDonald, the chauffeur and gardener, were brothers and lived in quarters over the garage. Oh, there was a laundress, too, but I don't remember her name. She didn't live in the house—only came in four days a week."

"You have described the entire household?"

"Yes."

"And the entire layout of the house?"

"Yes—well, with the exception of the service quarters. You reached them through a door at the back of the big hall—kitchen, laundry, servants' dining room and pantry, which opened also into the dining room. They ran across the back of the house. Do you want me to describe them further?"

"Thanks, no. We can go on with your story now. Did you see anyone but Mr. Ives on your way to the sand pile?"

"Not in the house. I passed Mrs. Daniel Ives on my way through the rose garden. She always used to work there after dinner until it got dark. She asked me as I went by if the children were asleep, and I told her that Mr. Ives was with them."

"What did you do then?"

"I found the book in the swing by the sand pile and went back across the lawn to the house. As I was starting up the steps, I heard Mrs. Patrick Ives's voice, speaking from the flower room at the left of the front door. She was speaking very softly, but the window on to the porch was open and I could hear her distinctly."

"Was she speaking to someone in the room?"

"No, she was telephoning. I think that I've already said that the downstairs 'phone is in that room. She was giving a telephone number—Rosemont 200."

"Were you familiar with that number?"

"Oh, quite. I had called it up for Mrs. Ives several times."

"Whose number was it, Miss Page?"

"It was Mr. Stephen Bellamy's telephone number."

The courtroom pulsed to galvanized attention, its eyes whipping to Stephen Bellamy's tired, dark face. It was lit with a strange, friendly, reassuring smile, directed straight at Susan Ives's startled countenance. For a moment she stared back at him soberly, then slowly the colour came back into her parted lips, which curved gravely to mirror that voiceless greeting. For a long moment their eyes rested on each other before they returned to their accustomed guarded inscrutability. As clearly as though they were shouting across the straining faces, those lingering eyes called to each other, "Courage!"

"You say that you could hear Mrs. Ives distinctly, Miss Page?"

"Very distinctly."

"Will you tell us just what she said?"

"She said"—Miss Page frowned a little in concentration and then went on steadily—"she said, 'Is that you, Stephen?... It's Sue—Sue Ives. Is Mimi there?... How long ago did she leave?... Are you sure she went there?... No, wait—this is vital. I have to see you at once. Can you get the car here in ten minutes?... No, not at the house. Stop at the far corner of the back road. I'll come through the back gate to meet you.... Elliot didn't say anything to you?... No, no, never mind that—just hurry.'"

"Is that all that she said?"

"She said good-bye."

"Nothing else?"

"Nothing else."

"What did you do then?"

"I turned back from the porch steps and circled the house to the right, going in by the side door and on up to the nursery."

"Why did you do that?"

"I didn't want Mrs. Ives to know that I had overheard her conversation. I thought if by any chance she saw me coming in through the side door, it would not occur to her that I could have heard it from there."

"I see. When you got up to the nursery was Mr. Ives still there?"

"Yes; he came out of the night nursery when he heard me and said that the children were quiet now."

"Did he say anything else to you?"

"Yes; he still had the boat in his hand, and he said there was something that he wanted to fix about the rudder, and that he'd bring it back in the morning."

"Did you say anything to him?"

"Yes."

"Please tell us what you said."

"I told him that I had just overheard a telephone conversation that his wife was having with Mr. Bellamy, and that I thought he should know about it."

44

"Did you tell him about it?"

"Not at that moment. As I was about to do so, Mrs. Ives herself called up from the foot of the stairs to ask Mr. Ives if he still intended to go to the poker game at the Dallases.... Shall I go on?"

"Certainly."

"Mr. Ives said yes, and Mrs. Ives said that in that case she would go to the movies with the Conroys, who had asked her before dinner. Mr. Ives asked her if he couldn't drop her there, and she said no—that it was only a short walk and that she needed the exercise. She went straight out of the front door, I think. I heard it slam behind her."

"What did you do then?"

"I said, 'Your wife has gone to meet Stephen Bellamy.'"

"And then what happened?"

"Mr. Ives said, 'Don't be a damned little fool.'"

Miss Page smiled meekly and appreciatively at the audible ripple from the other side of the railing.

"Did you say anything to that?"

"I simply repeated the telephone conversation."

"Word for word?"

"Word for word, and when I'd finished, he said, 'My God, somebody's told her.'"

"I object. Your Honour, I ask that that be stricken from the record!" Lambert's frenzied clamour filled the room. "What Mr. Ives said——"

"It may be stricken out."

Judge Carver's tone was the sternest of rebukes, but the unchastened prosecutor stood staring down at her demure face triumphant for a moment, and then, with a brief expressive gesture toward the defense, turned her abruptly over to their mercies. "That's all. Cross-examine."

"No lunch to-day either?"

"No, I've got to get these notes off."

The red-headed girl proudly exhibited an untidy pile of telegraph blanks and a much-bitten pencil. The gold pencil and the black leather notebook had been flung contemptuously out of the cab window on the way back to the boarding house the night before.

45

"Me too. We'll finish 'em up here and I'll get 'em off for you.... Here's your apple."

The red-headed girl took it obediently, a fine glow invading her. How simply superb to be working there beside a real reporter; such a fire of comradeship and good will burned in her that it set twin fires flaming in her cheeks. The newspaper game! There was nothing like it, absolutely. Her pencil tore across the page in a fever of industry.

It was almost fifty minutes before the reporter spoke again, and then it was only in reply to a question: "What—what did you think of her?"

"Think of whom?"

"Of Kathleen Page."

"Well, you don't happen to have a pat of the very best butter about you?"

"Whatever for?"

"To see if it would melt in her mouth."

"It wouldn't," said the red-headed girl; and added fiercely, "I hate her—nasty, hypocritical, unprincipled little toad!"

"Oh, come, come! I hope that you won't allow any of this to creep into those notes of yours."

"She probably killed Mimi Bellamy herself," replied the newest member of the Fourth Estate darkly. "I wouldn't put it past her for a moment. She——"

"The Court!"

The red-headed girl flounced to her feet, the fires still burning in her cheeks, eyeing Miss Page's graceful ascent to the witness box with a baleful eye. "I hope she's headed straight for all the trouble there is," she remarked between clenched teeth to the reporter.

For the moment it looked as though her wish were about to be gratified.

Mr. Lambert lumbered menacingly toward the witness box, his ruddy face grim and relentless. "You remember a great deal about that evening, don't you, Miss Page?"

"I have a very good memory." Miss Page's voice was the prettiest mixture of pride and humility.

"Do you happen to remember the book that you were reading?"

"Perfectly."

"Give us the title, please."

"The book was *Cytherea*, one of Hergesheimer's old novels."

"Was it your own book?"

"No, it came from Mr. Ives's study."

"Had he loaned it to you?"

"No."

"Had Mrs. Ives loaned it to you?"

"No one had loaned it to me; I had simply borrowed it from the study."

"Oh, you were given the run of the books in Mr. Ives's study? I see." Miss Page sat silent, eyeing him steadily, only a slight stain of colour under the clear, pale skin betraying the fact that she had heard him. "Were you?" demanded Mr. Lambert savagely, leaning toward her.

"Was I what?"

"Were you given the run of Mr. Ives's library?"

"I had never stopped to formulate it in that way. I supposed that there could be no possible objection to taking an occasional book."

"I see. You regarded yourself as one of the family?"

"Oh, hardly that."

"Did you take your meals with them?"

"No."

"Spend the evenings with them?"

"No."

Miss Page's fringed eyes were as luminous and steady as ever, but the stain in her cheeks had spread to her throat.

"You resented that fact, didn't you?"

The prosecutor's voice whipped out of the brief silence like a sword leaping from the scabbard: "I object to that question. To paraphrase my learned opponent, what possible relevance has Miss Page's sense of resentment or contentment got to do with the murder of this girl?"

"And to quote my witty adversary's reply, Your Honour, it has everything to do with it. We propose definitely to attack Miss Page's credibility. We believe we can show that she detested Mrs. Ives and would not hesitate to do her a disservice."

"Oh," said the prosecutor, with much deliberation, "that's what you propose to show, is it?"

Even the clatter of the judge's gavel did not cause him to turn his head an inch. He continued to gaze imperturbably at the occupant in the box, who, demure and pensive, returned it unswervingly. In the brief moment occupied by the prosecutor's skilful intervention the flush had faded entirely. Miss Page looked as cool and tranquil as a little spring in the forest.

"You may answer the question, Miss Page," said the judge a trifle sternly.

"May I have the question repeated?"

"I asked whether you didn't resent the fact that you were treated as a servant rather than as a member of the household."

"It never entered my head that I was being treated as a servant," said Miss Page gently.

"It never entered your head?"

"Not for a moment."

"You were perfectly satisfied with your situation in every way?"

"Oh, perfectly."

"No cause for complaint whatever?"

"None whatever."

"Miss Page, is this your writing? Don't trouble to read it—simply tell me whether it is your writing."

Miss Page bent docilely over the square of pale blue paper. "It looks like my writing."

"I didn't ask you whether it looked like it—I asked you if it was your writing."

"I really couldn't tell you that. Handwriting can be perfectly imitated, can't it?"

"Are you cross-examining me or am I cross-examining you?"

Miss Page permitted herself a small, fugitive smile. "I believe that you are supposed to be cross-examining me."

"Then be good enough to answer my question. To the best of your belief, is this your writing?"

"It is either my writing or a very good imitation of it."

The outraged Mr. Lambert snatched the innocuous bit of paper from under his composed victim's nose and proffered it to the clerk of the court as though it were something unclean. "I offer this letter in evidence."

"Just one moment," said the prosecutor gently. "I don't want to waste the Court's time with a lot of useless objections, but it seems to me that this letter has not yet been identified by Miss Page, and as you are evidently unwilling to let her read it, for some occult reason that I don't presume to understand, I must object to its being offered in evidence."

"What does this letter purport to be, Mr. Lambert?" inquired the judge amiably.

Mr. Lambert turned his flaming countenance on the Court. "It purports to be exactly what it is, Your Honour—a letter from Miss Page to her former employer, Mrs. Ives. And I am simply amazed at this hocus-pocus about her not being able to identify her own writing being tolerated for a minute. I———"

"Kindly permit the Court to decide what will be tolerated in the conduct of this case," remarked the judge, in a voice from which all traces of amiability had been swept as by a cold wind. "What is the date of the purported letter?"

"May 7, 1925."

"Did you write Mrs. Ives a letter on that date, Miss Page?"

"That's quite a time ago, Your Honour. I certainly shouldn't like to make any such statement under oath."

"Would it refresh your memory if you were to look over the letter?"

"Oh, certainly."

"I think that you had better let Miss Page look over the letter if you wish to offer it in evidence, Mr. Lambert."

Once more Mr. Lambert menacingly tendered the blue square, which Miss Page considered in a leisurely and composed manner in no way calculated to tranquillize the storm of indignation that was rocking him. Her perusal completed, she lifted a gracious countenance to the inflamed one before her. "Oh, yes, that is my letter."

Mr. Lambert snatched it ungratefully. "I again offer this in evidence."

"No objection," said the prosecutor blandly.

"Now that you have fortified yourself with its contents, Miss Page, I will ask you to reconcile some of the statements that it contains with some later statements of yours made here under oath this afternoon:

"MY DEAR MRS. IVES:

49

"I would like to call your attention to the fact that for the past three nights the food served me has evidently been that discarded by your servants as unfit for consumption. As you do not care to discuss these matters with me personally, I am forced to resort to this means of communication, and I ask you to believe that it is literally impossible to eat the type of meal that has been put before me lately. Boiled mutton which closely resembled boiled dishrags, stewed turnips, and a kind of white jelly that I was later informed was intended to be rice, and a savoury concoction of dried apricots, and sour milk was the menu for yesterday evening. You have made it abundantly clear to me that you regard me as a species of overpaid servant, but I confess that I had not gathered that slow starvation was to be one of my duties.

"Sincerely,
"KATHLEEN PAGE."

"Kindly reconcile your statement that it had never entered your head that you were being treated as a servant with this sentence: 'You have made it abundantly clear that you regard me as a species of overpaid servant.'"

"That was a silly overwrought letter written by me when I was still suffering from the effects of a nervous and physical collapse. I had completely forgotten ever having written it."

"Oh, you had, had you? Completely forgotten it, eh? Never thought of it from that day to this? Well, just give us the benefit of that wonderful memory of yours once more and tell us the effect of this letter on your relations with Mrs. Ives?"

"It had a very fortunate effect," said Miss Page, with her prettiest smile. "Mrs. Ives very kindly rectified the situation that I was indiscreet enough to complain of, and the whole matter was cleared up and adjusted most happily."

"What?" The astounded monosyllable cracked through the courtroom like a rifle shot.

"I said that it was all adjusted most happily," replied Miss Page sunnily and helpfully, raising her voice slightly.

Actual stupor had apparently descended on her interrogator.

"Miss Page, you make it difficult for me to credit my ears. Is it not the fact that Mrs. Ives sent for you at once on receipt of that note, offered you a month's wages in lieu of notice, and requested you to leave the following day?"

"Nothing could be farther from the fact."

Mr. Lambert's voice seemed about to forsake him at the calm finality of this reply. He opened his mouth twice with no audible results, but at the third effort something closely resembling a roar emerged: "Are you telling me that you did not go on your knees to Mrs. Ives in floods of tears and tell her that it would be signing your death warrant to turn you out then, and implore her to give you another chance?"

"I am telling you," said Miss Page equably, "that nothing remotely resembling that occurred. Mrs. Ives was extremely regretful and considerate, and there was not a word as to my leaving."

Apoplexy hovered tentatively over Mr. Lambert's bulky shoulder. "Do you deny that two days before this murder your insolence had once more precipitated a scene that had resulted in your dismissal, and that you were intending to leave on the following Monday?"

"Most certainly I deny it."

"A scene that arose from the fact that during Mrs. Ives's absence in town you ordered the car to take you and a friend of yours from White Plains for a three-hour drive in the country, and that when Mrs. Ives telephoned from town to have the car meet her, as she was returning that afternoon instead of the next day, she was informed that you were out in it and she was obliged to take a taxi?"

"That is not true either."

"It is not true that you went for a drive with a young man that afternoon?"

"Oh, that is quite true; but I had Mrs. Ives's permission to do so before she left."

For a moment Mr. Lambert turned his crimson countenance toward Susan Ives. She had lifted her head and was staring, steadily and contemptuously, at her erstwhile nursery governess, whose limpid eyes moved only from Mr. Lambert to Mr. Farr and back. Even the contempt could not extinguish a frankly diverted twist to her lips at the pat audacity of the gentle replies. Evidently Mr. Lambert could find no comfort there. He turned back to his witness.

"Miss Page, do you know what perjury is?"

"Your Honour——"

Miss Page's lightning promptitude cut through the prosecutor's voice: "It's a demonstrably false statement made under oath, isn't it?"

"Just wait a minute, please, Miss Page. Your Honour, I respectfully submit that this entire line of cross-examination by Mr. Lambert is extremely objectionable. I have let it go this far because I don't want to prolong this trial with a lot of unnecessary bickering; but, as far as I can see, he has simply been entertaining the jury with a series of exciting little episodes that there is not a shred of reason to believe are not the offspring of his own fertile imagination. According to Miss

Page, they are just exactly that. They are, however, skilfully calculated to prejudice her in the eyes of the jury, and when Mr. Lambert goes so far as to imply in no uncertain manner that Miss Page's denial of these fantasies is perjury, I can no longer——"

"Your Honour, do you consider this oration for the benefit of the jury proper?" Mr. Lambert's voice was unsteady with rage.

"I do not, sir. Nor do I consider it the only impropriety that has occurred. I see no legitimate place in cross-examination for a request for a definition of perjury. However, you have received your reply. You may proceed with your cross-examination."

"Miss Page, when you realized that Mrs. Ives was talking to someone on the telephone, why did you not go on into the house?"

"Because I was interested in what she was saying."

"So you eavesdropped, eh?"

"Yes."

"A very pretty, honourable, decent thing to do in your opinion?"

"Oh," said Miss Page, with her most disarming smile, "I don't pretend not to be human."

"Well, that's very reassuring. Can you tell us why Mrs. Ives didn't hear you outside on the porch, Miss Page?"

"I wasn't on the porch. I had just started to come up the steps when I stopped to listen. I had on tennis shoes, which wouldn't make any noise at all on the lawn."

"You say that you could hear Mrs. Ives distinctly?"

"Oh, quite."

"So that anybody else could have heard her distinctly too?"

"Anyone who was standing in that place could have—yes."

"She was making a secret rendezvous and yet was speaking in a tone sufficiently audible for any passer-by to hear?"

"She probably thought there would be no passer-by."

"Your Honour, I ask to have that stricken from the record as deliberately unresponsive."

"You were not asked as to Mrs. Ives's thoughts, Miss Page. Mr. Lambert asked you whether any passer-by could not have heard Mrs. Ives's conversation."

"Anyone who passed over the route that I did could have heard it perfectly."

"Mr. Patrick Ives could have heard it?"

"Mr. Patrick Ives was upstairs."

"That was not my question. I asked you if Patrick Ives could not have heard it quite as readily as you?"

"He could, if he had been there."

"Miss Page, will you be good enough to repeat that conversation for us once again?"

"The whole thing?"

"Certainly."

"Mrs. Ives said"—again the little frown of concentration—"she said, 'Is that you Stephen?... It's Sue—Sue Ives. Is Mimi there?... How long ago did she leave?... Are you sure she went there?... No, wait—this is vital—I have to see you at once. Can you get the car here in ten minutes?... No, not at the house. Stop at the far corner of the back road. I'll come through the back gate to meet you.... Elliot hasn't said anything to you?... No, no, never mind that—just hurry.... Good-bye.'"

Mr. Lambert beamed at her—a ferocious and colossal beam. "Now, that's very nice—very nice, indeed, Miss Page. Every word pat, eh? Almost as though you'd learned it by heart, shouldn't you say?"

"That's probably because I did learn it by heart," proffered Miss Page helpfully.

The beam forsook Mr. Lambert's countenance, leaving the ferocity. "Oh, you learned it by heart, did you? Between the front steps and the side door, I suppose?"

"Not exactly. I wrote it down before I went in the side door."

"You did what?"

"I wrote it down while Mrs. Ives was talking, most of it. The last sentence or so I did just before I came in."

Mr. Lambert took a convulsive grip on his sagging jaw. "Oh, indeed! Brought back a portable typewriter and a fountain pen and a box of notepaper from the sand pile, too, I suppose?"

Miss Page smiled patiently and politely.

"No; but I had some crayons of the children's in my sweater pocket."

"And half a dozen pads, too, no doubt?"

"No, I wrote it on the flyleaf of the book—*Cytherea*, you know."

"For what purpose did you write this down?" The voice of Mr. Lambert was the voice of one who has run hard and long toward a receding goal.

"It sounded important to me; I didn't want to make any mistakes."

"Quite so. So your story is that you took this information, which you admit you acquired by eavesdropping on the woman you claim had been invariably kind and generous to you, straight to her husband, in the fond expectation of ruining both their lives?"

"Oh, no, indeed—in the expectation of saving them. Mr. Ives had been even kinder to me than Mrs. Ives; I was desperately anxious to help them both."

"And this was your idea of helping them?"

"It was probably a stupid way," said Miss Page humbly. "But it was the only one that I could think of. I was afraid they were planning to elope, and I thought that Mr. Ives might be able to stop them. You see, I hadn't realized then the real significance of the telephone conversation."

"What real significance, if you please?"

"The fact that someone must have told Mrs. Ives all about Mr. Ives's affair with Mrs. Bellamy before she went out that night," said Miss Page softly.

"Your Honour," said the flagging voice—"Your Honour, I ask that that reply be stricken from the record as unresponsive."

"The Court does not regard it as unresponsive. You requested Miss Page to give her final interpretation of the telephone conversation and she has given it."

"May I have an exception, Your Honour?"

"Certainly."

"Then the story that you expect this jury to believe, Miss Page, is that nothing but affectionate zeal prompted you to spy on this benefactress of yours and to bear the glad tidings of her infidelity to her unsuspecting husband—tidings acquired through a reputed conversation of which you were the sole witness and the self-constituted recorder?"

"I hope that they will believe me," said Miss Page meekly. For one brief moment her ingenuous eyes rested appealingly on the twelve stolid and inscrutable countenances.

"And I hope that you are unduly optimistic," said Mr. Lambert heavily. "That is all, Miss Page."

"Just one moment," said the prosecutor easily. "Miss Page, when Mr. Lambert asked you whether anyone couldn't have overheard that conversation, he prevented you from explaining why no one was likely to. Let's first get that straight. Where was Mrs. Daniel Ives?"

"In the rose garden."

"That was where she usually went after dinner, wasn't it?"

"Always, I think. She used to work out there for an hour or so until it got dark, because that was the coolest part of the day."

"Was the rose garden visible from the study?"

"Quite clearly. A window overlooked the little paved terrace that led down into the rose garden."

"So that it would have been simple for Mrs. Ives to verify whether Mrs. Daniel Ives was in the garden?"

"Oh, quite."

"Where were the servants apt to be at that time?"

"They would be having their dinner in the back part of the house—they dined after the family."

"What about Mr. Patrick Ives?"

"Mrs. Ives knew that he had gone upstairs. He told me that she had been helping him to fasten the little pennant on in the study just before he came up."

"And she thought that you were upstairs, too, didn't she?"

"Oh, yes; I was not in the habit of coming down after dinner. I had my meals in the nursery."

"Did Mr. Ives use the study much—to write or to work in, I mean?"

"I don't know how much he worked in it; he had quite a collection of technical volumes in it, but I don't believe that he did much writing, though. He had a very large, flat-topped desk that he used as a kind of work bench."

"Where he made the boats and dollhouses?"

"Yes."

"Kept his tools and materials?"

"Yes."

"Was that desk visible from the door?"

"Yes; it was directly opposite the door into the hall."

"Would a person going from the flower room to the foot of the nursery stairs pass it?"

"They could not very well avoid doing so."

"Would the contents of the top of the desk be visible from the doorway?"

"Oh, surely. The study is not a large room."

The prosecutor made two strides toward the witness box. Something small and dark and bright glinted for a moment in his hand. "Miss Page, have you ever seen this knife before?"

Very delicately Miss Page lifted it in her slender fingers, eyeing it gravely and fastidiously. "Yes," she said quietly.

A little wind seemed to blow suddenly through the courtroom—a little, cold, ominous wind.

"Where?"

"On the desk in Mr. Patrick Ives's study on the afternoon of the nineteenth of June, 1926."

In a voice almost as gentle as her own, the prosecutor said, "That will be all, Miss Page. You may go."

And as lightly, as softly as she had come, Miss Page slipped from the witness box and was gone.

The second day of the Bellamy trial was over.

CHAPTER III

"Oh, I knew I would be—I knew it!" moaned the red-headed girl crawling abjectly over three irritated and unhelpful members of the Fourth Estate, dropping her pencil, dropping her notebook, dropping a pair of gray gloves and a squirrel scarf, and lifting a stricken face to the menacing countenance of Ben

Potts, king of court criers. "I've been late for every single thing that's happened since I got to this wretched town. It's like Alice in Wonderland—you have to run like mad to keep in the same place. Who's talking? What's happened?"

"Well, you seem to be doing most of the talking," replied the real reporter unkindly. "And about all that's happened has been fifteen minutes of as hot legal brimstone and sulphur as you'd want to hear in a thousand years, emitted by the Mephistophelean Farr, who thinks it would be nice to have a jackknife in evidence, and the inflammable Lambert, who thinks it would be horrid. Mr. Lambert was mistaken, the knife is in, and they're just opening a few windows to clear the air. Outside of that, everything's lovely. Not a soul's confessed, the day is young, and Mr. Douglas Thorne is just taking the stand. Carry on!"

The red-headed girl watched the lean, bronzed gentleman with sandy hair and a look of effortless distinction with approval. Nice eyes, nice hands.

"Mr. Thorne, what is your occupation?"

Nice voice: "I am a member of the New York Stock Exchange."

"Are you a relative of the defendant, Susan Ives?"

"Her elder brother, I'm proud to say."

His pleasant eyes smiled down at the slight figure in the familiar tweed suit, and for the first since she had come to court Sue Ives smiled back freely and spontaneously—a friendly, joyous smile, brilliant as a banner.

The prosecutor lifted a warning hand. "Please stick to the issue, Mr. Thorne, and we'll take your affection for your sister for granted. Are you the proprietor of the old Thorne estate, Orchards?"

"Yes."

"The sole proprietor?"

"The sole proprietor."

"Why did your sister not share in that estate, Mr. Thorne?"

"My father no longer regarded my sister as his heir after she married Patrick Ives. He took a violent dislike to Mr. Ives from the first, and it was distinctly against his wishes that Sue married him."

"Did you share this dislike?"

"For Patrick? Oh, no. At the time I hardly knew him, and later I became extremely fond of him."

"You still are?"

The pleasant gray eyes, suddenly grave, looked back unswervingly into the hot blue fire of the prosecutor's. "That is a difficult question to answer categorically. Perhaps the most accurate reply that I can give is that at present I am reserving an opinion on my brother-in-law and his conduct."

"That's hardly a satisfactory reply, Mr. Thorne."

"I regret it; it is an honest one."

"Well, let's put it this way: You are devoted to your sister, aren't you, Mr. Thorne?"

"Very deeply devoted."

"You admit that her happiness is dear to you?"

"I don't particularly care for the word 'admit'; I state willingly that her happiness is very dear to me."

"And you would do anything to secure it?"

"I would do a great deal."

"Anything?"

Douglas Thorne leaned forward over the witness box, his face suddenly stern. "If by 'anything,' Mr. Farr, you mean would I commit murder, my reply is no."

Judge Carver's gavel fell with a crash. "That is an entirely uncalled for conclusion, Mr. Thorne. It may be stricken from the record."

"Kindly reply to my question, Mr. Thorne. Would you not do anything in order to secure your sister's happiness?"

"No."

Once more Sue Ives's smile flew like a banner.

"Mr. Thorne, did your sister ever speak to you about her first two or three years in New York?"

"I have a vague general impression that we discussed certain aspects of it, such as living conditions there at the time, and——"

"Vague general impressions aren't what we want. You have no specific knowledge of where they were or what they were doing at the time?"

"I can recall nothing at the moment."

"Your sister, to whom you are so devoted, never once communicated with you during that time?"

"I received a letter from her about a week after she left Rosemont, stating that she thought that for the time being it would be better to sever all connections with Rosemont, but that her affection for all of us was unchanged."

"I haven't asked you for the contents of the letter. Is that the only communication that you received from her during those years in New York?"

"With the exception of Christmas cards, I heard nothing more for a little over two years. Then she began to write fairly regularly."

"Mr. Thorne, were you on the estate of Orchards at any time on June 19, 1926?"

"I was."

There was a sudden stir and ripple throughout the court room. "Now!" said the ripple. "Now! At last!"

"At what time?"

"I couldn't state the exact time at which I arrived, but I believe that it must have been shortly after nine in the evening."

The ripples broke into little waves. Nine o'clock—nine——

"And at what time did you leave?"

"That I can tell you exactly. I left the main house at Orchards at exactly ten minutes to ten."

The ripples broke into little waves. Ten o'clock—ten——

"Silence!" banged Judge Carver's gavel.

"Silence!" sang Ben Potts.

"Please tell us what you were doing at Orchards during that hour."

"It was considerably less than an hour. Mr. Conroy had telephoned me shortly before dinner, asking me to leave the keys at the cottage, which I gladly agreed to do, as I had been intending for some time to get some old account books I had left in my desk at the main house. I didn't notice the exact time at which I left Lakedale, but it must have been about half-past eight, as we dine at half-past seven, and I smoked a cigar before I started. I drove over at a fair rate of speed— around thirty-five miles an hour, say—and went straight to the main house."

"You did not stop at the gardener's cottage?"

"No; I——"

"Yet you pass it on your way from the lodge to the houses don't you?"

"No, coming from Lakedale I use the River Road; the first entrance off the road leads straight from the back of the place to the main house; the lodge gates are at the opposite end of the place on the main road from Rosemont. Shall I go on?"

"Certainly."

"It was just beginning to get dark when I arrived, and the electricity was shut off, so I didn't linger in the house—just procured the papers and cleared out. When I got back to the car, I decided to leave it there and walk over to the cottage and back. It was only a ten-minute walk each way, and it was a fine evening. I started off——"

"You say that it was dark at the time?"

"It was fairly dark when I started, and quite dark as I approached the cottage."

"Was there a moon?"

"I don't think so; I remember noticing the stars on the way home, but I am quite sure that there was no moon at that time."

"You met no one on your way to the cottage?"

"No one at all."

"You saw nothing to attract your attention?"

"No."

"And heard nothing?"

"Yes," said Douglas Thorne, as quietly and unemphatically as he had said no.

The prosecutor took a quick step forward. "You say you heard something? What did you hear?"

"I heard a woman scream."

"Nothing else?"

"Yes, a second or so afterward I heard a man laugh."

"A man laugh?" the prosecutor's voice was rough with incredulity. "What kind of a laugh?"

"I don't know how to characterize it," said Mr. Thorne simply. "It was an ordinary enough laugh, in a rather deep masculine voice. It didn't strike me as in any way extraordinary."

"It didn't strike you as extraordinary to hear a woman scream and a man laugh in a deserted place at that hour of the night?"

"No, frankly, it didn't. My first reaction was that the caretaker and his wife had returned from their vacation earlier than we had expected them; or if not, that possibly some of the young people from the village were indulging in some romantic trespassing—that's not unknown, I may state."

"You heard no words? No voices?"

"Oh, no; I was about three hundred feet from the cottage at the time that I heard the scream."

"You did not consider that that sound was the voice of a woman raised in mortal terror?"

"No," said Douglas Thorne. "Naturally, if I had, I should have done something to investigate. I was somewhat startled when I first heard it, but the laugh following so promptly completely reassured me. A scream of terror, a scream of pain, a scream of surprise, a scream of more or less perfunctory protest—I doubt whether anyone could distinguish between them at three hundred feet. I certainly couldn't."

The prosecutor shook his head irritably; he seemed hardly to be listening to this lucid exposition. "You're quite sure about the laugh—you heard it distinctly?"

"Oh, perfectly distinctly."

"Could you see the cottage from where you stood at the time?"

"No; the bend in the road and the high shrubbery hide it completely until you are almost on top of it."

"Then you don't know whether it was lighted when you heard the scream?"

"No; I only know that it was dark when I reached it a moment or so later."

"What did you do when you reached the cottage?"

"I noticed that it was dark as I ran up the steps, but on the off chance that it might have been the gardener that I had heard, I rang the bell half mechanically and tried the door, as I wanted to explain to him about Mr. Conroy's visit in the morning. The door was locked."

"You had the key on the ring, hadn't you?"

"Yes; but I had no reason in the world for going in if the gardener wasn't there."

"You heard no sound from within?"

"Not a sound."

"And nothing from without?"

"Everything was perfectly quiet."

"No one could have passed you at any time?"

"Oh, certainly not."

"Mr. Thorne, would it have been possible for anyone in the cottage to have heard you approaching?"

"I think that it might have been possible. The night was very still, and the main drive down which I was walking is of crushed gravel. The little drive off it that circles the house is of dirt; I don't know how clear footsteps would be on that, but of course anyone would have heard me going up the steps. I have a vague impression, too, that I was whistling."

"Could anyone have been concealed in the shrubbery about the house?"

"Oh, quite easily. The shrubbery is very high all about it."

"But you noticed no one?"

"No one."

"What did you do after you had decided that the house was empty?"

"I put the keys under the mat, as had been agreed, and returned to the main house. As I got into my roadster, I looked at my wrist watch by one of the headlights. It was exactly ten minutes to ten."

"What caused you to consult your watch?"

"I'd had a vague notion that I might run over to see my sister for a few minutes, as I was in the neighbourhood, but when I discovered that it was nearly ten, I changed my mind and went straight back to Lakedale."

"Mr. Thorne, you must have been perfectly aware when the news of the murder came out the next morning that you had information in your possession that would have been of great value to the state. Why did you not communicate it at once?"

Douglas Thorne met the prosecutor's gaze steadily, with a countenance free of either defiance or concern. "Because, frankly, I had no desire whatever to be involved, however remotely, in a murder case. I was still debating my duty in the matter two days later, when my sister and Mr. Bellamy were arrested, and the papers announced that the state had positive information that the murder was committed between quarter to nine and quarter to ten on the night of the nineteenth. That seemed to render my meagre observations quite valueless, and I accordingly kept them to myself."

"And I suppose you fully realize now that you have put yourself in a highly equivocal position by doing so?"

"Why, no, Mr. Farr; I may be unduly obtuse, but I assure you that I realize nothing of the kind."

"Let me endeavour to enlighten you. According to your own story, you must have heard that scream between nine-thirty and twenty-five minutes to ten, granting that you spent three or four minutes on the cottage porch and took ten minutes to walk back to the house. According to you, you arrived at the scene of action within three minutes of that scream, to find everything dark, silent and orderly. It is the state's contention that somewhere in that orderly darkness, practically within reach of your outstretched hand, stood your idolized sister. Quite a coincidence, isn't it?"

"It is quite a coincidence that that should be your contention," remarked Douglas Thorne, a dangerous glint in his eye. "But I know of no scandal attached to coincidence."

"Well, this particular type of coincidence has landed more than one man in jail as accessory after the fact," remarked the prosecutor grimly. "What time did you get back to Lakedale that night?"

"At ten-thirty."

"Did anyone see you?"

"My wife was on the porch when I arrived."

"Anyone else?"

"No."

"That's all, Mr. Thorne. Cross-examine."

Mr. Lambert approached the witness box at almost a prance, his broad countenance smouldering with ill-concealed excitement. "Mr. Thorne, I'll trouble you with only two questions. My distinguished adversary has asked you whether you noticed anything unusual in the neighbourhood of the cottage. I ask you whether in that vicinity you saw at any time a car—an automobile?"

"I saw no sign of a car."

"No sign of a small Chevrolet, for instance—of Mr. Bellamy's, for instance?"

"No sign of any car at all."

"Thank you, Mr. Thorne. That will be all."

Over Mr. Lambert's exultant carol rose a soft tumult of whispers. "There goes the state's story!" "Score 100 for the defense!" "Oh, boy, did you get that? He's fixed the time of the murder and run Sue and Steve off the scene all in one move." "The hand is quicker than the eye." "Look at Farr's face; that boy's got a mean eye——"

"Silence!" sang Ben Potts.

The prosecutor advanced to within six inches of the witness box, his eyes contracted to pin points. "You assure us that you saw no car, Mr. Thorne?"

"I do."

"But you are not able to assure us that no car was there?"

"Obviously, if a car was there, I should have seen it."

"Oh, no, believe me, that's far from obvious! If a car had been parked to the rear of the cottage on the little circular road, would you have seen it?"

"I should have seen its lights."

"And if its lights had been turned out?"

"Then," said Douglas Thorne slowly, "I should probably not have seen it."

"You were not in the rear of the cottage at any time, were you?"

"No."

"Then it is certain that you would not have seen it, isn't it?"

"I have told you that under those circumstances I do not believe I should have seen it."

"If a car had been parked on the main driveway between the lodge gates and the cottage, with its lights out, you would not have seen that either, would you, Mr. Thorne?"

"Possibly not."

"And you don't for a moment expect to have twelve level-headed, intelligent men believe that a pair of murderers would park their car in a clearly visible position, with all its lights burning for any passer-by to remark, while they accomplished their purpose?"

"I object to that question!" panted Mr. Lambert. "I object! It calls for a conclusion, Your Honour, and is highly——"

"The question is overruled."

"Very well, Mr. Thorne; that will be all."

Mr. Lambert, who had been following these proceedings with a woebegone countenance from which the recent traces of elation had been washed as though by a bucket of unusually cold water, pulled himself together valiantly. "Just one moment, Mr. Thorne; the fact is that you didn't see a car there, isn't it?"

"That is most certainly the fact."

"Thank you; that will be all."

"And the fact is," remarked the grimly smiling prosecutor, "that it might perfectly well have been there without your seeing it, isn't it?"

"Yes, that also is the fact."

"That will be all. Call Miss Flora Biggs."

The prosecutor's grim little smile still lingered.

"Miss Flora Biggs!"

Flora Biggs might have been a pretty girl ten years ago, before that fatal heaviness had crept from sleazy silk ankles to the round chin above the imitation pearls. Everything about Miss Biggs was imitation—an imitation fluff of something that was meant to be fur on the plush coat that was meant to be another kind of fur; an imitation rose of a washed-out magenta trying to hide itself in the masquerading collar; pearls the size of large bone buttons peeping out from too golden hair; an arrow of false diamonds catching the folds of the purple velvet toque that was not quite velvet; nervous fingers in suede gloves that were rather a bad grade of cotton clutching at a snakeskin bag of stenciled cloth—a poor, cheap, shoddy imitation of what the well-dressed woman will wear. And yet in those small insignificant features that should have belonged to a pretty girl, in those round china-blue eyes, staring forlornly out of reddened rims, there was something candid and touching and appealing. For out of those reddened eyes peered the good shy little girl in the starched white dress brought down to entertain the company—the good, shy little girl whose name had been Florrie Biggs. And little Florrie Biggs had been crying.

"Where do you live, Miss Biggs?"

"At 21 Maple Street, Rosemont." The voice was hardly more than a whisper.

"Just a trifle louder, please; we all want to hear you. Did you know Madeleine Bellamy, Miss Biggs?"

The tears that had been lurking behind the round blue eyes welled over abruptly, leaving little paths behind them down the heavily powdered cheeks. "Yes, sir, I did."

"Intimately?"

65

"Yes, sir. I guess so. Ever since I was ten. We went to school and high school together; she was quite a little younger than me, but we were best friends."

The tears rained down quietly and Miss Biggs brushed them impatiently away with the clumsy gloved fingers.

"You were fond of her?"

"Yes, sir, I was awful fond of her."

"Did you see much of her during the years of 1916 and '17?"

"Yes, sir; I just lived three houses down the block. I used to see her every day."

"Did you know Patrick Ives too?"

"Yes, sir; I knew him pretty well."

"Was there much comment on his attention to your friend Madeleine during the year 1916?"

"Everyone knew they had a terrible case on each other," said Miss Biggs simply.

"Were they supposed to be engaged?"

"No, sir, I don't know as they were; but everyone sort of thought they would be."

"Their relations were freely discussed amongst their friends?"

"They surely were."

"Did you ever discuss the affair with either Mr. Ives or Mrs. Bellamy?"

"Not ever with Pat, I didn't, but Mimi used to talk about it quite a lot."

"Do you remember what she said during the first conversation?"

"Well, I think that the first time was when we had a terrible fight about it." At memory of that far-off quarrel Florrie's blue eyes flooded and brimmed over again. "We'd been on a picnic and Pat and Mimi got separated from the rest of us, and by and by we went home without them; and it was awfully late that night when they got back, and I told Mimi that she ought to be carefuller how she went around with a fellow like Pat Ives, and she got terrible mad and told me that she knew what she was doing and she could look after herself, and that I was just jealous and to mind my own business. Oh, she talked to me something fierce."

Miss Biggs's voice broke on a great sob, and suddenly the crowded courtroom faded.... It was a hot July night in a village street and the shrill, angry voices of the two girls filled the air. Once more Mimi Dawson, insolent in her young beauty, was telling little Florrie Biggs to keep her small snub nose out of other people's affairs. All the injured woe of that far-off night was in her sob.

"Did she speak of him again?"

"Oh, yes, sir, she certainly did. She used to speak of him most of the time—after we made it up again, that is."

"Did she tell you whether they were expecting to be married?"

"Not in just so many words, she didn't, but she used to sort of discuss it a lot, like whether it would be a good thing to do, and if they'd be happy in Rosemont or whether New York wouldn't work better—you know, just kind of thinking it over."

Mr. Farr looked gravely sympathetic. "Exactly. Nothing more definite than that?"

"Well, I remember once she said that she'd do it in a minute if she were sure that Pat had it in him to make good."

"And did you gather from that and other remarks of hers that it was she who was holding back and Mr. Ives who was urging marriage?"

"Oh, yes, sir," said Miss Biggs, and added earnestly, "I think she meant me to gather that."

There was a warm, friendly little ripple of amusement, at which she lifted startled blue eyes.

"Quite so. Now when Mr. Ives went to France, Miss Biggs, what did your circle consider the state of affairs between them to be?"

"We all thought they was sure to get married," said Miss Biggs, and added in a low voice, "Some of us thought maybe they was married already."

"And just what made you think that?"

Miss Biggs moved restlessly in her chair. "Oh, nothing special, I guess; only they seemed so awfully gone on each other, and Pat was always hiring flivvers to take her off to Redfield and—and places. They never went much with the crowd any more, and lots of people were getting married then—you know, war marriages——" The soft, hesitant voice trailed off into silence.

"I see. Just what was Mr. Ives's reputation with your crowd, Miss Biggs? Was he a steady, hard-working young man?"

"He wasn't so awfully hard-working, I guess."

The distressed murmur was not too low to reach Patrick Ives's ears, evidently; for a brief moment his white face was lit with the gayest of smiles, impish and endearing. It faded, and the eyes that had been suddenly blue faded, too, back to their frozen gray.

"Was he popular?"

"Oh, everyone liked him fine," said Miss Biggs eagerly. "He was the most popular fellow in Rosemont, I guess. He was a swell dancer, and he certainly could play on the ukulele and skate and do perfectly killing imitations and—and everything."

"Then why did you warn your friend against consorting with this paragon, Miss Biggs?"

"Sir?"

"Why did you tell Mimi Dawson that she shouldn't play around too much with Pat Ives?"

"Oh—oh, well, I guess, like she said, I was just foolish and it wasn't none of my business."

"You said, a 'fellow like Pat Ives,' Miss Biggs. What kind of a fellow did you mean? The kind of a fellow who played the ukulele? Or did he play something else?"

"Well—well, he played cards some—poker, you know, and red dog and—well, billiards, you know."

"He gambled, didn't he?"

"Now, Your Honour," remarked Mr. Lambert heavily, "is this to be permitted to go on indefinitely? I have deliberately refrained from objecting to a most amazing line of questions——"

"The Court is inclined to agree with you, Mr. Lambert. Is it in any way relevant to the state's case whether Mr. Ives played the ukulele or the organ, Mr. Farr?"

"It is quite essential to the state's case to prove that Mr. Ives has a reckless streak in his character that led directly to the murder of Madeleine Bellamy, Your Honour. We contend that just as in those months before the war in the village of Rosemont, so in the year of 1926, he was gambling with his own safety and happiness and honour, and as in those days, with the happiness and honour and safety of a woman as well—with the same woman with whom he was renewing the affair broken off by a trick of fate nine years before. We contend——"

"Yes. Well, the Court contends that your questioning along these lines has been quite exhaustive enough, and that furthermore it doubts its relevance to the present issue. You may proceed."

"Very well, Your Honour.... When Mr. Ives returned in 1919, were you still seeing much of Miss Dawson?"

"No, sir," said Miss Biggs in a low voice. "Not any hardly."

"Why was that?"

"Well, mostly it was because she was starting to go with another crowd—the country-club crowd, you know. She was all the time with Mr. Farwell."

"Exactly. Did you renew your intimacy at any later period?"

"No, sir, not ever."

Once more the cotton fingers were busy with the treacherous tears, falling for Mimi, lost so many years ago—lost again, most horribly, after those unhappy years.

"Thank you, Miss Biggs. That will be all. Cross-examine."

Mr. Lambert's heavy face, turned to those drowned and terrified eyes, was almost paternal. "You say that for many years there was no intimacy between you and Mrs. Bellamy, Miss Biggs?"

"No, sir, there wasn't—not any."

"Mrs. Bellamy never took you into her confidence as to her feelings toward Mr. Ives after her marriage?"

"She never took me into her confidence about anything at all—no, sir."

"You never saw her after her marriage?"

"Oh, yes, I did see her. I went there two or three times for tea."

"Everything was pleasant?"

"She was very polite and pleasant—yes, sir."

"But there was no tendency to confide in you?"

"I didn't ask her to confide in me," said Miss Biggs. "I didn't ask her for anything at all—not anything."

"But if there had been anything to confide, it would have been quite natural to confide in you—girls generally confide in their best friend, don't they?"

"I guess so."

"And as far as you know, there were no guilty relations between Mrs. Bellamy and Mr. Ives at the time of her death?"

"I didn't know even whether she saw Mr. Ives," said Florrie Biggs.

Mr. Lambert beamed gratefully. "Thank you, Miss Biggs. That's all."

"Just one moment more, please." The prosecutor, too, was looking as paternal as was possible under the rather severe limitations of his saturnine countenance. "Mr. Lambert was just asking you if it would have been natural for her to confide in you, as girls generally confide in their best friends. At the time of this murder, and for many years previous, you weren't Mrs. Bellamy's best friend, were you, Miss Biggs?"

"No, sir, I guess I wasn't."

"There was very little affection and intimacy between you, wasn't there?"

"I don't know what you call between us," said Miss. Biggs, and the pretty, common, swollen face was suddenly invested with dignity and beauty. "I loved her better than anyone I knew. She was the only best friend I ever had—ever."

And swept by the hunger in that quiet and humble voice, the courtroom was suddenly empty of everyone but two little girls, warm cheeked, bright eyed, gingham clad—a sleek pig-tailed head and a froth of bright curls locked together over an inkstained desk. Best friends—four scuffed feet flying down the twilight street on roller skates—two mittened paws clutching each other under the shaggy robe of the bell-hung sleigh—a slim arm around a chubby waist on the hay cart— decorous, mischievous eyes meeting over the rims of the frosted glasses of sarsaparilla while brown-stockinged legs swung free of the tall drug-store stools—a shrill voice calling down the street in the sweet-scented dusk, "Yoo-hoo, Mimi! Mimi, c'mon out and play." Mimi, Mimi, lying so still with red on your white lace dress, come on out and——

"Thank you, Miss Biggs; that's all."

She stumbled a little on the step of the witness box, brushed once more at her eyes with impatient fingers and was gone.

"Call Mrs. Daniel Ives."

"Mrs. Daniel Ives!"

All through the Court went that quickening thrill of interest. A little old lady was moving with delicate precision down the far aisle to the witness box; the red-headed girl glanced quickly from her to the corner where Patrick Ives was sitting. He had half risen from his seat and was watching her progress with a passion of protest on his haggard young face. Well, even the prosecutor said that this reckless young man had been a good son, and it could hardly be a pleasant sight for the worst of sons to see his mother moving steadily toward that place of inquisition, and to realize that it was his folly that had sent her there. He sat down abruptly, turning his face toward the blue autumnal sky outside the window, against which the bare boughs of the tree spread like black lace. The circles under his eyes looked darker than ever.

As quietly as though it were a daily practice, Mrs. Ives was raising a neat black-gloved hand to take the oath and setting a daintily shod foot on the step of the witness box. She seated herself unhurriedly, opened the black fur collar at her throat, folded her hands on the edge of the box, and lifted a pair of dark blue

70

eyes, bravely serene, to the shrewd coolness of the prosecutor. There was just a glimpse of silver hair under the old-fashioned black toque with its wisp of lace and round jet pins; there was the faintest touch of pink in her cheeks and a small smile on her lips, shy and gracious. The kind of mother, decided the red-headed girl, that you would invent, if you were very talented.

"Mrs. Ives, you are the mother of Patrick Ives, are you not?"

"I am."

The gentle voice was as clear and true as a little bell.

"You heard Miss Biggs's testimony?"

"Oh, yes; my hearing is still excellent." The small smile deepened for a moment to friendly amusement.

"Were you aware of the state of affairs between Madeleine Bellamy and your son at the time that war broke out?"

"I was aware that he was paying her very marked attention, naturally, but I was most certainly not aware that they were seriously considering marriage. Both of them seemed absolute babies to me, of course."

"Had your son confided in you his intentions on the subject?"

"I believe that if he had had any such intentions he would have; but no, he had not."

"You were entirely in his confidence?"

"I hope so. I believe so." The deep blue eyes hovered compassionately over the averted face strained toward the window, and then moved tranquilly back to meet the prosecutor's.

"When this affair with Mrs. Bellamy was renewed in 1926, did he confide it to you?"

"Oh, no."

"Showing thereby that you were not entirely in his confidence, Mrs. Ives?"

"Or showing perhaps that there was nothing to confide," said Mrs. Daniel Ives gently.

The prosecutor jerked his head irritably. "The state is in possession of an abundance of material to prove that there was everything to confide, I assure you, Mrs. Ives. However, it is not my intention to make this any more difficult for you than is strictly necessary. How long ago did you come to Rosemont?"

"About fifteen years ago."

"You were a widow and obliged to support yourself?"

"No, that's hardly accurate. I was not supporting myself entirely and I was not a widow." The pale roses deepened a little under the black toque, but the voice was a trifle clearer than before.

"You mean that at the time you came to Rosemont your husband was still living?" The prosecutor made no attempt to disguise the astonishment in his voice.

"I do not know whether he was living or not. He had left me, you see, almost seventeen years before I came to Rosemont. I learned three years ago that he was dead, but not when he died."

"Mrs. Ives, I do not wish to dwell on a subject that must be painful to you, but I would like to get this straight. Were you divorced?"

"It is not at all painful to me," said Patrick Ives's mother gently, her small gloved hands wrung tightly together on the edge of the witness box. "It happened many years ago, and my life since has been full of so many things. We were not divorced. My husband was younger than I, and our marriage was not happy. He left me for a much younger woman."

"It was believed in Rosemont that you were a widow, was it not?"

"Everyone in Rosemont believed me to be a widow except Pat, who had known the truth since he was quite a little boy. It was foolish of me not to tell the truth, perhaps, but I had a great distaste for pity." She smiled again, graciously, at the prosecutor. "False pride was about the only luxury that I indulged in, in those days."

"You say that you were supporting both your son and yourself?"

"No. Pat was doing any little jobs that he could get, as he had done since he sold papers on the corner when he was six years old." For a moment the smile faded and she eyed the prosecutor steadfastly, almost sternly, as though daring him to challenge that statement, and for a moment it looked as though he were about to do exactly that, when abruptly, he veered.

"Were you in the garden the night of the nineteenth of June, Mrs. Ives?"

"In the rose garden—yes."

"Did you see Miss Page on her way to the sand pile?"

"I believe that I did, although I have nothing that particularly fixes it in my mind."

"Did you see your daughter-in-law?"

"Yes."

For a moment the faintest shadow passed over her face—a shadow of doubt, of hesitancy. Her glance went past the prosecutor to the place where her daughter-in-law was sitting, quietly attentive, and briefly, profoundly, their eyes met. The shadow passed.

"Which way was she going?"

"She was going past the rose garden toward the back gate of the house."

"Just one moment, Mrs. Ives. What is the distance between Mr. Ives's house and Orchards?"

"Well, that depends on how you approach it. By road it must be almost two miles, but if you use the little footpath that cuts across the meadows north of the house, it can't be less than a mile."

"Do you know where that path comes out?"

"I believe that it comes out by a little summerhouse or playhouse on the Thorne estate."

"Far from the gardener's cottage?"

"Oh, no—Miss Page said that it was quite near it, I think. She had been using it to take the children over to the playhouse on several occasions—and as it was quite without Mrs. Ives's knowledge, I spoke to my son about it."

"Did other members of the household make use of this path?"

"Not to my knowledge."

"Now, Mrs. Ives, when Mrs. Patrick Ives passed you in the garden, did she speak to you?"

"Yes."

"Just what did she say?"

"As nearly as I can remember, she said that she was going to the movies with the Conroys, and that she wasn't sure whether she would be back before I got to bed. She added that Pat was going to play poker."

"Nothing more?"

"That is all that I remember."

"Did you see her again that night?"

"Yes."

"Will you tell us when?"

"I saw her twice. Not more than two or three minutes after she passed me in the rose garden, she came back and went toward the house, almost running. I was at the far end of the garden by then, working on some trellises, and I didn't speak to her. She seemed in a great hurry, and I thought that she had probably forgotten something—her bag or a scarf for her hair, perhaps. She wasn't wearing any hat. A minute or so later she came out of the house and ran back down the path to the back gate."

"Was she wearing a scarf on her hair?"

"No."

"Had she a bag?"

"I don't remember seeing a bag, but she might well have had one."

"She did not speak to you?"

"No."

"And those were the two times that you refer to?"

"Oh, no," corrected Mrs. Ives gently. "I thought of those occasions as forming one time. I saw her again, a good deal later in the evening."

Once more the courtroom was filled with that strange stir—the movement of hundreds of bodies moving an inch nearer to the edges of chairs.

"Good Lord!" murmured the reporter devoutly. "She's going to give the girl an alibi! Look out, you old fox!"

The prosecutor, thus disrespectfully and inaudibly adjured, moved boldly forward. "At what time did you see your daughter-in-law, Mrs. Ives?"

"You've got to grant him nerve," continued the reporter, unabashed. "Or probably he's betting that the old lady wouldn't perjure herself even to save her son's wife. I'd rather bet it myself."

Mrs. Ives, who had been sitting silently studying her linked fingers, raised an untroubled countenance to the prosecutor's, but for the first time she spoke as though she were weighing her words: "It is difficult for me to give you the exact time, as I did not look at a clock. I had been in bed for quite a little while, however, and had turned out the light. I should say, roughly, that it might have been half-past ten. It was quite dark when I came into the house myself, I remember, and I believe that it stayed light at that time until long after nine."

"It was your habit to work in the garden until it was dark?"

"Yes; gardening is both my recreation and occupation." Mrs. Ives's tranquil eyes smiled at the prosecutor as though she expected to find in him an understanding soul. "Those hours after dinner were a great happiness to me, and often after it was too dark for any further work I would prolong them by sitting on a bench in the rose arbour and thinking over work well done. It was generally dark before I came in."

"And was on the night of the nineteenth of June?"

"Oh, yes; it had been dark for some time."

"Did you go straight to bed when you came in?"

"No; I stopped for a moment in the flower room to put away the basket with my tools and to tidy up a bit. Gardening is a grubby business." Again that delicate, friendly smile. "Just as I was coming out I saw Melanie, the waitress, turning out the lights in the living room, and I remember thinking that it must be ten o'clock, as that was the time that she usually did it if the family were not at home. Then I went on up to bed. It wasn't very long after I had turned out the light that I heard the front door close and thought, 'That must be Sue.'"

"It didn't occur to you that it might be your son?"

"Oh, no; Pat never got in before twelve if he was playing cards."

"You say that you saw Mrs. Ives. Did she come straight up to your room?"

"No; about five minutes after I heard the door close, I imagine. My room is in the left wing of the house, you understand, and I always leave my door a little ajar. Sue came to the door and asked in a whisper, 'Are you awake, Mother?' I said that I was and she came in, saying, 'I brought you your fruit; I'll just put it on the stand.'"

"Was she in the habit of doing that?"

"No, not exactly in the habit—that was Pat's task, but Sue is the most thoughtful child alive, and she had remembered that Pat wasn't there." Once more her eyes, loving and untroubled, smiled into Sue's.

"Did you turn on the light, Mrs. Ives?"

"No."

"Weren't you going to take the fruit?"

"Oh, no; I am not a very good sleeper, and I saved the fruit for the small hours of the morning."

"You were not able to see Mrs. Ives clearly, in that case?"

"I could see her quite clearly; there was a very bright light in the hall."

"You noticed nothing extraordinary in her appearance?"

"Nothing whatever."

"She was wearing the clothes that you had last seen her in?"

"She was wearing the dress, but she had taken off the coat, I believe."

"Ah-h!" sighed the courtroom under its breath.

"What kind of a coat, Mrs. Ives?"

"A little cream-coloured flannel coat." Not by the flicker of an eyelash did Mrs. Ives admit the sinister significance of that sigh.

"Did she say anything further?"

"Yes. I asked her whether she had enjoyed the movie, and she said that she had not gone to Rosemont, as she had met Stephen Bellamy in his car on her way to the Conroys' and he had given her a lift. He told her that the picture in Rosemont was an old one that they had both seen, and suggested that they drive over by the River Road and see what was running in Lakedale. When they got there they discovered that they had seen that film, too, so they drove around a little longer and then came home."

"That was all that she said?"

"She wished me sweet dreams, I believe, and kissed me good-night."

Under the gentle directness of her gaze, the prosecutor's face hardened. "Where was the fruit that you speak of usually kept, Mrs. Ives?"

"I believe that it was kept in a small refrigerator in the pantry."

"Was there a sink in that pantry?"

"Yes."

The prosecutor advanced deliberately toward the witness box, lowering his voice to a strangely menacing pitch: "Mrs. Ives, during the space that elapsed between the closing of the front door and Mrs. Patrick Ives's appearance in your bedroom, there would have been ample time for her to have washed her hands at that sink, would there not?"

"Oh, surely."

There was not even a second's hesitation in that swift reply, not a second's cloud over the lifted, slightly wondering face; but the little cold wind moved again through the courtroom. Over the clear, unfaltering syllables there was the sound of running water—of water that ran red, as Sue, the thoughtful, cleansed the hands that were to bear the fruit for the waiting mother.

"That will be all, Mrs. Ives," said the prosecutor. "Cross-examine."

She turned her face quietly toward Lambert's ruddy one.

"I'll keep you only a minute, Mrs. Ives." The rotund voice was softened to one of friendliest concern. "Mrs. Ives seemed quite herself when she came into the room?"

"Absolutely herself."

"No undue agitation?"

"She was not agitated in the slightest."

"Mr. Farr has asked you whether your son ever confided to you that he was having an affair with Mrs. Bellamy. I ask you whether he ever intimated that he was unhappy?"

"Not ever."

"Did Mrs. Ives?"

"Never."

"What was your impression as to their relations?"

"I thought——" For the first time the clear voice faltered, broke. She forced it back to steadiness relentlessly. "I thought that they were the happiest people that ever lived," said Patrick Ives's mother.

"Thank you, Mrs. Ives," said Mr. Lambert gently. "That will be all."

"Want me to bring back a sandwich?" inquired the reporter hospitably, gathering up his notes.

"Please," said the red-headed girl meekly.

"Sure you don't want to trail along? That drug store really isn't half bad."

"I'm always afraid that something might happen to me and that I mightn't get back," explained the red-headed girl. "Like getting run over, or arrested or kidnapped or something.... One with lettuce in it, please."

She sat contemplating the remaining occupants of the press seats about her with fascinated eyes. Evidently others were agitated by the same fears that haunted her. At any rate, three or four dozen were still clinging to their places, reading or writing or talking with impartial animation. They looked much nicer and less impersonal scattered about like that, but they still made her feel dreadfully shy and incompetent. They all knew one another so well; they were so casual and self-contained. Hurrying through the corridors, their ribald, salty banter broke over her in waves, leaving her drowned and forlorn.

She liked them awfully—that lanky, middle-aged man with the shrewd, sensitive face, jabbering away with the opulent-looking young creature in the sealskin cap and cloak; that Louisville reporter with her thin pretty face and little one-sided smile; that stocky youngster with the white teeth and the enormous vocabulary and the plaid necklace; that really beautiful girl who looked like an Italian opera singer and swore like a pirate, and arrived every day exactly an hour late in a flame-coloured blouse up to her chin and a little black helmet down to her eyebrows.

"Here's your sandwich," said the reporter—"two of 'em, just to show my heart's in the right place. The poisonous-looking pink one is currant jelly and the healthy-looking green one is lettuce. That's what I call a balanced ration! Fall to!"

The red-headed girl fell to obediently and gratefully.

"I do like the way newspaper people look," she said when only a few crumbs of the balanced ration remained.

"Ten thousand thanks," said the newspaper man. "Myself, I do like the way lady authoresses look."

"I mean I like them because they look so—so awfully alive," explained the red-headed girl sedately, keeping her eyes on the girl in the flame-coloured blouse lest the cocky young man beside her should read the unladylike interest that he roused in her.

"Ah, well, in that case, not more than one thousand thanks," said the reporter—"and those somewhat tempered. Look alive, do we? There's a glowing tribute for you! I trust that you'll be profoundly ashamed of yourself when I inform you that I meant nothing of the kind when I extolled the appearance of lady authoresses. Dead or alive, I like the way their hair grows over their ears, and their discreet use of dimples, and the useless length of their eyelashes. Meditate on that for a while!"

The red-headed girl meditated, while both her colour and her dimples deepened. At the end of her meditations she inquired politely, "Is it true that Mr. Bellamy's counsel broke his leg?"

"Couldn't be truer. Fell down the Subway stairs at eleven-forty-five last night and is safe in the hospital this morning. Lambert's taking over Bellamy's defense; he and those two important, worried-looking kids who sit beside him at the desk down there reading great big enormous law books and are assistant counsel—whatever that means.... Ah, here's Ben Potts! Fine fellow, Ben.... We're off!"

"Mr. Elliot Farwell!"

A thickset, broad-shouldered individual, with hair as slick as oiled patent leather, puffy eyes, and overprominent blue jowls, moved heavily toward the witness box. An overgaudy tie that looked as though it came from the ten-cent store and had actually come from France, a waistcoat that made you think vaguely of checks, though it was quite guiltless of them; a handkerchief with an orange-and-green monogram ramping across one corner—the stuff of which con men and race-track touts and ham actors and men about town are made. The red-headed girl eyed him severely. Thus she was wont to regard his little brother and big brother at the night clubs, as they leaned conqueringly across little tables, offering heavily engraved flasks to limp chits clad in shoulder straps and chiffon handkerchiefs.

"Mr. Farwell, where were you on the afternoon of the nineteenth of June at about five o'clock?"

"At the Rosemont Country Club."

Not a pleasant voice at all, Mr. Farwell's; a heavy, sullen voice, thickened and coarsened with some disreputable alchemy.

"What were you doing?"

"I was just hanging around after golf, having a couple of drinks."

"Did you see Mrs. Patrick Ives?"

"Yes."

"Talk with her?"

"Yes."

"Will you give us the substance of your conversation?"

Mr. Farwell shifted his bulk uneasily in his chair. "How do you mean—the substance of it?"

"Just outline what you said to Mrs. Ives."

"Well, I told her——" The heavy voice lumbered to silence. "Do I have to answer that?"

"Certainly, Mr. Farwell." Judge Carver's voice was edged with impatience.

"I told her that she'd better keep an eye on her husband," blurted Mr. Farwell desperately.

"Did you give her any reason for doing that?"

"Of course I gave her a reason."

"Well, just give it to us, too, will you?"

"I told her that he was making a fool of himself with Mimi."

"Nothing more specific than that?"

"Well, I told her that they were meeting each other secretly."

"Where?"

"At the gardener's cottage at Orchards." Those who were near enough could see the little beads of sweat on Mr. Farwell's forehead.

"How did you know that?"

"Orsini told me."

"And who is Orsini?"

"He's the Bellamys' man of all work—tends to the garden and furnace and all that kind of thing."

"Well, just how did Orsini come to tell you about this, Mr. Farwell?"

"Because I'd twice seen Mrs. Bellamy take the Perrytown bus, alone, and I told Orsini that I'd give him ten dollars if he found out for me where she was going. He said he didn't need to find out—he knew."

"Did he tell you how he knew?"

"Yes; he knew because it was he that loaned her the key to the cottage. She'd found out that he had the key, and she told him some cock-and-bull story about wanting to practise on the cottage piano that the gardener had there, and he used to loan it to her whenever she asked for it, and generally she'd forget to give it back to him till the next day."

"How did he happen to have it?"

"The Thornes' gardener was a friend of his, and he left it with Orsini when he went off on his vacation to Italy, because he'd left some kind of homebrew down in the cellar, and he wanted Orsini to keep an eye on it."

"Did you know when she had last borrowed it?"

"Yes; she'd borrowed it round noon on the nineteenth. I went by her house a little before one to see if she would take lunch with me at the club, and Orsini was fixing up the gate in the picket fence. He told me that Mimi had left about half an hour ago in their car, asking for the key, as she said she wanted to go to the cottage to practise. So I went after her."

"To the gardener's cottage?"

"Yes."

"Was she there?"

"No."

"How did you know that she wasn't there, Mr. Farwell?"

"Because there wasn't any car, nor any music either."

There was a surly defiance in Farwell's tone that the prosecutor blandly ignored.

"Did you go into the cottage?"

"No; it was locked."

"What did you do then?"

"It started to rain while I was standing on the porch and I stopped and tossed up a coin as to whether to go on to the club, hoping it would clear up enough for golf, or to go back to the bungalow. It came tails, so I waited for a minute or so and went on to the club."

"Whom did you find there?"

"Mrs. Bellamy, Dick Burgoyne, the Conroys, the Dallases, Sue Ives—all the crowd. It cleared up after lunch, and most of us went off to the links. Sue made up a foursome with the Conroys and Steve Bellamy, who turned up on the two o'clock train. Mimi played a round with Burgoyne, and I went with George Dallas. We all got round within a few minutes of each other and sat around, getting drinks and gabbing."

"Was it then that you told Mrs. Ives about this affair of her husband's?"

"It was around that time."

"Was Mr. Ives there?"

"No; he'd telephoned that he couldn't get out till dinner-time."

"Just what made you tell Mrs. Ives this story, Mr. Farwell?"

Elliot Farwell's heavy jowls became slightly more prominent. "Well, I'd had a drink too many, I guess, and I was good and fed up with the whole thing. I thought Sue was a peach, and it made me sick to see what Ives was getting away with."

"What did Mrs. Ives say?"

"She said that I was out of my head, and I told her that I'd bet her a thousand dollars to five cents that Mimi and Pat would tell some fairy stories about what they were doing that evening and meet at the cottage. And I told her that I'd waited behind the bushes at the lodge gates the week before when Sue was in New York, and seen both of them go up the drive—Mimi on foot and Ives ten minutes later in the car. That worried her; she wasn't sure how sober I was, but she cut out telling me I was crazy."

He paused and the prosecutor lifted an impatient voice. "Then what, Mr. Farwell?"

"Well, a little while after that George Dallas came over and said that if Sue wanted him to, he'd stop on the way home and show her how to make the new cocktail that he'd been telling her about, so that she could surprise Pat with it at dinner. And she said all right, and we all piled into our cars and headed for her place— all except Mimi and Bellamy. They'd left a few minutes before, because they had dinner early."

"Did you have any further conversation with Mrs. Ives on the subject?"

"Not anything that you'd call conversation. There was a whole crew jabbering around there at her place."

"Well, did she mention it again?"

"Oh, well, she came up to me just when I was going—I was looking around for my hat in the hall—and she said, 'Elliot, don't tell anyone else that you've told me about this, will you?' And I said, 'All right.' And she said, 'Promise. I don't want it to get back to Pat that I know until I decide what to do.' And so I said sure I'd promise. And then I cleared out."

In the hushed courtroom his voice sounded ugly and defiant, but he kept his face turned stubbornly away from Sue Ives's clear attentive eyes, which never once had left it, and which widened a little now, gravely ironic, as the man who had promised not to tell sullenly broke that promise.

"Oh," whispered the red-headed girl fiercely—"oh, the cad! He's trying to make it look as though she did it—as though she meant to do it even then."

"Oh, come on, now!" remonstrated the reporter judicially, "Give the poor devil his due! After all, he's on oath, and the prosecutor's digging into him with a pickax and spade. Here, look out, or we'll miss something!"

"And after you and Mr. Burgoyne had dined, Mr. Farwell?"

"Well, I had a rotten headache, so I decided that I wouldn't go over to Dallases' for the poker game after all, but that I'd turn in and read a detective story that I'd brought out with me. I called up George to ask if he'd have enough without me, and he said yes, so I decided that I'd call it a night and went up to my bedroom."

"Did you see Mr. Burgoyne before he left?"

"Yes, he stuck his head in the door just as I was putting on my bathrobe and asked if there was anything he could do, and I said nothing but tell George I was sorry."

"Have you any idea what time that was?"

"It must have been round quarter to nine; the party was to start about nine, and he was walking."

"Did you read for long after he left?"

"Yes, I read right along; but about half-past nine I got up for a cigarette, and I couldn't find a match, so I started hunting through the pockets of the golf suit I'd been wearing, for my lighter. It wasn't there. I remembered that I'd used it on the way over to the cottage—I kept it in my pocket with my loose change—and all of a sudden it came back to me that I'd pulled a handkerchief out of that pocket when I was getting that coin to toss up on the porch and I'd thought I heard something drop, and looked around a little, but I didn't pay much attention to it, because I thought probably it was just some change that had rolled off the porch. I realized then that it must have been the lighter, and I was sore as the devil."

"Will you tell us why, Mr. Farwell?"

"Because I didn't want anyone to know I'd been hanging round the cottage, and the lighter was marked on the inside."

"Marked with your name?"

"Marked with an inscription—Elliot, from Mimi, Christmas, 1918."

The coarse voice was suddenly shaken, the coarse face suddenly pale—Elliot from Mimi, Christmas, 1918.

"What did you do after you missed the lighter, Mr. Farwell?"

"Well, I cursed myself good and plenty and went on a hunt for matches downstairs. There wasn't one in the whole darned place, and I was too lazy to get into my clothes again, so I called Dick at the Dallases' and asked him to be sure to bring some home with him."

"What time did you telephone?"

"I didn't look at the time. It was half-past nine when I started to look for the matches. Quarter to ten—ten minutes to, maybe."

"Did you go back to bed?"

"Yes; but I went on reading for quite a while. I'd dozed off by the time Dick came in, though the light was still burning."

"What time was that?"

"A little after half-past eleven."

The prosecutor stood eyeing the heavy countenance before him speculatively for a moment, and then, with a quick shake of his narrow, sleek, finely poised head, took his decision. "Mr. Farwell, when did you first tell the story that you have been telling us?"

"On June twenty-first."

"Where did you tell it?"

"In your office."

"At whose request?"

"At——"

Mr. Lambert, who had been sitting twitching in his chair, emitted a roar of protest as he bounded to his feet that effectually drowned out any information Mr. Farwell was about to impart. "I object, Your Honour! I object! What does it matter whether this witness told his story in the prosecutor's office or the Metropolitan Opera House? The point is that he's telling it here, and anything else is deliberately beside the mark. I——"

"The Court is inclined to agree with you, Mr. Lambert. What is the object of establishing when, where, and why Mr. Farwell told this story, Mr. Farr?"

"Because, Your Honour, it is entirely owing to the insistence of the state that Mr. Farwell is at present making a series of admissions that if misinterpreted by the jury might be highly prejudicial to Mr. Farwell. There is not one chance in a hundred that the defense would have brought out under cross-examination the fact that Mr. Farwell was at the gardener's cottage on the nineteenth of June—a fact that I have deliberately elicited in my zeal to set all the available facts before the jury. But in common fairness to Mr. Farwell, I think that I should be permitted to bring out the circumstances under which I obtained this information."

Judge Carver paraded his fine, keen old eyes meditatively from the ruddy full moon of Mr. Lambert's countenance to the black-and-white etching of the prosecutor's, cold as ice, for all the fever of intensity behind it; on farther still to the bull-necked and blue-jowled occupant of the witness box. There was a faint trace of distaste in their depths as they returned to the prosecutor. Perhaps it was that distaste that swung back the pendulum. Judge Carver had the reputation of being as fair as he was hard.

"Very well, Mr. Farr. The Court sees no impropriety in having you state those circumstances as briefly as possible."

"May I have an objection to that, Your Honour?" Lambert's face had deepened to a fine claret.

"Certainly."

"On the morning of the twenty-first of June," said Mr. Farr, "I asked Mr. Farwell to come to my office. When he arrived I told him that we had information in our hands that definitely connected him with this atrocious crime, and that I sincerely advised him to make a clean breast of all his movements. He proceeded to do so promptly, and told me exactly the same story that he has told you. It came, frankly, as a surprise to me, but it in no way altered or modified the state's case. I therefore decided to put Mr. Farwell on the stand in order to let you have all the facts."

"Was the information that you possessed connecting Mr. Farwell with the crime the cigarette lighter, Mr. Farr?" inquired Judge Carver gravely.

"No, Your Honour; it was Mrs. Ives's telephone conversation with Stephen Bellamy, asking whether Elliot had not told him anything. There was no other Elliot in Mrs. Ives's circle of acquaintances."

"Is the lighter in the possession of the state at present?"

"No, Your Honour," remarked the prosecutor blandly. "The state's case would be considerably simplified if it were."

His eye rested, fugitive but penetrating, on Mr. Lambert's heated countenance.

"That is all that you desire to state, Mr. Farr?"

"Yes, Your Honour. No further questions, Mr. Farwell. Cross-examine."

"What kind of a cigarette lighter was this, Mr. Farwell?" There was an ominous rumble in Lambert's voice.

"A little black enamel and silver thing that you could light with one hand. They brought a lot of them over from England in '17 and '18."

"Had anyone ever suggested to you that this lighter might possibly prove a dangerous weapon against you if it fell into the hands of the defense?" inquired Mr. Lambert, in what were obviously intended to be silken tones.

"No," replied Mr. Farwell belligerently; "no one ever told me anything of the kind."

Mr. Farr permitted himself a fleeting and ironic smile in the direction of his adversary before he turned a countenance lit with splendid indignation in the direction of the jury.

"Mr. Farwell, you told the prosecutor that you had had a couple of drinks before you confided this story about her husband to Mrs. Ives. Was that accurate, or had you had more?"

"I'd had three or four, maybe—I don't remember."

"Three or four after you came off the links?"

"Well, what of it?" Farwell's jaw was jutting dangerously.

"Be good enough to answer my question, Mr. Farwell."

"All right, three or four after I came off the links."

"And three or four before you started?"

"I don't remember how many; we all had something at lunch."

"You had had too many, hadn't you, Mr. Farwell?"

"Too many for what?"

"Too many for Mimi Bellamy's good, let us say." Mr. Lambert caught a menacing movement from the chair occupied by the prosecutor and hurried on: "Would you have been quite so explicit to Mrs. Ives if you had not had those drinks?"

"I don't know whether I would or not." The little beads of sweat on the low forehead were suddenly larger. "I'd been thinking for quite a while that she ought to know what was going on."

"I see. And just what did you think was to be gained by her knowledge?"

"I thought she'd put a stop to it."

"Put a stop to it with a knife, Mr. Farwell?" inquired Mr. Lambert, ferociously genial.

And suddenly there leaped from the dull eyes before him a flame of such raw agony that Mr. Lambert took a hasty and prudent step backward.

"What do you take me for? I thought she'd make him cut it out."

"And it was absolutely essential to you that he should cut it out, wasn't it, Mr. Farwell?"

"What?"

"You were endeavoring to persuade Mrs. Bellamy to divorce Mr. Bellamy and marry you, weren't you, Mr. Farwell?"

Mr. Farwell sat glaring dumbly at his tormentor out of those strange eyes.

"Weren't you?"

"Yes." As baldly as though Mr. Farwell were stating that he had tried to get her to play a game of bridge.

"How long had it been since your affection for her had revived?"

"It hadn't revived. My affection for her, if that's what you want to call it, hadn't ever stopped."

"Oh, I see. And at the time of the murder you were not convinced that it was hopeless?"

"No."

"I see. But you were a good deal disturbed over this affair with Mr. Ives, weren't you?"

"Yes."

"And when you went home you had a few more drinks just to celebrate the fact that you'd fixed everything up, didn't you?"

"I had another drink or so."

"And when you went up to bed with the detective story you took a full bottle of whisky with you, didn't you?"

"I guess so."

"And it was three quarters empty the next morning, wasn't it?"

"How do I know?"

"Wasn't it found beside your bed almost empty next morning, Mr. Farwell?"

"I don't know. I'd taken a good deal of it."

"Mr. Farwell, are you sure that you didn't find that you had lost that cigarette lighter before nine-thirty—at a little after nine, say?"

"No, I told you that it was nine-thirty."

"What makes you so sure?"

"I looked at my watch."

"And just why did you do that?"

"Because I wanted to know the time."

"Why?"

"I don't know—I just wanted to know."

"It was very convenient that it happened to be just nine-thirty, wasn't it?"

"I don't know what you mean; it wasn't convenient at all, if it comes to that."

"You don't? And you don't see why it was convenient that you happened to call up the Dallas house at about ten minutes to ten, assuring them thereby that you were safe at home in your pajamas?"

"No, I don't."

"You have a Filipino boy who works for you, haven't you, Mr. Farwell?"

"Yes."

"Was he in the house after Mr. Burgoyne went on to the poker party?"

"No; he goes home after he finishes the dinner things—around half-past eight usually."

"So you were absolutely alone in the house?"

"Absolutely."

"Your car was outside, wasn't it?"

"It was in the garage."

"It never entered your head when you missed that lighter, the loss of which concerned you so deeply, to get into that automobile and take the five- or ten-minute drive to Orchards to recover it?"

"It certainly didn't."

"You didn't do anything of the kind?"

"Look here, I've already told you about twenty times that I didn't, haven't I?" Mr. Farwell's voice was straining perilously at the leash.

"I didn't remember that I'd asked you that before. At what time did you first hear of this tragedy, Mr. Farwell?"

"You mean the—murder?"

"Naturally."

Once more the dull eyes were lit by that strange flare of stupefied agony. "At about twelve o'clock Sunday morning, I guess—or half-past eleven—I don't know—sometime late that morning. George Dallas telephoned me. I was still half asleep."

"What did you do?"

"Do? I don't know what I did. It knocked me cold."

Mr. Lambert suddenly thrust his beaming countenance into the stolid mask before him. "However cold it might have knocked you, Mr. Farwell, don't you remember that within three quarters of an hour of the time that you received this news you locked yourself in the library and tried to blow your brains out?"

"Yes," said Elliot Farwell, "I remember that."

"You didn't succeed because your friend Richard Burgoyne had previously emptied the pistol?"

"Correct."

"And your Filipino boy, looking for you to announce lunch, noticed you through the window and set up the alarm, didn't he?"

"So I understand."

"What did you say to Mr. Burgoyne when he forced his way into the library, Mr. Farwell?"

"I don't remember."

"You don't remember that you said, 'Keep your hands off me, Dick; after what I've done, there's no way out but this'?"

"No, I don't remember it, but I probably said it. I don't remember what I said."

"What explanation do you offer for that remark, Mr. Farwell?"

"I'm not offering any explanations; if I said it, I said it. What difference does it make what I meant?"

"It makes quite a difference, I assure you. You have no explanation to offer?"

"No."

"Mr. Farwell, for the last time I ask you whether you were not at the gardener's cottage at Orchards on the night of June nineteenth?"

"No."

"At about nine-thirty?"

"No."

Mr. Lambert, the ruddy moon of his countenance suddenly alive with malice, shot his question viciously into the tortured mask: "It was not your laugh that Mr. Thorne heard coming from the cottage, Mr. Farwell?"

"You——"

Over the gasp of the courtroom rose the bellow of rage from the witness box, the metallic ring of the prosecutor's voice, the thunder of Judge Carver's gavel and Ben Potts's chant.

"Silence! Silence!"

"Your Honour, I would like to ask one question. Is Mr. Farwell on trial for his life here, or is this the case of the People versus Bellamy and Ives?"

"This Court is not given to answering rhetorical questions, Mr. Farr. Mr. Lambert, Mr. Farwell has already told you several times that he was not at Orchards on the night of June nineteenth. The Court has given you great latitude in your cross-examination, but it does not propose to let you press it farther along those lines. If you have other questions to put, you may proceed."

"No further questions, Your Honour." Mr. Lambert's voice remained buoyantly impervious to rebuke.

"One moment, Mr. Farwell." The prosecutor moved swiftly forward. The man in the witness box, who had lurched to his feet at that last outrage from the exultant Lambert, turned smouldering eyes on him. On the rim of the witness box, his hands were shaking visibly—thick, well groomed, insensitive hands, with a heavy seal ring on one finger. "You admit that you had been drinking heavily before you spoke to Mrs. Ives, do you not?"

"Yes—yes—yes."

"Did you regret that fact when you returned home that evening?"

"I knew I'd talked too much—yes."

"Did you regret it still more deeply when you received the news of the murder the following morning?"

"Yes."

"Wasn't that the reason for your attempted suicide?"

A long pause, and then once more the heavy tortured voice: "Yes."

"Because you realized that harm had come to her through your indiscretion?"

"Yes, I told you—yes."

"Thanks, that's all. Call Mr. Dallas."

"Mr. George Dallas!"

A jaunty figure in blue serge, with a smart foulard tie and curly blond hair just beginning to thin, moved briskly forward. Mr. Dallas was obviously a good fellow; there was a hearty timbre to his rather light voice, his lips parted constantly in an earnestly engaging smile over even white teeth, and his brown eyes were the friendliest ever seen out of a dog's head. If he had not had thirty thousand dollars a year, he would have been an Elk, a Rotarian, and the best salesman on the force.

He cast an earnestly propitiatory smile at Sue Ives, who smiled back, faintly and gravely, and an even more earnestly propitiatory one at the prosecutor, who returned it somewhat perfunctorily.

"Mr. Dallas, you were giving a poker party on the night of the nineteenth of June, were you not?"

"I was indeed."

Mr. Dallas's tone implied eloquently that it had been a highly successful party, lacking only the prosecutor's presence to make it quite flawless.

"You were present when Mr. Farwell telephoned Mr. Burgoyne?"

"Oh, yes."

"The telephone was in the room in which you were playing?"

"Yes, sir."

"About what time did the call come in?"

"Well, now let's see." Mr. Dallas was all eager helpfulness. "It must have been about quarter to ten, because every fifteen minutes we were making a jack pot, and I remember that we'd had the first and another was just about due when the 'phone rang and Dick held up the game for a while."

"Did you get Mr. Burgoyne's end of the conversation?"

"Well, not all of it. We were all making a good deal of a racket—just kidding along, you know—but I heard Dick say, 'Oh, put on your clothes and come over and we'll give you enough of 'em to start a bonfire.'"

"Did Mr. Burgoyne make any comments after he came back?"

"He said, 'Boys, don't let me forget to take some matches when I go. Farwell hasn't got one in the house.'"

"What time did he leave?"

"Oh, around eleven-fifteen, I guess; we broke up earlier than usual."

"Did you call Mr. Farwell up the following day around noon?"

"Yes, I did." Mr. Dallas's jaunty accents were suddenly tinged with gravity.

"Can you remember that conversation?"

"Well, I remember that when Elliot answered he still sounded half asleep and rather put out. He said, 'What's the idea, waking a guy up at this time of day?' And I said, 'Listen, Elliot, something terrible's happened. I was afraid you'd see it in the papers. Mimi Bellamy's been murdered in the gardener's cottage at Orchards.' He made a queer sort of noise and said, 'Don't, George! Don't, George!' Don't—don't—over and over again, as though he were wound up. I said, 'Don't what?' But he'd hung up, I guess; anyway he didn't answer."

"He seemed startled?"

"Oh, rather—he seemed absolutely knocked cuckoo." The voice hung neatly between pity and regret, the sober eyes tempering the flippant words.

"All right, Mr. Dallas—thanks. Cross-examine."

As though loath to tear himself from this interesting and congenial chatter, Mr. Dallas wrenched his expressive countenance from the prosecutor and turned it, flatteringly intent, on the roseate Lambert.

"Did other people overhear Mr. Burgoyne's remarks, Mr. Dallas?"

"Oh, I'm quite sure that they must have. We were all within a foot or so of each other, you know."

"Who was in the room?"

"Well, there was Burgoyne, and I had Martin and two fellows from New York who were out for the week-end, and—let's see——"

"Wasn't Mr. Ives in the room at the time?"

"Well, no," said Mr. Dallas, a curious, apprehensive shadow playing over his sunny countenance. "No, he wasn't."

"I see. What time had he arrived, Mr. Dallas?"

"Mr. Ives?"

"Yes."

Mr. Dallas cast a fleeting and despairing glance at the white-faced figure in the corner by the window, and Patrick Ives returned it with a steady, amused, indifferent air. "Oh—oh, well, he hadn't."

Mr. Lambert stopped, literally transfixed, his eyes bulging in his head. "You mean that he hadn't arrived at a quarter to ten?"

"No, he hadn't."

For the first time since the trial opened, Sue Ives stirred in her seat. She leaned forward swiftly, her eyes, urgent and imperious, on her stupefied counsel. Her lifted face, suddenly vivid with purpose, her lifted hand, cried a warning to him clearer than words. But Mr. Lambert was heeding no warnings.

"What time did he get there?"

"He—well, you see—he didn't get there."

Mr. Dallas again turned imploring eyes on the gentleman in the corner, whose own eyes smiled back indulgently, a little more indifferent, a little more amused.

"Had he let you know of this change of plans?"

"No," said Mr. Dallas wretchedly. "No, he hadn't—exactly."

"He simply didn't turn up?"

"That's it—he just didn't turn up." Mr. Dallas's voice made a feeble effort to imply that nothing could possibly be of less consequence between men of the world.

Mr. Lambert, stupor still rounding his eyes, made a vague gesture of dismissal, his face carefully averted from Sue Ives's sternly accusing countenance.

"No further questions."

Mr. Dallas scrambled hastily to his feet, his ingenuous gaze turned hopefully on the prosecutor.

The expression on the prosecutor's classic features, however, was not calculated to reassure the most optimistic. Mr. Farr was contemplating the amiable countenance of his late witness with much the look of astounded displeasure which must have adorned Medusa's first audience. He, too, sketched a slight gesture of dismissal toward the door, and Dallas, eager and docile, followed it.

The third day of the Bellamy trial was over.

CHAPTER IV

"Well, this is the time you beat me to it," commented the reporter approvingly. "That's the hat I like too. Want a pencil?"

"I always want a pencil," said the red-headed girl. "And I beat everybody to it. I'd rather get here at six o'clock than go through that howling mob of maniacs one single time more. Besides, I've been sleeping, so I might as well be here. Besides, I thought that if I got here early you might tell me whether it was Mr. Ives or Mr. Farwell who did it."

"Who did what?"

"Who killed Mrs. Bellamy."

"Oh, Lord!" groaned the reporter. "Why is it that every mortal soul at a murder trial spends his life trying to pin the crime on to anyone in the world but the people being tried for it. Talk about juries!"

"I'm not talking about juries," said the red-headed girl firmly. "I'm talking about Mr. Farwell, and Mr. Ives. Don't you think that it was funny that Mr. Farwell was there that day?"

"Oh, comical as all get out! Still and all, I believe that he was there precisely when he said he was. That poor devil was telling the truth."

"How do you know?" inquired the red-headed girl respectfully.

"Oh, you get hunches at this game when you've been at it long enough."

"That must be nice. Did you get a hunch about Mr. Ives?"

"About Pat Ives? I haven't heard him yet."

"What did it mean, his not being at that poker game?"

"Well, it might have meant anything in the world—or nothing. The only thing that's perfectly clear is that it meant that last night was undoubtedly one of wassail and carouse for Uncle Dudley Lambert."

"Why?"

"My dear child, didn't you see the look of unholy glee that flooded the old gentleman's countenance when he realized that young Mr. Ives hadn't a shadow of an alibi for that eventful evening?"

"Well, but why?"

"Because the only thing that Uncle Dudley would as soon do as save his angel goddaughter from the halter is to drape one around Pat Ives's neck. He's hated Pat ever since he dared to subject his precious Sue to a life of good healthy hardship in New York; he's never forgiven him for estranging her from her father; and since he found out that he betrayed her with the Bellamy girl, he's been simply imbecile with rage. And now, through some heaven-sent fluke, he's enabled to put his life in jeopardy. He's almost out of his head. He'd better go a bit warily, however. If I can read the human countenance—and it may interest you to know that I can read the human countenance—Mrs. Patrick Ives is not entirely in favour of sending her unworthy spouse to the gallows. She had a monitory look in her eye that bodes ill for Uncle Dudley if she ever realizes what he's doing."

The red-headed girl heaved an unhappy sigh. "Well, I don't believe that anyone did it," she remarked spaciously. "Not anyone here, I mean. Burglars, probably, or one of those funny organizations, or——"

"Silence, silence! The Court!"

Mr. Farr had a new purple necktie, sombre and impressive; Mr. Lambert was a trifle more frivolous, though the polka dots were discreet; Mrs. Ives wore the same tweed suit, the same copper-coloured hat. Heavens, it might as well be a uniform!

"Call Miss Cordier."

"Miss Melanie Cordier!"

The slim elegance of the figure in the severely simple black coat and black *cloche* hat was especially startling when one remembered that Miss Melanie Cordier was the waitress in the Ives household. It was a trifle more comprehensible when one remembered that she was as Gallic as her name implied. With her creamy skin, her long black eyes and smooth black curves of hair, her lacquer-red mouth exactly matching the lacquer-red camellia on her lapel, Miss Cordier bore a striking resemblance to a fashion magazine's cover designs. She mounted the witness box with profound composure and seated herself, elaborately at ease.

"Miss Cordier, what was your occupation on the nineteenth of June, 1926?"

"I was waitress in the employment of Mrs. Patrick Ives." There was only the faintest trace of accent in the clear syllables—a slight softening of consonants and broadening of vowels, becoming enough variations on an Anglo-Saxon theme.

"How long had you been in her employ?"

"A year and nine month—ten month. I could not be quite sure."

"How did you happen to go to Mrs. Ives?"

"It was through Mrs. Bellamy that I go."

"Mrs. Stephen Bellamy?"

"Yes, sir, through Mrs. Stephen Bellamy."

"Will you tell us just how that happened, Miss Cordier?"

"Assuredly. My little younger sister had been sent by an agency three or four years ago to Mrs. Bellamy directly when she land in this country. She was quite inexperience', you understand, and could not command a position such as one trained could demand; but Mrs. Bellamy was good to her and she work hard, and after a while she marries a young man who drives for the grocer and they——"

"Yes, quite so, Miss Cordier. My question was, how did Mrs. Bellamy happen to send you to Mrs. Ives?"

"Yes, that is what I explain." Miss Cordier, exquisitely unruffled, pursued the even tenor of her way. "Sometime when my sister was there with Mrs. Bellamy I would go out to show her what she should do. For me, I have been a waitress for eight years and am well experience'. Well, then I see Mrs. Bellamy and tell her that if some time she knows of a excellent position in that Rosemont, I would take it so that sometime I could see my little sister who is marrying that young man from the grocer's. And about two years ago, maybe, she write to me to say that her friend Mrs. Patrick Ives she is looking for a extremely superior waitress. So that is how I go to Mrs. Ives."

"Are you still in the employ of Mrs. Ives?"

"No. On June twentieth I resign, since I am not quite content with something that have happen."

"Did this occurrence have anything to do with the death of Mrs. Bellamy?"

"That I do not say. But I was not content."

"Miss Cordier, have you seen this book before? I call your attention to its title— *Stone on Commercial Paper*, Volume III."

Miss Cordier's black eyes swept it perfunctorily. "Yes, that book I know."

"When did you last see it?"

"The night of June nineteenth, about nine o'clock."

"Where?"

"In the study of Mr. Ives."

"What particularly brought it to your attention?"

"Because I take it out of the corner by the desk to look inside it."

"For what purpose?"

"Because I want to see whether a note I put there that afternoon still was there."

"And was that note still there, Miss Cordier?"

"No, monsieur, that note, it was gone."

The prosecutor tossed the impressive volume carelessly on to the clerk's desk. "I offer this volume in evidence, Your Honour."

"Any objections?" Judge Carver turned an inquiring eye on the bulky figure of Dudley Lambert, hovering uncertainly over the buckram-clad repository of correspondence.

Mr. Lambert, shifting from one foot to the other, eyed the volume as though he were endeavouring to decide whether it were an infernal machine or a jewel casket, and with one final convulsive effort arrived at a conclusion: "No objection."

"Miss Cordier, to whom was the note that you placed in the book addressed?"

"It was addressed to Mr. Patrick Ives."

"Was it written by you?"

"Ah, no, no, monsieur."

"Do you know by whom it was written?"

"Yes, monsieur."

"By whom?"

"By Mrs. Stephen Bellamy."

"And how did it happen that you were in possession of a note from Mrs. Bellamy to Mr. Ives?"

"It was the habit of Mrs. Bellamy to mail to me letters that she desire' to have reach Mr. Ives, without anyone should know. Outside there would be my name on the envelope; inside there would be a more small envelope with the name of Mr. Ives on it. That one I would put in the book."

"You had been doing this for some time?"

"For some time, yes—six months—maybe eight."

"How many notes had you placed there, to the best of your recollection?"

"Ah, that I am not quite sure—ten—twelve—twenty—who knows? At first once a month, maybe; that last month, two and three each week."

"At what time did you put the note there?"

"Maybe fifteen minutes before seven, maybe twenty. After half-past six, I know, and not yet seven."

"Was that your usual habit?"

"Oh, no, monsieur; it was my habit to put them there in the night, when I make dark the house. Half-past six, that was a very bad time, because quite easily someone might see."

"Then why did you choose that time, Miss Cordier?"

"Oh, but I do not choose. You see, it was like this: That night, when MacDonald, the chauffeur, bring in the letters a little bit after six, this one it was there for me, in a envelope that was write on it Urgent. On the little envelope inside it say Urgent—Very Urgent in letters with lines under them most black, and so I know that there is great haste that Mr. Patrick Ives he should get that letter quick. So I start to go to the study, but there in the hall is all those people who have come from the club, and Mrs. Ives she send me quick to get some *canapés*, and Mr. Dallas he come with me to show me what he want for the cocktails—limes and honey and all those thing, you know." She looked appealingly at the prosecutor from the long black eyes and for a moment his tense countenance relaxed into a grim smile.

"You were about to tell us why you placed the note there at that time."

"Yes; that is what I tell. Well, I wait and I wait for those people to go home, and still they do not go, but I dare not go in so long as across the hall from the study they all stay in that living room. But after a while I cannot wait any longer for fear that Mr. Patrick Ives should come and not find that most urgent note. So very quiet I slip in when I think no one look, and I put that note quick, quick in the book, and I start to come out in the hall; but when I get to the door I see there is someone in the hall and I step back again to wait till they are gone."

"And whom did you see in the hall, Miss Cordier?"

"I see in the hall Mr. Elliot Farwell and Mrs. Patrick Ives."

"Did they see you?"

Miss Cordier lifted eloquent shoulders. "How do I know, monsieur? Maybe they do, maybe they don't—me, I cannot tell. I step back quick and listen, and after a while their voices stop and I hear a door close, and I come out quick through the hall and into the door to the kitchen without I see no one."

"Did you hear what Mr. Farwell and Mrs. Ives were saying?"

"No, that I could not hear even when I listen, so low they talk, so low that almost they whisper."

"You heard nothing else while you were there?"

"Yes, monsieur. While I stand by the desk, but before I take out the book, I heard mademoiselle go through the hall with the children."

"Mademoiselle? Mademoiselle who?" The prosecutor's voice was expressionless enough, but there was a prophetic shadow of annoyance in his narrowed eyes.

"Mademoiselle Page."

"You say that she was simply passing through the hall?"

"Yes, monsieur—on her way to the stairs."

"You had not yet touched the book?"

"No, monsieur."

"You waited until she passed before you did so?"

"Yes."

"Was Mrs. Ives in the hall at the time that you placed the note in the book?"

"Ah, that, too, I do not say. I say only that she was there one minute—one half minute after I have put it there."

"Could she have seen you place it in the book from the position in which you saw her standing?"

"It is possible."

"Was she facing you?"

"No, monsieur; it is Mr. Farwell who face' me. Mrs. Ives had the back toward me."

Again that shadow of fierce annoyance, turning the blue eyes almost black. "Then what makes you say that she might have seen you?"

The dark eyes meeting his widened a trifle in something too tranquil for surprise—a mild, indolent wonder at the obtuseness of the human race in general, men in particular, and prosecutors more particularly still. "I say that because it might well be that in that little minute she have turn' the back to me, or if she have not, then it might be that she see in the mirror."

"There was a mirror?"

"But yes, on the other side of the hall from the study door there is a long, long chair—a what you call a bench—where the gentlemen they leave their hats. Over that there hangs the mirror. And it was by that bench that I see Mr. Farwell and Mrs. Ives."

"And the desk and the bookcase were reflected in the mirror?"

"Yes, monsieur."

"I see. Now did you notice anything at dinner, Miss Cordier?"

"Nothing at all; everything was as usual, of an entire serenity."

"It was at the usual hour?"

"At quarter past seven—yes."

"Who was present?"

"Mrs. Patrick Ives, Mrs. Daniel Ives, Mr. Ives, as usual."

"Do you recall the conversation?"

"Oh, no, monsieur, I recall only that everyone talk as always about small things. It is my practice, like an experience' waitress, serious and discreet, to be little in the dining room—only when serving, you understand." The serious and discreet waitress eyed her interrogator with a look of bland superiority.

"Nothing struck you as unusual after dinner?"

"No, no."

"You saw no one before you turned out the lights for the night?"

"Oh, yes, I have seen Mrs. Daniel Ives at that time, and she ask me whether Mrs. Ives have return, and I say no."

"No one else?"

"Only the other domestics, monsieur. At a little past ten I retire' for the night."

"You went to sleep immediately?"

"Yes, monsieur."

"Breakfast was just as usual the next morning?"

"As usual—yes."

"At what time?"

"At nine, as on all Sundays. Mrs. Patrick Ives have hers at half-past nine, when she gets home from church."

"Nothing unusual in that?"

"Oh, no; on the contrary, that is her habit."

"And after breakfast, nothing unusual occurred?"

"I do not know whether you call it unusual, but after breakfast, yes, something occurred."

"Just tell us what it was, please."

Miss Cordier spent an interminable moment critically inspecting a pair of immaculate cream-coloured gloves before she decided to gratify this desire: "It was just so soon as Mr. Ives and his mother have finish' breakfast, a few minutes before half-past nine. Mr. Ives he go directly to his study, and I go after him with the Sunday papers and before I go out I ask—because me, I am desirous to know—'Mr. Ives, you have got that note all right what I put in the book?' And he say——"

"Your Honour, I object! I object! What Mr. Ives said——"

This time there was no indecision whatever in the clamour set up by the long-suffering Lambert, and the prosecutor, eyeing him benevolently, raised a warning hand to his witness. "Never mind what he said, Miss Cordier. Just tell us what you said."

"I said, after he spoke, 'Oh, Mr. Ives, then if you have not got it, it is Mrs. Ives who have found it. She have seen me put it in the book while she stood there in the hall.'"

The prosecutor waited for a well-considered moment to permit this conveniently revelatory reply to sink in. "It was after this conversation with Mr. Ives that you decided you would no longer remain with Mrs. Ives?"

"No, monsieur, it was later in the morning that I decide that."

"Something occurred that made you decide it then?"

Miss Cordier's lacquer-red lips parted, closed, parted again. "Yes."

"What, Miss Cordier?"

"At half-past eleven I have heard that Mrs. Bellamy have been killed." The dark eyes slipped sidelong in the direction of the quiet young woman who had not so long since been her mistress. There she sat, leaning easily back in the straight, uncomfortable chair, ankles crossed, hands linked, studying the tips of her squarely cut little shoes with lowered eyes. The black eyes travelled from the edge of the kilted skirt to the edge of the small firm chin and then slid slowly back to the prosecutor: "When I heard that, I was not content, so I no longer stayed."

"Exactly." The prosecutor plunged his hands deep in his pockets and cocked a flagrantly triumphant eye at the agitated Lambert. "You no longer stayed. That will be all, Miss Cordier. Cross-examine."

"Miss Cordier, you knew perfectly that if for one second it came to Mrs. Ives's attention that you had been acting as go-between in the alleged correspondence between her husband and Mrs. Bellamy you would not have remained five minutes under her roof, did you not?"

Miss Cordier leaned a trifle farther over the edge of the witness box to meet the rough anger of Lambert's voice, something ugly and insolent hardening the creamy mask of her face.

"I know that when Mrs. Ives is angered she is quick to speak, quick to act—yes, monsieur."

At the fatal swiftness of that blow, the ruddy face before her sagged and paled, then rallied valiantly. "And so you decided that you had better leave before Mr. Ives questioned her about finding the note and you were turned out in disgrace, didn't you?"

"I have said already, monsieur, that I leave because I have heard that Mrs. Bellamy have been murdered and I am not content." The ominously soft voice pronounced each syllable with a lingering and deadly deliberation.

Mr. Lambert eyed her savagely and moved heavily on: "You say that you were cut off from escaping through the hall by the fact that you saw that it was occupied by Mr. Farwell and Mrs. Ives?"

"That is so."

"Why didn't you go back through the dining room to the pantry?"

"Because I hear Mr. Dallas and Mr. Burgoyne talking from the dining room, where they try one more cocktail."

"Why should they have thought it unusual to have you come from the study?"

"I think it more prudent that no one should know I have been in that study."

"You were simply staying there in order to spy on Mrs. Ives, weren't you?"

"I could not help see Mrs. Ives unless I close' my eyes."

Mr. Lambert was obliged to swallow twice before he was able to continue:

"Did you tell Mr. Ives that Mr. Farwell was in the hall also at the time that you saw Mrs. Ives there?"

"I do not remember whether I tell him or whether I do not."

"Mr. Farwell was facing you, was he not?"

"Yes."

"What made you so sure that it was Mrs. Ives who took the note, not Mr. Farwell?"

"Because, when I hear the door close, then I know that Mr. Farwell he has gone."

"And how did you know that?"

Once more Miss Cordier raised eloquent shoulders. "Because, monsieur, I am not stupid. I look out, he is standing by the hat stand; I go back, I hear a door close, I look out once more, and he is not there. But that is of the most elementary."

"You should be a detective instead of wasting your time waiting on tables," commented her courtly interrogator. "The plain truth is, isn't it, that anyone in the house might have gone out and closed that door while Mr. Farwell went back to the living room with Mrs. Ives?"

"If you say so, monsieur," replied Miss Cordier indifferently.

"And the plain truth is that Mr. Farwell was frantically infatuated with Mrs. Bellamy and was spying on her constantly, isn't it?"

"It is possible."

"Possible! Mr. Farwell himself stated it half a dozen times from this very witness box. It's a plain fact. And another plain fact is that any one of a dozen other people might have passed through the hall and seen you at work, mightn't they?"

"I should not believe so—no, monsieur."

"Whether you believe it or not, it happens to be the truth. Six or eight servants, eight or ten guests——What reason have you for believing that Miss Page herself did not notice something unusual in your attitude and turn back in time to see you place the note after you believed that she had passed?"

"No reason, monsieur—only the evidence of all five of my senses."

"You are a highly talented young woman, Miss Cordier, but you can't see with your back turned, can you?"

"Monsieur is pleased to jest," remarked Miss Cordier, in the tone of one frankly undiverted.

"Don't characterize my questions, please—answer them."

"Willingly. I do not see with my back turn'."

"So it comes down to the fact that ten—twelve—fourteen people might have seen you place this urgent and mysterious note that you so boldly charge Mrs. Ives with taking, doesn't it?"

"That is monsieur's opinion, not mine."

Monsieur glared menacingly at the not too subtle mockery adorning the witness's pleasing countenance.

"And furthermore, Miss Cordier, it comes down to the fact that we have only your word for it that the note was ever placed in the book at all, doesn't it?"

"Monsieur does not find that sufficient?"

Monsieur ignored the question, but his countenance testified eloquently that such was indeed the case.

"Just how did you happen to select a book in Mr. Ives's library as a hiding place for this correspondence?"

"Because that is a good safe place, where every night he can look without anyone to watch."

"What made you think that someone else might not take out that book to read?"

"That book? *Stone on Commercial Paper*, Volume III? Monsieur is pleased to jest!"

Monsieur, scowling unattractively at some openly diverted members of the press, changed his line of attack with some abruptness. "Miss Cordier, you know a man called Adolph Platz, do you not?"

Miss Cordier's lashes flickered once—twice. "Of a certainty."

"Did you see him in the afternoon of the nineteenth of June?"

"Yes."

"How did you come to know him?"

"He was for a time chauffeur to Mrs. Ives."

"Married, wasn't he?"

"Married, yes."

"Mrs. Platz was a chambermaid in Mrs. Ives's employ?"

"Yes."

"They left because Mrs. Platz quarrelled with you, did they not?"

"One moment, please." The prosecutor lifted an imperious voice. "Are we to be presented with an account of all the back-stairs quarrels, past and present, indulged in by Mrs. Ives's domestics? To the best of my belief, my distinguished adversary is entering a field, however profitable and entertaining it may prove, that I have left totally virgin. Does the court hold this proper for cross-examination?"

"The Court does not. The question is overruled."

"I ask an exception, Your Honour.... Miss Cordier, when you were turning out the lights that night, did you go into all the downstairs rooms?"

"Into all of them—yes."

"Did you see Mr. Patrick Ives in any of them?"

"No, monsieur."

Sue Ives leaned forward with a swift gesture, a sudden wave of colour sweeping her from throat to brow. Mr. Lambert looked diligently away.

"You have placed great stress on your skill, experience, and training as a waitress, Miss Cordier. Are you a waitress at present?"

"No."

"Just what is your present occupation?"

"At present I have no occupation. I rest."

"In the boarding house in Atlantic City where you have been occupied in resting for the past three or four months, you are not reposing under the name of Melanie Cordier, are you?"

The black eyes darted toward the prosecutor, who stood leaning, shrewd and careless, over the back of a tilted chair. "Is it particularly germane to this inquiry whether Miss Cordier chooses to call herself Joan of Arc, if she wants to?" he inquired.

"I propose to attack the credibility of this witness," said Mr. Lambert unctuously. "I propose to prove by this witness, that while she is posing here as a correct young person and a model servant she is actually living a highly incorrect life as a supposedly married woman.... Miss Cordier, I ask you whether for the past three months you have not been passing as the wife of Adolph Platz, having persuaded him to abandon his own wife?"

In the pale oval of her face the black eyes flamed and smoked. "And I tell you no, no, and again no, monsieur!"

"You do not go under the name of Mrs. Adolph Platz?"

"I do not persuade him to abandon that stupid doll, his wife. Long before I knew him, he was tired and sick of her."

"You do not go under the name of Mrs. Adolph Platz?"

"That is most simple. Monsieur Platz he have been to me a excellent friend and adviser. When I explain to him that I am greatly in need of rest he suggest to me that a woman young, alone, and of not an entire lack of attraction would quite possibly find it more restful if the world should consider her married. So he is amiable enough to suggest that if it should assist me, I might for this small vacation use his name. It is only thing I have take from him, monsieur may rest assured."

"You remove a great weight from my mind," Mr. Lambert assured her, horridly playful; "and from the minds of these twelve gentlemen as well, I am sure." The twelve gentlemen, who had been following the lady's simple and virtuous explanation of her somewhat unconventional conduct with startled attention, smiled for the first time in four days, shifting stiffly on their chairs and exchanging sidelong glances, skeptically jocose. "It is a pleasure to all of us to know that such chivalry as Mr. Platz has exhibited is not entirely extinct in this wicked workaday world. I hardly think that we can improve on your explanation as to why you are known in Atlantic City as Mrs. Adolph Platz, Miss Cordier. That will be all."

The prosecutor, who did not seem unduly perturbed by these weighty flights of sarcasm, continued to lean on his chair, though he once more lifted his voice: "You had saved quite a sum of money during these past years, hadn't you, Miss Cordier?"

"Yes, monsieur."

"It proved ample for your modest needs on this long-planned and greatly needed vacation, did it not?"

"More than ample—yes."

"Mr. Platz had left his wife some time before these unhappy events caused you to leave Mrs. Ives, hadn't he?"

"Of a surety, monsieur."

"That's all, thank you, Miss Cordier."

Miss Cordier moved leisurely from the stand, chic and poised as ever, disdaining even a glance at the highly gratified Lambert, and bestowing the briefest of smiles on Mr. Farr, who responded even more briefly. Many a lady, trailing sable and brocade from an opera box, has moved with less assurance and grace than Mrs. Ives's one-time waitress, the temporary Mrs. Adolph Platz. The eyes of the courtroom, perplexed, diverted, and faintly disturbed, followed her balanced and orderly retreat, the scarlet camellia defiant as a little flag.

"Call Miss Roberts."

"Miss Laura Roberts!"

Miss Laura Roberts also wore black, but she wore her black with a difference. A decent, sober, respectful apparel for a decent, sober, respectful little person— Miss Roberts, comely, rosy-faced, gray-eyed, fawn-haired and soft-voiced, had all the surface qualifications of an ideal maid, and she obviously considered that

106

those qualifications did not include scarlet lips and scarlet flowers. Under the neat black hat her eyes met the prosecutor's shyly and bravely.

"Miss Roberts, what was your occupation on June nineteenth, 1926?"

"I was maid and seamstress to Mrs. Patrick Ives, sir."

The pretty English voice, with its neat, clipped accent, fell pleasantly and reassuringly on the ears of the courtroom, which relaxed with unfeigned relief from the tensity into which her Gallic colleague had managed to plunge it during her tenure of the witness box.

"Did you see Mrs. Ives on the evening of the nineteenth?"

"Not after dinner—no, sir. I asked her before dinner if it would be quite all right for cook and me to go down to the village to church that night, and she said quite, and not to bother about getting home early, because she wouldn't be needing me again. So after church we met two young gentlemen that we knew and went across to the drug store and had some ices, and sat talking a bit before we walked home, so that it was well on to eleven when we got in, and all the lights were out except the one in the kitchen, so I knew that Mrs. Ives was in bed."

"What time did you leave the house for church, Miss Roberts?"

"Well, I couldn't exactly swear to it, sir, but it must have been around half-past eight; because service was at nine, and it's a good bit of a walk, and I do remember hurrying with dinner so that I could turn down the beds and be off."

"Were you chambermaid in the household as well as seamstress-maid?"

"Oh, no, sir; only it was the chambermaid's night off, you see, and then it was my place to do it."

"I see. So on this night you turned down all the beds before eight-thirty?"

"Yes, sir—all but Miss Page's, that is."

"That wasn't included in your duties?"

"Oh, yes, sir, it was. But that night when I got to the day nurse's door it was locked, and when I knocked, no one didn't answer at first, and then Miss Page called out that she had a headache and had gone to bed already——"

Miss Roberts hesitated and looked down at the prosecutor with honest, troubled eyes.

"Nothing extraordinary about that, was there?"

"Well, yes, sir, there was. You see, when I was coming down the hall I heard what I thought were voices coming out of those rooms, and crying, and I was afraid that the little girl was having more trouble with her ear. That's why I started to go in without knocking, but after I'd been standing there a minute, I heard that it was Miss Page crying herself, fit to break her heart. I never heard anyone cry so dreadful in all my life. It fairly gave me a turn, but the moment I knocked there wasn't a sound, and then after a minute she called out that she wouldn't need me, just as I told you, sir. So I went on my way, of course, though I was still a bit worried. She'd been crying so dreadful, poor thing, that I was afraid she would be right down sick."

"Yes, quite so. Very much upset, as though she'd been through an agitating experience?"

"Oh, yes, indeed, sir."

"You were mistaken about the voices weren't you? It was just Miss Page crying?"

"No, sir—I thought I heard voices, too." The soft voice was barely audible.

"The little girl's?"

"No, sir. It sounded—it sounded like Mr. Ives."

The prosecutor stared at her blankly.

"Mr. Patrick Ives?"

"Yes, sir."

"You could hear what he was saying?"

"No, sir, I couldn't; it stopped as soon as I tried the door. I thought he was talking to the little girl."

Mr. Farr continued to contemplate her blankly for a moment, and then, with an eloquent shrug of the shoulders, dismissed Mr. Ives, Miss Page, and the locked door for more fruitful pastures.

"Now, Miss Roberts, your duties included the care of your mistress's wardrobe, did they not?"

"Yes, sir."

"You are quite familiar with all its contents?"

"Oh, quite."

"Will you be good enough to tell us if it contains to-day all the articles that it contained on the nineteenth of June, 1926?"

"No, sir, it doesn't. Mrs. Ives gives away a lot of her things at the end of every season. We sent a big box off to a sick cousin she has in Arizona, and another to some young ladies in Delaware, and another to the——"

"Never mind about the things that you sent at the end of the season. Did you send anything at about the time of the murder—within a few weeks of it, say?"

The roses in Miss Roberts's cheeks faded abruptly, and the candid eyes fled precipitately to the chair where Susan Ives sat, playing idly with the crystal clasp of her brown suede bag. At the warm, friendly, reassuring little smile that she found waiting for her, Miss Roberts apparently found heart of grace. "Yes, sir, we did," she said steadily.

"On what date, please?"

"On the twentieth of June."

The courtroom drew in its breath sharply—a little sigh for its lost ease—and moved forward the inch that separated suspense from polite attention.

"To whom was the package sent?"

"It was sent to the Salvation Army."

"What was in it?"

"Well, there were two old sweaters and a swiss dress that had shrunk quite small, and a wrapper, and some blouses and a coat."

"What kind of a coat, Miss Roberts?"

"A light flannel coat—a kind of sports coat, you might call it," said Miss Roberts clearly; but those who craned forward sharply enough could see the knuckles whiten on the small, square, capable hands.

"Cream-coloured flannel?"

"Well, more of a biscuit, I'd call it," replied Mrs. Ives's maid judicially.

"The coat that Mrs. Ives had been wearing the evening before, wasn't it?"

"I believe it was, sir."

"Did you see the condition of this coat before you packed it, Miss Roberts?"

"No, sir, I didn't. It wasn't I that packed it."

"Not you? Who did pack it?"

"Mrs. Ives packed it herself."

"Ah, I see." In that sudden white light of triumph the prosecutor's face was almost beautiful—a cruel and sinister beauty, such as might have lighted the face of the youngest Spanish Inquisitionist as the stray shot of a question went straight to the enemy's heart. "It was Mrs. Ives who packed it. How did it come into your hands, Miss Roberts?"

"The package, sir?"

"Certainly, the package."

"It was this way, sir: A little before eight Sunday morning Mrs. Ives's bell rang and I went down to her room. She was all dressed for church, and there was a big box on her bed. She said, 'I rang for you before, Roberts, but you were probably at breakfast. Take this down to MacDonald and tell him to mail it when he gets the papers. The post office closes at half-past nine.'"

"Was that all that she said?"

"Oh, no, sir. She asked me for some fresh gloves, and then she said over her shoulder like as she was going out, 'It's those things that I was getting together for the Salvation Army. I put in the coat I was wearing last night too. I absolutely ruined it with some automobile grease on Mr. Bellamy's car.'"

"Nothing more?"

"Well, then I said, 'Oh, madam, couldn't it be cleaned?' And Mrs. Ives said, 'It isn't worth cleaning; this is the third year I've had it.' Then she went out, sir, and I took it down and gave it to MacDonald."

"Was it addressed?"

"Oh, yes, sir."

"How?"

"Just Salvation Army Headquarters, New York, N.Y."

"No address in the corner as to whom it came from?"

"Oh, no, sir. Mrs. Ives never———"

"Be good enough to confine yourself to the question. You are not aware, yourself, of the exact nature of these stains, are you, Miss Roberts?"

"Yes, sir, I am," said the pink-cheeked Miss Roberts firmly. "They were grease stains."

"What?" The prosecutor's startled voice skipped half an octave. "Didn't you distinctly tell me that you didn't see this coat?"

"No, sir, no more I did. It was Mrs. Ives that told me they were grease stains."

The prosecutor indulged in a brief bark of mirth that indicated more relief than amusement. "Then, as I say, you are unable to tell us of your own knowledge?"

"No, sir," replied Miss Roberts, a trifle pinker and a trifle firmer. "Mrs. Ives told me that those stains were grease stains, so I'm certainly able to say of my own knowledge that it was absolutely true if she said so."

There was something in the soft, sturdy voice that made the grimy courtroom a pleasanter place. Sue Ives's careless serenity flashed suddenly to that of a delighted child; Stephen Bellamy's fine, grave face warmed and lightened; the shadows lifted for a moment from Pat Ives's haunted eyes; there was a grateful murmur from the press, a friendly stir in the jury. The quiet-eyed, soft-voiced, stubborn little Miss Roberts was undoubtedly the heroine of the moment.

Mr. Farr, however, was obviously unmoved by this exhibition of devotion and loyalty. He permitted more than a trace of annoyance to penetrate his clear, metallic voice. "That's all very pretty and touching, naturally, Miss Roberts, but from a crudely legal standpoint we are forced to realize that your statement as to the nature of the stains has no weight whatever. It is a fact, is it not, that you never laid eyes on the stained coat that Mrs. Ives sent out of her house within a few hours of the time that this murder was committed?"

"Yes, sir, that is a fact."

"No further questions, Miss Roberts. Cross-examine."

"It is a fact, too, that Mrs. Ives frequently sent packages in just this way, isn't it, Miss Roberts?" inquired Mr. Lambert mellifluously.

"Oh, yes, indeed, she did—often and often."

"Was she in the habit of putting her address on packages sent to charitable institutions?"

"No, sir. She didn't want to be thanked for her charities—not ever."

"Precisely. That's all, Miss Roberts—thanks."

"Call Orsini."

"Loo-weegee Aw-see-nee!"

Luigi Orsini glanced darkly at Ben Potts as he mounted the witness stand, and Mr. Potts returned the glance with Nordic severity.

"What was your occupation on June 19, 1926, Orsini?"

"I work for Miz' Bell'my."

"In what capacity?"

"What you say?"

"What was your job?"

"I am what you call handy—do everything there is to do."

The spacious gesture implied Gargantuan labours and super-human abilities. A small, thick, stocky individual, swarthy and pompadoured, with lustrous eyes, a glittering smile, and a magnificent barytone voice, he suggested without any effort whatever infinite possibilities in the rôle of either tragedian or comedian. The redoubtable Farr eyed him with a trace of well-justified apprehension.

"Well, suppose you tell us what your principal activities were on the nineteenth of June."

"Ah, well, that day me, I am very active, like per usual. At six o'clock I arise and after some small breakfast I take extra-fine strong wire and some very long sticks——"

"No, no, you can skip all that. You heard Mr. Farwell's testimony, didn't you?"

"For sure I hear that testimony."

"Was it correct that he stopped around noon at the Bellamys' and asked for Mrs. Bellamy?"

"All correct, O.K."

"Did he tell you where he was going?"

"Yes, sair, he then he say he get her at that cottage."

"Nothing else?"

"Not one other thing else."

"You didn't see him again?"

"No, no; I do not see him again evair."

"When did you last see Mrs. Bellamy?"

"It is about eight in the evening—maybe five minute before, maybe five minute after."

"How do you fix the time?"

"I have look at my watch—this watch you now see, which is a good instrument of entirely pure silver, but not always faithful."

The prosecutor waved away the bulky shining object dangled enticingly before his eyes with a gesture of almost ferocious impatience. "Never mind about that. Why did you consult your watch?"

The owner of the magnificent but unfaithful instrument swelled darkly for a moment, but continued to dangle his treasure. "That you shall hear—patience. I produce the instrument at this time so that you note that while the clock over the door it say twenty minutes before the hour, this watch it say nine minute—or maybe eight. You judge for yourself. It is without a doubt eccentric. But on that night still I have consult it to see if I go to New York at eight-twenty. I wait to decide still when I see Mrs. Bell'my run down the front steps and come down to the gate where I stand."

"Did she speak to you?"

"Oh, positive. She ask, 'What, Luigi, you do not go to New York?'"

"How did she know that you were going to New York?"

"Because already before dinner I have ask permission from Mr. Bell'my if I can go to New York that evening to see a young lady from Milan that I think perhaps I marry, maybe. Miz' Bell'my she is in the next room and she laugh and call out, 'You tell Marietta that if she get you, one day she will find herself marry to the President of these United State'.' I excuse myself for what may seem like a boast, but those are the words she use."

And suddenly, as though he found the memory of that gay, mocking young voice floating across the heavy air of the courtroom more unbearable than all the blood and shame and horror that had invaded it, Stephen Bellamy's face twisted to a tortured grimace and he lifted an unsteady hand to lowered eyes.

"Look!" came a penetrating whisper. "He's crying, ain't he? Ain't he, Gertie?"

And the red-headed girl lowered her own eyes swiftly, a shamed and guilty flush reaching to the roots of her hair. How ugly, how contemptible, one's thoughts could sound in words!

"What reply did you make to Mrs. Bellamy?"

"I tell to her that I think maybe I had better not go, as that afternoon I have invest my money in a small game of chance with the gardener next door and the investment it have prove' unsound. I say that how if I go to New York to see my young lady, it is likely that I must request of her the money to return back to Rosemont—and me, who am proud, I find that in-delicate. So Miz' Bell'my she laugh out and look quick in the little bag that she carry and give me three dollar'— to make the course of true love run more smooth, she say—and then she call back over her shoulder, 'Better hurry, Luigi, or you miss that train.' So I hurry, but all the same I miss it—by two small minute, because, chiefly, this watch he is too eccentric."

In spite of its eccentricity, he returned it tenderly to his vest pocket, after a final flip in the direction of the harassed Farr and the enraptured audience.

"Did you notice anything else in the bag when Mrs. Bellamy opened it?"

"Oh, positive. The eyes of Luigi they miss nothing what there is to see. All things they observe. In that bag of Miz' Bell'my there are stuff, stuff in two, three letters—I dunno for sure—maybe four. But they make that small little bag bulge out so—very tight, like that." Mr. Orsini's eloquent hands sketched complete rotundity.

"You never saw Mrs. Bellamy again?"

"Not evair—no, no more—not evair."

For a moment the warm blood under the swarthy Southern skin seemed to run more slowly and coldly; but after a hasty glance at the safe, reassuring autumn sunlight slanting across the crowded room, the colour flowed boldly back to cheek and lip.

"You say that you missed the train to New York. What did you do then?"

"Then I curse myself good all up and down for a fool that is a fool all right, and I go back to my room in the garage and get into my bed and begin to read a story in a magazine that call itself *Honest Confession* about a bride what——"

"Never mind what you were reading. Did you notice anything unusual on your return?"

"Well, maybe you don't call it nothing unusual, but I notice that the car of Mr. Bell'my it is no longer in the garage. That make me surprise' for a minute, because I have heard Mr. Bell'my tell Nellie, the house girl, that it is all right for her to go home early to her mother, where she sleep, because he will be there to answer the telephone if it should ring. But all the same, I go on to bed. I just think he change his mind, maybe."

"What time did you get back to the garage?"

"At twenty-two minutes before nine I am in my room. That I verify by the alarm clock that repose on the top of my bureau, and which is of an entire reliability; I note it expressly, because I am enrage' that I have miss' that train by so small an amount."

"Orsini, do you know what kind of tires Mr. Bellamy was using on his car?"

"Yes, sair, that, too, I know. There are three old tires of what they call Royal Cord make—two on back and one on front. On the left front one is a good new Silvertown Cord, what I help him to change about a month before all these things have happen. For spare, he carry a all new Ajax. And that is all there is."

"You're perfectly sure that the Ajax wasn't on?"

"Oh, surest thing."

"When did you last see the car?"

"When I go down to the gate, round half-past seven."

"And the Ajax was still on as a spare?"

"That's what."

"Did you see Mr. Bellamy again on the evening of the nineteenth?"

"Yes, that evening I have seen Mr. Bell'my again."

"At what time?"

"At five before ten."

"Was he alone?"

"No; with him there was a lady."

"Did you recognize her?"

"Yes, sair, I have recognize' her."

"Who was this lady, Orsini?"

"This lady, sair, was Miz' Patrick Ives."

At those words, pronounced with exactly their proper dramatic inflection by that lover of the drama, Mr. Luigi Orsini, every head in the courtroom pivoted to the spot where Mrs. Patrick Ives sat with the autumn sun warming her hair to something better than gold. And quite oblivious to the ominous inquiry in those straining eyes, she turned toward Stephen Bellamy, meeting his startled eyes with a small, rueful smile, lifted brows and a little shake of the head that came as near to saying "I told you so" as good sportsmanship permitted.

"You are quite positive of that?"

"Oh, without one single doubt."

"How were you able to identify her?"

"Because I hear her voice, as clear as I hear you, and I see her clear as I see you too."

"How were you able to do that?"

"By the lights of Mr. Bell'my's car, when she get out and look up at my window, where I stand and look out."

"Tell us just how you came to be standing there looking out, please."

"Well, after a while, I began to get sleepy over that magazine, and I look at the clock and it say ten minutes to ten, and I think, 'Luigi, my fine fellow, to-morrow you rise at six to do the work that lies before you, and at present it is well that you should sleep.' So I arise to turn out the light, which switch is by the window, and just when I get there to do that I hear a auto car turn in at the gate. I think, 'Ah-ha! There now comes Mr. Bell'my.' And then I look out of that window, for I am surprise'. It is the habit of Mr. Bell'my to put away that car so soon as he come in, but this time he don't do that. He stop in front of the house and he help out a lady. She stand there looking up at my window, and I see her clear like it is day, but it is all dark inside, so she can see nothing. Then she say, 'I still could swear that I have seen a light,' and Mr. Bell'my he say, 'Sue, don't let this get you. I tell you that there is no one here—I saw him headed for the train. Maybe perhaps it was the shine from our own lamps what you see. Come on.' And she say, 'Maybe; but I could swear——' And then I don't hear any more, because they go into the house, and me, I stand there like one paralyze', because always I have believe Mr. Bell'my to be a man of honour who love——"

"Yes—never mind that. Did you see them come out?"

"Yes, that I see, too. In five-ten minutes they come out and get quick into the car, and drive away without they say one word. They start off very fast, so that the car it jump."

"Do you know at what time Mr. Bellamy returned that night?"

"No; because then I wake only half up from sleep when I hear him drive that car into the garage, and I do not turn to look at the clock."

"It was some time later?"

"Some time—yes. But whether one hour—three hours—five hours, that I cannot say. What I am not sure of like my life, that I do not say."

"Exactly; very commendable. That's all, thanks. Cross-examine."

Orsini wheeled his lustrous orbs in the direction of Mr. Lambert, whose ruddy countenance had assumed an expression of intense inhospitality, though he managed to inject an ominous suavity into his ample voice. "With those vigilant and all-seeing eyes of yours, Mr.—er—Mr. Orsini, were you able to note the garments that Mrs. Bellamy was wearing when she went past you at the gate?"

"Oh, positive. A white dress, all fluffy, and a black cape, quite thin, so that almost you see through it—not quite, maybe, but almost."

"Any hat?"

"On the head a small black scarf that she have wrap' also around her neck, twice or mebbe three time. The eyes of Luigi——"

"Exactly. Could you see whether she had on her jewels?"

"Positive. Always like that in the evening, moreover, she wear her jewels."

"You noticed what they were?"

"Same like always—same necklace out of pearls, same rings, diamond and sapphire, two on one hand, one the other—I see them when she open that bag."

"Mr. Bellamy was a person of moderate means, wasn't he, as far as you know?"

"Oh, everybody what there is around here knows he wasn't no John P. Rockfeller, I guess."

"Do you believe that the stones were genuine?"

Mr. Orsini, thus appealed to as an expert, waxed eloquent and expansive. "Oh, positive. That I know for one absolute sure thing."

"Tell us just how, won't you?"

"Well, that house girl, Nellie, one night she tell me that Miz' Bell'my have left one of her rings at the club where she wash her hands, but that Miz' Bell'my just laugh and say she should worry herself, because all those rings and her pearls they are insure big, and if she lose those, she go out and buy herself a new house and a auto car, and maybe a police dog too."

"I see. Had it ever occurred to you that Mrs. Bellamy was using the cottage at Orchards for other purposes than piano practice, Mr. Orsini?"

Orsini's smile flashed so generously that it revealed three really extravagant gold fillings. "Well, me, I don't miss many things, maybe you guess. After she get that key three-four times, I think to myself, 'Luigi, it is funny thing that nevair she give you back that key until the day after, and always those evenings she go out by herself—most generally when Mr. Bell'my he stay in town to work.' So one of those nights when she ask for that key I permit myself to take a small little stroll up the road in Orchards, and sure thing, there is a light in that cottage and a auto car outside the door. Sufficient! I look no further. Me, I am a man of the world, you comprehend."

"Obviously."

"Just a moment, Mr. Lambert," interrupted Judge Carver. "Is your cross-examination going to take some time?"

"Quite a time, I believe, Your Honour."

"Then I think it best that we adjourn for the noon recess, as it is already after twelve. The Court stands adjourned until one-ten."

"Well, here's where we get our comic relief," said the reporter with unction. "That son of sunny Italy is going to give us an enviable imitation of a three-ringed circus and a bag of monkeys before he and Lambert get through with each other, or I miss my guess. He's got a look in his eye that is worth the price of admission alone. What's your mature opinion of him?"

"I think that he's beguiling," said the red-headed girl somewhat listlessly. Little shadows were under her gray eyes, and she curled small limp paws about a neglected notebook. Something in the drooping shoulders under the efficient jacket suggested an exhausted baby in need of a crib and a bottle of hot milk and a firm and friendly tucking in. She made a half-hearted effort to overtake an enormous yawn that was about to engulf her, and then surrendered plaintively.

"Bored?" inquired the real reporter, his countenance illuminated by an expression of agreeable surprise.

"Bored?" cried the lady beside him in a voice at once scornful and outraged. "Bored? I'm half destroyed with excitement. I can't sleep any more. I go back to the boarding house every night and sit up in front of a gas stove with an orange-and-magenta comforter over my shoulders that ought to warm the dead, writing up my notes until all hours; and then I put a purple comforter over my knees and a muffler over my nose, and get an apple and sit there alternately gnawing the apple and my fingers and trying to work out who did it until even the cats stop singing under my window and the sky begins to get that nice, appealing slate colour that's so prettily referred to as dawn. And even then I don't know who did it."

"Don't you, indeed?" inquired the reporter severely, looking irritated and anxious. "Haven't you any sense at all, you little idiot? Listen, I know a place just two blocks down where you can get some fairly decent hot soup. You go and drink about a quart of it and then trot along home and turn in, and I'll do your notes for you to-night so well that your boss will double your salary in the morning— and if you're very good and sleep eighteen hours, I may tell you who did the murder."

The red-headed girl, who had shuddered fastidiously at the offer of fairly decent soup, eyed him ungratefully as she extracted a packet of salted peanuts from the capacious pouch that served her as handbag, commissary, and dressing table.

"Thank you kindly," she said. "My boss wrote me two special-delivery letters yesterday to say that I was doing far the best stuff that was coming up out of

Redfield—far. He said that the three clippings that I sent him of your stuff showed promise—he did, honestly.... I think that soup's terrible, and this is the first time in my life that I've been able to stay up as late as I pleased without anyone sending me to bed. I'm mad about it.... Have some peanuts?"

"No, thanks," said the reporter, rising abruptly. "Anything I can get you outside?"

"You're cross!" wailed the red-headed girl, her eyes round with panic and contrition. "You are—you are—you're absolutely furious. Wait, please—please, or I'll hang on to your coat tails and make a scene. The real reason I don't go out and get soup is because I don't dare. If I went away even for a minute, something might happen, and then I wouldn't ever sleep again. Someone might get my seat—didn't you see that fat, sinful-looking old lady who got the *Gazette* girl's place yesterday? She wouldn't go even when three officers and the sheriff told her she had to, and the *Gazette* girl had to sit on a stool in the gallery, and she said she had such a rushing of rage in her ears that she couldn't hear anything that anyone said all afternoon. So, you see——And I would like a ham sandwich and I think that you write better than Conrad, and I apologize, and if you'll tell me who did the murder, I'll tell you. And please hurry, because I hope you won't be gone long."

"You're a nice little nut," said the reporter, and he beamed on her forgivingly, "and I like you. I like the way your nose turns up and your mouth turns down, and I like that funny little hat you wear.... I'll make it in two jumps. Watch me!"

The red-headed girl watched him obediently, her face pink and her eyes bright under the funny little hat. When the door opened to let him out, she plunged her eyes apprehensively for a moment into the silent, pushing, heaving mob behind the policeman's broad blue shoulders, shivered, and turned them resolutely away.

"If I were convicted of murder to-morrow," thought the red-headed girl passionately, "they'd shove just like that to see me hanged. Ugh! What's the matter with us?"

She eyed with an expression of profound distaste the plump lady just beyond her, conscientiously eating stuffed eggs out of a shoe box. So smug, so virtuous, so pompadoured and lynx-eyed——Her eyes moved hastily on to the pair of giggling flappers exchanging powder puffs and anecdotes over a box of maple caramels; on to the round-shouldered youth with the unattractive complexion and unpleasant tie; on to the pretty thing with overflushed cheeks and overbright eyes above her sable scarf and beneath her Paris hat. The red-headed girl wrenched her eyes back to the empty space where there sat, tranquil and aloof, the memory of the prisoner at the bar.

It was good to be able to forget those hot, hungry, cruel faces, so sleek and safe and triumphant, and to remember that other face under the shadow of the small felt hat, cool and controlled and gay—yes, gay, for all the shadows that beset it. Only—what thoughts were weaving behind that bright brow, those steady lips?

Thoughts of terror, of remorse, of bitterness and horror and despair? If you were strong enough to strike down a laughing girl who barred your path, you would be strong enough to keep your lips steady, wouldn't you?

The red-headed girl stared about her wildly; she felt suddenly small and cold and terrified. Where was the reporter? What a long time——Oh, someone had opened a window. It was only the wind of autumn that was blowing so cold then, not the wind of death. What was it those little news-boys were calling outside, yelping like puppies in the gray square?

"Extra, Extra! All about the mysterious——"

"Well," said the reporter's voice at her elbow, tense with some suppressed excitement, "this is the time he did it! No enterprising Filipino and housemaid around this time. Read that and weep!"

Across the flimsy sheet of the Redfield *Home News* it ran in letters three inches high: Ex-fiancé of Murdered Girl Blows Out Brains. Prominent Clubman Found Dead in Garden at Eleven Forty-five This Morning.

"I've got a peach of a story started over the wires this minute," said the reporter exultantly. "Here, boy, rush this stuff and beat it back for more. I couldn't get your sandwich."

"Well," said the red-headed girl in a small awed voice—"well, then, that means that he did it himself, doesn't it? That means that he couldn't stand it any longer because he killed her, doesn't it?"

"Or it means that he good and damn well knew that Susan Ives did it," muttered the reporter, shaken from Olympian calm to frenzied activity. "Here, boy! Boy! Hi, you, rush this—and take off the ear muffs. It's a hundred-to-one bet that he knew that Sue'd done it, and that he'd as good as put the knife in her hand by telling her where, when, and why it should be managed.... Here, boy!"

"He didn't!" said the red-headed girl fiercely. "He didn't know it. How could——"

"The Court!" sang Ben Potts.

"How could he know whether she——"

"Silence!" intoned Ben reprovingly.

Mr. Orsini and Mr. Lambert were both heading purposefully for the witness box.

"Now you've just told us, Mr. Orsini, that you were able to see Mrs. Ives's face when you looked down from your window in the garage as clearly as you see mine. Can you give us an idea of the approximate distance from the garage to the house?"

"Positive. The distance from the middle of the garage door to the middle of the front porch step, it is"—he glanced earnestly at a small slip of paper hitherto concealed in one massive paw, and divulged a portion of its contents to his astounded interrogator—"it is forty-seven feet five inches and one half inch."

"What?"

Mr. Orsini contemplated with pardonable gratification the unfeigned stupor that adorned the massive countenance now thrust incredulously forward. "Also I can now tell you the space between the front gate and the door—one hunnerd forty-three feet and a quarter of a inch," he announced rapidly and benevolently. "Also from the fence out to the road—eleven feet nine inch and a——"

Judge Carver's gavel fell with a crash over the enraptured roar that swept the courtroom. "One more demonstration of this kind and I clear the Court. This is a trial for murder, not a burlesque performance. You, sir, answer the questions that are put to you, when they are put. What's that object in your hand?"

Mr. Orsini dangled the limp yellow article hopefully under the judge's fine nose. "The instrument with which I make the measure," he explained, all modest pride. "What you call a measure of tape. The card on which I make the notes as well."

Judge Carver schooled his momentarily shaken countenance to its customary rigidity and turned a lion tamer's eye on the smothered hilarity of the press. The demoralized Lambert pulled himself together with a mighty effort; a junior counsel emitted a convulsive snort; only Mr. Farr remained entirely unmoved. Pensive, nonchalant and mildly sardonic, he bestowed a perfunctory glance on the measure of tape and returned to a critical perusal of some notes of his own, which he had been studying intently since he had surrendered his witness to his adversary. The adversary, his eyes still bulging, returned once more to the charge.

"May I ask you what caused you to burden yourself with this invaluable mass of information?"

"Surest thing you may ask. I do it because me, I am well familiar with the questions what all smart high-grade lawyers put when in the court—like, could you then tell us how high were those steps, and how many were those minutes, and how far were those walls—all things like that they like to go and ask, every time, sure like shooting."

"I see. A careful student of our little eccentricities. How has it happened that your crowded life has afforded you the leisure to make so exhaustive a study of our habits?"

"Once again, more slow?" suggested the student affably.

"How have you happened to become so familiar with court life?"

"Oh, me, I am not so familiar with it as that. Once—twice—that is enough for one who know how to use his eyes and ear—more is not necessary."

"No, as you say, once or twice ought to be enough; it's a pity that you've found it necessary to extend your experience. Orsini, have you ever been in jail?"

"Who—me?" The glittering smile with which Mr. Orsini was in the habit of decorating his periods was not completely withdrawn, but it became slightly more reticent. His lambent eyes roved reproachfully in the direction of Mr. Farr, who seemed more absorbed than ever in his notes. "In what kind of a jail you mean?"

Mr. Lambert looked obviously disconcerted. "I mean jail—any kind of a jail."

"Was it up on a hill, perhaps, this jail?" inquired his victim helpfully.

"On a hill? What's that got to do with it? How should I know whether it was on a hill?"

"A high hill, mebbe, with trees all about it?" Once more Orsini's hands were eloquent.

"All right, all right, were you ever in a jail on a hill with trees around it?"

Orsini gazed blandly into the irate and contemptuous countenance thrust toward him. "No, sair," he replied regretfully. "If that jail was up on a hill with trees around it, then I was not in that jail."

Once more the courtroom, reckless of the gavel, yielded to helpless and hilarious uproar, and for this time they were spared. One look at Mr. Lambert's countenance, a full moon in the throes of apoplexy, had undermined even Judge Carver's iron reserves. The gavel remained idle while he indulged himself in a severe attack of coughing behind a large and protective handkerchief. The red-headed girl was using a more minute one to mop her eyes when she paused, startled and incredulous. Across the courtroom, Patrick and his wife Susan were laughing into each other's eyes, for one miraculous moment the gay and care-free comrades of old; for one moment—and then, abruptly, memory swept back her lifted veil and they sat staring blankly at the dreadful havoc that lay between them, who had been wont to seek each other in laughter. Slowly, painfully, Sue Ives wrenched her eyes back to their schooled vigilance, and after an interminable breath, Pat Ives turned his haunted ones back to the window, beyond which the sky was still blue. Only in that second's wait the red-headed girl had seen the dark flush sweep across his pallor, and the hunger in those imploring eyes, frantic and despairing as those of a small boy who had watched a beloved hand slam a heavy door in his face.

"Why, he loves her!" thought the red-headed girl. "He loves her dreadfully!" Those few scattered seconds when laughter and hope and despair had swept across a court—how long—how long they seemed! And yet they would have scantily sufficed to turn a pretty phrase or a platitude on the weather. They had just barely served to give the portly Lambert time to recover his breath, his voice, and his venom, all three of which he was now proceeding to utilize simultaneously and vigorously.

"I see, I see. You're particular about your jails—like them in valleys, do you? Now be good enough to answer my question without any further trifling."

"What question is that?"

"Have you ever been in jail?"

Mr. Orsini's expression became faintly tinged with caution, but its affability did not diminish. "When?" he inquired impartially.

"When? Any time! Will—you—answer—my—question?"

Thus rudely adjured, his victim yielded to the inevitable with philosophy, humour, and grace. "Not any time—no, no! That is too exaggerate'. But sometimes—yes—I do not deny that sometimes I have been in jail."

Under the eyes of the entranced spectators, Mr. Lambert's rosy jowls darkened to a fine, deep, full-bodied maroon. "You don't deny it, hey? Well, that's very magnanimous and gratifying—very gratifying indeed. Now will you continue to gratify us by telling us just why you went to jail?"

Mr. Orsini dismissed his penal career with an eloquent shrug. "Ah, well, for what thing do you not go to jail in these days? If you do not have money to pay for fine, it is jail for you! You drink beer what is two and three quarter, you shake up some dice where you think nobody care, you drive nine and one-half mile over a bridge where it say eight and one half——"

"That will do, Orsini. In 1911 did you or did you not serve eight months in jail for stealing some rings from a hotel room?"

"Ah, that—that is one dirty lie—one dirty plant is put on me! I get that——"

From under the swarthy skin of the erstwhile suave citizen of the world there leaped, sallow with fury, livid with fear, the Calabrian peasant, ugly and vengeful, chattering with incoherent rage. Lambert eyed him with profound satisfaction.

"Yes, yes—naturally. It always is. Very unfortunate; our jails are crowded with these errors. It's true, too, isn't it, Orsini, that less than three weeks before the murder you told Mr. Bellamy that the reason you hadn't asked your little Milanese friend to marry you was that you couldn't afford to buy her an engagement ring?"

"You—you——"

"Just one moment, Orsini." The prosecutor's low voice cut sharply across the thick, violent stammering. "Don't answer that question.... Your Honour, I once more respectfully inquire as to whether this is the trial of Mr. Bellamy and Mrs. Ives or of my witnesses, individually and en masse?"

"And the Court has told you once before that it does not reply to purely rhetorical questions, Mr. Farr. You are perfectly aware as to whose trial this is, and while the Court is inclined to agree as to the impropriety of the last question, it does not believe that it is in error in stating that it is some time since you have seen fit to object to any of the questions put by Mr. Lambert to your witness."

"Your Honour is quite correct. It being my profound conviction that I have an absolutely unshakable case, I have studiously refrained from injecting the usual note of acrimonious bickering into these proceedings that is supposed to be the legal prerogative. This kind of thing causes me profoundly to regret my forbearance, I may state. About two out of three witnesses that I've put on the stand have been practically accused of committing or abetting this murder. Whether they're all supposed to be in one gigantic conspiracy or to have played lone hands is still a trifle hazy, but there's no doubt whatever about the implications. Miss Page, Miss Cordier, Mr. Farwell, Mr. Ives, Mr. Orsini—it'll be getting around to me in a minute."

"I object to this, Your Honour, I object!" The choked and impassioned voice of Mr. Dudley Lambert went down before the clear, metallic clang of the prosecutor's, roused at last from lethargy.

"And I object, too—I object to a great many things! I object to the appalling gravity of a trial for murder being turned into a farce by the kind of thing that's been going on here this morning. I'm entirely serious in saying that Mr. Lambert might just as well select me as a target for his insinuations. I used to live in Rosemont. I have a good sharp pocket knife—my wife hasn't a sapphire ring to her name—I've been arrested three times—twice for exceeding a speed limit of twenty-two miles an hour and once for trying to reason with a traffic cop who had delusions of grandeur and a——"

"That will do, Mr. Farr." There was a highly peremptory note in Judge Carver's voice. "The Court has exercised possibly undue liberality in permitting you to extend your observations on this point, because it seemed well taken. It does not believe that you will gain anything by further elaboration. Mr. Lambert your last question is overruled. Have you any further ones to put to the witness?"

Mr. Lambert, looking a striking combination of a cross baby and a bulldog, did not take these observations kindly. "Am I denied the opportunity of attacking the credibility of the extraordinary collection of individuals that Mr. Farr chooses to produce as witnesses?"

"You are not. In what way does your inquiry as to Mr. Orsini's inability to provide a young woman with an engagement ring purport to attack his credibility?"

"It purports to show that Orsini had a distinct motive for robbery and——"

"Precisely. And precisely for that reason, since Mr. Orsini is not on trial here, the Court considers the question irrelevant and incompetent, as well as improper. Have you any further ones to put?"

"No." The rage that was consuming the unchastened Mr. Lambert choked his utterance and bulged his eyes. "No further questions. May I have an exception from Your Honour's ruling?"

"Certainly."

Orsini, stepping briskly down from the witness box, lingered long enough to bestow on his late inquisitor a glance in which knives flashed and blood flowed freely—a glance which Mr. Lambert, goaded by frustrated rage, returned with interest. The violence remained purely ocular, however, and the obviously disappointed spectators began to crawl laboriously to their feet.

"Call for Turner."

"Joseph Turner!"

A bright-eyed, brown-faced, friendly-looking boy swung alertly into the box and fired a pair of earnest young eyes on the prosecutor.

"What was your occupation on June nineteenth of this year, Mr. Turner?"

"I was bus driver over the Perrytown route."

"Still are?"

"No, sir; driving for the same outfit, but over a new route—Redfield to Glenvale."

"Ever see these before, Turner?"

The prosecutor lifted a black chiffon cape and lace scarf from the pasteboard box beside him and extended them casually toward the witness.

The boy eyed them soberly. "Yes, sir."

"When?"

"Two or three times, sir; the last time was the night of the nineteenth of June."

"At what time?"

"At about eight-thirty-five."

"Where did you pick Mrs. Bellamy up?"

"At about a quarter of a mile beyond her house, toward the club. There's a bus stop there, and she stepped out from some deep shadows at the side of the road and signalled me to stop."

"Did you know Mrs. Bellamy by name at that time?"

"No, sir; I found out later. That's when I learned where her house was too."

"Was yours the first bus that she could have caught?"

"If she missed the eight o'clock bus. Mine was the next."

"Did anything particularly draw your attention to her?"

"Yes, sir. She had her face all muffled up in her veil, the way she always did, but I specially noticed her slippers. They were awfully pretty shiny silver slippers, and when I let her out at the corner before Orchards it was sort of muddy, and I thought they sure were foolish little things to walk in, but that it was a terrible pity to spoil 'em like that."

"How long did it take you to cover the distance between the point from which you picked Mrs. Bellamy up to the point at which you set her down?"

"About eight minutes, I should say. It's a little over two miles—nearer two and a half, I guess."

"Did she seem in a hurry?"

"Yes, sir, she surely did; when she got out at the Orchards corner she started off almost at a run. I pretty nearly called to her to look out or she'd trip herself, but then I decided that it wasn't none of my business, and of course it wasn't."

"How do you fix the date and the time, Turner?"

"Well, that's easy. It was my last trip that night to Perrytown, see? And about the date, next morning I saw how there had been the—a—well, a murder at Orchards, and I remembered her and those silver slippers, and that black cloak, so I dropped in at headquarters to tell 'em what I knew—and it was her all right. They made me go over and look at her, and I won't forget that in a hurry, either— no, sir."

The boy who had driven her to Orchards set his lips hard, turning his eyes resolutely from the little black cloak. "I got 'em to change my route the next day," he said, his pleasant young voice suddenly shaken.

"You say that you had driven her over several times before?"

"Well, two or three times, I guess—all in that last month too. I only had the route a month."

"Same time—half-past eight?"

"That's right—eight-thirty."

"Anything in particular call your attention to her?"

"Well, I should think she'd have called anyone's attention to her," said Joe Turner gently. "Even all wrapped up like that, she was prettier than anything I ever saw in my whole life." And he added, more gently still: "About twenty times prettier."

The prosecutor stood silent for a moment, letting the hushed voice evoke once more that radiant image, lace-scarfed, silver-slippered, slipping off into the shadows. "That will be all," he said. "Cross-examine."

"No questions." Even Lambert's voice boomed less roundly.

"Next witness—Sergeant Johnson."

"Sergeant Hendrick Johnson!"

Obedient to Ben Pott's lyric summons, a young gentleman who looked like a Norse god inappropriately clothed in gray whipcord and a Sam Browne belt strode promptly down the aisle and into the witness box.

"Sergeant Johnson, what was your occupation on the nineteenth of June, 1926?"

"State trooper—sergeant."

"When did you first receive notification of the murder at Orchards?"

"At a little before ten on the morning of the twentieth of June. I'd just dropped in at headquarters when Mr. Conroy came in to report what he'd discovered at the cottage."

"Please tell us what happened then."

"I was detailed to accompany Mr. Dutton, the coroner, Dr. Stanley and another trooper, Dan Wilkins, to the cottage. Mr. Dutton took Dr. Stanley along with him in his roadster, and Wilkins rode with me in my side car. We left headquarters at a little after ten and got to the cottage about quarter past."

"Just one moment. Do I understand that the state troopers have headquarters in Rosemont?"

"That's correct, sir."

"Of which you are in charge?"

"That's correct too."

"Who had the key to the cottage?"

"I had it; Mr. Conroy had turned it over to me. I unlocked the door of the cottage myself, and we all went in together." The crisp, assured young voice implied that a murder more or less was all in the day's work to the state police.

"Did you drive directly up to the cottage door?"

"No; we left the motorcycle and the car just short of the spot where the little dirt road to the cottage hits the gravel road to the main house and went in on foot, using the grass strip that edges the road."

"Any special reason for that?"

"There certainly was. We didn't want to mix up footprints and other marks any more than they'd been mixed already."

"What happened after you got in the house?"

"Well, Mr. Dutton and the doctor took charge of the body, and we helped them to move it into the dining room across the hall, after a careful inspection had been made of the position of the body. As a matter of fact, a chalk outline was made of it for further analysis, if necessary, and I took a flash light or so of it so that we'd have that, too, to check up with later. I helped to carry the body to the other room and place it on the table, where it was decided to keep it until the autopsy could be performed. I then locked the door of the parlour so that nothing could be disturbed there, put the key in my pocket, and went out to inspect the marks in the dirt road. I left Mr. Dutton and Dr. Stanley with the body and sent Wilkins down the road to a gas station to telephone Mr. Bellamy that his wife had been found in the cottage. There was no telephone in the cottage, and the one at the main house had been disconnected."

"Sergeant, was Mr. Bellamy under suspicion at the time that you telephoned him?"

"I didn't do the telephoning," corrected Sergeant Johnson dispassionately; and added more dispassionately still; "Everyone was under suspicion."

"Mr. Bellamy no more than another?"

"What I said was," remarked the sergeant with professional reticence, "that everyone was under suspicion."

Mr. Farr met the imperturbable blue eye of his witness with an expression in which irritation and discretion were struggling for supremacy. Discretion triumphed. "Did you discover any tracks on the cottage road?"

"I surely did."

"Footprints?"

"No; there were some prints, but they were too cut up and blurred to make much out of. What I found were tire tracks."

"More than one set?"

"There were traces of at least four sets, two of them made by the same car."

"All equally distinct?"

"No, they varied considerably. The ground in the cottage road is of a distinctly clayey character, which under the proper conditions would act almost as a cast."

"What would be a proper condition?"

"A damp state following a rainstorm, followed in turn by sufficient fair weather to permit the impression to dry out."

"Was such a state in existence?"

"In one case—yes. There was a storm between one and three on the afternoon of the nineteenth. We'll call the tire impressions A, B 1 and 2, and C. A showed only very vague traces of a very broad, massive tire on a heavy car. It was almost obliterated, showing that it must have been there either before or during the downpour."

"Would those tracks have corresponded to the ones on Mr. Farwell's car?"

"There were absolutely no distinguishing tire marks left; it could have been Mr. Farwell's or any other large car. C had come much later, when the ground had had time to dry out considerably. They were the traces of a medium-sized tire on fairly dry ground. They cut across the tracks left by both A and B."

"Could they have been made by Mr. Conroy's car?"

"I think that very likely they were. I checked up as well as possible under the conditions, and they corresponded all right."

"What about the B impressions?"

"Both the B impressions were as sharp and distinct as though they had been made in wax. They were made by the same car; judging from the soil conditions, at an interval of an hour or so. We made a series of tests later to see how long it retained moisture."

"Of what nature were these impressions, sergeant?"

"They were narrow tires, such as are used on the smaller, lighter cars," said Sergeant Johnson, a slight tinge of gravity touching the curtness of his unemotional young voice. "Two of the tires—the ones on the front right and rear left wheels had the tread so worn off that it would be risky to hazard a guess as to their manufacture. The ones on the front left and rear right were brand new, and the impressions in both cases were as clear cut as though you'd carved them. The impressions of B 2 were even deeper than B 1, showing that the car must have stood much longer at one time than at another. We experimented with that, too, but the results weren't definite enough to report on positively."

"What makes you so clear as to which were B 2?"

"At one spot B 2 was superimposed on B 1 very distinctly."

"What were the makes of the rear right and left front tires, sergeant?"

"The rear right was a new Ajax tire; the front left was a practically new Silvertown cord."

"Did they correspond with any of the cars mentioned so far in this case?"

"They corresponded exactly with the tires on Mr. Stephen Bellamy's car when we inspected it on the afternoon of June twentieth."

"No possibility of error?"

"Not a chance," said Sergeant Johnson, succinctly and gravely.

"Exactly. Had the car been washed at the time you inspected it, Sergeant?"

"No, sir, it had not."

"Was there mud on the tires?"

"Yes, but as it was of much the same character as the mud in Mr. Bellamy's own drive, we attached no particular importance to it."

"Was there any grease on the car?"

"No, sir; we made a very thorough inspection. There was no trace of grease."

"Did you find anything else of consequence on the premises, sergeant?"

"I picked up a kind of lunch box in the shrubbery outside, and in the dining room, on a chair in the corner, I found a black cape—chiffon, I expect you call it—a black lace scarf and a little black silk bag with a shiny clasp that looked like diamonds."

"Did you keep a list of the contents of the bag?"

"I did."

"Have you it with you?"

"I have."

"Let's hear it, please?"

"'Contents of black purse found in dining room of Thorne Cottage, June 20, 1926,'" read Sergeant Johnson briskly, "'One vanity case, pale green enamel; one lip stick, same; one small green linen handkerchief, marked Mimi; leather frame inclosing snapshot of man in tennis clothes, inscribed For My Mimi from Steve; sample of blue chiffon with daisies; gold pencil; two theatre-ticket stubs to Vanities, June eighth; three letters, written on white bond paper, signed Pat.'"

"That's all?"

"That's all."

"Are these the articles found in the dining room, sergeant?"

Sergeant Johnson eyed the contents of the box placed before him somewhat cursorily. "Those are the ones."

"Just check over the contents of the bag, will you? Nothing missing?"

"Not a thing."

"I ask to have these marked for identification and offer them in evidence, Your Honour."

"No objections," said Mr. Lambert unexpectedly.

Mr. Farr eyed him incredulously for a moment, as though he doubted the evidence of his ears. Then, rather thoughtfully, he produced another object from the inexhaustible maw of his desk and poised it carefully on the ledge under the sergeant's nose. It was a box—a nice, shiny tin box, painted a cheerful but decorous maroon—the kind of a box that good little boys carry triumphantly to school, bursting with cookies and apples and peanut-butter sandwiches. It had a neat handle and a large, beautiful, early English initial painted on the top.

"Did you recognize this, sergeant?"

"Yes. It's a lunch box that I picked up back of the shrubbery to the left of the Orchards cottage."

"Had it anything in it?"

"It was about three-quarters empty. There was a ham sandwich and some salted nuts and dates in it, and a couple of doughnuts."

"What should you say that the initial on the cover represented?"

"I shouldn't say," remarked the sergeant frankly. "It's got too many curlicues and doodads. It might be a D, or it might be P, or then again, it mightn't be either."

"So far as you know, it hasn't been identified as anyone's property?"

"No, sir."

"It might have been left there at some previous date?"

"Well, it might have been; but the food seemed pretty fresh, and there were some new twigs broken off, as though someone had pressed way back into the shrubbery."

"I offer this box in evidence, Your Honour, not as of any evidential value, but merely to keep the record straight as to what was turned over by the police."

"No objections," said Mr. Lambert with that same surprising promptitude, his eyes following the shiny box somewhat hungrily.

"Very well, sergeant, that's all. Cross-examine."

"Did you examine the portion of the drive to the rear of the cottage, sergeant?" inquired Mr. Lambert with genial interest.

"Yes, sir."

"Find any traces of tires?"

"No, sir."

"No further questions," intoned Mr. Lambert mellifluously.

Mr. Farr turned briskly to an unhappy-looking young man crouching apprehensively in a far corner. "Now, Mr. Oliver, I'm going to get you just to read these three letters into the record. I'm unable to do it myself, as I've been subjected to considerable eye strain recently."

"Do I start with the one on top?" inquired the wretched youth, who looked as though he were about to die at any moment.

"Start with the first in order of date," suggested Mr. Farr benevolently. "May twenty-first, I think it is. And just raise your voice a little so we'll all be able to hear you."

"Darling, darling," roared Mr. Oliver unbelievably, and paused, staring about him wildly, flame coloured far beyond the roots of his russet hair. "May twenty-first," he added in a suffocated whisper.

> DARLING, DARLING:
>
> I waited there for you for over an hour. I couldn't believe that you weren't coming—not after you'd promised. And when I got back and found that hateful, stiff little note——Mimi, how could you? You didn't mean it to say, "I don't love you"? It didn't say that, did it? It sounded so horribly as though that was what it was trying to say that I kept both hands over my ears all the time that I was reading it. I won't believe it. You do—you

132

must. You're the only thing that I've ever loved in all my life, Mimi; I swear it. You're the only thing that I'll ever love, as long as I live.

You say that you're frightened; that there's been talk—oh, darling, what of it? "They say? What say they? Let them say!" They're a lot of wise, sensible, good-for-nothing idiots, who haven't anything better to do in the world than wag their heads and their tongues, or else they're a pack of young fools, frantic with jealousy because they can't be beautiful like Mimi or lucky like Pat. If their talk gets really dangerous or ugly we can shut them all up in ten seconds by telling them that we're planning to shake the dust of Rosemont from our heels any minute, and live happy ever after in some "cleaner, greener land."

Do you want me to tell them that I've asked you fifteen thousand and three times to burn all our bridges and marry me, Mimi? Or didn't you hear me? You always look then as though you were listening to someone else—someone with a louder voice than mine, saying "Wait—not yet. Think again—you'll be sorry. Be careful—be careful." Don't listen to that liar, Mimi—listen to Pat, who loves you.

To-morrow night, about nine, I'll have the car at the back road. I'll manage to get away somehow, and you must too. Wear that frilly thing that I love—you know, the green one—and the slippers with butterflies on them, and nothing on your hair. The wickedest thing that you ever do is to wear a hat. No, I'm wrong, you can wear something on your hair, after all. On the two curls right behind your ears—the littlest curls—my curls—you can wear two drops of that stuff that smells like lilacs in the rain. And I'll put you—and your curls—and your slippers—and your sweetness—and your magic—into my car and we'll drive twenty miles away from those wagging tongues. And, Mimi, I'll teach you how beautiful it is to be alive and young and in love, in a world that's full of spring and stars and lilacs. Oh, Mimi, come quickly and let me teach you!

PAT.

The halting voice laboured to an all too brief silence. Even the back of Mr. Oliver's neck was incandescent—perhaps he would not have flamed so hotly if he had realized how few eyes in the courtroom were resting on him. For across the crowded little room, Sue Ives, all her gay serenity gone, was staring at the figure by the window with terrified and incredulous eyes, black with tears.

"Oh, Pat—oh, Pat," cried those drowning eyes, "what is this that you have done to us? Never loved anyone else? Never in all your life? What is this that you have done?"

And as though in answer to that despairing cry, the man by the window half rose, shaking his head in fierce entreaty.

"Don't listen! Don't listen!" implored his frantic eyes....

"Now the next one, Mr. Oliver," said Mr. Farr.

ROSEMONT, JUNE 8TH.

MIMI DARLING, DARLING, DARLING:

It's after four o'clock and the birds in the vines outside the window are making the most awful row. I haven't closed my eyes yet, and now I'm going to stop trying. What's the use of sleeping, when here's another day with Mimi in it? Dawn—I always thought it was the worst word in the English language, and here I am on my knees waiting for it, and ranting about it like any fool—like any happy, happy fool.

I'm so happy that it simply isn't decent. I keep telling myself that we're mad—that there's black trouble ahead of us—that I haven't any right in the world to let you do this—that I'm older and ought to be wiser. And when I get all through, the only thing I can remember is that I feel like a kid waking up on his birthday to find the sun and the moon and the stars and the world and a little red wagon sitting in a row at the foot of his bed. Because I have you, Mimi, and you're the sun and the moon and the stars and the world—and a little red wagon too, my beautiful love.

Well, here's the sun himself, and no one in Rosemont to pay any attention to him but the milkman and me. "The sun in splendour"—what comes after that, do you remember? Not that it makes any difference; the only thing that makes any difference is that what will come after that in just a few minutes will be a clock striking five—and then six and then seven and it will be another day—another miraculous, incredible day getting under way in a world that holds Mimi in it. Lucky day, lucky world, lucky, lucky me, Mimi, who will be your worshipper while this world lasts.

Good morning, Beautiful.

YOUR PAT.

The eyes of the Court swung avidly back to the slim figure in the space before them, but for once that bright head was bowed. Sue Ives was no longer looking at Mimi's worshipper.

"And the next?" murmured Farr.

ROSEMONT, JUNE 9TH.

MY LITTLE HEART:

I went to bed the minute I got home, just as I promised, but it didn't do much good. I did go to sleep for a bit, but it was only to dream that you were leaning over me again with your hair swinging down like two lovely clouds of fire and saying over and over in that small, blessed voice—that voice that I'd strain to hear from under three feet of sod—"It's not a dream, love, it's not a dream—it's Mimi, who's yours and who's sweeter than all the dreams you'll dream between here and heaven. Wake up. Wake up! She's waiting for you. How can you sleep?" And I couldn't sleep; no, it's no use. Mimi, how can I ever sleep again, now that I have you?

It wasn't just a dream that between those shining clouds that are your hair your eyes were bright with laughter and with tears, was it, Mimi? No, that was not a dream. To think that anyone in the world can cry and still be beautiful! It must be an awful temptation to do it all the time—only I know that you won't. Darling, don't cry. Even when you look beautiful and on the edge of laughter, it makes me want to kill myself. It's because you're afraid, isn't it—afraid that we won't be able to make a go of it? Don't be afraid. If you will come to me—really, forever, not in little snatched bits of heaven like this, but to belong to me all the days of my life—if you will believe in me and trust me, I swear that I'll make you happy. I swear it.

I know that at first it may be hideously hard. I know that giving up everything here and starting life all over somewhere with strangers will be hard to desperation. But it will be easier than trying to fight it out here, won't it, Mimi? And in the end we'll hold happiness in our hands—you'll see, my blessed. Don't cry, don't cry, my little girl—not even in dreams, not even through laughter. Because, you see, like the Prince and Princess in the fairy tale, we're going to live happy ever after.

YOUR PAT.

"That concludes the letters?" inquired Judge Carver, hopefully, his eyes on the bowed head beneath his throne.

"That concludes them," said Mr. Farr, removing them deftly from the assistant prosecutor's palsied fingers. "And as it is close to four, I would like to make a suggestion. The state is ready to rest its case with these letters, but an extremely unfortunate occurrence has deprived us so far of one of our witnesses, who is essential as a link in the chain of evidence that we have forged. This witness was stricken three weeks ago with appendicitis and rushed to a New York hospital. I was given every assurance that he would be able to be present by this date, but late last week unfavourable symptoms developed and he has been closely confined ever since.

"I have here the surgeon's certificate that he is absolutely unable to take the stand to-day, but that it is entirely possible that he may do so by Monday. As this is Friday, therefore, I respectfully suggest that we adjourn to Monday, when the state will rest its case."

"Have you any objections, Mr. Lambert?"

"Every objection, Your Honour!" replied Mr. Lambert with passionate conviction. "I have two witnesses myself who have come here at great inconvenience to themselves and are obliged to return at the earliest possible moment. What about them? What about the unfortunate jury? What about the unfortunate defendants? I have most emphatic objections to delaying this trial one second longer."

"Then I can only suggest that the trial proceed and that the state be permitted to produce its witness as soon as is humanly possible, in which case the defense would necessarily be permitted to produce what witnesses it saw fit in rebuttal."

Mr. Lambert, still flown with some secret triumph, made an ample gesture of condescension.

"Very well, I consider it highly irregular, but leave it that way—leave it that way by all means. Now, Your Honour——"

"You say you have a certificate, Mr. Farr?"

"Yes, Your Honour."

"May we have its contents?"

"Certainly." Mr. Farr tendered it promptly. "It's from the chief surgeon at St. Luke's. As you see, it simply says that it would be against his express orders that Dr. Barretti should take the stand to-day, but that, if nothing unfavourable develops, he should be able to do so by Monday."

"Yes. Well, Mr. Farr, if Mr. Lambert has no objections you may produce Dr. Barretti then. You have no further questions?"

"None, Your Honour."

"Very well, the Court stands adjourned until to-morrow at ten."

"What name did he say?" inquired the reporter in a curiously hushed voice. "Dr. What?"

"It sounded like Barretti," said the red-headed girl, getting limply to her feet.

"The poor fool!" murmured the reporter in the same awe-stricken tones.

"What?"

"Lambert. Did you get that? The poor blithering fool doesn't know who he is and where he's heading."

"Well, who is he?" inquired the red-headed girl over her shoulder despairingly. She felt that if anything else happened she would sit on the floor and cry, and she didn't want to—much.

"It's Barretti—Gabriel Barretti," said the reporter. "The greatest finger-print expert in the world. Lord, it means that he must have their——What in the world's the matter? D'you want a handkerchief?"

The red-headed girl, nodding feebly, clutched at the large white handkerchief with one hand and the large blue serge sleeve with the other. Anyway, she hadn't sat on the floor.

The fourth day of the Bellamy trial was over.

CHAPTER V

"He couldn't look so cocky and triumphant and absolutely sure of himself as that if he didn't actually know that everything was all right," explained the red-haired girl in a reasonable but tremulous whisper, keeping an eye in desperate need of reassurance on the portly and flamboyant Lambert, who was prowling up and down in front of the jury with an expression of lightly won victory on his rubicund countenance and a tie that boasted actual checks under a ruddy chin. Every now and then he uttered small, premonitory booms.

"He could look just exactly like that if he were a God-forsaken fool," murmured the reporter gloomily. "And would, and undoubtedly does. Whom the gods destroy they first make mad. Look out, there he goes!"

"Your Honour," intoned Mr. Lambert with unction, "gentlemen of the jury, I am not going to burden you with a lengthy dissertion at this moment. In my summing up at a later time I will attempt to analyze the fallacious and specious reasoning on which my brilliant opponent has constructed his case, but at present something else is in my mind; or perhaps I should be both more candid and more accurate if I say that something else is in my heart.

"We have heard a great deal of the beauty, the charm, the enchantment, and the tragedy of the young woman whose dreadful death has brought about this trial. Much stress has been laid on her appalling fate and on the pitiful horror of so much loveliness crushed out in such a fashion. It is very far from my desire to deny or to belittle any of this. Tragic and dreadful, indeed, was the fate of Madeleine Bellamy; not one of us can think of it unmoved.

"But, gentlemen, when its horror grips you most relentlessly, I ask you to think of another young woman whose fate, to my mind, has been bitterer still; who, many times in these past few days, would have been glad to change places with that dead girl, safe and quiet now, beyond the reach of the slings and arrows of outrageous fortune that have been raining about her own unprotected head. I ask you to turn your thoughts for one moment to the fate of Susan Ives, the prisoner at the bar.

"Not so many weeks ago there is not one of you who would not have thought her an object of profound envy. Sue Ives, the adored, the cherished, the protected; Sue Ives, moving safe and happy through a world of flowers and blue skies that held no single cloud; Sue Ives, the lucky and beloved, the darling of the gods. There she sits before you, gentlemen, betrayed by her husband, befouled by every idle tongue that wags, torn from her children and her home, pilloried in every journal in the land from the most lofty and impeccable sheet to the vilest rag in Christendom, branded before the world as that darkest, most dreadful and most abject of creatures—a murderess.

"A murderess! This girl, so loyal and generous and honest that those who knew her believed her to be of somewhat finer clay than the rest of this workaday world; so proud, so sensitive and so fastidious that those who loved her would rather a thousand times have seen her dead in her grave than subjected to the ugly torture that has been her lot these past few days. What of her lot, gentlemen? What of her fate? What has brought her to this dreadful pass? Lightness or disloyalty or bad repute or reckless indiscretion or evil intent? Your own wife, your own daughter, your own mother, could not be freer of any taint of scandal or criticism.

"Accusations of this nature have been made in this court, but not by me and not against her. Of these sins, Madeleine Bellamy, the girl for whom all your pity has been invoked, has stood accused. She is dead. I, too, invoke your pity for her and such forgetfulness as you can mete out for the folly and dishonour that led to her death. For if she had not gone to that cottage to meet her lover, death would not have claimed her. She met death because she was there, alone and unprotected.

Whether she was struck down by a thief, a blackmailer, an old lover or a new one, is not within my province to prove or in yours to decide. My intent is only to show you that so slight is the case against Susan Ives and Stephen Bellamy that a stronger one could be made out against half a dozen people that have been paraded before you in order to defame her.

"What is this case against her? I say against her, because if you decide that Mrs. Ives is not guilty, the case against Stephen Bellamy collapses automatically. It is not the contention of the state that he committed this crime. The evidence produced shows, according to the state, that he and Mrs. Ives were together throughout the evening, at her instigation. If she had nothing whatever to do with the crime, it follows inevitably that neither did her companion. I again, therefore, turn your attention to Mrs. Ives, and ask you once more what is this case against her?

"This: You are asked to believe that this girl—many of you have daughters older than Susan Ives—that this girl, gently born, gently bred and gentle-hearted, upon receiving information from a half-intoxicated and infatuated suitor of Mimi Bellamy's that Mimi was carrying on an affair with her husband, Patrick Ives, dined peacefully at home, rose from the table, summoned Mrs. Bellamy's adoring husband to meet her down a back lane, procured a knife from a table in her husband's study and straightway sallied forth to remove the encumbrance that she had discovered in her smooth path by the simple and straightforward process of murdering her—murder, you note, premeditated, preconceived, and prearranged. Roughly, an hour and a half elapsed between the time that Susan Ives set out and the moment that the scream fixes as that of the murder.

"Presumably some of that time was occupied in convincing Mr. Bellamy of the excellence of her scheme and some of it in idle conversation—the time must have been occupied somehow; the actual rise and fall of a knife is no lengthy matter. Mr. Bellamy, we gather, was so entertained by the death of his idolized wife that he yielded to hearty laughter—Mr. Thorne has told you of that laugh, I believe.

"The lamp has gone out, so in total darkness they proceed to collect the jewels and wait peacefully until Mr. Thorne has put his keys under the doormat—the door is locked; they have thought of everything, you see—when once more they venture forth, enter an automobile that has the convenient quality of becoming either visible or invisible as serves them best, and return promptly and speedily to the house of Mr. Stephen Bellamy.

"Possibly you wonder why they do that. It is barely ten, and almost anyone might see them, thereby destroying their carefully concocted movie alibi, but possibly they thought that the Bellamy house would be a nice place to hide the pearls and talk things over. We are left a trifle in the dark as to their motives here, but undoubtedly the prosecutor will clear all that up perfectly. Ten minutes later they come out, and still together start off once more, presumably in the direction of Mrs. Ives's home so that everyone there can get a good look at them together,

139

while Mrs. Ives still has the knife and the bloodstained coat in her possession. There they part, Mrs. Ives to straighten up a little before she takes some fruit up to Mrs. Daniel Ives, Mr. Bellamy presumably to return to his own home and a night of well-earned repose.

"In the morning Mrs. Ives rises sufficiently early to pack up the blood drenched garments in a large box for the Salvation Army; she turns them over to a maid to turn over to a chauffeur, requests a fresh pair of gloves and sets forth to early church—the service which she has attended every Sunday of her life since she was a mite of six, with eyes too big for her face, hair to her waist, skirts to her knees and little white cotton gloves that would fit a doll if it weren't too big. The prosecutor leaves her there telling her God that last night she had had to kill a girl who was liable to make a nuisance of herself before she got through by cutting down Sue Ives's monthly income considerably. Of course it all may seem a trifle incomprehensible to us, but it's undoubtedly perfectly clear to God and the prosecutor.

"I think that that is a fair and accurate statement of the state's case, though Mr. Farr undoubtedly can—and will—make it sound a great deal more plausible when he gets at it. But that's what it boils down to, and all the specious reasoning and forensic and histrionic ability in the world won't make it one atom less preposterous. That's their case.

"And on what evidence are we asked to believe this incredible farrago? I'll tell you. We have the word of a hysterical and morbidly sensitive girl with a supposed grievance that she overheard a telephone conversation; we have the word of a vindictive young vixen who is leading nothing more nor less than a life of sin that she planted a note and failed to find it again; we have the disjointed narrative of an unfortunate fellow so far gone in drink, and love that he was half out of his senses at the time that he is supposed to be reporting these crucial events and has since blown his brains out; we have the word of an ex-jailbird who might well have more reasons than one for directing the finger of suspicion at a convenient victim; we have a trooper, eager for credit and prominence, swearing to you that he can as clearly recognize and identify a scrap of earth bearing the imprint of a bit of tire as though it were the upturned countenance of his favourite child—a bit of tire, gentlemen, which undoubtedly has some hundreds of millions of twins in this capacious country of ours.

"It is on this evidence, fantastic though it may sound, that my distinguished adversary is asking you to condemn to death a gentle lady and an honest gentleman. On the testimony of a neurotic, a love thief, a jailbird, and a drunkard! These are plain words to describe plain truths. I propose to produce witnesses of unimpeachable record to substantiate every one of them.

"It is, frankly, a great temptation to me to rest the case for the defense here and now; because in all honesty I cannot see how it would take any twelve sane men in this country five consecutive minutes to reach and return a verdict of not guilty. Remember, it does not devolve on me to prove that Susan Ives and

Stephen Bellamy are innocent, but on the state to prove that they are guilty. If they have proved that these two are guilty, then they have proved that I am. I believe absolutely that one is not more absurd than the other.

"On that profound conviction I could, I say, rest this case. But there is a bare possibility that some minor aspects of the case are not so clear to you as they are to me—there is a passionate desire on my part to leave not one stone unturned in behalf of either of my clients—and there is also, I confess, a very human desire to confront and confound some of the glib crew who have mounted the steps to that stand day after day somewhat too greatly concerned to swear away two human lives. It will not be a lengthy and exhausting performance, I promise. Four or five honest men and women will suffice, and you will find, I believe, that truth travels as fast as light.

"Nor shall I produce the hundreds upon hundreds of character witnesses that I could bring before you to tell you that of all the fine and true and gallant souls that have crossed their paths, the most gallant, the finest and the truest is the girl that this very sovereign state is asking you to brand as a murderess. In the case of the People versus Susan Ives I shall call only one character witness into that box—Susan Ives herself. And if, after you have listened to her, after you have seen her, after you have heard her tell her story, you do not believe that society and the law and the people themselves, clamouring for a victim, have made a frightful and shocking error, it will be because I am not only a bad lawyer but a bad prophet as well. Gentlemen, it is my profound and solemn conviction that whatever I may be as a lawyer, I am in very truth a good prophet!"

"I don't believe he's a bad lawyer," said the red-headed girl breathlessly. "He's a good lawyer. He is! He makes everyone see just how ridiculous the case against them is. That's being a good lawyer, isn't it. That's making a good speech, isn't it? That's——"

"He's a pompous old jackass," said the reporter unkindly. "But he loves his Sue, and he did just a little better than he knows how. Not so good at that either. You don't make a case ridiculous by jeering at it. If——"

"Call Mrs. Platz!" boomed the oblivious object of his strictures.

"Mrs. Adolph Platz!"

Mrs. Platz, minute and meek, with straw-coloured hair and straw-coloured lashes and a small pink nose in a small white face, advanced toward the witness stand with no assurance whatever.

"Mrs. Platz, what was your position on June 19, 1926?"

"I was chambermaid-waitress with Mrs. Alfred Bond at Oyster Bay."

"Had you been formerly in the employ of Mrs. Patrick Ives?"

"Yes, sir, I was, for about six months in 1925. I just did chamber work there, though."

"Was your husband there at the time?"

"Yes, sir. Adolph was there as what you might call a useful man. He helped with the furnace and garden and ran the station wagon—things like that."

"How long had you been married?"

"Not very long, sir—not a year, quite." Mrs. Platz's lips were suddenly unsteady.

"Mrs. Platz, why did you leave Mrs. Ives's employ?"

"Do I have to answer that, sir?"

"I should very much like to have you answer it. Was it because you were discontented with your work?"

"Oh, no, indeed, it wasn't that; nobody in this world could want a kinder mistress than Mrs. Ives. It was because—it was because of Adolph."

"What about Adolph, Mrs. Platz?"

"It was because——" She shook her head despairingly, fighting down the shamed, painful flush. "I don't like talking about it, sir. I'm not one for talking much."

"I know. Still, the only thing that can help any of us now is truth. I'm sure that you want to help to give us that."

"Yes, sir, I do. All right then—it was because of the way Adolph was carrying on with Mrs. Ives's waitress, Melanie."

"How did you know that?"

"Oh, I think they wanted me to know it," said Adolph Platz's wife, her soft voice suddenly hard and bitter. "He was more like a lunatic over her than a sane, grown-up man—he was indeed. I caught him kissing her twice—once in the pantry and once just behind the garage. They wanted me to catch them."

"What did you do when you made this discovery?"

"The first time I didn't do anything; I was too scared and sick and surprised. I didn't know men did things like that—you know, not the men you married—not decent ones that were your brother's best friends, like Adolph. Other men, might, but not them. I didn't do anything but cry some at night. But the next time I saw them I wasn't so surprised, and I was mad right through to my bones. I jumped right in and told both of them what I thought of them, and then I went right straight to Mrs. Ives and told her I was leaving the minute she could get someone else, and I told her why too. I told her she could keep Adolph, but not me."

142

"What happened then?"

"Then she sent for Melanie and Adolph and they both said it wasn't so."

"Your Honour——"

"Never mind what anyone said, Mrs. Platz; just tell us what happened."

"I couldn't do that without telling you what we were all saying, sir. We were all talking at once, you see, and——"

"Yes. Well, suppose you just tell us what happened as a result of this conference?"

"Adolph and I left, sir. I wouldn't have stayed no matter what happened after all that—not with me a laughingstock of all those servants for being such a dumbbell about what was going on. And Mrs. Ives didn't want Adolph without me, so he came too. There wasn't any way Mrs. Ives could tell which of us was speaking the truth, so she didn't try; but all the same, she gave Melanie as good a dressing down as——"

"Yes, yes, exactly. Now just what happened after you left Mrs. Ives, Mrs. Platz?"

"Well, after that, sir, we had a pretty hard time. We weren't happy, you see. I couldn't forget, and that made it bad for us; and I guess he couldn't either. Maybe he didn't want to."

The flood gates, long closed, were open at last. The small, quiet, tidy person in the witness box was pouring out all her sore heart, oblivious to straining ears, conscious only of the ruddy and reassuring countenance before her.

"I'm sorry, Mrs. Platz, but we aren't permitted to learn the opinions that you formed or the conclusions that you reached. We just want the actual incidents that occurred. Now will you just try to do that?"

The frustrated, troubled eyes met his honestly. "Well, I'll try, but that sounds pretty hard, sir. What was it you wanted to know?"

"Just what you did when you left Mrs. Ives."

"Yes, sir. Well, first we tried to get a job together, but we didn't get much of a one. It was a family of seven, and we did all the work, and Dolph didn't like it at all; so when spring came he decided to take a position as gardener on Long Island at Oyster Bay, where they wanted a single man to sleep in the garage. We fixed it up so that I was to take a job at Locust Valley as chambermaid, and we'd spend Sundays together, and evenings, too, sometimes. It looked like a pretty good plan, the way things were going, and it didn't work out so bad until I got that letter."

"You haven't told us about any letter, Mrs. Platz."

"No, sir, I haven't, that's a fact. Do you want that I should tell you now?"

"Well, I don't want you to get ahead of your story. Before you go on, I'd like to clear up one thing. What was the date on which your husband took this position?"

"It was the first of April, 1926. I didn't get mine till about two weeks later."

"Did you consider that he had left you for good at that time—deserted you, I mean?"

"I certainly didn't understand any such a thing." A spark shone in Mrs. Platz's mild eye. "He came to see me every Sunday of his life just like clockwork, and about once a week besides."

"He had talked of leaving you?"

"He certainly didn't, except once in a while when both of us was mad and didn't mean anything we said—like he'd say if I didn't quit nagging he'd walk out and leave me cold, and I'd say nothing would give me any more pleasure—you know, like married people do sometimes."

Mr. Lambert permitted himself a wintry smile.

"Quite. Divorce was not contemplated by either of you?"

"No, sir, we couldn't contemplate anything like that. Divorces cost something dreadful; and besides, we hadn't been married no more than a year about." Mrs. Platz blinked valiantly through the straw-coloured lashes, her mouth screwed to a small, watery smile.

"So, at the time you were speaking of, your relations with your husband were amiable enough, were they?"

"Yes, sir; I don't have any complaints to make. Everything was nicer than it had been since the fall before."

"What changed your relations?"

Mrs. Platz, the painful flush mounting once more, fixed her eyes resolutely on the little patch of floor between her and Mr. Lambert.

"It was that——"

"Just a little louder, please. We all want to hear you, you know."

"It was that waitress of Mrs. Ives'. She sent for him to come back."

"How do you know that?"

"Well, I'll tell you how I know it." Mrs. Platz leaned forward confidentially. It was good, said her quick, eager voice—after all these weary months of silence, it was good to find a friend to listen to this ugly story. "This was the way: Sunday evening came around and he hadn't never turned up at all."

"Sunday of what date?"

"Sunday, June twentieth, sir. I didn't know what in the world to make of it, but Tuesday morning, what do I get but a letter from Dolph saying that——"

"Have you still got that letter?"

"Yes, sir."

"Have you got it with you?"

"Yes, sir." Mrs. Platz dipped resourcefully into her shiny black leather bag and produced a soiled bit of blue notepaper.

"This is the original document?"

"Oh, yes, sir."

"In your husband's handwriting?"

"Yes."

"Your Honour, I ask to have this note marked for identification, after which I offer it in evidence."

"Just one moment, Your Honour. May I ask on what grounds the correspondence of the Platz family is being introduced into this case?"

"If Your Honour will permit me, I'll explain why these documents are being introduced," remarked Mr. Lambert briskly. "They are being introduced in order to attack the credibility of one of the prosecutor's star witnesses; they are being introduced in order to prove conclusively and specifically that Miss Melanie Cordier is a liar, a perjurer, and a despoiler of homes. I again offer this letter in evidence—I shall have another one to offer later."

Judge Carver eyed the blue scrap in Mr. Lambert's fingers with an expression of deep distaste. "You say that this proves that the witness was guilty of perjury?"

"I do, Your Honour."

"Very well, it may be admitted."

Mr. Farr permitted himself a gesture of profound annoyance, hastily buried under a resigned shrug. "Very well, Your Honour, no objection."

"The envelope containing this letter is postmarked Atlantic City, June 20, 1926," remarked Mr. Lambert with unction. "It says:

"DEAR FRIEDA:

"Well, you will be surprised to get this, I guess, and none too pleased either, which I am not blaming you for. The fact is that I have decided that we had better not see anything more of each other, because Melanie and I, we have decided that we can't get along any longer without each other and so she has come to me and I have got to look after her.

"The reason that I did not come to see you this week-end was that I went out to Rosemont to see her and she had got in wrong with Mrs. Ives and she was in a dreadful state about this Mrs. Bellamy being killed, and she is very delicate, so I am going to see that she gets a good rest.

"I hope that you will not feel too bad, as this is the best way. Melanie does not know that I am writing, as she is of a very jealous nature and does not want me writing any letters to you, so no more after this one, but I want everything to be square and aboveboard, because that is how I am. It won't do you any good to look for me, so you can save yourself the trouble, because no matter how often you found me, I wouldn't come back, as Melanie is very delicate and needs me. Hoping that you have no hard feelings toward me, as I haven't any toward you,

"Yours truly,
"ADOLPH PLATZ."

Adolph Platz's wife sat listening to this ingenuous document with an inscrutable expression on her small, colourless face. It was impossible to tell whether, in spite of the amiable injunctions of the surprising Mr. Platz, she yielded to the indulgence of hard feelings or not.

"Have you ever seen Mr. Platz since the receipt of this letter, Mrs. Platz?"

"No, sir."

"Did you ever try to find him?"

"No, sir, I didn't; but my brother Gus did. He was set on finding him, and he spent all his holidays looking in Atlantic City. He said that he hadn't any hard feelings against him, but it certainly would be a real treat to break every bone in his body."

"And did he?"

"Oh, no, sir, I don't believe that he broke any bones—not actually broke them."

"I mean—did he find him?"

"Oh, yes, sir, he found him in a very nice boarding house called Sunrise Lodge."

"Yes, exactly. Was Miss Cordier with him?"

The colourless face burned suddenly, painfully. "Yes, sir, she was."

"Now did you ever hear from this husband of yours again, Mrs. Platz?"

"Yes."

"When?"

"In September—over a month ago."

"Have you got the letter with you?"

"I have, sir—right here."

"I offer this in evidence too."

"No objection," said Mr. Farr bitterly. "I should appreciate the opportunity of inspecting these letters after Court adjourns, however."

"Oh, gladly, gladly," cried Mr. Lambert, sonorously jocose. "More than happy to afford you the opportunity. Now the envelope of this letter is postmarked New York, September 21, 1926. It says:

"DEAR FRIEDA:

"Well, this is to say that by the time you get this I will be on my way to Canada. I have a first-class opportunity to get into a trucking business up there that has all kinds of possibilities, if you get what I mean, and I think it is better for all concerned if I start in on a new life, as you might say, as the old one was not so good. Melanie thinks so, too, as she is very sensitive about all these things that have happened, and she thinks that it would be much nicer to start a new life too. She will join me when she is through being subpœnaed for this Bellamy trial, which is all pretty fierce, wouldn't you say so too. She doesn't know that I am writing you, because she is still jealous, but I thought I would like you to know for the sake of old times, as you might say, and also so that you can let Gus know that it won't do him any good to go looking for me any more. He will probably see that if you explain how I am starting this new life in Canada. Hoping that this finds you as it leaves me,

"Yours truly,
"ADOLPH PLATZ."

"Have you ever heard from your husband since you received this letter, Mrs. Platz?"

147

"No, sir."

"Ever heard of him?"

"No, sir."

"Thank you, that will be all. Cross-examine."

"No questions," said Mr. Farr indifferently, and the small, unhappy shadow that had been Adolph Platz's wife was gone.

"Well," said the reporter judicially to the red-headed girl, "you have to grant him one thing. He knows when to leave bad enough alone."

"Call Mrs. Shea."

"Mrs. Timothy Shea!"

Mrs. Timothy Shea advanced belligerently toward the witness box, her forbidding countenance inappropriately decorated with a large lace turban enhanced with obese violets and a jet butterfly. She seated herself solidly, thumped a black beaded bag on to the rail before her and breathed audibly through an impressive nose.

"Mrs. Shea, what is your occupation?"

"I keep a boarding house in Atlantic City—known far and wide as the decentest in that place or in any other, as well as the most genteel and the best table."

"Yes. Just answer the question, please. Never mind the rest. Were you——"

"I'll thank you to let me be after telling the truth," said Mrs. Shea, raising her voice to an unexpected volume. "It's the truth I swore to tell and the truth I'm after telling. The decentest and the——"

"Yes, undoubtedly," said Mr. Lambert hastily. "But what I wanted to know was whether you were in court at the time that Miss Cordier was testifying?"

"I was there. It will be a long day before I forget that day, and you may well say so."

"Had you seen her before?"

"Had I seen her before?" inquired Mrs. Shea with a loud and melodramatic laugh. "Every day of my life for close on three months, mincing around with her eyes on the ground and her nose in the air as fine as you please, more shame to her."

"Did you know her as Miss Cordier?"

"I did not."

"Under what name did you know her?"

"Under the name she gave me and every other living soul in the place—the name of Mrs. Adolph Platz, that ought to have burned the skin off her tongue to use it."

"She and Mr. Platz lived with you as man and wife?"

"Well, I ought to have lived in this world long enough to know that no man and his wife would go on forever playing the love-sick fools like those two," remarked Mrs. Shea grimly. "But I thought they were new wed and would soon be over it."

"Was Mr. Platz staying with you regularly?"

"Seven days and nights of the week."

"Did he pay you regularly?"

"He did that!"

"Did he seem to have a regular profession?"

"Well, that's all whether you'd call bootlegging a regular profession."

"Now, Your Honour," remonstrated Mr. Farr, who had been following this absorbing recital with an air of possibly fictitious boredom, "I don't want to indulge in any legal hair-splitting, but surely a line should be drawn somewhere when it comes to this type of baseless slander and innuendo."

"Do I understand that you have evidence of Mr. Platz's activities?" inquired Judge Carver severely.

"The evidence of two eyes and two ears and a nose," remarked Mrs. Shea with spirit. "Goings and comings and doings such as——"

"That will do, Mrs. Shea. The question hardly seems material. It is excluded. You may take your exception, Mr. Lambert."

Mr. Lambert, thus prematurely adjured, stared indignantly about him and returned somewhat uncertainly to his task.

"Is it a fact that Mr. Platz's relationship with Miss Cordier during their sojourn under your roof was simply that of a friend?"

"Fact!" Mrs. Shea snorted derisively. "'Tis a black-hearted lie off a black-hearted baggage. Friend, indeed!"

"That will do, Mrs. Shea," said Judge Carver ominously. "Mr. Lambert, I request you to keep your witness in hand."

"It is my endeavour to do so," replied Mr. Lambert with some sincerity and much dignity. "I will be greatly obliged, Mrs. Shea, if you omit any comments or characterizations from your replies. Will you be good enough to give us the day when you first discovered that Mrs. Cordier and Mr. Platz were not married?"

"September seventeenth."

"Have you any way of fixing the date?"

"You may well say so. Wasn't it six years since Tim Shea died, and didn't that big tall Swede come roaring down there saying that the two of them was no more married than Jackie Coogan and the Queen of Spain, and that he was going to beat the life out of his dear brother-in-law, Mr. Adolph Platz? And didn't he go and do it, without so much as by your leave or saving your presence, and in the decentest and——"

"Madam!" Judge Carver's tone would have daunted Boadicea.

"And are those what you call comments and characterizations?" inquired Mrs. Shea indignantly. "Well, God save us all!"

"That will be all, thank you, Mrs. Shea," said Mr. Lambert hastily. "Cross-examine."

"No questions," said Mr. Farr with simple fervour. Mrs. Shea, looking baffled but menacing, moved forward with a majestic stride, leaving the courtroom in a state of freely expressed delight. Across the hum of their voices boomed Mr. Lambert's suddenly impressive summons.

"Mr. Bellamy, will you be good enough to take the stand?"

Very quietly he came, the man who had been sitting there so motionless for so many days for them to gape their fill at, moving forward now to afford them better fare. Dark-eyed, low-voiced, courteous, and grave, he advanced toward the place of trial with an unhurried tread. In the lift of his head there was something curiously and effortlessly noble, thought the red-headed girl. Murderers should not hold their heads like that.

"Mr. Bellamy, where were you on the night of June nineteenth at nine-thirty o'clock?"

The proverbial dropped pin would have made a prodigious clatter in the silence that hovered over the waiting courtroom.

"I was in my car on the River Road, about a mile or so from Lakedale."

"You were not in the neighbourhood of the Thorne estate, Orchards?"

"Not within ten miles—twelve, perhaps, would be more accurate?"

"Was anyone with you?"

"Yes; Mrs. Patrick Ives was with me."

"You have a way of fixing the time?"

"I have."

"I will ask you to do so later. Will you tell us now at what time you left the Rosemont Country Club?"

"At a little before six, I think. We dined at quarter to seven, and my wife always dressed before dinner."

"Had you noticed Mr. Farwell in conversation with Mrs. Ives before you left?"

"Yes; my wife had called my attention to the fact that they seemed deeply absorbed in a conversation on the club steps."

"Just how did she call your attention to it?"

"She said, 'Oh, look, El's got another girl!'"

"Did you make any comment on that?"

"Yes; I said, 'That's clear gain for you, darling'——" He caught himself up, olive skin a tone paler, teeth deep in his lip. "I said, 'That's clear gain for you, but a bit hard on Sue.'"

"You were aware of Mr. Farwell's devotion to your wife?"

Behind Stephen Bellamy's tragic eyes someone smiled, charming, tolerant, ironic—and was gone.

"It was impossible to be unaware of it. Mr. Farwell was candour itself on the subject, even with those who would have been more grateful for reticence."

"Your wife made no attempt to conceal it?"

"To conceal it? Oh, no. There was nothing whatever to conceal; his infatuation for Mimi was common property. She laughed about it, though I think that sometimes it annoyed her."

"Did she ever mention getting a divorce in order to marry Farwell?"

"A divorce? Mimi?" His eyes, blankly incredulous, met Mr. Lambert's inquiring gaze. After a moment, he said, slowly and evenly, "No, she never mentioned a divorce."

"If she had asked for one, would you have granted it to her?"

"I would have granted her anything that she asked for."

"But you would have been surprised?"

Stephen Bellamy smiled with white lips. "'Surprised' is rather an inadequate word." He sought for one more adequate—failed—and dismissed it with an eloquent motion of his hands. "I should have been more—well, astounded than it is possible for me to say."

"So you had no inkling that your wife was contemplating any such action?"

"Not the faintest, not the——" Once more he pulled himself up, and after a moment's pause, he leaned forward. "That, too, sounds ridiculously inadequate. I should like to make myself quite clear; apparently I haven't succeeded in doing so. I believed my wife to be completely happy. You see, I believed that she loved me."

He was pale enough now to gratify the most exigent reporter of emotions, but his pleasant, leisurely voice did not falter, and it was the ruddy Lambert, not he, who seemed embarrassed.

"Yes, quite so—naturally. I wished simply to establish the fact that you were not in her confidence as to her—er—attitude toward Mr. Ives. Now, Mr. Bellamy, I am going to ask you to tell us as directly and concisely as possible just what happened from the time that you and Mrs. Bellamy finished dinner that evening up to the time that you retired for the night."

"I did not retire for the night."

"I beg your pardon?"

"I said that I did not retire for the night. Sleep was entirely out of the question, and I didn't care to go up to our—to my room."

"Naturally—quite so. I will reframe my question. Will you be good enough to tell us what occurred on the evening of June nineteenth from the conclusion of dinner to, say, eleven o'clock?"

"I will do my best. I'm afraid that I haven't an especially good memory for details. Mimi had said on the way home from the club that she had told the Conroys that she would join them after dinner at the movies in Rosemont. Quite a party were going, and I asked if they were going to stop by for her. She said no; that she had arranged to meet them at the theatre, as there was no room in their car. I suggested that I drive her over, and she said not to bother, as I'd have to walk back, because she wanted to keep the car; but I told her that I didn't mind the walk and that I wanted to pick up some tobacco and a paper in the village.

"After dinner we went out to the garage together; the self starter hadn't been working very well, and just as I got it started, Mimi called my attention to the fact that one of the rear tires was flat. She asked what time it was, and when I told her that it was five minutes to eight, she said that there wouldn't be time to change the tire, but that if she hurried she could catch the Conroys and make them give her a lift, even if they were crowded. They lived only about five minutes from us."

"North of you or south of you, Mr. Bellamy?"

"North of us—away from the village, toward the club. I wanted to go with her, but she said that it would be awkward for me to get away if I turned up there, and it was only a five-minute walk in broad daylight. So then I let her go."

He sat silent, staring after that light swift figure, slipping farther away from him—farther—farther still.

"You did not accompany her to the gate?"

Stephen Bellamy jerked back those wandering eyes. "I beg your pardon?"

"You didn't accompany her to the gate?"

"No. I was looking over the tire to see whether I could locate the damage; I was particularly anxious to get it in shape if I could, because we were planning to motor over next day to a nursery in Lakedale to get some things for the garden—some little lilacs and flowering almonds and some privet for a hedge that we——" He broke off abruptly, and after a moment said gently, "I beg your pardon; that's got absolutely nothing to do with it, of course. What I was trying to explain was that I was endeavouring to locate the tire trouble. In a minute or so I did."

"You ascertained its nature?"

"Yes; there was a cut in it—a small, sharp cut about half an inch long."

"Is that a usual tire injury?"

"I am not a tire expert, but it seemed to me highly unusual. I didn't give it much thought, however, except to wonder what in the world I'd gone over to cause a thing like that. I was in a hurry to get it fixed, as I said, and I remembered that I'd seen Orsini standing by the gate as we went by to the garage. I went out to ask him to get me a hand, but he'd started down the road toward Rosemont. I could see him quite a bit off, hurrying along, and I remembered that we'd given him the evening off. So I went back to the garage, took my coat off and got to work myself. I'd just got the shoe off when I heard——"

"Just a minute, Mr. Bellamy. Did you see Mrs. Bellamy again when you went to the gate?"

"Oh, no; she'd been gone several minutes; and in any case there is a jog in the road two or three hundred feet north of our house that would have concealed her completely."

"She was headed in the general direction of Orchards?"

"In the direction of Orchards—yes."

"It was along this route that the Perrytown bus passed?"

"Yes."

"Please continue."

"As I was saying, I had succeeded in getting the shoe off when I heard the telephone ringing in the library of our house. I dropped everything and went in to answer it, as there was no one else in the house."

"Who was on the telephone, Mr. Bellamy?"

"It was Sue—Mrs. Ives. She wanted to know if Mimi was at home."

"Will you give us the conversation, to the best of your recollection?"

"Yes. I said that she was not; that she had gone to the movies in Rosemont with the Conroys. Mrs. Ives asked how long she had been gone. I told her possibly ten or fifteen minutes. She asked me if I was sure that she had gone there, and I said perfectly sure, and asked her what in the world she was talking about. She said that it was essential to see me at once, and asked if I could get there in ten minutes. I said not quite as soon as that, as I was changing a tire, but that I thought that I could make it in fifteen or twenty. She asked me to meet her at the back road, and then—yes, then she asked me if Elliot had said anything to me. I said, 'Sue, for God's sake, what's all this about?' And she said never mind, to hurry, or something like that, and rang off before I could say anything more."

"What did you do next, Mr. Bellamy?"

"Well, for a minute I didn't know what to do—I was too absolutely dumfounded by the entire performance. And then, quite suddenly, I had a horrible conviction that something had happened to Mimi, and that Sue was trying to break it to me. I felt absolutely mad with terror, and then I thought that if I could get Mrs. Conroy on the telephone there was just a chance that they mightn't have left yet, or that maybe some of the servants might have seen Mimi come in and could tell me that she was all right.

"Anyway, I rang up, and Nell Conroy answered the 'phone, and said no, that Mimi hadn't turned up; and that anyway they had told her not to meet them till eight-thirty, because the feature film didn't go on till then. I said that Mimi must have made a mistake—that she'd probably gone to the theatre—something—anything—I don't remember. All that I do remember is that I rang off somehow and stood there literally sweating with terror, trying to think what to do next. I remember putting my hand up to loosen my collar and finding it drenched; I'd forgotten all about Sue. All I could remember was that something must have happened to Mimi, and that she might need me, and that I didn't know where she was. And then I remembered that Sue had told me to hurry and that she could explain everything. I tore out to the garage and went at the new tire like a maniac; it didn't take me more than about eight minutes to get it on, and not more than three or four more to get over to the back road where I was to meet Sue. I didn't pay much attention to speed limits."

"Just where is this road, Mr. Bellamy?"

"Well, I don't know whether I can make it clear. It's a connecting road out of Rosemont between the main highway—the Perrytown Road, you know—and a parallel road about five miles west, called the River Road, that leads to Lakedale. It runs by about a quarter mile back of the Ives' house."

"Did you arrive at this back road before Mrs. Ives?"

"No. Mrs. Ives was waiting for me when I got there. I asked her whether she had been there long, and she said only a minute or two. I asked her then whether anything had happened to Mimi. She said, 'What do you mean—happened to her?' I said an accident of any kind, and added that I'd been practically off my head ever since she had telephoned, as I had called up the Conroys and discovered that she wasn't there. Sue said, 'So Elliot was right!' She had been standing by the side of the car, talking, but when she said that, she looked around her quickly and stepped into the seat beside me. She said, 'I'd rather not have anyone see us just now. Let's drive over to the River Road. Mimi hasn't been hurt, Steve. She's gone to meet Pat at Orchards.' I was so thunderstruck, and so immensely, so incalculably, relieved that Mimi wasn't hurt that I laughed out loud. That sounds ridiculous, but it's true. I laughed, and Sue said, 'Don't laugh, Steve; Mimi's having an affair with Pat—she's been having one for weeks. They don't love us—they love each other.' I said, 'That's a damned silly lie. Who told it to you—Elliot Farwell?'"

"Were you driving at the time that this conversation took place?"

"Oh, yes, we were well up the back road. I'd started the minute she asked me to. Shall I go on?"

"Please."

"Do you want the whole conversation?"

"Everything that was said as to the relations of Mrs. Bellamy and Mr. Ives."

"Very well. She told me that unfortunately it was no lie; that for several weeks they had been using the gardener's cottage at Orchards for a place of rendezvous, and that Farwell had even seen them going there. I said that it made no difference to me whatever what Farwell had seen—that I wouldn't believe it if I had seen it myself. I asked her if Farwell hadn't been drinking when he told her this, and she said yes—that unless he had been he wouldn't have told her. I asked her if she didn't know that Elliot Farwell was an abject idiot about Mimi, and she said, 'Oh, Stephen, not so abject an idiot as you—you who won't even listen to the truth

155

that you don't want to hear.' I said 'I'll listen to anything that you want to tell me, but truth isn't what you hear—it's what you believe. I don't believe that Mimi doesn't love me.'

"She said, 'Where is she now, Steve?' And I said, 'At the movies. She probably met someone on the road who gave her a lift; or else she decided to walk straight there, as she knew that the Conroys' car would be crowded.' She said, 'She's not at the movies. She's waiting for Pat in the gardener's cottage.' I said, 'And has Pat gone to meet her?' And she said, 'No, this time he hasn't gone to meet her.' I said, 'What makes you think that?' Sue said, 'I don't think it; I know it.' I said, 'Oh, yes, he was going to Dallases to play poker, wasn't he?' And after a moment she said, 'Yes, that's where he said he was going. I happened to know that there's been a slip in their plan to meet to-night.'

"Then she told me that she believed they were planning to run away, and that the reason she had wanted to see me was to tell me that she would never give Pat a divorce as long as she lived, and she thought if I told Mimi that before it was too late it might stop her.

"We'd reached the River Road by this time, and were well on our way to Lakedale, and I said, 'Sue, we've talked enough nonsense for to-night; I'll tell you what we'll do. We're running low on gas, and when we get to Lakedale we'll get some, turn around and head back for Rosemont. We can see whether the movies are out as we go through the village, and if they aren't, you can come back to our house and wait for a minute or so until Mimi gets there. Then you can put the whole thing up to her and take your punishment like a lady when you find what a goose you've been. Is that a bargain?' And she said, 'All right, that's a bargain.'

"We'd been driving pretty slowly, so that it was after nine when we got into Lakedale; there were two or three people ahead of us at the gas station—Saturday night, you know—and Sue was very thirsty, so we asked the man at the gas pump if he could get her some water, and he did. I noticed him particularly, because he had the reddest hair that I've ever seen on a human being. We were at the station about ten minutes, and I looked at my watch just as we left. It said twenty minutes past nine."

"Was your watch correct, Mr. Bellamy?"

"Absolutely! I check it every day at the station."

"How long a drive is it from Lakedale to Rosemont?"

"Under half an hour—it's around nine miles."

"And to Orchards from Lakedale?"

"It's close to twelve—Orchards is about three miles north of Rosemont."

"Quite so. Now will you be good enough to continue with your story?"

156

"We hardly talked at all on our way back to Rosemont. I remember that Sue asked whether we wouldn't get there before the film was over, and I said, 'Probably.' But as a matter of fact, we didn't. We got to Rosemont at about five minutes to ten, and the theatre was dark. There were no cars in front of it and the doors were locked. I said, 'She'll probably be at the house,' and Sue said, 'If she isn't, I think that it will look decidedly queer to have me dropping in there at this time of night.' I said, 'There'll be no one there to see you; Nellie's gone home to her mother and Orsini went to New York at eight-fifteen.'

"It takes only three or four minutes from the theatre to the house, and just as we started to turn in at the gate Sue said, 'You're wrong; there's a light in the garage.' I looked up quickly, and there wasn't a sign of a light. I laughed and said, 'Don't let things get on your nerves, Sue; I tell you that I saw him going to the train.' And I helped her out of the car. There was a light in the hall, and as I opened the door I called 'Mimi!' No one answered, and then I remembered that I'd left it burning when I went out. I said, 'Come in. She must be over at the Conroys'. I'll call up and get her over.'"

"So far so good," said the reporter contentedly. "If Mr. Stephen Bellamy isn't telling the truth, he's as fertile and resourceful a liar as has crossed my trail in these many moons. Do you feel better?"

"Better than best," the red-headed girl assured him fervently. "Only I wish that Bellamy girl had died a long time ago."

"Do you indeed?"

"Yes, I do indeed—about twenty years ago, before she got out of socks and hair ribbons and started in breaking men's hearts. Elliot Farwell and Patrick Ives and Stephen Bellamy—even that little bus driver looked bewitched. Of course I ought to be sorry she's dead—but truly she wasn't good for very much, was she?"

"Not very much. The ones who are good for very much aren't generally particularly heartbreaking."

"You'd probably be as bad as any of them," said the red-headed girl darkly, and relapsed into silence.

"I'm universally rated rather high on susceptibility," admitted the reporter with modest pride. "Did you sleep better last night?"

"Not any better at all."

"Look here, are you telling me that after reducing me to a state of apprehension that resulted in my spending six dollars and thirty-five cents, and two hours and twenty minutes of invaluable time in a hired flivver in order to cure you of insomnia, you went back to that gas log of yours and worked half the night and had it again? Didn't you solemnly swear———"

"I'm not ever solemn when I swear. I didn't work after twelve. If you paid six thousand dollars for it, it was a tremendous bargain. It was the nicest ride I ever took. That was why I didn't sleep."

"Mollifying though mendacious," said the reporter critically. "Are you by any chance a flirt?"

The red-headed girl eyed him thoughtfully. After quite a lengthy period of contemplation she seemed to arrive at a decision. "No," she said gravely, "I'm not a flirt."

"In that case," said the reporter quite as gravely, "I'm going to get you some lunch. And if Sue Ives decides to confess to the entire newspaper fraternity that it really was she who did it, after all, I'm not going to be there—I'm going to be bringing your lunch back to you because you're not a flirt. Do I make myself clear?"

"Yes, thank you," said the red-headed girl.

She sat staring after him with round bright eyes that she was finding increasingly difficult to keep open. What was it that she had said that first day—that day that seemed so many, many days ago? Something about a murder story and a love story being the most enthralling combination in the world?

Well———The red-headed girl looked around her guiltily, wondering if she looked as pink as she felt. It was frightful to be so sleepy. It was frightful and ridiculous not to be able to sleep any more because of the troubles and passions of half a dozen people that you'd never laid eyes on in your life, and didn't really know from Adam and Eve—or Cain and Abel were better, perhaps. What's he to Hecuba or Hecuba to him? What indeed? She yawned despairingly.

No, but that wasn't true—you did know them—a hundred times—a thousand times better than people that lived next to you all the days of their lives. That was what gave a trial its mysterious and terrible charm; curiosity is a hunger in everyone alive, and here the sides of the houses were lifted off and you saw them moving about as though they were alone. You knew—oh, you knew everything! You knew that little Pat Ives had sold papers in the streets and that he carved ships, and that once he had played the ukulele and had taken Mimi Dawson riding on spring nights.

You knew that Sue Ives had gone to church in little cotton gloves when she was six years old, and that she had a coat of cream-coloured flannel, and poor relations in Arizona, and a rose garden beyond the study window. You knew that Stephen Bellamy dined at quarter to seven and had a small car, and flowering almonds in his garden, and a wife who was more beautiful than a dream, with

158

silver slippers and sapphire-and-diamond rings. You knew that Laura Roberts turned down the beds on the chambermaid's night out and had a gentleman friend in the village and that—and that——

"Wake up!" said the reporter's voice urgently. "Here are the sandwiches. I broke both legs trying to get back through that crowd.... Oh, Lord, here's the Court! Too late—hide 'em!"

The red-headed girl hid them with a glance of unfeigned reluctance.

"Mr. Bellamy," inquired Mr. Lambert happily, "you were telling us that you went into your house. What occurred next?"

"I went straight to the telephone and called up Mrs. Conroy. She answered the telephone herself, and I said, 'Can I speak to Mimi for a moment, Nell?' She said, 'Why, Steve, Mimi isn't here. The show got out early and we waited for about five minutes to make sure that she wasn't there. I thought that she must have decided not to come.' I said, 'Yes, that's what she must have decided.' And I rang off. That same terror had me again; I felt cold to my bones. I said. 'She's not there. I was right the first time—something's happened to her.' Sue said, 'Of course she's not there. She went to the cottage.' I said, 'But you say that Pat didn't go. She'd never wait there two hours for him. Maybe we'd better call up Dallas and make sure he's there.'"

The even voice hesitated—was silent. Mr. Lambert moved forward energetically. "And what did Mrs. Ives say to that?"

"She said—she said, 'No, that's no good. He's not at the Dallases'; he's home.' I said, 'Then let's call him up there.' Sue said, 'No, I'd rather not do that. I don't want him to know about this until I decide what to do next. I give you my word of honour that he's there. Isn't that enough?' I said all right, then, I'd call up the police court and the hospital to see if any accidents had been reported. I remember that Sue said something about its being premature, but none of her business. Neither the station nor the hospital had any information."

"Did you give your name?"

"Naturally. I asked them to communicate with me at once if they heard anything."

"And then what, Mr. Bellamy?"

"Then—then, after that, I don't remember much. All the rest of it was sheer nightmare. I do remember Sue saying that we might retrace the route that Mimi started over toward the Conroys, on the bare chance that she had had some kind of collapse at the roadside. But that was no good, of course. And finally we decided that there was nothing more to do till morning, and that I'd better get Sue home. I drove her back to the house——"

"To your house?"

"No, no; the Ives' house. I dropped her at the front gate. I didn't drive in. I asked her to let me know if Pat was there, and she said that if he were she'd turn on the light in the study twice. I waited outside by the car for what seemed a hundred years, and after a long time the light in the study went on once, and off, and on again and off, and I got in the car and drove away."

"What time was that, Mr. Bellamy?"

"I'm not sure—about quarter to eleven, perhaps. Mrs. Ives had asked me what time it was when we stopped at the gate. It was shortly after ten-thirty."

"Did you go straight home?"

"Not directly—no. I drove around for quite a bit, but I couldn't possibly tell you for how long. It's like trying to remember things in a delirium."

"But it was only after you heard that Mrs. Bellamy had not been at the movies that you were reduced to this condition—before that everything is quite clear?"

"Oh, quite."

"And you are entirely clear that at the time fixed for the murder you and Mrs. Ives were a good ten miles away from the gardener's cottage at Orchards?"

"Nearer twelve miles, I believe."

"Thank you, Mr. Bellamy; that will be all. Cross-examine."

Mr. Farr arrived in the center of the arena where sat his victim, pale and patient, with a motion so sudden that it suggested a leap. Not once had he lifted his voice during that long, laboriously retrieved narration. Now the courtroom was once more filled with its metallic clang, arresting and disturbing.

"Mr. Bellamy, you've told us that the tools in the garage belonged to Orsini. They were perfectly accessible to anyone else, weren't they?"

"Perfectly."

"Was Mrs. Bellamy in the garage at any time before you left?"

"Why, yes, I believe that she was. I remember meeting her as she came into the house just as I came downstairs to dinner—I'd gone up to wash my hands. She said she'd been out to the garage to see whether she'd left a package with some aspirin and other things from the drug store in the car. They weren't there, and she asked me to call up the club the next day to see whether she had left them there."

"So that she would have been perfectly able to have made that incision of that tire herself?"

"I should think so."

"She did not at any time suggest that you accompany her either to the movies or the Conroys, did she?"

"Oh, no."

"She countered such suggestions on your part, did she not, by saying that you would have to walk back, that it would be awkward for you to get away, and other excuses of that nature?"

"Yes. My wife knew that the pictures hurt my eyes, and she never urged me to——"

"No, never mind that, Mr. Bellamy. Please confine yourself to yes or no, whenever it is possible. It will simplify things for both of us. It would have been entirely possible for your wife to injure that tire in order to keep you from accompanying her, wouldn't it?"

"Yes."

"Now, Mr. Bellamy, I want to get this perfectly correctly. You claim that at nine-thirty you were on the River Road twelve miles from Orchards. Do you mean twelve miles by way of the back road, Rosemont and the Perrytown Road?"

"Yes."

"Retracing your way over the route that you had previously taken?"

"Yes."

"But surely you know that there is another and shorten route from Lakedale to Orchards, Mr. Bellamy?"

"I know that there is another route—yes. I was not aware that it was much shorter."

"Well, for your information I may state that it is some three miles shorter. Can you describe this route to us?"

"Not very well, I'm afraid. I'm not at all familiar with it. I believe that it is the road that Mr. Thorne was speaking of having taken that night, leading into the back of Orchards."

"Your supposition is entirely correct. Now, will you tell us just how you get there?"

"As I said, I'm not sure that I can. I believe that you continue on down the River Road until you turn off down a rather narrow, rough little road that leads directly to the back gates of Orchards. It's practically a private road, I believe, ending at the estate."

"What is its name?"

"I'm not sure, but I believe that it's something like Thorne Path, or Road, or Lane—I'm pretty clear that it has the name Thorne in it."

"Oh, you're clear about that, are you, in spite of the fact that you've never been near it?"

"You misunderstood me evidently. I never said that I had never been near it. As a matter of fact, I have been over it several times—two or three anyway."

"And yet you wish us to believe that you have no idea of either the name or the distance?"

"Certainly. It's been a great many years since I've used it—ten, perhaps. It was at a time that I was going frequently to Orchards, when Mr. Thorne, Senior, was alive."

"And you have never used it since?"

"No. It's not a road that anyone would use unless he were going to Orchards. It's practically a blind alley."

"Again I must ask you to refrain from qualifications and elaborations. 'No' is a reply to that question. The fact remains, doesn't it, that here was an unobtrusive short cut to Orchards that you haven't seen fit to tell us about?"

Stephen Bellamy smiled slightly—that gracious and ironic smile, so oddly detached as to be disconcerting. "I'm afraid that I can't answer that either yes or no—either would be misleading. I had completely forgotten that there was such a road."

"Completely forgotten it, had you? Had Mrs. Ives forgotten it too?"

"I'm sure that I don't know."

"Mr. Bellamy, is not this road, known as Thorne Lane, the one that you and Mrs. Ives took to reach Orchards the night of the murder?"

Mr. Bellamy frowned faintly in concentration. "I beg your pardon?"

"Did you not use Thorne Lane to reach Orchards on the night of the murder?"

The frown vanished; for a moment, Mr. Bellamy looked frankly diverted. Were these, inquired his lifted brows, the terrors of cross-examination? "We certainly did nothing of the kind. I thought that I'd already explained that I hadn't been over that road in ten years."

"I heard your explanation. Now, will you kindly explain to us why you didn't use it?"

"Why?" inquired Stephen Bellamy blankly.

"Why, consumed with anxiety as you were for the safety of your wife, didn't it occur to you to go to this gardener's cottage, where you were assured that she was having a rendezvous with another man?"

"I was not assured of any such thing. I was most positively assured that Mr. Ives had not gone there to meet her. Nor was I in anxiety at all about my wife during my drive with Mrs. Ives. I believed that she had gone to the movies."

"Very well, when you found out that she wasn't at the movies, why didn't you go then to the cottage?"

"Mrs. Ives gave me her word of honour that Mr. Ives was at home. It seemed incredible to both of us that she would have waited there for over two hours."

"Incredible to both of you that she could have waited? I thought you wished us to believe that you had such entire confidence in her love for you that you were perfectly convinced that she had never been near the cottage."

"I"—the whitened lips tightened resolutely—"I did not believe that she had been. It was simply a hypothesis that I accepted in desperation—a vain attempt to believe that she might be safe, after all."

"It would have consoled you to know that she was safe in the gardener's cottage with Patrick Ives?"

"I would have given ten years of my life to have believed that she was safe and happy anywhere in the world."

"Your honour meant nothing to you?"

"My honour? What had my honour to do with it?"

"Do you not consider that when a man's wife has betrayed him, his honour is involved and should be avenged?"

"I believe nothing of the kind. My honour is involved only by my own actions, not by those of others."

"You would have let her go to her lover with your blessing?"

Something flared in the dark eyes turned to the prosecutor's mocking blue ones, and died. "I did not say that," said Stephen Bellamy evenly.

Judge Carver leaned forward abruptly, "Mr. Bellamy is entirely correct," he said sternly. "He said nothing of the kind."

"I regret that I seem to have misunderstood him," said the prosecutor with ominous meekness.

"You would have prevented her?"

"I would have begged her to try to find happiness with me."

"And if that had not succeeded, you would have prevented her?"

"How could I have prevented her?"

The prosecutor took a step forward and lowered his voice to that strange pitch that carried farther than a battle cry. "Quite simply, Mr. Bellamy. As simply as the person who drove that knife to Madeleine Bellamy's heart prevented her joining her lover—as simply as that."

Judge Carver's gavel fell with a crash. "Let that remark be stricken from the record!"

Stephen Bellamy's head jerked back, and from somewhere an arm flashed out to catch him. He motioned it away, steadying himself carefully with an iron grip on the witness box. His eyes, the only things alive in his frozen face, met his enemy's unswervingly.

"I did not drive that knife to her heart." His voice was as ominously distinct as the prosecutor's.

"But you did not raise a hand to prevent it from striking?"

"I could not raise a hand—I was not there."

"You did not raise a hand?"

"Your Honour!"

Bellamy's eyes swung steadily to the clamorous and distracted Lambert. "Please—I'd rather answer. I have told you already that I was not there, Mr. Farr. If I had been I would have given my life—gladly, believe me—to have prevented what happened."

Farr turned a hotly incredulous countenance to Judge Carver's impassive one. "Your Honour, I ask to have that stricken from the record as deliberately unresponsive."

"It is not strictly responsive," conceded His Honour dispassionately. "However, the Court feels that you had already received a responsive answer, so were apparently pressing for an elaboration. It may remain."

"I defer to Your Honour's opinion," said Mr. Farr in a tone so far from deferential that His Honour regarded him somewhat fixedly. "Mr. Bellamy, what reason did Mrs. Ives give you for believing that Mr. Ives was at home?"

"She did not give me a reason; she gave me her word of honour."

"You did not press her for one?"

"No; I considered her word better than any assurance that she——"

"Your Honour, I have repeatedly requested the witness to confine himself to yes and no. I ask with all deference to have the Court add its instructions to that effect."

"Confine yourself to a direct answer whenever possible, Mr. Bellamy. You are not permitted to enter into explanations."

"Very well, Your Honour."

"Nothing was said about an intercepted note, Mr. Bellamy?"

"No."

"You were perfectly satisfied that she had some mysterious way of ascertaining that he had not gone out at all that evening?"

"Yes."

"But at some time during the evening that assurance on your part evaporated?"

"I don't follow you."

"I'll be clearer. By the time you reached Mrs. Ives's home—I believe that you've told us that that was at about ten-thirty—your confidence in her infallibility had so diminished that you suggested that she signal to you if Mr. Ives were actually there?"

"I believe that that was her suggestion."

"Her suggestion? After she had given you her word of honour that he was there?"

"Yes."

"You wish that to be your final statement on that subject?"

"Wait a moment." He looked suddenly exhausted, as though he had been running for a long time. "I told you that things were very confused from the time that I found that Mimi hadn't gone to the movies. I'm trying to get it as straight as possible. It was some time after we had left my house—after ten, I mean—and before we got to hers, that I suggested there was just a chance that she was mistaken and that Pat had gone to meet her after all. Sue said she couldn't be mistaken, and that, anyway, they'd never dare stay at the cottage so late—it wouldn't fit in with the movie story. I suggested then that possibly she had been right in her idea that they had been planning to run away together. Possibly that was what they had done to-night. She said, 'Steve, you sound as though you wish they had.' I said, 'I wish to God they had.' Then she said, 'I know that Pat hasn't been out, but I'll let you know definitely when we go home.' It was then that she suggested the lights."

"It all comes back very clearly now, doesn't it, Mr. Bellamy?"

"Yes."

"Very convenient, remembering all those noble bits about how you wished to God that they'd eloped, isn't it?"

"I don't know that it's particularly noble or convenient. It's the truth."

"Oh, undoubtedly. Mr. Bellamy, at what time——"

"Your Honour, I protest these sneers and jeers that Mr. Farr is indulging in constantly. I——"

"I simply remarked that Mr. Bellamy was undoubtedly telling the truth," said Mr. Farr in dangerously meek tones. "Do you regard that as necessarily sarcastic?"

"I regard your tone as sheerly outrageous. I protest——"

"It might be just as well to make no comments on the witness's replies, of either a flattering or an unflattering nature," remarked Judge Carver drily. "Is there a question before the witness?"

"No, Your Honour. I was not permitted to complete my question."

"It may be completed." There was a hint of acerbity in the fine voice.

"Mr. Bellamy, at what time, after you left Mrs. Ives at her house, did you return to your own?"

"I don't know." The voice was weary to the point of indifference.

"You don't know?"

"No; the whole thing's like a nightmare. Time doesn't mean much in a nightmare."

"Well, did this nightmare condition permit you to ascertain whether it was after twelve?"

"I believe that it was later."

"After one?"

"Later."

"How do you know that it was later?"

"I don't know—because the sky was getting lighter, I suppose."

"You mean that dawn was breaking?"

"I suppose so."

"You are telling us that you drove about until dawn?"

"I am telling you that I don't remember what I did; it was all a nightmare."

"Mr. Bellamy, why didn't you go home to see whether your wife had returned?"

For the first time the eyes fixed on the prosecutor wavered. "What?"

"You heard me, I believe."

"You want to know why I didn't go back to my house?"

"Exactly."

"I don't know—because I was more or less out of my head, I suppose."

"You were anxious to know what had become of her, weren't you?"

"Anxious!" The stiff lips wrenched themselves into something dreadfully like a smile.

"Yet from eleven o'clock on you never went near your house to ascertain whether she had come home or been brought home?"

"No."

"You didn't call up the police?"

"I told you I'd already called them up."

"Nor the hospital?"

"I'd called them too."

"Where were they to notify you in case they had news to report?"

"At my house."

"How were you to receive this information—this vital information—if you were roaming the country in an automobile?"

"I don't know."

"Weren't you interested to know whether she was dead or alive?"

"Yes."

"Then why didn't you go home?"

"I have told you—I don't know."

"That's your best answer?"

"Yes."

"Let's see whether I can't help you to a better one. Isn't the reason that you didn't go home or call up the police or the hospital because you knew perfectly well that any information that anyone in the world could give you would be superfluous?"

Stephen Bellamy focussed his weary eyes intently on the sardonic face only a few inches from his. "I'm sorry—I don't understand what you mean."

"Don't you? I'll try to make it clearer. Wasn't the reason that you didn't go home the perfectly simple one that you knew that your wife was lying three miles away in a deserted cottage, soaked in blood and dead as a doornail?"

"Oh, for God's sake!" At the low, despairing violence of that cry some in the courtroom winced and turned away their faces from the ugly triumph flushing the prosecutor's cold face. "I don't know, I tell you, I don't know. I was half crazy; I wasn't thinking of reasons, I wasn't thinking of anything except that Mimi was gone."

"Is that your best answer."

"Yes."

"At what time the next morning did you hear of the murder of your wife, Mr. Bellamy?"

Slowly, carefully, fighting inch by inch back to the narrow plank of self-control that lay between him and destruction, Stephen Bellamy lifted his tired voice, his tired eyes. "I believe that it was about eleven o'clock."

"Who notified you?"

"A trooper, I think, from the police station."

"Please tell us what he said."

"He said that Mrs. Bellamy's body had been found in an empty cottage on the old Thorne estate, and that while it had already been identified, headquarters thought I had better go over and confirm it. I said that I would come at once."

"And did so?"

"Yes."

"You saw the body?"

"Yes."

"Identified it?"

"Yes."

"It was clothed?"

"Yes."

"In these garments, Mr. Bellamy?"

And there, incredibly, it was again, that streaked and stiffened gown with its once airy ruffles, dangling over the witness box in reach of Stephen Bellamy's fine long-fingered hand. After the first convulsive movement he sat motionless, his eyes dilated strangely under his level brows. "Yes."

"These shoes?"

Lightly as butterflies they settled on the dark rim of the box, so small, so gay, so preposterous, shining silver, shining buckles. The man in the box bent those strange eyes on them. After a moment, his hand moved forward, slowly, hesitantly; the fingers touched their rusted silver, light as a caress, and curved about them, a shelter and a defense.

"These shoes," said Stephen Bellamy.

Somewhere in the back of the hall a woman sobbed loudly and hysterically, but he did not lift his eyes.

The prosecutor asked in a voice curiously gentle: "Mr. Bellamy, when you went into the room, was the body to the right or the left of the piano?"

"To the left."

"You're quite sure?"

"Absolutely."

"Oh, God!" whispered the reporter frantically. "Oh, God, they've got him!"

"It's strange that you should be so sure, Mr. Bellamy," said the prosecutor more gently still. "Because there was no piano in the room to which you were taken to see the body."

"What?" The bent head jerked back as though a whip had flicked.

"There was no piano in the dining room to which they had removed the body, Mr. Bellamy. The piano was in the parlour across the hall, where the body was first discovered."

"If that is so I must have seen it when I came in and confused it somehow."

"You couldn't very well have seen it when you came in, I'm afraid. The door to the parlour was closed and locked so that the contents of the room would not be disturbed."

"Well, then—then I must remember it from some previous occasion."

"A previous occasion? When you were never in the cottage before?"

"No, no, I never said that. I never said anything like that." The desperate voice rose slightly in its intensity. "I couldn't have; it isn't true. I've been there often— years ago, when I used to go over to play with Doug Thorne when we were kids. There was a playhouse just a few hundred feet from the cottage, and we used to run over to the cottage and get bread and jam and cookies from the old German gardener. I remember it absolutely; that's probably what twisted me."

"But the old German gardener didn't have any piano, Mr. Bellamy," explained the prosecutor patiently. "Don't you remember that Orsini particularly told us how the Italian gardener had just purchased it for his daughter before they went off on their vacation? It couldn't have been the old German gardener."

The red-headed girl was weeping noiselessly into a highly inadequate handkerchief. "Horrid, smirking, disgusting beast!" she intoned in a small fierce whisper. "Horrid——"

"No? Well, then," said the dreadful, hunted voice, "probably Mimi told me about it. She——"

"Mrs. Bellamy?" There was the slightest inflection of reproach in the soothing voice. "Mrs. Bellamy told you that her body was lying to the left of the piano as you entered the room? It isn't just the piano, you see—I'm afraid that you're getting a little confused. It's the position of the body in relation to the piano. You're quite correct about the position, of course—quite. But won't you tell us how you were so sure of it?"

"Wait, please," said Stephen Bellamy very clearly and distinctly. "You're quite right about the fact that I'm confused. I can see perfectly that I'm making an absolute mess of this. It's principally because I haven't had any sleep since God knows when, and when you don't sleep, you——"

"Mr. Bellamy, I'm sorry that I can't let you go into that. Will you answer my question?"

"I can't answer your question. But I can tell you this, Mr. Farr—I can tell you that as God is my witness, Susan Ives and I had nothing more to do with this murder than you had. I——"

"Your Honour! Your Honour!"

"Be silent, sir!" Judge Carver's voice was more imperious than his gavel. "You are completely forgetting yourself. Let that entire remark be stricken from the record.

Mr. Lambert, be good enough to keep your witness in hand. I regard this entire performance as highly improper."

Mr. Lambert, a pale ghost of his rubicund self, advanced haltingly from where he had sat transfixed during the last interminable minutes. "I ask the Court's indulgence for the witness, Your Honour. He took the stand to-day against the express advice of his physicians, who informed him that he was on the verge of a nervous breakdown. As it is now almost four, I ask that the court adjourn until to-morrow, when Mr. Bellamy will again take the stand if the prosecutor wishes to continue the cross-examination."

Judge Carver leaned forward, frowning.

"If it please Your Honour," said the prosecutor, briskly magnanimous, "that won't be necessary. I've finished with Mr. Bellamy, and unless my friend wishes to ask him anything on redirect——"

"Nothing on redirect," said Mr. Lambert hollowly, his eyes on the exhausted despair of the face before him. "That will be all, Mr. Bellamy."

Slowly, stiffly, as though his very limbs had been wrenched by torture, Stephen Bellamy moved down the steps from the box, where there still rested Mimi Bellamy's lace dress and silver slippers. When he stood a foot or so from his chair, he stopped for a moment, stared about him wildly, turning on the girl seated a little space away a look of dreadful inquiry. There she sat, slim and straight, with colour warm on her cheeks and bright in her lips, smiling that gay, friendly smile that was always waiting just behind the serene indifference of her eyes. And painfully, carefully, Stephen Bellamy twisted his stiffened lips to greet it, turned his face away and sat down. Even those across the courtroom could watch the ripple in his cheeks as his teeth clenched, unclenched, clenched.

"If Your Honour has no objection," the prosecutor was saying in that smooth new voice, "the witness that I spoke of yesterday is now in the court. He is still under his doctor's orders, but he had an unusually good night, and is quite able to take the stand; he is anxious to do so, in fact, as he is supposed to get off for a rest as soon as possible. His testimony won't take more than a few moments."

"Very well, let him take the stand."

"Call Dr. Barretti."

"Dr. Gabriel Barretti."

Dr. Barretti, looking much more like a distinguished diplomat than most distinguished diplomats ever look, mounted the stand with the caution of one newly risen from a hospital cot and settled himself comfortably in the uncomfortable chair. A small, close-clipped gray moustache, a fine sleek head of graying hair, a not displeasing touch of hospital pallor, brilliant eyes behind pince-nez on the most inobstrusive of black cords, and the tiny flame of the Legion of

171

Honour ribbon lurking discreetly in his buttonhole—Dr. Barretti was far from suggesting the family physician. He turned toward the prosecutor with an air of gravely courteous interest.

"Dr. Barretti, what is your profession?"

"I believe that I might describe myself, without too much presumption, as a finger-print expert."

There was no trace of accent in Dr. Barretti's finely modulated voice, and only the neatest touch of humourous deprecation.

"The greatest authority in the world to-day, aren't you, Doctor?"

"It would ill become me to say so, sir, and I might find an unflattering number to disagree with me."

"Still, it's an undisputed fact. How long has finger-printing been your occupation?"

"It has been both my occupation and my hobby for about thirty-two years."

"You started to make a study of it then?"

"A little before that. I studied at the time, however, with Sir Francis Galton in England and Bertillon in France. I also did considerable experimental work in Germany."

"Sir Francis Galton and Bertillon were the pioneers in the use of finger prints for identification, were they not?"

"Hardly that. Finger prints for the purpose of identification were used in the Far East before history was invented to record it."

Mr. Farr frowned impatiently. "They were its foremost modern exponents as a means of criminal identification?"

"Perfectly true. They were pioneers and very distinguished authorities."

"Shortly before his death in 1911, did Sir Francis Galton write a monograph on some recent developments in finger-print classification?"

"He did."

"Did the dedication read 'To Gabriel Barretti, My Pupil and My Master'?"

"Yes. Sir Francis was more than generous."

"Are you officially associated with any organization at present?"

"Oh, yes. I am very closely associated with the work of the Central Bureau of Identification in New York, and with the work of the Army and Navy Bureau in Washington."

"You are the court of final appeal in both places, are you not?"

"I believe so. I am also an official consultant of both Scotland Yard and the Paris Sûreté."

"Exactly. Is there any opportunity of error in identification by means of finger prints?"

"Granted a moderately clear impression and an able and honest expert to read it, there is not the remotest possibility of error."

"The prints would be identical?"

"Oh, no; no two prints are ever identical. The pressure of the finger and the temperature of the body cause infinite minute variations."

"But they do not interfere with identification?"

"No more than the fact that you raise or lower your voice alters the fact that it is your voice."

"Precisely. Now, Dr. Barretti, I ask you to identify these two photographs and to tell us what they represent."

Dr. Barretti took the two huge cardboard squares with their sinister black splotches and inspected them gravely. The jury, abruptly and violently agog with interest, hunched rapidly forward to the edges of their chairs.

From over Mr. Farr's shoulder came an old, shaken voice—the voice of Dudley Lambert, empty of its erstwhile resonance as a pricked drum: "One moment— one moment! Do I understand that you are offering these in evidence?"

"I don't know whether you understand it or not," remarked Mr. Farr irritably. "It's certainly what I intend to do as soon as I get them marked for identification. Now, Dr. Barretti——"

"Your Honour, I object to this—I object!"

"On what grounds?" inquired Judge Carver somewhat peremptorily, his own eyes fixed with undisguised interest on the large squares.

"On the grounds that this entire performance is utterly irregular. I was not told that the witness held back by the prosecutor was a finger-print expert, nor that— —"

"You did not make any inquiries to that effect," the judge reminded him unsympathetically.

173

"I consider the entire performance nothing more or less than a trap, Your Honour. I know nothing about this man. I know nothing about finger prints. I am not a police-court lawyer, but a———"

"Do you desire further to qualify Dr. Barretti as an expert by cross-examination?" inquired His Honour with more than his usual hint of acerbity.

"I do not, Your Honour; as I stated, I am totally unable to cross-examine on the subject."

"I am sure that Dr. Barretti will hold himself at your disposal until you have had the time to consult or produce finger-print experts of your own," said Judge Carver, bending inquiring eyes on that urbane gentleman and the restive prosecutor.

"Oh, by all means," said Mr. Farr. "One day—two days—three days—we willingly waive cross-examination until my distinguished adversary is completely prepared. May I proceed, Your Honour?"

"You may."

"They represent two greatly enlarged sets of finger prints, enlarged some fifty to sixty times—both the photographs and the initialled enlargements are in the lower left-hand corners—by my photographer and myself."

"Both made at the same time?"

"The photographs were made at the same time—yes."

"No, no—were the finger prints themselves?"

"Oh, no, at quite different times. The set at the right is a photograph of official prints—prints made especially for our file; the one at the left, sometimes known as a casual print, was obtained from a surface at another date entirely."

"A clear impression?"

"A remarkably clear impression. I believe that I may say without exaggeration— a beautiful impression."

"Each shows five fingers?"

"The official one shows five fingers, the casual print shows four fingers distinctly—the fifth, the little finger, is considerably blurred, as apparently no pressure was exerted by it."

"Only one finger print is necessary in order to establish identity?"

"A section of a finger print, if it is sufficiently large, will establish identity."

"These prints are from the same hand?"

"From the same hand."

"It should be obvious even to the layman in comparing them that the same hand made them?"

"I should think that it would be inescapable."

"No two people in the world have ever been discovered to have the same arrangement of whorls or loops or arches that constitute a finger print?"

"No two in the world."

"How many finger prints have been taken?"

"Oh, millions of them—the number increases so rapidly that it would be folly to guess at it."

"I'm going to ask you to give these prints to the jury, Dr. Barretti, so that they may be able to compare them at their leisure. Will you pass them on, Mr. Foreman, after you have inspected them?... Thanks."

The foreman of the jury fell upon them with a barely restrained pounce, the very glasses on his nose quivering with excitement. Finger prints! Things that you read about all your life, that you wondered and speculated and marvelled over—and here they were, right in your lucky hands. The rest of the jury crowded forward enviously.

"Dr. Barretti, on what surface were these so-called casual prints found?"

Through the courtroom there ran a stir—a murmur—that strange soaring hum with which humanity eases itself of the intolerable burden of suspense. Even the rapt jury lifted its head to catch it.

"From the surface of a brass lamp—the lamp found in the gardener's cottage on the Thorne estate known as Orchards."

"Will you tell us why it was possible to obtain so sharply defined a print from this lamp?"

"Certainly. The hand that clasped the lamp was apparently quite moist, either from natural conditions of temperature or from some emotion. It had clasped the base, which was about six inches in diameter before it swelled into the portion that served as reservoir, quite firmly. The surface of the lamp had been lacquered in order to obviate polishing, making an excellent retaining surface. Furthermore, the impression was developed within twenty-four hours of the time of the murder, and the surface was at no time tampered with. The kerosene that had flowed from it freely flowed away from the base, and, in any case, the prints were on the upper portion of the base. All these circumstances united in making it possible to obtain an unusually fine print."

"One that leaves not the remotest possibility of error in comparison and identification?"

"Not the remotest."

"Whose hand made those two sets of impressions, Dr. Barretti?"

"The hand in both cases," said Dr. Barretti, gravely and pleasantly, "was that of Mrs. Patrick Ives."

After a long time Mr. Farr said softly, "That is all, Dr. Barretti. Cross-examine."

And as though it had travelled a great distance and were very tired, the old strange voice that Mr. Lambert had found in the courtroom that afternoon said wearily, "No questions now. Later, perhaps—later—not now."

The fifth day of the Bellamy trial was over.

CHAPTER VI

The reporter looked from the clock to the red-headed girl and back again, with an expression in which consternation and irritation were neatly blended. The red-headed girl's hat was well over one eye, her nose was undeniably pink, she had a fluff of hair over her ear, a fiery spot burning in either cheek and two or more in her eyes. The clock said ten-thirty-five.

"Well, you're a fine one," said the reporter in tones that belied the statement. He removed an overcoat, a woolly scarf, a portable typewriter, seven tabloid newspapers, and a gray felt hat from the seat next to him and waited virtuously for appropriate expressions of gratitude. None were forthcoming. The red-headed girl scrambled unceremoniously over his feet, sank into the seat, and abandoned herself to a series of minute but audible pants varied by an occasional subdued sniff.

"What in the world—" began the reporter.

"Don't speak to me!" said the red-headed girl in a small fierce voice, and added even more fiercely: "What's happened?"

"That's what I want to know!" remarked the reporter with some emphasis. "What in the world was that perfectly ungodly racket going on outside in the hall?"

"Me," said the red-headed girl. "Who's been on the stand?"

"You? For the Lord's sake, what were you doing?"

"Screaming," said the red-headed girl. "Who's been on the stand?"

"Just a guy from a prison out West to prove that Orsini had served a jail sentence for robbery. What were you screaming about?"

"Because they wouldn't let me in.... Who's on now?"

"That red-headed fellow, Leo Fox, from the gas station. He's through with his direct, and Farr has him now.... Why wouldn't they let you in?"

"Because——No, I can't tell you all that now. Later—at lunch. Listen, won't you——"

"It was Saturday night, wasn't it, Mr. Fox?"

"Sure it was Saturday night."

Mr. Fox, who was lavishly decorated with freckles, whose coat was about three inches too tight for him, and whose tie was about three shades too green, shifted his chewing gum dexterously to the other cheek and kept a wary eye on Mr. Farr.

"There were a good many cars getting gas at your station on fine Saturday nights in June, weren't there?"

"Sure there were."

"Yet this car and its occupants are indelibly stamped on your memory?"

"If you mean do I remember the both of them, sure I do. They wasn't just getting gas; the dame—the lady—she wanted a drink of water, and it was me who got it for her. That was what made me remember them, see?"

"And all you know is that it was some time after nine, because you didn't come on duty until nine?"

"That's right. I don't never come on until then; and sometimes I'm a couple of minutes late, at that."

"But it might have been two minutes past nine instead of twenty-five minutes past, as Mrs. Ives claims?"

"No, sir, it couldn't have been nothing of the kind. People don't get eight gallons of gas, and pay for it, and get change, and ask for glasses of water and get them, and drink them and get away all in two minutes. It must have been more than ten minutes past, no matter if they were the first ones to come along after I checked in."

Mr. Farr contemplated him with marked disfavour. "I didn't ask you for a speech, Mr. Fox. The only fact you are able to state to us positively as to the time is that you came on duty at nine o'clock, and that Mrs. Ives and Mr. Bellamy appeared after you had arrived."

"That's right."

"Then that will be all. You may stand down."

"Call Mr. Patrick Ives," said Mr. Lambert.

"Mr. Patrick Ives!"

From the corner by the window where he had sat, hour after hour and day after day, with his mother's small gloved hand resting lightly and reassuringly on his knee, Patrick Ives rose and moved slowly forward toward the witness box.

How tall he was, thought the red-headed girl—how tall and young, for all the haggard misery and bitterness of that white and reckless face. He stood staring about him for a moment, his black head towering inches above those about him; then, with one swift stride, he was in his place.

"Mr. Ives, will you be good enough to tell us as concisely as possible just what happened on the night of June 19, 1926, from the time that you arrived at your home to the time that you retired for the night?"

"Oh," said Patrick Ives indifferently, "I doubt whether I could do anything along that line at all. I have a notoriously bad memory, and I'd simply be faking a lot of stuff that wouldn't do either of us any good. Besides, most of that ground has been gone over by other witnesses, hasn't it?"

The casual insolence of the conversational tone had had the effect of literally hypnotizing Mr. Lambert, Mr. Farr, and the redoubtable Carver himself into a state of stupefied inaction. As the voice ceased, however, all three emerged from coma into violent energy. It was difficult to tell which of the three was the more profoundly moved, though Mr. Lambert's protestations were the most piercing. Fortified by his gavel, however, Judge Carver managed to batter the rest into silence.

"Let that answer be stricken from the record! It is totally improper, Mr. Ives. This is not a debating society. You will kindly refrain from expressing your opinions on any subject whatsoever, and will confine yourself to the briefest replies possible."

"If Mr. Lambert will put a definite question to me I'll see whether I can give him a definite answer," replied Mr. Ives, looking entirely unchastened and remotely diverted.

"Very well," said Lambert, choking with ill-concealed wrath. "Will you be so kind as to tell us whether anything out of the ordinary occurred during that evening, Mr. Ives?"

"No."

"Before dinner?"

"No."

"After dinner?"

"No."

Mr. Ives flung him the monosyllables like so many very bare bones tossed at a large, hungry, snapping dog.

"Miss Page testified that she met you at the nursery door with a ship model in your hand at about eight o'clock. Is that correct?"

"Yes."

"When did you see her again?"

"About a quarter of an hour later."

"Was her testimony as to what followed correct?"

"Oh, it was correct enough as far as it went."

"It went further than she told us?"

"Considerably," said Mr. Ives, a grimly reminiscent smile flitting across his haggard young face.

"In what direction?"

"In the direction of violent hysterics and general lunacy," said Mr. Ives unfeelingly.

"What was the cause of these—er—manifestations?"

"Miss Page," said Mr. Ives with great clarity and precision, "is a high-strung, unbalanced, hysterical little idiot Mrs. Ives had——"

"Does Your Honour consider that a responsive reply?" inquired Mr. Farr with mild interest.

"The Court has already warned the witness to keep strictly to the question. It repeats that warning. As for the reply, it may be stricken from the record."

"I consider it an absolutely responsive reply," cried Mr. Lambert with some heat. "Mr. Ives was explaining why Miss Page——"

"You may take your exception and put the question again, Mr. Lambert. The Court has ruled on the reply."

"What caused the hysteria you speak of?" inquired Mr. Lambert through gritted teeth.

"The fact that Mrs. Ives had told her that her services were no longer required, and that she had better make her preparations to leave on Monday. Miss Page wished me to intervene in her behalf, as I had already done on two occasions."

"Did you acquiesce?"

"On the contrary," said Pat Ives—and at the tone of chilled steel in his voice the red-headed girl felt a flash of something like pity for her pet detestation, the flower-faced Miss Page—"I told her that in my opinion Sunday was a better day than Monday, and that I'd send Roberts to help with the packing."

"Why was Miss Page so anxious to stay, Mr. Ives?"

"How should I know?" inquired Mr. Ives. "She probably realized that it was a very excellent job that she was losing."

"That is the only explanation that occurs to you?"

"It is the only explanation that it occurs to me to give you," said Mr. Ives gently, a small, dangerous smile playing about the corner of his mouth.

Mr. Lambert eyed him indecisively for a moment, and prudently decided on another tack. "Did that conclude your conversation?"

"Oh, no," replied Mr. Ives, the smile deepening. "That started it."

"Will you give us the rest of it, please?"

"I'm afraid I can't. As I told you, I have a bad memory. If it doesn't betray me, however, I believe that it was largely an elaboration of the two original themes."

"What themes?"

"The themes of her departure and my intervention."

"Miss Page said nothing about a note?"

"A note?" There was a look of genuine surprise in the lifted brows.

"She did not mention having intercepted a note from Mrs. Stephen Bellamy—having abstracted it from a book in the library?"

"I see," said Mr. Ives, the brows relaxing, the smile returning, a little deeper and more dangerous. "No, I don't believe that she mentioned that. It would probably have made an impression on me if she had."

"Had you any reason to believe that Miss Page was jealous of Mrs. Bellamy, Mr. Ives?"

"Jealous of Mrs. Bellamy? Why should Miss Page have been jealous of Mrs. Bellamy?"

"I thought that possibly you might be able to tell us."

"You were in error," said Mr. Ives, leaning a little forward in his chair. "I am totally unable to tell you."

He did not lift his voice, but Mr. Lambert moved back a step somewhat precipitately.

"Yes—exactly. Now, Mr. Ives, Melanie Cordier has testified that you told her that you had not found the note she claims to have placed there. Was that correct?"

"That is what I told her, certainly."

"And it was an accurate statement on your part?"

Mr. Farr rose leisurely to his feet. "Just one moment, please. I'm becoming a little confused from time to time as to whether this is direct or cross-examination. It looks as though Mr. Lambert were going to leave me very little to do. Possibly I'm in error, but it certainly sounds to me as though he were impeaching the veracity of his own witness."

"The Court is inclined to agree with you. Do you object to the question?"

"I don't particularly object to the question, but it strikes me as totally out of place."

"Very well. You need not reply to that question, Mr. Ives."

"Thanks—with Your Honour's permission, I prefer to. I'm sure that Mr. Lambert will be glad to know that my reply to Melanie Cordier was entirely accurate."

"How many of these notes had you received previously?" inquired Mr. Lambert, and the expression that inflamed his countenance was not one of gratitude.

"Six or eight, possibly."

"Over what period?"

"Over a period of about two months."

"Are you aware that Miss Cordier testified that she had placed possibly twenty there over a much more extended period?"

"Well, if she testified that," said Patrick Ives indifferently, "she lied."

"What was the tenor of these notes?"

"They were largely suggesting appointments at the cottage."

"How often were these appointments carried through?"

"Twice."

"Only twice?"

At the flat incredulity of Lambert's face something flared in Patrick Ives's heavy blue eyes.

"Twice, I said—twice."

"Will you give us the dates?"

"I'm afraid I can't—once in the latter part of May, again about a week before the murder. That's about the best that I can do."

"Mr. Ives, there has been some talk here of this knife, State Exhibit 6. Miss Page has identified it as belonging to you. Is that correct?"

"Quite."

"Will you tell us when you last saw it?"

"The last time that I remember seeing it before it was produced here in court was on the afternoon of my wife's arrest—Monday the twenty-first."

"Have you any idea where it was on the night of June nineteenth at half-past nine?"

"I have a very definite and distinct idea," said Patrick Ives, and for the first time since he had mounted the stand the haggard restlessness of his face relaxed to something curiously approaching gaiety. "It was in my right-hand trousers pocket."

Mr. Lambert's exultant countenance was turned squarely to the jury. "How did it come to be there?"

"It was there because that's where I stuck it when I took the boat upstairs to Pete at eight o'clock that evening, and it stayed there until I put it back on the desk Sunday morning after breakfast."

"No chance of an error on that?"

"Not a chance."

"No possibility of its being in the possession of Mrs. Ives at any time that evening?"

"Not a possibility."

"Mr. Ives, where were you that evening at nine-thirty o'clock?"

The careless gaiety departed abruptly from Patrick Ives's face. For a long moment he sat staring at Lambert, coolly and speculatively. His eyes, still speculating, shifted briefly to the hundreds of eager countenances straining toward his, and at the sight of their frantic attention his mouth twisted somewhat mirthlessly. "Unkind, isn't it," mocked his eyes, "to keep you waiting!"

"I was at home," said Patrick Ives.

"What were you doing?"

"Smoking a pipe and looking through a magazine, I think, though I shouldn't like to swear to the exact time. I wasn't using a stop watch."

"In what room?"

"Well, I'm afraid that I can't help you there much either. I moved about from one room to another, you see. I did a little more work on the boat, smoked, read—I didn't follow any set programme. I wasn't aware at the time that it would have been judicious to do so."

"You are aware now, however, that Melanie Cordier said that you were not in any of the lower rooms when she made her rounds at ten?"

"Then I must have been in one of the upper rooms," said Patrick Ives gently.

"You are also aware that Mrs. Daniel Ives has told us that you didn't bring her her fruit that night because you were not in the house?"

"Well," said Pat Ives gently still, "this is probably the first time in her life that she was ever mistaken. I was in the house."

"What caused you to change your mind as to attending the poker party, Mr. Ives?"

"Circumstances arose that made it impossible." The inscrutability of Mr. Ives's countenance suggested that he would be a formidable addition to any poker party.

"What circumstances?"

"Circumstances," said Mr. Ives, "that I shouldn't dream of discussing either here or elsewhere. I am able to assure you, however, that they were not even remotely connected with the murder."

"What circumstances?" repeated Mr. Lambert, with passionate insistence.

"Now, what," asked Mr. Farr with languid pathos, "I again inquire, is my distinguished adversary leaving for a mere prosecutor to do?"

"Mr. Lambert," said Judge Carver austerely, "it strikes the Court that you are most certainly pressing the witness unduly in view of the fact that this is direct examination, and you are therefore bound to abide by his answer. The Court——"

"He has refused to give me an answer," replied Mr. Lambert, with some degree of justice and a larger degree of heat. "I may state to Your Honour that I regard the witness's manner as distinctly hostile and——"

"The Court fails to see wherein he has proved hostile," remarked Judge Carver critically, "and it therefore requests you to bear in mind henceforth that you are dealing with your own witness. You may proceed with the examination."

Mr. Lambert turned his richly suffused countenance back to his own witness, avoiding Sue Ives's eye, which for the last half hour had not once wavered from the look of passionate indignation that she had directed toward him at the outset of his manœuvres.

"Mr. Ives," said Mr. Lambert, "you heard Miss Roberts testify that she believed that it was your voice that she heard as she tried the door to the day nursery, did you not?"

"Yes, I heard her testify to that effect."

"Was she mistaken?"

"No," said Patrick Ives, spacing his words with cool deliberation, "she was not mistaken."

"Was she mistaken in believing that the door was locked?"

"No, she was not mistaken."

"Which of you locked the door, Mr. Ives?"

"If you will tell me what that has to do with the murder of Mimi Bellamy," said Mr. Ives with even greater deliberation, "I will tell you who locked the door."

"You refuse to answer my question?"

"Most assuredly I refuse to answer your question."

"Your Honour——" choked the frenzied Lambert.

"The Court also fails to see what the question has to do with the case," said Judge Carver, in a tone by no means propitiatory. "It is excluded. Proceed."

"It is being made practically impossible for me to proceed in any direction," remarked Lambert, in a voice unsteady with indignation. "Impossible! Mr. Ives, all that any occupant of that room had to do in order to get out of the house was to unlock that door and go, wasn't it?"

"Absolutely all," acquiesced the hostile witness cordially.

"No one would have been likely to see either one or the other or both depart, would they?"

"I think it highly unlikely."

"No one saw either you or Miss Page in the house between nine and ten, did they?"

"Not a soul—not a single solitary soul," said Mr. Ives, and his voice was almost blithe.

"How long would it take to get from your house to the cottage at Orchards?"

"On foot?"

"On foot, yes."

"Oh, ten-fifteen minutes, perhaps. There's a short cut across the fields behind the house that comes out close to there."

"The one that Miss Page used to take the children to the playhouse?"

"That's the one, yes."

"She knew of this path?"

"Well, obviously." The grim smile flashed for a moment to open mockery.

"And you knew of it?"

"And I knew of it."

"How?"

"My mother had told me that Miss Page was taking the children there, and I'd requested her not to do so as I knew Sue's feeling about the place."

"Mr. Ives, were your relations with your wife happy?"

For a moment Patrick Ives sat perfectly still, fighting back the surge of crimson that flooded his pale mockery. When he spoke, his voice, for all its clearness, sounded as though it had travelled back from a great distance.

"Yes," he said, "they were happy."

"In so far as you know, she was unaware that you had ceased to care for her?"

"She could hardly have been aware of it," said Patrick Ives. "From the moment that I first saw her I have loved her passionately—and devotedly—and entirely."

After a long, astounded silence, Lambert's voice asked heavily, "You expect us to believe, in the face of the evidence that has been presented to us here, that you have been faithful to Mrs. Ives?"

"It's a matter of supreme indifference to me what you believe," said Patrick Ives. "I don't regard fidelity to Sue as particularly creditable. The fool of the world would have enough sense for that."

"You are saying that you never ceased to love her?"

"I am saying that since I met her I've never given another woman two thoughts except to wish to God that she was somewhere else."

"That was why you went to meet Madeleine Bellamy at the gardener's cottage?"

"That," said Mr. Ives imperturbably, "is precisely why I went to meet Madeleine Bellamy at the gardener's cottage."

Before the cool indifference of his eye the ugly sneer on Lambert's countenance wavered for a moment, deepened. "You deny that you wrote these letters?"

Pat Ives bent on the small packet flourished beneath his eye a careless glance. "Not for a moment."

"Were they or were they not written after rendezvous had taken place between you and Mrs. Bellamy?"

"Two of them were written after what you are pleased to describe as rendezvous had taken place—one before."

"And where, Mr. Ives, was your wife at the time of these meetings—on June eighth, June ninth and May twenty-second?"

"I don't know."

"She was in New York, wasn't she?"

"I haven't the faintest idea. I'd never met her, you see."

Lambert goggled at him above his sagging jaw. "You'd never met her?"

186

The courtroom throng blinked, shivered, stared wildly into one another's eyes. No, no, that wasn't what he had said—that couldn't be what he had said. Or perhaps he was going mad before their eyes, sitting there with those reckless eyes dark in his white face....

"No; those letters were written in 1916. I didn't meet Sue until the spring of 1919."

"Ha!" exhaled Lambert in a great breath of contemptuous relief. "Written in 1916, eh? And may I ask why Mrs. Bellamy was carrying them around in her bag in 1926?"

"You may ask," Pat Ives assured him, "and what's more, I'll tell you. She was selling them to me."

"Selling them to you? What for?"

"For a hundred thousand dollars," said Patrick Ives.

Over the stupefied silence of the courtroom soared Lambert's incredulous voice: "You expect us to believe that?"

"I wish to the Lord you'd stop asking me that," said his witness with undisguised irritation. "It's not my business to decide what you'll believe or what you won't believe. What I'm telling you is the truth."

"It is your contention that these letters of yours, which you now claim were written in 1916, were being used for purposes of blackmail by Mrs. Bellamy?"

"You choose your own words," said Pat Ives. "Personally, I'd chose prettier ones. Mimi undoubtedly considered that I would be getting value received in the letters. She was right. She also may have considered that I owed her something. She was right again."

"You owed her something?"

"I owed her a great deal for not having married me," said Pat Ives. "As she didn't, I owe her more happiness than most men even dream of."

Lambert made a sound that strongly suggested a snort. "Very pretty—very pretty indeed. What it comes down to, however, is that you accuse this dead girl, who is not here to defend herself, of deliberately stooping to blackmailing the man she loved for a colossal sum of money—that's it, isn't it?"

"Well, hardly. She didn't love me, of course—she never loved anyone in her life but Steve. She told me that she wanted the money because she thought that he was sick; that he was working himself to death and getting nothing out of it. She was going to persuade him that an aunt in Cheyenne had left her the money, and that she wasn't happy here, and that they ought to start out again in a place that she'd heard of in California. She had it all worked out very nicely."

"One moment, Mr. Ives." Judge Carver lifted an arresting hand. "As it is after twelve, the Court will at this time take its customary recess for luncheon. We will reconvene at one-fifteen."

The reporter viewed the recessional through the doors behind the witness box with an expression of unfeigned diversion. "Watch Uncle Dudley," he adjured the red-headed girl. "He's not going to have any luncheon; he's going to stay right here where nobody can get at him to give him any unwelcome instructions before he gets through with Mr. Patrick Ives. There, what did I tell you?"

Mr. Lambert, who had followed somewhat perfunctorily in the wake of his clients, now wheeled about briskly and returned to his well-laden desk, where he proceeded to plunge into a large stack of papers before him with virtuous abandon. He apparently found them of the most absorbing interest, although from time to time he permitted himself a slightly apprehensive glance at the closed door.

Finally it opened, and one of the amiable and harassed-looking young men who shared the desk with him entered purposefully. An animated though inaudible colloquy ensued, punctuated by much emphatic head wagging by Lambert. Finally the young man departed more precipitately than he had come, Mr. Lambert returned to his studies, and the reporter and the red-headed girl emerged from the fascinated hush in which they had been contemplating this silent drama.

"Ten to one she doesn't get in a syllable to him before he gets through with Ives," said the reporter.

"Who doesn't?" The red-headed girl's tone was a trifle abstracted. She was wondering if her nose was still pink, and if the young man beside her was one of the young men who consider face powder more immoral than tooth powder.

"Sue Ives, goose! What were you screaming about?"

"I was screaming," said the red-headed girl, memory lighting a reminiscent glitter in her eye, "because they wouldn't let me in, and I thought that if I made enough noise they might."

"Why wouldn't they let you in?"

"Because a fat fiend made a snatch at my ticket and tore it in two and I had only half a one to show them." She relinquished the powder box regretfully and exhibited a blue scrap about two inches square. "Next time," she remarked with grim pride, "they'll know whom this ticket belongs to. Two policemen snatched at me, and I told them if they laid one finger on me, I'd have them up for assault and battery. So they didn't lay a finger on me."

"It will probably be a life work—and an uphill job, at that—to eliminate a marked lack of emotional control that is your distinguishing characteristic," said the reporter meditatively. "However, did you enjoy the picnic?"

"I adored it!" said the emotionally uncontrolled young woman beside him.

"It was a fair picnic," conceded the reporter. "And for a person whose height should be measured in inches rather than feet; you're a very fair hiker. Too bad there's only one Sunday to a trial. You have rather a knack with bacon sandwiches too. How are you with scrambled eggs?"

"Marvellous!" said the red-headed girl frankly.

"Though, if things keep up the way they've been going this morning, we're liable to have another trial started before this one is over. The people versus Patrick Ives! I can see it coming."

"You don't think he did it, do you?" inquired the red-headed girl anxiously.

"Oh, when it comes to murder trials, I don't think. But I'll tell you this: If Steve Bellamy didn't do it, he thinks that Pat Ives did. And if Pat didn't he thinks that Sue did. And I don't envy any of them their thoughts these days.... Ah, here we are again!"

***

"Mr. Ives, do I understand that you were perfectly willing to pay a hundred thousand dollars for two or three letters that you protest are perfectly innocent?"

"I don't protest anything of the kind. I think they're damned incriminating letters—just exactly the kind of stuff that a sickening, infatuated, fatuous young fool would write. And you're flattering me when you say that I was perfectly willing. It took me about two months to get even moderately resigned to the situation, and at that, I didn't regard it with marked favour."

"Still, you were willing to pay a hundred thousand dollars to keep the letters out of your wife's hands?"

"Five hundred thousand dollars, if I could put my hands on it, to keep pain and sorrow and ugliness out of her way."

"You were not convinced, then, that she would accept your story as to when the letters were written?"

"I didn't want her to know that they had ever been written. I'd never told her of the degree of—intimacy that had existed between Mimi and myself."

"Exactly. Now Miss Cordier had told us that the notes from Mrs. Bellamy had been increasing in frequency at the time of the murder. Is that true?"

"Yes; I'd have about three in ten days."

"Her demands were becoming more insistent?"

"Considerably." Again that small grim smile, curiously unsuggestive of mirth.

"So that it had become essential for you to do something at once if you were to prevent these letters from reaching your wife?"

"It was necessary for me to produce the money at once, if that is what you mean."

"Don't trouble to analyze my meanings, if you please. Just answer my question."

Patrick Ives's eyes narrowed slightly. "Your question was ambiguous," he commented without emphasis.

"I asked you if it was not imperative for you to act promptly in order to prevent these letters from reaching your wife?"

"It's still ambiguous. As I said before, however, it was necessary to pay for the letters pretty promptly, and I brought out the money on the night of the nineteenth with that end in view."

"Oh!" said Lambert, in a heavily disconcerted voice. "You brought it out, did you? In what form?"

"I got it out of my safety box at noon—eighty-five thousand in Liberty Bonds and fifteen in municipal bonds."

"Did anyone know that you were doing this?"

"Naturally not."

"Where did you place this sum on your return, Mr. Ives?"

"Well, I put it first in the back of the desk drawer in my study just before dinner. I intended to put it upstairs in a wall safe behind a panel in my dressing room, but while I was looking through it in the study to make sure that it was all there, Sue called to me from the hall that our guests were going, and I went out on the porch to say good-bye to them. We didn't go upstairs before dinner, so that I didn't get a chance to transfer them until later in the evening."

"No one knew they were in the house?"

"Not so far as I know."

"What did you do with them subsequently?"

"I returned them to my safety-deposit box on Monday at noon."

"Anyone know of that transaction?"

"Not a soul."

"So you are the only person able to attest that you ever had any intention of paying that money to Mrs. Bellamy?"

"Well, whom do you want better?" inquired Pat Ives agreeably.

Mr. Lambert bestowed on him an enigmatic smile that was far from agreeable. "Did this sum represent a substantial portion of your capital?"

"It certainly would be no exaggeration to say that it made a large dent in it."

"You say that it had taken you a long time to decide to pay it?"

"A moderately long time—two months."

"Why didn't you take it to Mrs. Bellamy that evening, Mr. Ives?"

"I had no appointment with her. She was to let me know if she was able to get away, and at what time."

"It didn't occur to you to look in the book to see whether there was a note?"

"It most assuredly did occur to me. I went in for that specific purpose at the time that Sue called me from the hall."

"So that you didn't look?"

"Oh, yes, I did look when I came back five minutes later. There was no note."

"Aha!" said Mr. Lambert, and the red-headed girl, watching with horrified eyes the reckless progress of young Mr. Ives across the spread nets, made a mechanical note that never except in a book had she heard a human being say "Aha" before.

"So you looked in the book, did you? And there was no note, was there?"

"Right both times," said Mr. Ives.

"Now that's very interesting," beamed Mr. Lambert—"very interesting, indeed. But if there had been a note in that book, you'd have found it, wouldn't you?"

"Well, not being a blithering idiot, that's a fairly safe proposition."

"And if you had found it, you would have gone to the rendezvous, wouldn't you?"

"I'd certainly have made every effort to."

"Cancelling your poker engagement?"

191

"Presumably."

"Taking the short cut across the fields?"

"I don't know how I'd have gone. It's slightly academic, isn't it?"

"And in that gardener's cottage you would have found waiting for you the unfortunate girl with those letters that it was so vitally necessary for you to obtain?"

"Why don't you ask him whether he would still have had the knife in his pocket?" inquired Mr. Farr gently. "And why don't you ask him what he would have done with it? You don't want to leave anything like that out."

Lambert, thus rudely checked in his exultant career, turned bulging eyes and a howl of outraged protest in the direction of Judge Carver's unresponsive countenance.

"Your Honour, in a somewhat protracted career at the bar, I have yet to encounter as flagrant a breach——"

Judge Carver cut sharply across these strident objurgations: "And in a somewhat protracted career at the bar, Mr. Lambert, this Court has yet to encounter as extraordinary a conduct of an examination as you have permitted yourself, and as the Court, in the absence of protests from either the witness or the prosecution, has permitted you. Mr. Farr's objection was not put in a proper form, but is otherwise quite legitimate. The questions that you are putting to the witness involve a purely supposititious case, and as such, the witness is entirely at liberty to refuse to answer them. You may proceed."

"I'll answer it," said Pat Ives. "If I'd found the note, I'd have gone to the cottage, given Mimi the money, got the letters, and none of us would have spent these last weeks thinking what a nice pleasant place hell would be for a change. I wish to God I'd found it. Is that what you wanted to know?"

It was very far indeed from what Mr. Lambert wanted to know. However, he turned a wary eye on the jury, who were contemplating soberly and not too sympathetically the bitter, insolent face of the young gentleman in the witness box. Flippancy was obviously an evil stench in their nostrils. Mr. Lambert rattled the letters still clenched in his hand reminiscently.

"There are two or three things in these letters that I'd like to have you reconcile with the statement that they were written in 1916. First, what does it mean, Mr. Ives, when you say: 'I keep telling myself that we're mad—that there's black trouble ahead of us—that I haven't any right in the world to let you do this'—do what, Mr. Ives?"

"Carry on the highly indiscreet affair that we were indulging in," said Pat Ives, his white face a shade whiter. "We'd both completely lost our heads. She wasn't willing to marry me because she was afraid that I hadn't it in me to make good. There was a lot of ugly gossip going on, and it had upset her."

"Quite so," smiled Mr. Lambert dreadfully; "oh, quite so. Now in the one that begins: 'Mimi darling, darling, darling, it's after four o'clock and——'"

"Are you going through those letters again?" inquired Patrick Ives, his hands clenched on the edge of the box.

"Just one or two little things that I'd like cleared up, and I'm sure that these gentlemen would too. It goes on: 'Dawn—I always thought that was the worst word in the English language and here I am on my knees waiting for it, and ranting like——'

"You needn't go on," said Patrick Ives, "if what you're really after is when they were written. The sun that rose at 4:30 that morning in June in 1916 would have kept me waiting exactly one hour and six minutes longer in 1926. You and Mimi and I had forgotten just one thing, Mr. Lambert—we'd forgotten that in 1916 there was no such thing as daylight saving."

And through the staggered silence that invaded some three hundred-odd people who had forgotten precisely the same thing, there rose a little laugh—a gay, excited, triumphant little laugh, as though somewhere a small girl had suddenly received a beautiful and unexpected present. It came from just behind Mr. Lambert's sagging shoulders—it came from——The startled eyes of those in the courtroom jerked in that direction, staring unbelievingly at the quiet figure, so quiet, so cool, so gravely aloof. But the red-headed girl felt idiotic tears sting swiftly beneath her lids. Under the lowered barrier of Sue Ives's lashes there still danced the echo of that joyous truant, shameless and unafraid. It was she who had laughed, after all.

Mr. Lambert was not laughing. "You are a little late in recalling this," he remarked heavily.

"Oh, a good deal late," agreed Patrick Ives. "But, you see, I hadn't been going in for watching the sun rise for some time previous to the murder. Since then I have. And when I heard that letter read in court the other day, something clicked in my head. Not five o'clock, and the sun was up! Something wrong there. I went back to New York and looked it up in the public library. On Friday, June 9, 1916, the sun rose at four twenty-two A. M. On Wednesday, June 9, 1926, the sun rose at five twenty-eight. So that's that."

"Have you a certified statement to that effect?" inquired Lambert, forlornly pompous.

"No," said Mr. Ives. "But I can lend you a World Almanac."

"You seem to find a trial for murder a very amusing affair," remarked Lambert heavily, his eyes once more on the jury.

"You're wrong," said Patrick Ives briefly. "I don't."

"I do not believe that your attitude makes farther examination desirable," commented Lambert judicially. "Cross-examine."

Farr rose casually from his chair, his hands in his pockets, his head cocked a trifle to one side. "Mr. Ives," he said leisurely, "I'm going to ask you the one question that Mr. Lambert didn't. Did you murder Madeleine Bellamy?"

After a pause that seemed interminable, Pat Ives lifted his eyes from their scrutiny of his hands, locked at the edge of the witness box. "No," he said tonelessly.

"No further questions," remarked Mr. Farr, still more leisurely resuming his seat.

Lambert glared—swallowed—glared again, and turned on his heel. "Mrs. Ives, will you be good enough to take the stand?"

She was on her feet before the words were off his lips, brushing by him with her light, swift step and a look of contemptuous anger that was bright and terrible as a sword.

"Looks as though his precious Sue was going to give Uncle Dudley a bad half hour," murmured the reporter exultantly.

"Why?" whispered the red-headed girl. "Why did she look like that?"

"Because I rather fancy that Lambert has just a scrap exceeded his authority in his efforts to speed Pat Ives to the gallows. The old walrus made out a fairly damaging case against him, even if he did snort himself purple. If——"

"Mrs. Ives, I'm going to ask you to tell us in your own words just what occurred on the evening of the nineteenth of June, from the time that Mr. Farwell spoke to you at the club. I won't interrupt unless I feel that something is not quite clear. At what time did the conversation with Mr. Farwell take place?"

She looked so small, sitting there—so small and young and fearless, with her dark, bright eyes and her lifted chin and the pale gold wings of her hair folded under the curve of the little russet hat. She had no colour at all—not in her cheeks, not in her lips.

"It was a little after five," said Sue Ives, and the red-headed girl gave a sigh of sheer delight. Once or twice in a lifetime a voice like that falls on our lucky ears— a voice clear and fresh as running water, alive and beautiful and effortless. The girl in the box did not have to lift it a half tone to have it penetrate to the farthest corner of the gallery. "We got in from the links just at five, and Elliot came up and asked me if he could bring me something to drink. I said yes, and when he came back he suggested that we go over and sit on the steps, as he had a splitting headache, and everyone was making a good deal of a racket. We hadn't been there more than five minutes before he told me."

"Before he told you what?" prompted Lambert helpfully.

"Before he told me that Pat was having an affair with Mimi Bellamy." She did not vouchsafe him even a glance, but kept the clear, stern little face turned squarely to the twelve attentive ones lifted to hers. "At first I thought that it was simply preposterous nonsense—I told him so. Everyone knew that Elliot was absolutely out of his head over Mimi, and I thought that he really was going a little mad. I could see that he'd been drinking, of course, and I wasn't even as angry as I ought to have been, because he was so unhappy—dreadfully unhappy. And then he said that he'd spied on them—that he'd seen them go to the cottage together. Well, that—that was different. That didn't sound like the kind of thing that you'd invent or imagine, no matter how unbalanced you were."

"You believed it?"

"No, not at first—not quite. But it bothered me dreadfully all the way home from the club—all the time that we were standing around in our living room waiting for the cocktails. I couldn't get it out of my head. And then Pat came in."

She paused, frowning a little at the memory of that sick perplexity.

"You say that Mr. Ives came in?"

"Yes. He was looking dreadfully tired and—excited. No, that's not the word. Keyed up—different. Or perhaps it was just that I expected him to look different. I don't know. Anyway, Elliot started to go then, and I went into the hall after him, because he'd been drinking a good deal more, and I was afraid that he'd talk as indiscreetly to someone else as he had to me. I couldn't think very clearly yet, but I was quite sure that that ought to be stopped. So I asked him to be careful, and he said that he would."

"Did you notice Melanie Cordier in the library?"

"No. I was watching Elliot. He looked so wretchedly unhappy that I was really worried about him. Well, anyway, he went off without even saying good-bye, and I went back toward the living room. Just as I came up to it I heard George Dallas say, 'We can count on you for the poker party to-night, can't we?' And Pat said, 'I'll surely try to make it, but don't count on me.' Something inside my head went click, and all the pieces in the puzzle fell into place. I walked straight into the room and up to where he was standing. He'd gone over to the table and was pouring out another of those new cocktails. Everyone was making a dreadful racket, laughing and talking. I said, 'Nell Conroy wanted us to go to the movies to-night. Don't you think that it would be rather fun?' And he said, 'Sorry, but I told George that I'd run over for a poker game. Tell Nell that you'll go, and then I won't worry about you being lonely.' I said, 'That's a good idea.' And Pat said, 'Be back in a minute. I have some papers I want to get rid of.'

"He went across the hall; I could hear his steps. I felt just exactly as though I'd taken poison and I stood there waiting for it to begin to work. Someone came up to me to say good-bye—I think it was the Conroys, and then everyone else began to go, too, the way they always do. I started to go out to the porch with them, and while I was passing through the hall I saw Pat standing by the desk. He was looking at some papers in his hand. I went on toward the porch, calling back over my shoulder that everyone was leaving. In a minute, he came out too. I looked to see whether he still had the papers in his hand, but he hadn't. While we were both standing there watching them drive off, Melanie came out, announced dinner, and we went in. Pat stopped behind in the study for a moment, but he didn't go near the desk drawer—I could see it from my place at the table."

"Could you have seen him take a book from the corner shelf?"

"No—the screen between the rooms cut off that corner."

"Nothing unusual occurred at dinner?"

"No. That made it worse. Nothing unusual occurred at all. Pat talked and laughed a good deal, but that's what he always did."

"And after dinner?"

"After dinner Mother Ives went out into the garden, and Pat asked me to come into the study to look at the clipper ship that he'd been making for Pete. All the time that I was supposed to be looking at it, I couldn't take my eyes off the desk, wondering what he'd done with those papers—wondering what they were. There had been quite a little pile of them. After a while I couldn't stand it any longer, and I said, 'If you want to say good-night to Pete and Polly, you'll have to hurry. They ought to be asleep by now.' He said, 'Lord, that's true!' He snatched up the boat and started for the door, and I called after him, 'I'm not coming. I kissed them good-night before dinner.' I waited until I heard his footsteps on the stairs——"

She paused for a moment, pushing the bright hair back from her brow as though she found it suddenly heavy.

"And then, Mrs. Ives?"

"Then," said Sue Ives steadily, "I did something disgusting. I searched the desk, I pushed the door to, so that none of the servants could see me if they passed through the hall, and I hurried like mad. I don't know exactly what I expected to find, but I thought that maybe those papers were letters from Mimi, and then I knew that Pat kept his check book there, too, and I thought that there might be entries of some kind that would tell me something; I could bear anything but not knowing. It was like a—like a frenzy. Oh, it was worse! The top drawer on the left-hand side of the desk was locked."

She paused again for a moment, staring down as curiously and intently at the upturned faces below her as they stared up at her; then, with a quick, impatient shake of her head she went on: "But that didn't make any difference, because I knew where the key was. I used the top right-hand drawer myself for my household accounts and bills and loose silver, and I kept it locked because, whenever Pat brought home gold pieces from his directors' meetings, we used to put them there. We saved them up until we had enough to get a present for the house, something beautiful and——No, that doesn't make any difference. We called the drawer the bank, and Pat showed me where he kept the key so that I could always get into it."

"Where did he keep this key?"

"In a tobacco jar on top of the bookcase. I found it and opened the drawer, and there were the papers, quite a thick packet of them, pushed way back in the drawer. They were bonds—eighty-five thousand Liberty, fifteen thousand municipal. I counted them twice to make sure." For the first time since she had mounted the stand she turned her dark and shining eyes on the perturbed Lambert. "You were very anxious to know whether anyone but Pat had seen that money, weren't you? Well, I saw it. And I was just as sure that Pat had taken it out of our safe-deposit box in order to run away with Mimi Bellamy as I was that I was standing there counting it—just as sure as that. I put it back and locked the drawer and dropped the key back into the tobacco jar and went to the flower room to telephone to Stephen Bellamy. The clock in the hall said five minutes past eight. I hadn't been in the study for more than ten minutes." Once more she lifted her hands to that bright hair. "Do you want me to repeat the telephone conversation?"

"Was it substantially the same as Miss Page gave it?"

"Exactly the same, word for word."

"Then I hardly think that that will be necessary. Just tell us what you did after you finished telephoning."

"I went to the foot of the nursery stairs and called up to ask Pat if he had absolutely decided to go to the poker game. He called back yes, and asked if he couldn't drop me at the Conroys'. I told him that I'd rather walk. I got that flannel coat out of the closet and started off for the gate at the back of the house that led to the back road. I was almost running."

"Had you planned any course of action?"

"No, I hadn't any definite plan, but I knew that I had to get to Stephen and make him stop Mimi, and that every minute was precious. Just as I got to the gate, I noticed that a wind had sprung up—quite a cold wind—and I remembered that Mother Ives had told me at dinner that Polly's ear had been hurting her, and that she slept right by the window where that wind would blow on her, so I turned back to the house to tell Miss Page to be sure to put a screen around the head of her crib. I saw Mother Ives at the far end of the rose garden, but I thought that it would take as long to call her and explain as it would to do it myself. So I ran on to the house, and I was half-way up the nursery stairs before I heard Pat's voice. I thought he was talking to the babies, and I hurried up the last few steps. I was almost at the nursery door when I heard another voice—Kathleen Page's. It wasn't coming from the nursery; it was coming from her room. She was saying, 'Don't let her send me away from you—don't, don't! All I want——'"

"Your Honour——"

Farr's warning voice was hardly swifter than Judge Carver's: "I am afraid that you cannot tell us what you heard, Mrs. Ives."

"I cannot tell you what I heard Kathleen Page saying?"

The wonder in the clear, incredulous voice penetrated the farthest corner of the courtroom.

"No. Simply confine yourself to what you did."

"Did? I did nothing whatever. I could no more have moved a step nearer to the door than if I had been nailed to the floor. She was crying dreadfully, in horrid little pants and gasps. It was absolutely sickening. Pat said, 'Keep quiet, you little lunatic. Do you want——'"

"Mrs. Ives, the Court has already warned you that you are not able to tell us what was said."

"Why am I not able to tell you what was said? I told you what we said downstairs."

Judge Carver leaned toward her, his black sleeves flowing majestically over the edge of the rail. "No objection was raised as to that conversation. Mr. Farr objects to this and the Court sustains him. For your own sake, the Court requests you to conform promptly to its rulings."

For a moment the two pairs of dark eyes met in an exchange of glances more eloquent than words; a look of grave warning and one of fearless rebellion.

"I do not understand your rules. What am I permitted to tell of the things that I am asked to explain?"

"Simply tell us what you did after you heard the voices in the room."

"Very well; I will try again. I stood there for a moment, staring at the door to the day nursery. The key was on the outside so that the babies couldn't lock themselves in. I don't remember moving, but I must have moved, because suddenly I had the door knob in my hand. I jerked it toward me and slammed the door so hard that it nearly threw me off my feet. The key——"

"Yes, yes," cut in Lambert, his face suffused with a sudden and terrifying premonition. "We needn't go too much into all these details, you know. We want to stick to our story as closely as possible. You didn't say anything, did you?"

"No."

"Just went on downstairs to meet Stephen Bellamy, didn't you?"

"No."

"You did not?" Mr. Lambert's blank query was enough to wring commiseration from a stone. Sue Ives did not look particularly merciful, however. She had turned in her chair so that she faced her devoted adversary squarely. She leaned forward a little now, her lovely mouth schooled to disdain, her eyes under their level brows bright with anger.

"No, not then. I was telling you what I did. I turned the key in the lock and put it in my pocket. You didn't want me to say that, did you, Uncle Dudley? You wanted everyone to believe that it was Pat who murdered Mimi, didn't you?"

"Mrs. Ives—Mrs. Ives——"

"Silence! Silence!"

"Mrs. Ives!"

Over the outraged clamour of the law, her voice rose, clear and triumphant: "He didn't murder her, because he was locked in those rooms until quarter to eleven that night, and I had the key in my pocket. Now, you can all strike that out of the record!"

"Mrs. Ives!" Over the last crash of the gavel, Judge Carver's voice was shaken with something deeper than anger. "Mrs. Ives, if you are not immediately silent, the Court will be obliged to have you removed."

"Removed?" She was on her feet in an instant, poised and light. "You wish me to go?"

"I wish you to get yourself in hand immediately. You are doing yourself untold injury by pursuing this line of conduct. The rules that you are refusing to obey were made largely for your own protection."

"I don't want to be protected. I want to tell the truth. Apparently no one wants to hear it."

"On the contrary, you are permitted to take the stand for that express purpose."

"For that purpose? To tell the truth?" The scorn in her voice was almost gay.

"Precisely. The limits that are imposed are for your benefit, and you are injuring your co-defendant as well as yourself by refusing to abide by them."

"Stephen?" She paused at that, considering gravely. "I don't want to do that, of course. Very well, I will try to go on." She turned back to her chair, and a long sigh of incredulous relief trembled through the courtroom.

"I have forgotten where I stopped."

"You were about to tell us what you did after you came down the nursery stairs?" Lambert's shaken voice was hardly audible.

"Yes. Well, then—then we did exactly what Stephen said we did. We drove through the back road to the River Road, where we turned to the left and went into Lakedale in order to get more gasoline. I distinctly remember the time, because we had been discussing whether the movies would be out by the time that we got back. It was twenty-five minutes past nine. After that we retraced our steps—down the River Road to the back road, down to the place in the back road where I had met Stephen, past our house into the main street of the village, past the movie house, which was dark, and up the main street, which runs into the Perrytown Highway—up the Perrytown Highway to the Bellamy house.

"I was absolutely sure that I saw a light over the garage, but it certainly wasn't there a minute or so afterwards, and I decided that I might as well go in anyway. I was beyond bothering much about any minor conventions, and I thought that if Mimi were actually there, it would be a heavenly relief to put all the cards on the table and have it out with her once and forever. Mimi wasn't there, of course; it was then that Steve called up the Conroys. When he found that she wasn't there, I was really terrified at his condition. He was as quiet as usual, but he didn't seem to understand anything at all that was said to him. He didn't even bother to listen. He had some kind of a chill, and he just sat there shivering, while I reassured and argued and explained.

"I could have saved my breath. He didn't even hear me. He did finally rouse himself to telephone the police and the hospital; the rest of the time he just sat there staring and shivering. He wanted me to call up Pat and the Dallases, and of course I knew that that wouldn't do any good—Pat was locked up two stories away from a telephone. Finally I asked, 'Did you see what direction she was going in when she left?' He shook his head. I said, 'But she told you that she was going toward the Conroys'?' He nodded. I said, 'Well, maybe she turned her ankle and fainted somewhere along the side of the road—she always wears such dreadfully high heels. We might take the car and turn the headlights along the edge of the road and see if we can get any trace of her. Come on!'

"I knew that that was perfect nonsense, but I was desperate, and I thought that there was just a chance that it might rouse him. It did. It was exactly as though you'd put a galvanic shock through him. He jerked out of his chair. He was out in the hall without even waiting to look back at me, and I had to run to get to the car before he started it.

"We got off with such a jerk that it nearly threw me out of the car, and I was really afraid that he was going to dash us against one of the gateposts. I said, 'If we're going to find Mimi, Steve, we must go slowly, mustn't we? We must look carefully.' He said, 'That's right!' And after that we literally crept, all the way to the Conroys'."

"How far was that?"

"Oh, not far—not half a mile—just a little way. It wasn't until after we got past their entrance that we decided that——" She paused for a moment, her eyes dilated strangely in her small pale face; then she wrung her hands together more closely as though in that hard contact she found comfort, and continued steadily in her low voice. "We decided that we might as well go on."

Lambert, paler than she, said just as steadily, "Might as well go on where, Mrs. Ives?"

"Go on to the gardener's cottage at Orchards," said Susan Ives.

In the gray light of the courtroom, the faces of the occupants looked gray, too—sharpened, fearful, full of an ominous unease. More than one of them glanced swiftly over a hunched shoulder at the blue-coated guardians of the door, and then back again, with somewhat pinched and rueful countenance, at the slight occupant of the witness box. The figure sat so quietly there in the gathering shadows; to many who watched it seemed that there slanted across her lifted face another shadow still—the shadow of the block, of the gallows, of the chair....

"Is she confessing?" asked the red-headed girl in a small colourless voice.

"Wait!" said the reporter. "God knows what she's doing."

Judge Carver leaned suddenly toward Lambert.

"Mr. Lambert, it is already considerably past four. Is this testimony likely to continue for some time?"

"For some time, Your Honour."

"In that case," said Judge Carver gravely, "the Court considers it advisable to adjourn until ten to-morrow. Court is dismissed."

The small figure moved lightly down from the witness stand into the deeper shadows—deeper still—she was gone. The sixth day of the Bellamy trial was over.

CHAPTER VII

The reporter cast an anxious eye at the red-headed girl.

"You've been crying," he said accusingly.

The red-headed girl looked unrepentant.

"Of all the little idiots! What's Sue Ives to you?"

"Never mind," said the red-headed girl with dignity. "I can cry if I want to. I can cry all night if I want to. Keep quiet. Here she is!"

"Mrs. Ives, what made you decide to go on to the cottage?" Lambert's voice was very gentle.

"I think that it was Stephen's idea, but I'm not absolutely sure. I was at my wit's end by this time, you see. But I believe that it was Steve who suggested that maybe she had been taken ill or perhaps even fallen asleep at the cottage. I remember agreeing that it was stupid of us not to have thought of that before. At any rate, we both agreed to go on to the cottage."

She stopped again and sat for a moment locking and unlocking her fingers, her eyes fixed on something far beyond the courtroom door.

"What time did you arrive at the cottage?"

"At about quarter past ten, I believe—twenty minutes past perhaps. It isn't more than a five-minute drive. We drove the car up through the lodge gates and then turned off the little dirt road to the cottage. We drove it right up to the front steps, and then I said, 'It's no good; there's no light in the place. She isn't here.' Steve said, 'Maybe she left a note saying where she was going,' and I said, 'That's perfectly possible. Let's go in and see.' He helped me out, and just as we got to the door, I said, 'Well, we'll never know. The place will be locked, of course.' Steve had his hand on the door knob, and he pushed it a little. He said, 'No, it's open. That's queer.' I said, 'Probably she thought that he might come later.' And he opened the door and we went in."

She sat staring with that curious, intent rigidity at that far-off spot beyond the other closed door, and the courtroom followed her glance with uneasy eyes.

"And then?"

"Yes. And then when we got in there wasn't any light, of course. Steve asked, 'Do you know where the switch it?' And I told him, 'There isn't any switch.

Douglas has always been talking about putting electricity in these cottages, but he never has.' Steve said, 'Well, there must be a light somewhere, and I said, 'Oh, of course there is. There always used to be an old brass lamp here in the corner by the front door—let's see.' It was right there on the same table. There were matches there, too, and I struck one of them and lit it. Steve had stepped by me into the room; he was standing by the door, and he stood aside to let me pass. There was a little breeze from the open door, and I had put up one hand to shield the light and keep it from flickering. I was looking at the piano, because I'd never remembered seeing a piano there before. I was half-way across the room before I—before I——" The voice shuddered slowly away to silence.

After a long pause, Lambert asked, "Before you did what, Mrs. Ives?"

She gave a convulsive start, as though someone had let fall a heavy hand across the nightmare. "Before I—saw her."

The voice was hardly a whisper, but there was no one in the room beyond the reach of its stilled horror.

"It was Mrs. Bellamy that you saw?"

"Yes, I——" She swallowed—tried to speak—swallowed again, and lifted a hand to her throat. "I'm sorry. Might I have a glass of water? Is that all right?"

In all that room no one stirred save the clerk of the Court, who poured a glass of water with careful gravity and handed it up to her over the edge of the box. She drank it slowly, as though she found in this brief respite life itself. When she had finished it, she put it down gently and said, "Thank you," in a voice once more clear and steady.

"You were telling us that you saw Mrs. Bellamy."

"Yes.... I must have dropped the lamp immediately; all I remember was that we were standing there in the dark. I heard Stephen say, 'Don't move. Where are the matches?' He needn't have told me not to move. If I could have escaped death itself by stepping aside one inch I could not have moved that inch. I said, 'I have them here—in my pocket.' He said, 'Strike one.' I tried three times. The third time it lit, and he went by me and knelt down beside her. He touched her wrist and said, 'Mimi, did it hurt? Did it hurt, darling?' The match went out and I started to strike another. He said, 'Never mind. She's dead.' I said, 'I know it. Dead people can't close their eyes, can they?' He said, 'I have closed them. She's been murdered. I got you into this, Sue, and I'll get you out of it. Where are you?' I tried to say, 'Here,' but I couldn't. And then I thought that I heard something move—outside—in the bushes—and I screamed.

"I'd never done that before in my life. It didn't sound like me at all. It sounded like someone quite different. Steve whispered, 'For God's sake, be still.' I said, 'I heard someone moving.' He said 'It was I, coming toward you. Give me your hand.' His was so cold on my wrist that it was horrible.

"I put my hand over my mouth to keep from screaming again, and he pulled me through the hall and on to the porch. I said, 'Steve, we can't leave her there like that—we can't.' He said, 'She doesn't need us any more. Get in the car.' I pulled back, and he said, 'Listen to me, Sue. It doesn't make any difference how innocent we are, if it is ever known that we were in that room this evening, we'll never be able to make one human being in God's world believe that we aren't guilty—and we'll have to make twelve of them believe. I've got to get you home. Get into the car.' So I got in, and he drove me home."

She was silent, and the courtroom was silent too. To the red-headed girl, it seemed as though for a space everyone had foregone even the habit of breath and held it suspended until that voice should finish its dreadful tale. She could see Patrick Ives in his corner by the window. A long time ago he had buried his black head in his hands, and he did not lift it now. His mother had placed one small gloved hand on his knee. It rested there lightly, but she was not looking at him; her eyes had never wavered from Sue Ives's white face. Long ago the winter roses had faded in her own, but it was as gravely and graciously composed as on that first day.

"Did you drive straight home, Mrs. Ives?"

"Straight home. Stephen spoke two or three times; I don't remember saying anything at all. He told me to say that we'd driven over to Lakedale, and then he said that everything would be all right, because no one would know that Elliot had spoken to me, and no one could possibly know that we had gone to the cottage. I remember nodding, and then we were at our gate. Stephen said, 'You might as well give me that signal that we decided on before to let me know whether Pat's there; will you, Sue?' I said, 'Yes.' He said, 'You might ask him whether he heard from her this evening.' I said, 'Steve, it isn't us that this is happening to, is it? It isn't us—not Pat and you and I and Mimi?' He said, 'Yes, it's us. I'll wait right here. Hurry, will you?'

"I went into the house. All the lights were out except one in the hall, but I went out through the study and the dining room to the pantry. It connects with the servants' quarters, and I wanted to make sure that none of them were about, as I had to go up and unlock the day nursery, and I was afraid that Kathleen Page might make a scene. It was all dark and quiet; there wasn't anyone there. I passed the ice box as I came back, and I could see the fruit through the glass door. I remembered that Pat couldn't have taken it to Mother Ives, and I put some on a plate and went upstairs. Her door was open; she always left it open so that we could say good-night if we came in before eleven."

"Were you with her long?"

"Oh, no, only a minute. I told her that Steve and I had driven over to Lakedale instead of going to the movies, and kissed her good-night. Then I went around the gallery and on up to the nursery wing. I unlocked the door and pushed it open, but I didn't go in. Pat was sitting by the table, reading. The door to Miss

Page's room was closed. He sat there looking at me for a moment, and then he stood up and came into the hall, pulling the nursery door to behind him. He said, 'I didn't know that you had it in you to play an ugly trick like that, Sue.' I said, 'I didn't know it either.' I went down to the study and lit the light—twice. I waited until I heard the car start, and then I went up to my room and took off my clothes and went to bed. There were several lights in the room, and I kept every one of them burning until after the sun was up. In the morning I got up and dressed and went to church, and it was just a little while after I got home that we heard that Mimi's body had been found. And Monday evening both Stephen and I were put under arrest."

She was silent for a moment, and then said in a small, exhausted voice, "That's all. Must I wait?"

Lambert said gravely and gently, "I'm afraid so. When was the first time that you told this story, Mrs. Ives?"

"Night before last—to you—after they found my finger print, you know."

"It is the full and entire account of how you spent the evening of the nineteenth of June, 1926?"

"Yes."

"To the best of your knowledge, you have omitted nothing?"

"Nothing."

"Thank you; that will be all. Cross-examine."

Mr. Farr advanced leisurely toward the witness box and stood staring thoughtfully for a long moment at its pale occupant. Under those speculative eyes, the sagging shoulders straightened, the chin lifted.

"You were perfectly familiar with the gardener's cottage, were you not, Mrs. Ives?"

"Perfectly."

"You remembered even where the lamp stood in the hall?"

"Yes. I used to go there often as a child."

"Nothing had been changed since then?"

"I don't know. I was only there for a few seconds."

"Not long enough to notice a change of any kind whatever?"

"There was the piano; I remember that."

She sat very straight, watching him with those wide, bright eyes as though he were some strange and dangerous beast.

"Were you familiar with the back entrance from the River Road—to the Thorne estate, Mrs. Ives?"

"Yes."

"You could have found it at night quite easily?"

"You mean by the lights of the automobile?"

"Exactly."

"Yes."

"Were you aware that it was a shorter way to reach Orchards than going back by way of Rosemont?"

"Oh, yes; it was about three miles shorter."

"Why didn't you take it?"

"Because when we were in Lakedale we had no idea of going to the cottage. We didn't think of it until long after we had returned to Rosemont."

"But why didn't you think of it before? You knew that in all probability Mrs. Bellamy was waiting for your husband at the cottage, didn't you?"

The question was asked in tones of the gentlest consideration, but the sentinel watching from the dark eyes was suddenly alert.

"No, I didn't know that at all. In the first place, I wasn't sure that she had gone there; in the second place, I wasn't sure that she had waited, even if she had gone."

"There was no harm in making sure, was there?"

"I thought there was. My idea in seeing Stephen was to get him to talk to Mimi; I hadn't the faintest desire to take part in the humiliating and painful scene that would have been inevitable if I had confronted her."

"I see. Still, you were willing to confront her in her own home, weren't you?"

"Yes." She bit her lip in an effort to concentrate on that. "But that wouldn't have been tracking her down and spying on her, and by then——"

"'Yes' is an answer, Mrs. Ives."

"You mean that it's all the answer that you want?"

"Exactly."

"You didn't really want to know why I did it?"

Under the level irony of her glance the prosecutor's eyes hardened. "For your own good, Mrs. Ives, I suggest that you do not attempt to bandy language with me. You were not only willing to see her in her home but not long after you went to seek her in the cottage, did you not?"

"Yes. By that time we were both desperately worried and I put my own wishes aside."

"You wish us to understand that you went there on an errand of mercy?"

"I am not asking you to understand anything. I was simply telling you why we went."

"Exactly. Now, when you got to the cottage, Mrs. Ives, you say there was no light?"

"There was no light."

"But you fortunately remembered that this lamp was in the hall?"

"Fortunately?" repeated Susan Ives slowly, "I remembered that there was a lamp in the hall."

"How long has it been since you were at Orchards?"

"I have not been there since my marriage—not for seven years."

"How long since you were in the cottage?"

"I'm not sure—possibly a year or so before that."

"Were you a child nine years ago?"

"A child? I was over twenty."

"I thought you told us that it was as a child that you went to the cottage."

"I went occasionally after I was older. I was very fond of the old gardener and his wife. They were German and very sensitive after the outbreak of the war. We all used to go down from time to time to try to cheer them up."

"Very considerate indeed—another errand of mercy. But about this lamp, now, that you remembered so providentially after nine years. You are quite sure that it wasn't in the front parlour?"

"Absolutely sure."

"It couldn't have been standing on the little table that was overturned by Mimi Bellamy's fall?"

"How could it possibly have been standing there?"

"I was asking you. You are perfectly sure that it wasn't standing on that table, lighted, when you came in?"

"I see." The unwavering eyes burned brighter with that clear disdain. "I didn't quite understand. You mean am I lying, don't you? I have told you the truth; the lamp was on the table in the hall."

"Your Honour, I ask to have that reply stricken from the record as unresponsive."

"It may be stricken from the record to the point where the witness says, 'The lamp was on the table in the hall.'" Judge Carver stared down with stern, troubled eyes at the clear, unflinching face lifted to his. "Mrs. Ives, the Court again assures you that you do yourself no service by such replies and that they are entirely out of order. It requests that you refrain from them."

"I will try to, Your Honour."

"Mrs. Ives, you have told us that when you were standing in darkness you heard a sound that frightened you. Was it someone trying the door?"

"Oh, no; the door was open. It wasn't anything as clear as that. I thought first that it was someone moving in the bushes, but it was probably simply my imagination."

"You didn't hear anyone whistling?"

"No."

"You are quite sure that neither of you locked the door?"

"Absolutely. Why should we lock the door?"

"I must remind you again, Mrs. Ives, that it is I who am examining you. Now, you say that you went into the room ahead of Mr. Bellamy?"

"Yes."

"How far were you from the body when you first saw it?"

In the paper-white face the eyes dilated, suddenly, dreadfully. "I don't know. Quite near—three feet—four feet."

"You suspected that she was dead?"

"I knew that she was dead. Her eyes were wide open."

"You did not go nearer to her than those three or four feet?"

"No." She forced the word through her lips with a dreadful effort.

"You did not touch her?"

"No—no."

"Then how did the bloodstains get on your coat?"

At the sharp clang of that triumphant cry she shuddered and turned and came back to him slowly from the small, haunted room. "Bloodstains? There were no bloodstains on my coat."

"Do you still claim that the coat that you smuggled out of your house Sunday morning was stained with grease from Mr. Bellamy's car?"

"No—no, I don't claim that."

"That's prudent of you, as Sergeant Johnson has testified that there was no grease whatever on the car."

"I meant to explain that before," said Sue Ives simply. "Only there were so many other things that I forgot. It was kerosene from the lamp—the coat was covered with it. I didn't know how to explain it, so I thought that I had better get rid of it."

"I see," said the prosecutor grimly, "You're a very resourceful young woman, aren't you?"

"No," said the clear, grave voice. "I don't think that I'm particularly resourceful."

"I differ from you.... Mrs. Ives, you didn't intend to tell this jury that you had been in the gardener's cottage on the night of the nineteenth of June, did you?"

"Not if I could avoid doing so without perjuring myself."

"You decided to do so only when you were literally forced to it by information that you found was in the state's possession?"

"It is hard for me to answer that by yes or no," said Susan Ives. "But I suppose that the fairest answer to it is yes."

"You had decided to withhold this vitally important information because you and Stephen Bellamy had together reached the conclusion that no twelve sane men could be found to accept the fantastic coincidence that you and he were in the room in which this murder was committed within a few minutes of this crime, and yet had nothing whatever to do with it?"

"I think that again the answer should be yes."

"You are still of that opinion?"

"I no longer have any opinion."

"Why should you have changed your opinion that twelve sane men could not possibly believe your story?"

"I do not know whether they will believe me or not," said Sue Ives, her eyes, fearless and unswerving, on the twelve stolid, inscrutable countenances raised to hers. "You see, I don't know how true truth sounds."

"I should imagine not," said the prosecutor, his voice cruelly smooth. "No further questions."

And at that Parthian shot the white lips in the white face before him curved suddenly and amazingly into the lovely irony of a smile, a last salute over the drawn swords before they were sheathed.

"That will be all," said Lambert's voice gently. "You may stand down."

For a moment she did not move, but sat staring down with dark eyes to which the smile had not quite reached, at the twelve enigmatic countenances before her—at the slack, careless young one on the far end; the grim elderly one next to it; the small, deep-set eyes above the heavy jowls of that flushed one in the centre; the sleek attentive pallor of the one next to the door. She opened her lips as though to speak again, closed them with a small shake of her head, swept up gloves, bag and fur with one swift gesture, and without a backward glance was gone, moving across the cluttered space between her chair and the box with that light, sure step that seemed always to move across green grass, through sunlight and a little wind. She did not even look at Stephen Bellamy, but in the little space between their chairs their hands met once and clenched in greeting and swung free.

"Your Honour," said Lambert, in the quiet, tired voice so many leagues removed from the old boom, "in view of Mrs. Ives's evidence, I would like to have Mr. Bellamy take the stand once more. I have only one or two questions to put to him."

"He may take the stand," said Judge Carver impassively.

He took it steadily, the white face of horror that he had turned from the day before schooled once more to the old courtesy and quiet.

"Mr. Bellamy, you have heard Mrs. Ives's evidence as to the circumstance that led up to your visit to the gardener's cottage and of the visit to the cottage itself. Is her description is accord with your own recollection?"

"In complete accord."

"You would not change it in any particular?"

"No. It is absolutely accurate."

"Nor add to it?"

"Yes. There is something that I believe that I should add. Mrs. Ives was not aware of the fact that I returned to the cottage again that night."

If Lambert also was not aware of it, he gave no sign. "For what purpose?"

"I had no definite purpose—I did not wish to leave my wife alone in the cottage."

"At what time did you return?"

"Very shortly after I left Mrs. Ives at her home. I actually didn't know what I was doing. I took the wrong turn in the back road and drove around for a bit before I got straightened out, but it couldn't have been for very long."

"How long did you stay?"

"Until it began to get light; I didn't look at the time."

"You did not disturb the contents of the cottage in any way?"

"No; I left everything exactly as it was."

"Nor remove anything?"

"Nothing—nothing whatever."

"Thank you, Mr. Bellamy. That will be all, unless Mr. Farr has any questions."

"As a matter of fact, I have one or two questions," remarked Mr. Farr, leisurely but grim. "You, too, are highly resourceful, Mr. Bellamy, aren't you?"

"I should hardly say that I had proved myself so."

"Well, you can reassure yourself. That extra set of automobile tires had to be accounted for, hadn't they?"

"I should have accounted for them in any case."

"Should you, indeed? That's very interesting, but hardly a responsive answer to my question. I'll be grateful if you don't make it necessary for me to pull you up on that again. Now, you say that you didn't touch anything in the cottage?"

"I said that I did not disturb anything."

"Oh, you touched something, did you?"

"Yes."

"What?"

"I touched her hand."

211

"I see. You were looking for the rings?"

"No. I didn't think of the rings."

"They were still there?"

"Until you asked me this minute I had not thought of them. I do not believe that they were there."

"Mr. Bellamy, I put it to you that you returned to that cottage with the express purpose of removing those rings, the necklace, and any traces that you or Mrs. Ives may have left behind you in your previous flight?"

"You are wrong; I did not return for any of those purposes."

"Then for what purpose?"

"Because I did not wish to leave my wife alone."

"You consider that a plausible explanation?"

"Oh, no; simply a true one."

"She was dead, wasn't she?"

"She was dead."

"You knew that?"

"Yes."

"You knew that you couldn't do anything for her, didn't you?"

"I wasn't sure." The voice was as quiet as ever, but once more the ripple of the clenched teeth showed in the cheek. "She was afraid of the dark."

"Of the dark?"

"Yes; she was afraid to be alone in the dark."

"She was dead, wasn't she?"

"Yes—yes, she was dead."

"You ask us to believe that you spent hours in momentary danger of arrest for murder because a woman who was stone dead had been afraid of the dark when she was alive?"

"No. I don't ask you to believe anything," said Stephen Bellamy gently. "I was simply telling you what happened."

"You say that you didn't touch anything else in the cottage?"

"Nothing else."

"How could you find your way about without a light?"

"I had a light; I took the flashlight from my car."

"So that you could make a thorough search of the premises for anything that had been left behind?"

"We had left nothing behind."

"But you couldn't have been sure of that, could you? A knife, perhaps? A knife's an easy thing to lose."

"We had no knife."

Mr. Farr greeted this statement with an expression of profound skepticism. "Now, before I ask you to step down, Mr. Bellamy, I want to make sure that you haven't one final installment to add for our benefit. That's all that you have to tell us?"

"That is all."

"Sure?"

"Quite sure."

"This continued story that you have been presenting to us from day to day has reached its absolutely ultimate installment?"

"I have already said that I have nothing to add to my statement."

"And this is the same story that you were so sure that no twelve sane men in the world would believe, isn't it?"

"Yes. It isn't necessary to prove to me that I have been the fool of the world," said Stephen Bellamy quietly. "I willingly admit it. My deepest regret is that my folly has involved Mrs. Ives too."

"You have had no cause to revise your opinion as to the skepticism that your account of that night's doings would arouse in any twelve sane men, have you?"

"Oh, yes, I have had excellent reason completely to revise it."

The low, pleasant voice seemed to jar on the prosecutor as violently as a bomb. "And what reason, may I ask?"

"At the time that I arrived at that conclusion I had naturally had no opportunity to hear Mrs. Ives on the witness stand. Now that I have, it seems absolutely impossible to me that anyone could fail to believe her."

"That must be extremely reassuring for you," remarked Mr. Farr in a voice so heavily charged with irony that it came close to cracking under the strain. "That will be all, thank you, Mr. Bellamy."

Mr. Lambert rose slowly to his feet. "The defense rests," he said.

The red-headed girl watched them filing out through the door at the back without comment, and without comment she accepted the cake of chocolate and the large red apple. She consumed them in the same gloomy silence, broken only by an occasional furtive sniff and the application of a minute and inadequate handkerchief.

"You promised me last night," said the reporter accusingly, "that if I'd go home you'd stop crying and be reasonable and sensible and——"

"I'm not crying," said the red-headed girl—"not so that anybody would notice anything at all if they weren't practically spying on me. It's simply that I'm a little tired and not exactly cheerful."

"Oh, it's simply that, is it? Would you like my handkerchief too?" The red-headed girl accepted it ungratefully.

"The worst thing about a murder trial," she said, "is that it practically ruins everybody's life. It's absolutely horrible. They're all going along peacefully and quietly, and the first thing they know they're jerked out of their homes and into the witness box, and things that they thought were safe and hidden and sacred are blazoned out in letters three inches tall in every paper in the ... That poor little Platz thing, and that wretched Farwell man, and poor little Mrs. Ives with her runaway husband, and Orsini with his jail sentence—it isn't decent! What have they done?"

The reporter said, "What, indeed?" in the tone of one who has not heard anything but the last three words. After a moment he inquired thoughtfully. "Have you ever thought about getting married?"

The red-headed girl felt her heart miss two beats and then race away like a wild thing. She said candidly, "Oh, often—practically all the time. All nice girls do."

"Do they?" inquired the reporter in a tone of genuine surprise. "Men don't— hardly ever." He continued to look at her abstractedly for quite a long time before he added, "Only about once in their lives."

He was looking at her still when the door behind the witness box opened.

"Your Honour"—the lines in Mr. Lambert's face stood out relentlessly, but his voice was fresh and strong—"gentlemen of the jury, it is not my intention to take a great amount of your time, in spite of the fact that there devolves on me as solemn a task as falls to the lot of any man—that of pleading with you for the precious gift of human life. I do not believe that the solemnity of that plea is enhanced by undue prolixity, by legal hair-splitting or by a confusion of issues essentially and profoundly simple. The evidence in the case has been intricate enough. I shall not presume to analyze it for you. It is your task, and yours alone, to scrutinize, weigh, and dispose of it. On the other hand, the case presents almost no legal intricacies; any that are present will be expounded to you by Judge Carver when the time comes.

"When all is said and all is done, gentlemen, it is a very simple question that you have to decide—as simple as it is grave and terrible. The question is this: Do you believe the story that Stephen Bellamy and Susan Ives have told you in this courtroom? Is their story of what happened on that dreadful night a reasonable, a convincing and an honest explanation as to how they became involved in the tragic series of events that has blown through their peaceful homes like a malignant whirlwind, wrecking all their dearest hopes and their dearest realities? I believe that there can be but one answer to that question, and that not so long from now you will have given that answer, and that every heart in this courtroom will be the lighter for having heard it.

"These two have told you precisely the same story. That Stephen Bellamy did not go quite to the end with it in the first instance is a circumstance that I deplore as deeply as any one of you, but I do not believe that you will hold it against him. He did not, remember, utter one syllable that was not strictly and accurately truthful. It had been agreed between them that if it were necessary to swerve one hairbreadth from the truth, they would not swerve that hairbreadth.

"In persuading Mrs. Ives that her only safety lay in not admitting that she had been in the cottage that night, Mr. Bellamy made a grave mistake in judgment, but it was the mistake of a chivalrous and distraught soul, literally overwhelmed at the ghastly situation into which the two of them had been so incredibly precipitated.

"As for Susan Ives, she was so shaken with horror to the very roots of her being—so stunned, so confused and confounded—that she was literally moving through a nightmare during the few days that preceded her arrest; and, gentlemen, in a nightmare the best of us do not think with our accustomed clarity and cogency. She did what she was told to do, and she was told that it would make my task easier if I did not know that she had been near the cottage that night. That, alas, settled it for her once and for all. She has always sought to make my tasks easier.

215

"Stephen Bellamy undoubtedly remembered the old precept that it takes two to tell the truth—one to speak it and one to hear it. Possibly he believed that if there were two to speak it and twelve to hear it, it would be a more dangerous business. I do not agree with him. I believe that twelve attentive and intelligent listeners—as you have amply proved yourselves to be—make the best of all forums at which to present the truth, the whole truth and nothing but the truth. That is my belief, that was my considered advice, and it is my profound conviction that before many hours have passed I shall be justified of my belief.

"Perhaps you have guessed that my relations to Susan Ives are not the ordinary relations of counsel to client. Such, at any rate, is the case, and I do not shirk one of its implications. There is no tie of blood between us, but I am bound to her by every other tie of affection and admiration. I can say that I believe she is as dear to me as any daughter,—dearer, perhaps, than any daughter, because she is what most men only dream that their daughter may be. For the first time in my life I have offended her since I came to this court—offended her because she believed that I was more loyal to her welfare than her wishes. But she will forgive me even for that, because she knows that I am only a stupid old man who would give every hope that he has of happiness to see hers fulfilled, and who, when he pleads for her life to-day, is pleading for something infinitely dearer to him than his own.

"If, later, you say to one another and to yourselves, 'The old man is prejudiced in her favour; we must take that into account,' I say to you, 'And so you must—and so you must—well into account.' I am prejudiced because I have known her since she was so small that she did not come to my knee; because I have watched her with unvarying wonder and devotion from the days that she used to cling to me, weeping because her black kitten had hurt its paw, or radiant because there was a new daisy in her garden; because I have watched her from those bright, joyous days to these dark and terrible ones, and never once have I found a trace of alloy in her gold. I have found united in her the traits we seek in many different forms—all the gallantry and honesty of a little boy, all the gaiety and grace of a little girl, all the loyalty and courage of a man, all the tenderness and beauty of a woman. If you think I am prejudiced in her favour you will be right, gentlemen. And if that fact prejudices me in your eyes, make the most of it.

"Of Stephen Bellamy I will say only this: If I had a daughter I would ask nothing more of destiny than that such a man should seek her for his wife—and you may make the most of that too.

"On this subject I will not touch again, I promise. It is not part and parcel of the speech of counsel for the defense to the jury in a murder trial to touch on his feeling toward his clients. I am grateful for the indulgence of both the Court and the prosecution in permitting me to dwell on them at some length. During the course of Mrs. Ives's examination something as to our relation was inadvertently disclosed. In any case, I should have considered it my duty to inform you of it, as well as of every other fact in this case. I have now done so.

"A few days ago I said to you that Susan Ives was rich in many things. When I said that I was not thinking of money; I was referring to things that are the treasured possessions, the precious heritage, of many a humble and modest soul. Love, peace, beauty, security, serenity, health—these the least of us may have. As I have said, I am pretty close to being an old man now, and in my time I have heard much talk of class feeling and class hatred. I have even been told that it is difficult to get justice for the rich from the poor or mercy for the poor from the rich. I believe both these statements to be equally vile and baseless slanders.

"In this great country of which you and I are proud and privileged citizens, we are all rich—rich in opportunity and in liberty—and there is no room in our hearts for grudging envy, for warped malice. We do not say, 'This woman is rich; she has breeding; she has intelligence and culture and position, therefore she is guilty.' We do not say, 'This man is a graduate of one of our greatest universities. Five generations of his ancestors have owned land in this country, and have lived on it honourably and decently, gentlefolk of repute and power in their communities; he is the possessor of a distinguished name and a distinguished record, therefore he is a murderer!' We do not say that. No; you and I and the man in the street say, 'It is impossible that two people with this life behind them and a richer and finer one before them should stoop to so low and foul a weapon as an assassin's knife and a coward's blow in the dark.'

"But even in the strictly material sense of wealth, Mrs. Ives is not a wealthy woman. I should like, in the simple interests of truth, to dispel the legends of a marble heart moving through marble halls that has been growing about her. She has lived for several happy years in what you have heard described to you as a farm house—a simple, unpretentious place that she made lovely with bright hangings and open fires and books and prints and flowers. If you had rung her doorbell before that fatal day in June, no powdered flunky would have opened it to you. It might have been opened by Mrs. Ives herself, or by Mr. Ives's mother, or by a little maid in a neat dark frock and a white apron. Whoever had opened it to you, you would have found within a charming and friendly simplicity that might well cause you a little legitimate envy; you would have found nothing more.

"Sue Ives had what all your wives have, I hope—flowers in her garden, babies in her nursery, sunshine in her windows. With these any woman is rich, and so was she. As for Stephen Bellamy, he had no more than any good clerk or mechanic— a little house, a little car, a little maid of all work to help his pretty wife. That much for the legend of pride and pomp and power and uncounted millions that has grown up about these two. In the public press this legend has flourished extravagantly; it is of little concern to you or to any of us, save in so far as the preservation of truth is the concern of every one of us.

"The story that you have heard from the lips of Mrs. Ives and Mr. Bellamy is a refutation of every charge that has been brought against them. It is a fearless, straightforward, circumstantial and coherent account of their every action on the evening of that terrible and momentous night. Granted that every witness produced by the state here in order to confound and confuse them has spoken the absolute and exact truth—a somewhat extravagant claim, some of you may feel—granted even that, however, still you will find not one word of their testimony that is not perfectly consistent with the explanation of their actions that evening offered you by the defendants.

"Not only does the state's testimony not conflict with ours—it corroborates it. The overheard telephone conversation, the knife from the study, the stained flannel coat, the visit to Stephen Bellamy's house, the tire tracks in the mud outside the cottage, the fingerprints on the lamp within—there is the state's case, and there also, gentlemen, is ours. These sinister facts, impressive and terrible weapons in the state's hands, under the clear white light of truth become a very simple, reasonable and inevitable set of circumstances, fully explained and fully accounted for. The more squarely you look at them, the more harmless they become. I ask you to subject them to the most careful and severe scrutiny, entirely confident as to the result.

"The state will tell you, undoubtedly, that in spite of what you have heard, the fact remains that Susan Ives and Stephen Bellamy had the means, the motive, and the opportunity to commit this crime. It is our contention that they had nothing of the kind. No weapon has been traced to either of them; it would have been to all intents and purposes physically impossible for them to reach the gardener's cottage, execute this murder and return to Stephen Bellamy's house between the time that the gasoline vender saw them leave Lakedale and the time that Orsini saw them arrive at Mr. Bellamy's home—a scant forty minutes, according to the outside figures of their own witnesses; not quite twenty-five according to ours.

"But take the absolute substantiated forty-minute limit—from 9:15 to 9:55. You are asked to believe that in that time they hurled themselves in a small rickety car over ten miles, possibly more, of unfamiliar roads in total darkness, took a rough dirt cut-off, groped their way through the back gates of the Thorne place to the little road that led to the cottage, got out, entered the cottage, became involved in a bitter and violent scene with Mimi Bellamy which culminated in her death by murder; remained there long enough to map out a campaign which involved removing her jewels from her dead body, while fabricating an elaborate alibi— and also long enough to permit Mr. Thorne, who has arrived on the piazza, ample time to get well on his way; came out, got back into the invisible automobile and arrived at Mr. Bellamy's house, three miles away, at five minutes to ten. Gentlemen, does this seem to you credible? I confess that it seems to me so incredible—so fantastically, so grotesquely incredible—that I am greatly inclined to offer you an apology for going into it at such length. So much for the means, so much for the opportunity; now for the motive.

"There, I think, we touch the weakest point in the state's case against these two. That the state itself fully grasps its weakness, I submit, is adduced from the fact that not one witness they have put on the stand has been asked a single question that would tend to establish either of the motives ascribed to them by the state—widely differing motives, alike only in their monstrous absurdity. It is the state's contention, if it still cleaves to the theory originally advanced, that Madeleine Bellamy was murdered by Susan Ives because she feared poverty, and that she was aided and abetted by Stephen Bellamy in this bloody business because he was crazed by jealousy.

"I ask you to consider these two propositions with more gravity and concentration than they actually merit, because on your acceptance or rejection of them depends your acceptance or rejection of the guilt of these two. You cannot dismiss them as too absurd for any earthly consideration. You cannot say, 'Oh, of course that wasn't the reason they killed her, but that's not our concern; there may have been another reason that we don't know anything about.' No, fortunately for us, you cannot do that.

"These, preposterous as they are, are the only motives suggested; they are the least preposterous ones that the state could find to submit to you. If you are not able to accept them the state's case crumbles to pieces before your eyes. If you look at it attentively for as much as thirty seconds, I believe that you will see it crumbling. What you are asked to believe is this: That for the most sordid, base, mercenary and calculating motives—the desire to protect her financial future from possible hazard—Susan Ives committed a cruel, wicked, and bloody murder.

"For two hours you listened to Susan Ives speaking to you from that witness box. If you can believe that she is sordid, base, calculating, mercenary, cruel, and bloody, I congratulate you. Such power of credulity emerges from the ranks of mere talent into those of sheer genius.

"Stephen Bellamy, you are told, was her accomplice—driven stark, staring, raving mad by the most bestial, despicable, and cowardly form of jealousy. You have heard Stephen Bellamy, too, from that witness box, telling you of the anguish of despair that filled him when he thought that harm had befallen his beloved—if you can believe that he is despicable, cowardly, bestial, and mad, then undoubtedly you are still able to believe in a world tenanted by giants and fairies and ogres and witches and dragons. Not one of them would be so strange a phenomenon as the transformation of this adoring, chivalrous, and restrained gentleman into the base villain that you are asked to accept.

"The state's case, gentlemen! It crumbles, does it not? It crumbles before your eyes. Means, motives, opportunity—look at them steadily and clearly and they vanish into thin air.

"If means, motives, and opportunity constitute a basis for an accusation of murder, this trial might well end in several arrests that would be as fully justified as the arrests of Susan Ives and Stephen Bellamy. I make no such accusations; I am strong and sure and safe enough in the proved innocence of these two to feel no need of summoning others to the bar of justice. That is neither my duty nor my desire, but it would be incompatible with the desire for abstract truth not to point out that far stronger hypothetical cases might be made out against several whose paths also have crossed the path of the ill-starred girl who died in that cottage.

"We come as close to establishing as perfect an alibi as it is likely that innocent people, little suspecting that one will be called for, would be able to establish. What alibi had practically anyone who has appeared against these two for that night? The knife that Dr. Stanley described to you might have been one of various types—such a knife as might have been well discovered in a tool chest, in a kitchen drawer, in the equipment of a sportsman.

"You have analyzed the motives ascribed to the defendants. I submit that, taken at random, three somewhat solider motives might be robbery or blackmail or drunken jealousy. When one possible witness removes himself to Canada, when another takes his life—they are safely out of reach of our jurisdiction, but not beyond the scope of our speculations. I submit that these specifications are at least fruitful of interest. Abandoning them, however, I suggest to you that that girl, young, beautiful, fragile, and unprotected in that isolated cottage with jewels at her throat and on her fingers, was the natural prey of any nameless beast roving in the neighbourhood—one who had possibly stalked her from the time that she left her house, one who had possibly been prowling through the grounds of this deserted estate on some business, sinister or harmless. Ostensibly this was a case of murder for robbery; it remains still the simplest and most natural explanation—too simple and too natural by half for a brilliant prosecutor, an ambitious police force, and frenzied public, all clamouring for a victim.

"Well, they have had their victims; I hope that they do not sleep worse at night for the rest of their lives when they think of the victims that they selected.

"Two things the state has made no attempt to explain—who it was that stole the note from Patrick Ives's study and who it was that laughed when Madeleine Bellamy screamed. Whoever took the note, it was not Susan Ives. She had no possible motive in denying having taken it; she freely admitted that she searched the study for some proof of her husband's duplicity, and she also admitted that Elliot Farwell had informed her that he believed her husband was meeting Madeleine Bellamy at the cottage that very night. The note, which we presume was making a rendezvous, would in no way have added to her previous information. Any one of six or eight servants or six or eight guests may have intercepted it; whoever did so knew when and where Madeleine Bellamy was to be found that night.

"The laugh is more baffling and disconcerting still; the state must find it mightily so. It will be instructive to see whether they are going to ask you to believe that it was uttered by Stephen Bellamy as he saw his wife fall. In my opinion only a degenerate or a drunken monster would have chosen that moment for mirth. Possibly it is Mr. Farr's contention that he was both. Providentially, that is for you and not for him to decide.

"The state has still another little matter to explain to your satisfaction. According to its theory, Stephen Bellamy and Susan Ives arrived at the scene of the crime in a car—in Mr. Bellamy's car. The murderer of Madeleine Bellamy did not arrive in a car—or at any rate, no car was visible two minutes later in that vicinity. There were no tire tracks in the space behind the house, and the state's own witnesses have proved that on both Stephen Bellamy's visits his car was left squarely in front of the cottage door. If someone left an unlighted car parked somewhere down the main drive, as the state contends, it was not he. His car would have been clearly visible to any human being who approached the cottage. It will, as I say, be instructive to see how the state disposes of this vital fact.

"I have touched on these matters because I have desired to make clear to you two or three factors that are absolutely incompatible with any theory that the state has advanced. If they are to be disposed of in the most remotely plausible fashion, some other theory must be evolved, and I believe that you will agree with me that it is rather late in the day to produce another theory. I have not touched on them—and I wish to make this perfectly clear—on the ground that they are in no way necessary to our defense. That defense is not dependent on such intriguing details as who took the note, or who laughed, or whether the murderer approached his goal on foot or in a car. The defense that I advance is simple and staightforward and independent of any other circumstances.

"Of all the things that I have said to you, there is only one that I hold it essential that you carry in the very core of your memory when you leave this room on as solemn an errand as falls to the lot of any man. This only: That the sole defense that I plead for Stephen Bellamy and Susan Ives is that they are innocent—as entirely and unequivocally innocent as any man of you in whose hands rests their fate; that this foul and brutal murder was against their every wish, hope, or desire; that it is to them as ghastly, as incredible, and as mysterious as it is to you. That and that only is their defense.

"It is not my task, as you know—as in time Judge Carver will tell you—to prove them innocent. It is the state's to prove them guilty. A heavy task they will find it, I most truly believe. But I would have you find them something more than not guilty. That is the verdict that you may render with your lips, but with your hearts I ask you to render another more generous and ungrudgingly. 'Innocent'—a lovely, valiant, and fearless word, a word untainted by suspicion or malice. A verdict that has no place in any court, but I believe that all who hear your lips pronounce "Not guilty" will read it in your eyes. I pray that they may.

"I said to you that when you left this room you would be bound on the most solemn of all errands. I say to you now that when you return you may well be bound on the most beautiful one imaginable—you will return in order to give life to two who have stood in the shadow of death. Life!

"You cannot give back to Susan Ives something that she has lost—a golden faith and care-free security, a confidence in this world and all its works. You cannot give back to Stephen Bellamy the dead girl who was his treasure and delight,

221

about whose bright head clustered all his dreams. You cannot give back to them much that made life sweetest, but, gentlemen, you can give them life. You can restore to them the good earth, the clean air, the laughter of children, the hands of love, starlight and firelight and sunlight and moonlight—and brightest of all, the light of home shining through windows long dark. All these things you hold in your hands. All these things are yours to give. Gentlemen, I find it in my heart to envy you greatly that privilege, to covet greatly that opportunity."

He sat down, slowly and heavily, and through the room there ran an eager murmur of confidence and ease, a swift slackening of tension, a shifting of suspense. And as though in answer to it, Farr was on his feet. He stood silent for a moment, his hands clasped over the back of the chair before him, his eyes, brilliantly inscrutable, sweeping the upturned faces before him. When he lifted his voice, the familiar clang was muted:

"Your Honour, gentlemen, when my distinguished adversary rose to address you an hour or so ago, he assured you that he was about to take very little of your time. We would none of us grudge him one moment that he has subsequently taken. He is waging a grim and desperate battle, and moments and even hours seem infinitesimal weapons to interpose between those two whose defense is intrusted to him, and who stand this day in peril of their lives on the awful brink of eternity itself.

"The plea that has made to you is as eloquent and moving a one as you will hear in many a long day; it is my misfortune that the one that I am about to make must follow hard on its heels, and will necessarily be shorn of both eloquence and emotion. It will be the shorter for lack of them, but not the better. What I lack in oratory I shall endeavour to supply in facts: facts too cold, hard, and grim to make pleasant hearing—still, facts. It is my unwelcome duty to place them before you; I shall not shrink from it. It will not be necessary for me to elaborate on them. They will speak for themselves more eloquently than I could ever hope to do, and I propose to let them do so.

"Before I marshal them before you, I will dispose as briefly as possible of two or three issues that Mr. Lambert has seen fit to raise in his speech to you. First, as to the wealth of Mrs. Ives. I cannot see that the fact that she is wealthy is in any way a vital issue in this case, but Mr. Lambert evidently considered it sufficiently important to dwell on at considerable length. He managed very skilfully to place before you the picture of a modest little farmhouse with roses clambering over a cottage gate, presided over by an even more modest chatelaine. Very idyllic and utterly and absolutely misleading.

"The little farmhouse is a mansion of some twenty-odd rooms, the roses grow in a sunken garden as large as a small park; not many cottages boast a swimming pool, a tennis court, a bowling green and a garage for five cars—but Mrs. Ives's cottage took these simple improvements as a matter of course. Mr. Lambert drew your attention to the fact that if you had rung a doorbell the lady herself might have hastened to welcome your summons, and, he implies, to welcome you in to see how simply she lived.

"I doubt profoundly whether Mrs. Ives ever opened her door in her life unless she was intending to pass through it, and I doubt even more profoundly whether you would ever have been requested to cross the threshold of her home. Mr. Lambert did admit that the bell might have been answered by a little maid, but he failed to specify which one of the five little maids it might have been. He added, in an even more lyric vein, that Susan Ives had no more than any of your wives—no more than roses in her garden, sunlight in her windows, babies in her nursery. I confess myself somewhat taken aback. Are your wives the possessors of an acre of roses, a hundred windows to let in sunshine, a day and night nursery for your babies to play in, with a governess in still a third room to supervise their play? If such is the case, you are fortunate indeed.

"As for Stephen Bellamy, Mr. Lambert has assured you that any mechanic in the land was as well off as he. Well, possibly. The mechanics that I know don't have maids to help their pretty wives, and gardeners to sleep over their pretty garages, but perhaps the ones that you know do.

"So much for the wealth of the defendants. I said at the outset that it was a matter of no great importance, and in one sense it is not; in a deeper sense, it is of the greatest possible significance. Not that Susan Ives was, in the strictest sense of the word, a wealthy woman, but because of the alchemy that had been wrought in her by the sinister magic of what we may call the golden touch.

"You all know the legend of Midas, I am sure—the tale of that unhappy king who wished that every object that his fingers rested on might turn to gold, and whose fingers strayed one day to his little daughter's hair and transformed her into a small statue—beautiful, shining, brilliant, but cold and hard and inhuman as metal itself. Long ago Curtiss Thorne's fingers must have rested on his little daughter's hair, and what he made of his child then the woman is to-day. The product of pride, of power, of privilege, of riches—Susan Ives, proud, powerful, privileged, and rich—the golden girl, a charming object of luxury in the proper surrounding, a useless encumbrance out of them.

"No one knew this better than the golden girl herself—she had had bitter cause to know it, remember; and on that fatal summer afternoon in June a drunken breath set the pedestal rocking beneath her feet. She moved swiftly down from that pedestal, with the firm intention of making it steady for all time. It is not the gold that we hold in our hands that is a menace and a curse, gentlemen—not the shining counters that we may change for joy and beauty and health and mercy—it is the cold metal that has grown into our hearts. I hold no brief against wealth itself. I hold a brief against the product of the Midas touch.

"Mr. Lambert next introduced to you most skilfully a very dangerous theme—the theme of the deep personal interest that he takes in both defendants, more especially in Susan Ives. The sincerity of his devotion to her it is impossible to doubt. I for one am very far from doubting it. He loved the little girl before the fingers of Midas had rested heavy on her hair; he sees before him still only those bright curls of childhood clustering about an untarnished brow. Many of you who have daughters felt tears sting in your eyes when he told you that he loved her as his daughter—I, who have none, felt the sting myself.

"But, gentlemen, I ask you only this: Are you, in all truth and fairness, the most unbiased judges of your daughter's characters? Would you credit the word of an archangel straight from heaven who told you that your daughter was a murderess, if that daughter denied it? Never—never, in God's world, and you know it! If, in your hearts, you say to yourself, 'He has known Susan Ives and loved her for many years; he loves her still, so she must be all he thinks,' then Mr. Lambert's warm eloquence will have accomplished its purpose and my cold logic will have failed.

"But I ask you, gentlemen, to use your heads and not your hearts. I ask you to discount heavily not Mr. Lambert's sincerity, nor his affection, nor his eloquence, but his judgment and his credulity. Platitudes are generally the oldest and profoundest of truths; one of the most ancient and most profound of all is the axiom that Love is blind.

"So much for two general challenges that it has been my duty to meet; the more specific ones of the note, the car, and the laugh, I will deal with in their proper places. We are now through with generalizations and down to facts.

"These fall into two categories—the first including the events leading up to and precipitating the crime, the second dealing with the execution of the crime itself.

"I propose to deal with them in their logical sequence. In the first category comes the prime factor in this case—motive. Mr. Lambert has told you that that is the weakest factor in the state's case; I tell you that it is the strongest. There has never come under my observation a more perfect example of an overwhelming motive springing from the very foundation of motivation—from character itself.

"I want you to get this perfectly straight; it is of the most vital importance. There is never any convincing motive for murder, in that that implies an explanation that would seem plausible to the sane and well-balanced mind. There is something in any such mind that recoils in loathing and amazement that such a solution of any problem should seem possible. It makes no difference whether murder is committed—as it has been committed—for a million dollars or for five—in revenge for a nagging word or for bestial cruelty—for a quarrel over a pair of dice or over a pair of dark eyes—to us it seems equally abhorrent, grotesque, and incredible. And so it is. But in some few cases we are able to study the deep springs in which this monster lurks, and this is one of them.

"I ask you to concentrate now on what you have learned as to the character of Susan Ives, from her own lips and from the lips of others—the undisputed evidence that has been put before you. Forget for a moment that she is small and slight, sweet-voiced, clear-eyed—a lady. Look within.

"From the time that we first see her, on the very threshold of girlhood, to the time that you have seen her with your own eyes here, she has shown a character that is perfectly consistent—a character that is as resolute, as lawless, and as ruthless as you would find in any hardened criminal in this land. At the first touch of constraint or opposition she is metamorphosed into a dangerous machine, and woe to the one that stands in its way.

"Seven years ago, over the bitter opposition of her adoring father, she decided to marry the man who had previously been Madeleine Bellamy's lover, and who had, deservedly or undeservedly, somewhat of the reputation of the village scamp and ne'er-do-well. Her marriage to him broke her father's heart. Shortly thereafter the old man died, and so bitter, relentless, and unforgiving is the heart of this daughter, whom he had longed to cherish and protect, that not once since she left it in pride and anger has she set foot within the boundaries of her childhood's home.

"She returned, however, at the first opportunity to Rosemont; the arrogance that consumed her like a flame made it essential that she should be triumphantly reestablished on the grounds of her first defeat. And the triumph was a rich and intoxicating one. Wealthy, courted, admired, surrounded by a chorus of industrious flatterers, no wonder that she became obsessed with a sense of her power and importance. She was, in fact, undisputed queen of the little domain in which she lived, and her throne seemed far more secure than most.

"She was not precisely a benevolent monarch; poor little Kathleen Page and Melanie Cordier have testified to that, but then they had made the dangerous error of murmuring protests at the rule. A little judicious browbeating and starvation reduced them to the proper state of subjection, and all was well once more. Graciousness and generosity itself to all who bent the knee at the proper angle, as her mother-in-law and maid have testified, still, it required the merest flicker of insubordination to set the steel fingers twitching beneath the velvet glove.

"Nothing more than fugitive rebellions had penetrated this absolute monarchy, however, up to that bright summer afternoon when news reached its sovereign that there was an aspirant to the throne—a powerful pretender—an actual usurper, with the keys to the castle itself in her hand. The blood of Elizabeth of England, of Catherine of Russia, of Lucrezia of Italy rose in the veins of this other spoiled child to meet that challenge. And, gentlemen, we know too well the fate that befell those rash and lovely pretenders of old.

"Enough of metaphor. From the moment that Susan Ives knew that the beautiful daughter of the village dressmaker was trespassing on her property, Madeleine Bellamy was doomed.

"So much for the motive. Now for the means. We will take Susan Ives's own account of that evening—the account that was finally wrung from her when she found, to her terror and despair, that the state had in its hands evidence absolutely damning and conclusive. The telephone call, Orsini's vigil at the window, the tire tracks, the finger prints—all these successive blows brought successive changes in the fabric that the defendants were weaving for your benefit.

"It became evident early in the trial that their original tale of absolute innocence and ignorance would not bear inspection one minute, but they continued industriously to cut their cloth to fit our case until they were confronted with two or three little marks on the base of a lamp. Then and then only they saw the hopelessness of their plight, discarded the whole wretched, patched, tattered stuff, and tried frantically to replace it by a fabric bearing at least the outer pattern of candour. What candour under those circumstances is worth is for you to decide.

"Mr. Lambert assures you that they had both decided to stop short of perjury. If the conclusion of Stephen Bellamy's first story on that stand was not in fact black perjury, whatever it may have been technically, is again for you to decide. I have little doubt of that decision.

"But in Mrs. Ives's account of that evening's doings, you have the outward and visible sign of truth, if not the inward and spiritual state. The story that she finally told you I believe to be substantially correct as far as outward events go—up to the point where she entered the cottage door. From then on I believe it to be the sheerest fabrication. Let us follow it to that point.

"From the moment that Elliot Farwell informed her that Mimi Bellamy was carrying on an intrigue with her husband, her every act is a revelation. It is no pleasant task to inspect from then on the conduct of this loyal, gentle, generous and controlled spirit, but let us set ourselves to it. She has heard that her reign is threatened—what does she do?

"She returns to her home, concealing the rage and terror working in her like a poison under a flow of laughter and chatter—and cocktails. Susan Ives is a lawless individual, gentlemen—the law was made for humbler spirits than hers. In her house, in this court, in that darkened cottage, she has shown you unhesitatingly her defiance and contempt of any law made by man—and of one made by God.

"She is not as yet quite sure that Farwell has told her the truth; there is too much arrogance in her to believe that danger actually threatens her from that direction—but, under the smiling mask, behind the clenched teeth, the poison is working. She goes to the hall to bid Farwell good-bye and to warn him not to give knowledge of the intrigue away—perhaps already a prophetic sense of her share in this dreadful business is formulating. And while she is speaking to him she sees in the mirror Melanie Cordier, placing the note in the book. It is the work of a minute to step into the study after Melanie has left, abstract the note, master the contents, and return to the living room, her guests, and Patrick. On the way back, she stopped in the hall long enough to eavesdrop and get her cue. With that cue as to the prospective poker game in her possession, her course was already clear. She went up to Patrick Ives with a lie on her lips and a blacker one in her heart, and told him that she was going to the movies that night with the Conroys.

"She then followed him again into the hall to spy on him while he counted the bonds; she followed him back to the study after dinner to spy on him again, to see where he put them; she got rid of him with a lie, broke into his desk, confirmed her worst suspicions, and decided definitely on a course of action. A telephone message to Stephen Bellamy, another lie from the foot of the stairs to her unsuspecting husband, and she was on her way.

"Before she reached the gate, something went wrong, and she returned to the house—possibly for the reason that she gave you, possibly for another. At any rate, within a minute or so she was at her old task of eavesdropping and spying, and a minute or so later than that Patrick Ives was safely locked up, well out of the running when it came to protecting the foolish girl at the cottage or the maddened one on her way there. Susan Ives had successfully disposed of the greatest menace to the execution of her scheme. Perhaps fuel was added to the flame by what she heard from the room off the day nursery; perhaps she heard nothing at all and merely wanted to get Patrick out of the way. It is a matter of no great importance. She had accomplished her purpose and was on her way again, to meet Stephen Bellamy.

"It is the state's contention that she went to that rendezvous with a knife in her pocket and murder in her heart. Patrick Ives has told you that the knife that the state put in evidence was not out of his possession that evening; it is for you to decide whether you believe him or not. But which knife struck the blow is of no great importance either. The knife that murdered Madeleine Bellamy was, as you have been told, a perfectly ordinary knife—such a knife as might be found in any of your homes—in the kitchen, in the pantry, in the tool chest. From any of these places Susan Ives might have procured one, cleansed it and replaced it. We need not let which one she actually procured give us great concern.

"Susan Ives herself has touched very briefly on that drive with Stephen Bellamy through the quiet, starlit summer night; she merely confirms Stephen Bellamy's account, which is neither very coherent nor very convincing. The gist of it was that Sue Ives was occupied in proving Mimi's guilt and he with denying it. Some such conversation may well have taken place.

"The part that Stephen Bellamy played in the actual commission of this murder is a more enigmatic one than that of Susan Ives, if not less sinister. From the outset, it must have been perfectly clear to Mrs. Ives's exceptionally shrewd mind that, if she did not want Stephen Bellamy at her heels as an avenging husband, she must lure him into the rôle of an accomplice. This, by means best known to herself, she accomplished. We have it on Stephen Bellamy's own word that he entered that little room with her and left it with her, and we know that he sits beside her in this dock because they have elected to hang or go free together.

"Now as to what Mr. Lambert is pleased to refer to as their alibi, and then I have done.

"Of course, they have neither of them the shred of an alibi. Accepting the fact that they left the gas station shortly after nine and reached Stephen Bellamy's at about ten, they would have had ample time to reach the Thorne place by the River Road, confront the waiting girl with the intercepted note, murder her, make good their escape, and return to Bellamy's by ten o'clock. Later, Bellamy returns to the cottage alone to get the jewels, in order to give colour to the appearance of robbery and to remove any traces of the crime that they may have left behind them. Possibly it was then that he brought the lamp from the hall and smashed it at the dead girl's feet. By then they had had time to work out a story in the remote possibility of their eventual discovery pretty thoroughly. At any rate, he took Susan Ives home and returned alone. I repeat, they have no alibi.

"'Well, what of the laugh?' you say. 'What of the car that was not there?' To which I echo, 'What of them, indeed?'

"Gentlemen, just stop to think for one minute. Who heard that laugh? Who failed to see that automobile? Who fixed the hour for this murder at the moment that would come closest to establishing an alibi for these two? Why, the brother of Susan Ives—the loving, the devoted, the adoring brother, who stood up here in this room and told you that he would do anything short of murder to protect his sister——"

Lambert was on his feet, his eyes goggling in an ashen countenance. "He said nothing of the kind! Your Honour——"

"He did not say that he would not commit murder?"

"He did not say that he would do anything short of it. Of all the——"

"Then my memory is at fault," remarked Mr. Farr blandly. "It was certainly my impression that such was the substance of his remarks. If it gives offense I withdraw it, and state simply that the person who has fixed the hour of the murder for you is Mrs. Patrick Ives's brother, Mr. Douglas Thorne. There is not a shred of evidence save his as to the moment at which the murder took place—not a shred. You are entirely at liberty to draw your own conclusions from that. If you decide that he was telling the absolute truth, I will concede even that possibility.

"Mr. Thorne simply tells you that at about nine-thirty on the evening of the nineteenth of June he heard a woman scream and a man laugh somewhere in the neighbourhood of the gardener's cottage at Orchards. He adds that at the time he attached no particular importance to it, as he thought that it may have been young people sky-larking in the neighbourhood—and he may have been perfectly

228

right. It no more establishes the hour of Madeleine Bellamy's murder than it establishes the hour of the deluge.

"It is, in fact, perfectly possible that the murder took place after ten o'clock, after the visit to the Bellamy home and the alleged search along the road to the Conroys. Only one thing is certain: If it was nine-thirty when Mr. Thorne walked up those cottage steps, and if at that time there was no car in sight, then the hour of the murder was not nine-thirty. It may have been before that hour, it may have been after it. It was not then.

"So much for Mr. Lambert's trump cards, the laugh and the car. There remains the theft of the note, which he claims Mrs. Ives had no interest in denying. Of course she had every interest in denying it. If she admitted that she had found the note, then she would be forced to admit to the jury that she knew positively that Mimi was waiting in the cottage, and that did not fit in with her story at all. So she simply denies that she took it. And there goes their last trump.

"Stripped of glamour, of emotion, of eloquence, it is the barest, the simplest, the most appallingly obvious of cases, you see. There is not one single link in the chain missing—not one.

"Unless someone came to you here and said, 'I saw the knife in Susan Ives's hand, I saw it rise, I saw it fall, I heard the crash of that girl's body and saw the white lace of her frock turn red'—unless you heard that with your own ears, you could not have a clearer picture of what happened in that room. Not once in a thousand murder cases is there an eyewitness to the crime. Not once in five hundred is there forged so strong a chain of evidence as now lies before you.

"There was only one person in all the world to whom the death of Madeleine Bellamy was a vital, urgent, and imperative necessity. The woman to whom it was all of this—and more, far more, since words are poor substitutes for passions— has told you with her own lips that at ten o'clock on that night she stood over the body of that slain girl and saw her eyes wide in the dreadful and unseeing stare of death. When Susan Ives told you that, she told you the truth; and she told you the truth again when she said that when you knew that she had stood there, she did not believe that it would be possible for you to credit that the one fact had no connection with the other. Nor do I believe it, gentlemen—nor do I believe it.

"By her side, in that room, stood Stephen Bellamy. By his own confession it was he who closed the eyes of that slain girl, he who touched her hand. By his own confession he has told you that he did not believe it possible that you would credit that he stood there at that time and yet had no knowledge of her death. Nor do I believe it, gentlemen—nor do I believe it.

"Mr. Lambert has told you that to him has fallen the most solemn task that can fall to the lot of any man—that of pleading for the gift of human life. There is a still more solemn task, I believe, and that task has fallen to me. I must ask you not for life but for death.

"The law does not exact the penalty of a life for a life in the spirit of vengeance or of malice. It asks it because the flame of human life is so sacred a thing that it is business of the law to see that no hand, however powerful, shall be blasphemously lifted to extinguish that flame. It is in order that your wives and daughters and sisters may sleep sweet and safe at night that I stand before you now and tell you that because they lifted that hand, the lives of Stephen Bellamy and Susan Ives are forfeit.

"These two believed that behind the bulwarks of power, of privilege, of wealth, and of position, they were safe. They were not safe; they have discovered that. And if those barriers can protect them now, if still behind them they can find shelter and security and a wall to shield them as they creep back to their ruined hearthstones, then I say to you that the majesty of the law is a mockery and the sacredness of human life is a mockery, and the death penalty in this great state is a mockery.

"There was never in this state a more wicked, brutal, and cold-blooded murder than that of Madeleine Bellamy. For Susan Ives and Stephen Bellamy, the two who now stand before you accused of that murder, I ask, with all solemnity and fully aware of the tragic duty that I impose on each one of you, the verdict of guilty of murder in the first degree. If you can find it in your hearts, in your souls, or your consciences to render any other verdict, you are more fortunate than I believe you to be."

In the hushed silence that followed his voice, all eyes turned to the twelve who sat there unmoving, their drawn, pale faces, tired-eyed and tight-lipped, turned toward the merciless flame that burned behind the prosecutor's white face.

The red-headed girl asked in a desolate small voice that sounded very far away, "Is it all over now? Are they going now?"

"No—wait a moment; there's the judge's charge. Here, what's Lambert doing?"

He was on his feet, swaying a little, his voice barely audible.

"Your Honour, a note has been handed to me this moment. It is written on the card of the principal of the Eastern High School, Mr. Randolph Phipps."

"What are the contents of this note?"

Lambert settled his glasses on his nose with a shaken hand. "It says—it says:

> "MY DEAR MR. LAMBERT:
>
> "Before this case goes to the jury, I consider it my duty to lay before them some knowledge of the most vital importance that is my possession, and that for personal reasons I have withheld

230

up to the present time, in the hope that events would render it unnecessary for me to take the stand. Such has unfortunately not been the case, and I therefore put myself at your disposal. Will you tell me what my next step should be? The facts are such as make it imperative that I should be permitted to speak.

"RANDOLPH PHIPPS."

Judge Carver said slowly, "May I see the note?" Lambert handed it up in those shaking fingers. "Thank you. A most extraordinary performance," commented the judge dispassionately. After a moment he said more dispassionately still:

"The Court was about to adjourn in any case until to-morrow morning. It does not care to deliver its charge to the jury at this late hour of the day, and we will therefore convene again at ten to-morrow. In the meantime the Court will take the note under advisement. See that Mr. Phipps is present in the morning. Court is dismissed."

"I don't believe that I'll be here in the morning," said the red-headed girl in that same small monotone.

"Not be here?" The reporter's voice was a howl of incredulity. "Not be here, you little idiot? Did you hear what Lambert read off that card?"

"I don't think that I'll live till morning," said the red-headed girl.

The seventh day of the Bellamy trial was over.

CHAPTER VIII

The red-headed girl had not realized how tired she was until she heard Ben Potts's voice. He stood there as straight as ever, but where were the clear bugle tones that summoned the good burghers of Redfield morning after morning? A faint, a lamentable, echo of his impressive "Hear ye! Hear ye!" rang out feebly, and the red-headed girl slumped back dispiritedly in her chair, consumed with fatigue as with a fever.

"Sleep well?" inquired the reporter with amiable anxiety.

The red-headed girl turned on him eyes heavy with scorn. "Sleep?" she repeated acidly. "What's that?"

Judge Carver looked as weary as Ben Potts sounded, and the indefatigable Mr. Farr looked blanched and bitten to the bone with something deeper than fatigue. Only Mr. Lambert looked haler and heartier than he had for several interminable days; and the faces of Stephen Bellamy and Susan Ives were as pale, as controlled, and as tranquil as ever.

Judge Carver let his gavel fall heavily. "The Court has given careful consideration as to the advisability of admitting the evidence in question last night, and has decided that it may be admitted. Mr. Lambert!" Mr. Lambert bounded joyfully forward. "Is the Court correct in understanding that Mr. Phipps is your witness?"

"Quite correct, Your Honour."

"Let him be called."

"Mr. Randolph Phipps!"

The principal of Eastern High School was a tall man; there was dignity in the way he held his head and moved his long, loose limbs, but all the dignity in the world could not still the nervous tremor of his hands or school the too sensitive mouth to rigidity. Under straight, heavy brows, the eyes of a dreamer startled from deep sleep looked out in amazement at a strange world; the sweep of dark hair above the wide brow came perilously close to being Byronic; only the height of his cheek bones and the width of his mouth saved him from suggesting a matinée idol of some previous era. He might have been thirty-five, or forty, or forty-five. His eyes were eighteen.

"Mr. Phipps, it is the understanding of this court that you have a communication to make of peculiar importance. You understand that in making that statement you will, of course, be subject to the usual course of direct and cross-examination?"

"I understand that—yes."

"Very well. You may proceed with the examination, Mr. Lambert."

"Mr. Phipps, where were you on the night of the nineteenth of June?"

"On the night of the nineteenth of June," said Mr. Phipps, in the clear, carrying voice of one not unaccustomed to public speaking, "I spent about three hours on the Thorne estate at Orchards. Some things occurred during that time that I feel it my duty to make known to the jury in this case."

"What were you doing on the Thorne place?"

"I suppose that I was doing what is technically known as trespassing. It did not occur to me at the time that it was a very serious offense, as I knew the place to be uninhabited—still, I suppose that I was perfectly aware that I had no business there."

"You had no especial purpose in going there?"

"Oh, yes; I went there because I had selected it as a pleasant place for a picnic supper."

"You were alone?"

"No—no, I was not alone." Mr. Phipps suddenly looked forty-five and very tired.

"Other people were accompanying you on this—this excursion?"

"One other person."

"Who was this other person?"

"A friend of mine—a young lady."

"What was the name of this young woman?"

"Is it necessary to give her name? I hope—I hope with all my heart—that that will not be necessary." The low, urgent, unhappy voice stumbled in its intensity. "My companion was quite a young girl. We both realize now that we committed a grave indiscretion, but I shall never forgive myself if my criminal stupidity has involved her."

"I am afraid that we shall have to have her name."

"I am a married man," said Mr. Phipps, in a clear voice that did not stumble. "I am placing this information before the Court at no small sacrifice to myself. It seems to me to place too heavy a penalty on my decision to come forward at this moment if you ask me to involve another by so doing. The girl who was with me that evening was one of my pupils; she is at present engaged to a young man to whom she is entirely devoted; publicity of the type that this means is in every way abhorrent to her. I request most urgently that she shall not be exposed to it."

"Mr. Phipps," said Judge Carver gravely, "you have been permitted to take the stand at your own request. It is highly desirable that any information, of the importance that you have implied that in your possession to be, should be as fully corroborated as possible. It is therefore essential that we should have the name of this young woman."

"Her name is Sally Dunne," said Mr. Phipps.

"Is she also prepared to take the stand?"

"She is prepared to do whatever is essential to prevent a miscarriage of justice. She is naturally extremely reluctant to take the stand."

"Is she in court?"

"She is."

"Miss Dunne will be good enough not to leave the courtroom without the Court's permission. You may proceed, Mr. Phipps."

"We arrived at Orchards at a little after eight," said Mr. Phipps. "Miss Dunne took the half-past-seven bus from Rosemont, left it a short distance beyond Orchards, and walked back to the spot where I had arranged to meet her, just inside the gate. We did not arrive together, as I was apprehensive that it might cause a certain amount of gossip if we were seen together."

"How had you come to choose Orchards, Mr. Phipps?"

"Miss Dunne had on several occasions commented on the beauty of the place and expressed a desire to see it more thoroughly, and it was in order to gratify that desire that the party was planned. As I say, we met at the gate and walked on up the drive past the lodge and the little driveway that leads to the gardener's cottage to a small summerhouse, about five hundred feet beyond the cottage itself. It contained a little furniture—a table and some chairs and benches—and it was there that we decided to have our supper. Miss Dunne had brought a luncheon box with her containing fruit and sandwiches, and we spread it on the table and began to eat. Neither of us was particularly hungry, however, and we decided to keep what remained of the food—about half the contents of the box, I think—in case we wanted it later, and to do some reading before it got too dark to see. I had brought with me the *Idylls of the King*, with the intention of reading it aloud."

"The book is of no importance, Mr. Phipps."

"No," said Mr. Phipps, in a tone of slight surprise. "No, I suppose not. You are probably quite right. Well, in any case, we read for quite a while, until it began to get too dark to see, and after that we sat there conversing."

The fluent voice with its slightly meticulous pronunciation paused, and Lambert moved impatiently. "And then, Mr. Phipps?"

"Yes. I was trying to recollect precisely what it was that caused us to move from the summerhouse. I think that it was Miss Dunne who suggested that it was rather close and stuffy there, because of the fact that the structure was smothered in vines; she asked if there wasn't somewhere cooler that we could go to sit. I said: 'There's the gardener's cottage. We might try the veranda there.' You could just see the roof of it through the trees. I pointed it out to her, and we started——"

"You were familiar with the layout of the estate?"

"Oh, quite. That was one of the principal reasons why we had gone there. I had once done some tutoring in Latin and physics with Mr. Thorne's younger son Charles—the one who was killed in the war. We had been in the habit of using the summerhouse, which was his old playhouse, as a schoolroom."

234

"That was some time ago?"

"About fifteen years ago—sixteen perhaps. I had just graduated from college myself, and Charles Thorne was going to Princeton that fall."

"But you still remembered your way about?"

"Oh, perfectly. I was about to say that we did not approach it from the main drive, but cut across the lawns, pushed through the shrubbery at the back and came up to it from the rear. We had just reached the little dirt drive back of the cottage, and were perhaps a hundred feet away from the house itself, when we heard voices, and Miss Dunne exclaimed: 'There's someone in the cottage. Look, the side window is lighted.' I was considerably startled, as I had made inquiries about the gardener and knew that he was in Italy.

"I stood still for a moment, debating what to do next, when one of the voices in the cottage was suddenly raised, and a woman said quite clearly, 'You wouldn't dare to touch me—you wouldn't dare!' Someone laughed and there was a little scuffling sound, and a second or so after that a scream—a short, sharp scream— and the sound of something falling with quite a clatter, as though a chair or a table had been overturned.

"I was in rather a nervous and overwrought state of mind myself that evening, and before I thought what I was doing I laughed, quite loudly. Miss Dunne whispered, 'Be careful! They'll hear you.' Just as she spoke, the light went out in the cottage and I said, 'Well, Sally, evidently we aren't the only indiscreet people around here this evening. I'd better get you out of this.'

"Just as I was speaking I heard steps on the main driveway and the sound of someone whistling. The whistling kept coming closer every second, and I whispered, 'Someone's coming in here. We'd better stand back in those bushes by the house.' There were some very tall lilacs at the side of the house under the windows, and we tiptoed over and pushed back into them. After a minute or so, we heard someone go up the steps, and then a bell rang inside the house. There wasn't any sound at all for a minute; then we could hear the steps coming down the porch stairs again, and a moment later heard them on the gravel, and a moment later still they had died away.

"I said, 'That was a close call—too many people around here entirely. Let's make it two less.' We tiptoed out past the cottage to the main road and started back toward the lodge gates, walking along the grass beside the road in order not to make any noise. We were almost back to the gates when Miss Dunne stopped me."

"Do you know what time it was, Mr. Phipps?"

"I am not sure of the time. I looked at my watch last when it began to get too dark to read—shortly before nine. We did not start for the cottage until a few minutes later, and it is my impression that it must have been between quarter to

235

ten and ten. We had been walking very slowly, but even at that pace it should not take more than twenty minutes."

"It was dark then?"

"Oh, yes; it had been quite dark for some time, though it was possible to distinguish the outline of objects. It was a very beautiful starlight night."

"Quite so. What caused Miss Dunne to stop you?"

"She exclaimed suddenly, 'Oh, good heavens, I haven't got my lunch box! I must have left it in the bushes by the cottage.' I said, 'Perhaps you left it in the summerhouse,' but she was quite sure that she hadn't, as she remembered distinctly thinking just before we reached the cottage that it was a nuisance lugging it about. She was very much worried, as it had her initial stenciled on it in rather a distinctive way, and she was afraid that someone that she knew might possibly find it and recognize it, and that if they returned it, her parents might learn that she had been at Orchards that night."

"Her parents were not aware of this expedition?"

"They were not, sir. They had both gone to New Hampshire to attend the funeral of Mr. Dunne's mother."

"Proceed, Mr. Phipps."

"Miss Dunne seemed so upset over the loss of the box that I finally agreed to go back with her to look for it, though there seemed to me a very slight chance of anyone identifying it, and I did not particularly care to risk arousing anyone who still might be in the cottage. I had a flashlight, however, and we decided to make a hurried search as quietly as possible; so we started back, retracing our steps and keeping a sharp lookout for the box.

"When we got to the dirt cut-off leading to the cottage from the main driveway, we took it and approached as quietly as possible, standing for a moment just at the foot of the steps where the lilac bushes began and listening to see whether we could hear anything within. Miss Dunne said, 'There's not a sound, and no light either. I don't believe there's a soul around.'

"I said, 'Someone has closed the windows and pulled down the shades in this front room. It was open when we were here before.' Sally said, 'Well, never mind—let's look quickly and get away from here. I think it's a horrid place.' I turned on the flashlight and said, 'We were much farther back than this.' She said, 'Yes; we were beyond these windows. Look! what's this?'

"Something was glittering in the grass at the side of the steps, and I bent down and picked it up. It was a small object of silver and black enamel. I turned the light on it, and Miss Dunne said, 'It's one of those cigarette lighters. Look, there is something written on it. It says, *Elliot from Mimi, Christmas*.'

"Just then I heard a sound that made me look up. I said, 'Listen, that's a car.' And I no more than had the words out of my mouth when I saw its headlights coming around the corner of the cut-off. I whispered, 'Stand still—don't move!' because I could see that the headlights wouldn't catch as, as we were standing far back from the road; but Miss Dunne had already pushed back into the shrubbery about the house. I stood stock-still, staring at the car, which had drawn up at the steps. It was a small car—a runabout, I think you call it———"

"Could you identify the make, Mr. Phipps?"

"No, sir; I am not familiar with automobiles. Just a small dark, ordinary-looking car. Two people got out of it—a man and a woman. They stood there for a moment on the steps, and when I saw who they were I came very close to letting out an exclamation of amazement. They went up the steps toward the front door."

"Were they conversing?"

"Yes, but in low voices. I couldn't hear anything until he said quite clearly, 'No, it's open—that's queer.' They went in, and I whispered to Miss Dunne, 'Do you know who that was? That was Stephen Bellamy, with Mrs. Patrick Ives.' Just as I spoke I saw a light go on in the hall, and a second or so later it disappeared and one sprang up behind the parlour shades. I was just starting over toward Miss Dunne when there was a crash from the parlour—a metallic kind of a crash, like breaking glass, and the light went out. I whispered, 'Come on Sally; I'm going to get out of this!' She started to come toward me, and someone inside screamed—a most appalling sound, as though the person were in mortal terror. I assure you that it froze me to the spot, though it was only the briefest interval before I again heard voices on the porch."

"Could you see the speakers, Mr. Phipps?"

"No; not until they were getting into the car. I was at this time standing just around the corner of the house, and so could not see the porch."

"Could you distinguish what they were saying?"

"Not at first; they were both speaking together, and it was very confusing. It wasn't until they appeared again in the circle of the automobile lights that I actually distinguished anything more than a few fragmentary words. Mr. Bellamy had his hand on Mrs. Ives's wrist and he was saying———"

Mr. Farr was on his feet, but much of the tiger had gone out of his spring. "Does the Court hold that what this witness claims that he heard one person say to another person is admissible evidence?"

"Of course it is admissible evidence!" Lambert's voice was frantic with anxiety. "Words spoken on the scene of the crime, within a few minutes of the crime——What about the rule of *res gestæ*?"

Mr. Farr made an unpleasant little noise. "A few minutes? That's what you call three quarters of an hour? When ejaculations made within two minutes have been ruled out after *res gestæ* has been invoked?"

"It has been interpreted to admit whole sentences at a much——"

"Gentlemen"—Judge Carver's gavel fell with an imperious crash—"you will be good enough to address the Court. Am I correct in understanding that what you desire is a ruling on the admissibility of this evidence, Mr. Farr?"

"That is all that I have requested, Your Honour."

"Very well. In view of the gravity of this situation and the very unusual character of the testimony, the Court desires to show as great a latitude as possible in respect to this evidence. It therefore rules that it may be admitted. Is there any objection?"

"No objection," said Mr. Farr, with commendable promptness, rallying a voice that sounded curiously flat. "It has been the object—and the sole object—of the state throughout this case to get at the truth. It is entirely willing to waive technicalities wherever possible in order that that end may be obtained.... No objection."

"You may proceed, Mr. Phipps."

"Mr. Bellamy was saying, 'It makes no difference how innocent we are. If it were ever known that we were in that room to-night, you couldn't get one person in the world to believe that we weren't guilty, much less twelve. I've got to get you home. Get into the car.' And they got into the car and drove off."

"And then, Mr. Phipps?"

"And then, sir, I said to Miss Dunne, 'Sally, that sounds like the voice of prophecy to me. If no one would believe that they were innocent, no one would believe that we are. Never mind the lunch box; I'm going to get you home too.'"

"You were aware that a murder had been committed?"

"A murder? Oh, not for one moment!" The quiet voice was suddenly vehement in its protest. "Not for one single moment! I thought simply that for some inexplicable reason Mr. Bellamy and Mrs. Ives had been almost suicidally indiscreet and had fortunately become aware of it at the last moment. It brought my own most culpable indiscretion all too vividly home to me, and I therefore proceeded to escort Miss Dunne back to her home, where I left her."

"Yes—exactly. Now, Mr. Phipps, just one or two questions more. On your first visit to the cottage, when you heard the woman's voice cry, 'Don't dare to touch me,' both the front and the rear of the cottage were under your observation, were they not?"

"At different times—yes."

"Would it have been possible for an automobile to be at any spot near the cottage while you were there without your attention being drawn to the fact?"

"It would have been absolutely impossible."

"It could not have stood there without your seeing it?"

"Not possibly."

"Nor have left without your hearing it?"

"Not possibly."

"Did you hear or see such a car on that visit to the cottage, Mr. Phipps?"

"I saw no car and heard none."

"Thank you, Mr. Phipps; that will be all."

"Well, not quite all," said Mr. Farr gently. Mr. Phipps shifted in his chair, his eyes under their dark brows luminous with apprehension. "Mr. Phipps, at what time did you reach your home on the night of the nineteenth of June?"

"I did not return to my home. It was closed, as my family—my wife and my two little girls—were staying at a little place on the Jersey coast called Blue Bay. I had taken a room at the Y. M. C. A."

"At what time did you return to the Y. M. C. A.?"

"I did not return there," said Mr. Phipps, in a voice so low that it was barely audible.

"You did not return to the Y. M. C. A.?"

"No. By the time that I had left Miss Dunne at her home I decided that it was too late to return to the Y. M. C. A. without rendering myself extremely conspicuous, and as I was not in the least sleepy, I decided that I would take a good walk, get a bite to eat at one of the hand-out places in the vicinity of the station, and catch the first train—the four-forty-five—to New York, where I could get a boat to Blue Bay and spend Sunday with my family."

"You mean that you did not intend to go to bed at all?"

"I did not."

"And you carried out this plan?"

"I did."

"What time did you leave Miss Dunne at her home, Mr. Phipps?"

"At about quarter to one."

"What time did you start from the Orchards for home?"

"We started from the lodge gates at a little before eleven."

"How far is it from there to Miss Dunne's home in Rosemont?"

"Just short of four miles."

"It took you an hour and three-quarters to traverse four miles?"

"Yes. The last bus from Perrytown to Rosemont goes by Orchards at about quarter to eleven. We missed it by five or six minutes and were obliged to walk."

"It took you over an hour and three quarters to walk less than four miles?"

"We walked slowly," said Mr. Phipps.

"So it would seem. Now, did anyone see you leave Miss Dunne at her door, Mr. Phipps?"

"No one."

"You simply said good-night and left her there?"

"I said good-night," said Mr. Phipps, "and left her at her door."

"You did not go inside at all?"

Mr. Phipps met the suave challenge with unflinching eyes. "I did not set my foot inside her house that night."

"Your Honour," asked Mr. Lambert, in a voice shaken with righteous wrath, "may I ask where these questions are leading?"

"The Court was about to ask the same thing.... Well, Mr. Farr?"

"I respectfully submit that it is highly essential to test the accuracy of Mr. Phipps' memory as to the rest of the events on the night which he apparently remembers in such vivid detail," said Mr. Farr smoothly. "And I assume that he is open to as rigorous an inspection as to credibility as the defense has seen fit to lavish on the state's various witnesses. If I am in error, Your Honour will correct me."

"The Court wishes to hamper you as little as possible," said Judge Carver wearily. "But it fails to see what is to be gained by pressing the question further."

"I yield to Your Honour's judgment. Did anyone that you know see you after you left Miss Dunne that night, Mr. Phipps?"

"Unfortunately, no," said Mr. Phipps, in that low, painful voice. "I saw no one until I reached my wife in Blue Bay at about eleven o'clock the following morning."

"Did you tell your wife of the events of the night?"

"No. I told my wife that I had spent the night in New York with an old classmate and gone to the theatre."

"That was not the truth, was it, Mr. Phipps?" inquired the prosecutor regretfully.

"That was a falsehood," said Mr. Phipps, his eyes on his locked hands.

Mr. Farr waited a moment to permit this indubitable fact to sink in. When he spoke again, his voice was brisker than it had been in some time. "How did you recognize Mr. Bellamy, and Mrs. Ives, Mr. Phipps?"

"They were standing in the circle of light cast by their headlights. I could see them very distinctly."

"No, I mean where had you seen them before."

"Oh, I had seen them quite frequently before. Mrs. Ives I saw often when she was Miss Thorne and I was tutoring at Orchards, and I had seen her several times since as well. Indeed, I had been in her own house on two occasions in regard to some welfare work that the school was backing."

"You were aware then that Mrs. Ives was a very wealthy woman?"

Mr. Phipps looked at him wonderingly. "Aware? I knew of course that——"

"Your Honour, I object to that question as totally improper."

"Objection sustained," said Judge Carver, eyeing the prosecutor with some austerity.

"And as to Mr. Bellamy?" inquired that gentleman blandly.

"Mr. Bellamy was a director of our school board," said Mr. Phipps. "I was in the habit of seeing him almost weekly, so I naturally recognized him."

"Oh, you knew Mr. Bellamy, too, did you?" Mr. Farr's voice was encouragement itself.

"I knew him—not intimately, you understand, but well enough to admire him as deeply as did all who came in contact with him."

"He was deeply admired by all the members of the board?"

"Undoubtedly."

"It will do you no damage with the board, then, when they learn of your testimony in this case?"

"Your Honour——"

"Please," said Mr. Phipps quietly, "I should like to answer that. Whether it would do me damage or not is slightly academic, as I have already handed in my resignation as principal of the Eastern High School. I do not intend to return to Rosemont; my wife, my children, and I are leaving for Ohio to-morrow."

"You have resigned your position? When?"

"Last night. My wife agreed with me that my usefulness here would probably be seriously impaired after I had testified."

"You are a wealthy man, Mr. Phipps?"

"On the contrary, I am a poor man."

"Yet you are able to resign your position and go West as a man of independent means?"

"Are you asking me whether I have been bribed, Mr. Farr?" asked Mr. Phipps gravely.

"I am asking you nothing of the kind. I am simply——"

"Your Honour! Your Honour!"

"Because if you are," continued Mr. Phipps clearly over the imperious thunder of the gavel, "I should like to ask you what sum you yourself would consider sufficient to reimburse you for the loss of your private happiness, your personal reputation, and your public career?"

"I ask that that reply be stricken from the record, Your Honour!"

The white savagery of Mr. Farr's face was not an agreeable sight.

"Both your question and the witness's reply may be so stricken," said Judge Carver sternly. "They were equally improper. You may proceed, Mr. Farr."

Mr. Farr, by a truly Herculean effort, managed to reduce both voice and countenance to a semblance better suited to so ardent a seeker for truth. "You wish us to believe then, Mr. Phipps, that on the night of the nineteenth of June, for the first time in over ten years, you went to the gardener's cottage at Orchards at the precise moment that enabled you to recognize Susan Ives and Stephen Bellamy standing in the circle of their automobile lights?"

"That is exactly what I wish you to believe," said Mr. Phipps steadily. "It is the truth."

Mr. Farr bestowed on him a long look in which irony, skepticism, and contemptuous pity were neatly blended. "No further questions," he said briefly. "Call Miss Dunne."

"Miss Sally Dunne!"

Miss Sally Dunne came quickly, so tall, so brave, so young and pale in her blue serge dress with its neat little white collar and cuffs, that more than one person in the dark courtroom caught themselves wondering with a catch at the heart how long it had been since she had coiled those smooth brown braids over her ears and smoothed the hair ribbons out for the last time. She was not pretty. She had a sad little heart-shaped face and widely spaced hazel eyes, candid and trustful. These she turned on Mr. Lambert, and steadied her lips, which were trembling.

"Miss Dunne, I just want you to tell us one or two things. You heard Mr. Phipps' testimony?"

"Yes, sir." A child's voice, clear as water, troubled and innocent.

"You were with him on the night of June nineteenth from eight until one or thereabouts?"

"Yes, sir."

"Was his testimony as to what happened accurate?"

"Oh, yes, indeed, sir. Mr. Phipps," said the little voice proudly, "has a very wonderful memory."

"You were with him on his first visit to the cottage?"

"I was with him every minute of the evening."

"You saw no car near the cottage?"

"There wasn't any car there," said Miss Dunne.

"You saw Mr. Bellamy and Mrs. Ives on your second visit to the cottage, some time after ten o'clock?"

"Just when they came out," said Miss Dunne conscientiously. "I didn't see their faces when they went in."

"Did you hear them speak?"

"I heard Mr. Bellamy say, 'Sue, no matter how innocent we are, we'll never get one person to believe that we aren't guilty if they know that we were in that room, much less twelve. I've got to get you home."

"Yes. Are you engaged to be married, Miss Dunne?"

243

"I don't know," said Miss Dunne simply. "I was engaged, but my—my fiancé didn't want me to testify in this case. You see, he's studying for the ministry. I think perhaps that he doesn't consider that he's engaged any longer."

"Were you yourself anxious to testify?"

"I was anxious to do what Mr. Phipps thought was right for us to do," said Miss Dunne. "But I am afraid that I was not very brave about wanting to testify."

"Were you in the habit of going on these—these picnic expeditions with Mr. Phipps?"

"Oh, no, sir. We had taken only two or three quite short little walks—after school, you know. He was helping me with my English literature because I wanted to be a writer. The party that night was a farewell party."

"A farewell party?"

"Yes. School had closed on Friday, and we—Mr. Phipps thought that perhaps it would be better if we didn't see each other any more. It was my fault that we went to Orchards that night. It was all my fault," explained Miss Dunne carefully in her small, clear voice.

"Your fault?"

"Yes. You see, Mr. Phipps thought that I was very romantic indeed, and that I was getting too fond of him, so that we had better stop seeing each other. I am very romantic," said Sally Dunne gravely, "and I was getting too fond of him."

"How often have you seen Mr. Phipps since that evening, Miss Dunne?"

"Twice; once on the Tuesday following the—the murder—only for about five minutes in the park. I begged him not to say anything about our having been there unless it was absolutely necessary. And again last night when he said that it was necessary."

"Yes, exactly. Thank you, Miss Dunne; that will be all. Cross-examine."

"It was not the state that is responsible for the pitiless publicity to which this unfortunate young girl has been exposed," said Mr. Farr, looking so virtuous that one sought apprehensively for the halo. "And it is not the state that proposes to prolong it. I ask no question."

Judge Carver said, in answer to the look of blank bewilderment in the clear eyes, "That will be all. You may step down, Miss Dunne."

The red-headed girl, who thought that nothing in the world could surprise her any more, felt herself engulfed in amazement.

"Well, but what did he let her go for?"

"He let her go," explained the reporter judicially, "because he's the wiliest old fox in Bellechester County. He knows perfectly well that while he has a fair sporting chance of instilling the suspicion in the twelve essential heads that Mr. Phipps is a libertine and a bribe taker and a perjurer, he hasn't the chance of the proverbial snowball to make them believe that Sally Dunne could speak anything but the truth to save her life or her soul. That child could make the tales of Munchausen sound like the eternal verities. The quicker he can get her off the stand, the more chance he has of saving his case."

"Save it? How can he save it?"

"Well, that's probably what he'd like to know. As the prosecutor is supposed to be a seeker after truth, rather than a bloodhound after blood, he has rather a tough row to hoe. And here's where he starts hoeing it."

"The state has no comment to make on the testimony that you have just heard," Mr. Farr was saying to the twelve jurors with an expression of truly exalted detachment, "other than to ask you to remember that, after all, these two last witnesses are no more than human beings, subject to the errors, the frailties, and the weaknesses of other human beings. If you will bear that in mind in weighing their evidence, I do not feel that it will be necessary to add one other word."

Judge Carver eyed him thoughtfully for a moment over the glasses that he had adjusted to his fine nose. Then, with a perfunctory rap of his gavel, he turned to the papers in his hand.

"Gentlemen of the jury, the long and anxious inquiry in which we have been engaged is drawing to a close, and it now becomes my duty to address you. It has been, however painful, of a most absorbing interest, and it has undoubtedly engaged the closest attention of every one of you. You will not regret the strain that that attention has placed upon you when it shortly becomes your task to weigh the evidence that has been put before you.

"At the very outset of my charge I desire to make several things quite clear. You and you alone are the sole judges of fact. Any comment that the Court may make as to the weight or value of any features of the evidence is merely his way of suggestion, and is in no possible way binding on the jury. Nor do statements made by counsel as to the innocence or guilt of the defendants, or as to any other conclusions or inferences drawn by them, prove anything whatever or have any effect as evidence.

"It is not necessary for any person accused in a court in this county to prove that he is not guilty. It devolves on the state to prove that he is. If you have a reasonable doubt as to whether the state has proved his guilt, it is your duty to return a verdict of not guilty. That is the law of the land.

"Now, having a reasonable doubt does not mean that by some far-fetched and fantastic hypothesis you can arrive at the conclusion of not guilty because any other conclusion is painful and distasteful and abhorrent to you. There is hardly anything that an ingenious mind cannot bring itself to doubt, granted sufficient industry and application. A reasonable doubt is not one that you would conjure up in the middle of a dark, sleepless, and troubled night, but one that would lead you to say naturally when you went about your business in clear daylight, 'Well, I can't quite make up my mind about the real facts behind that proposition.' Not beyond any possible doubt—beyond a reasonable doubt—bear that in mind.

"To convict either of the defendants under this indictment, the state must prove to your satisfaction beyond reasonable doubt:

"First, that Madeleine Bellamy is dead and was murdered.

"Second, that this murder took place in Bellechester County.

"And third, that such defendant either committed that murder by actually perpetrating the killing or by participating therein as a principal.

"That Madeleine Bellamy is dead is perfectly clear. That she was murdered has not been controverted by either the state or the defense. That the murder took place in Bellechester County is not in dispute. The only actual problem that confronts you is the third one: Did Mrs. Ives and Mr. Bellamy participate in the murder of this unfortunate girl?

"The state tells you that they did, and in support of that statement they advance the following facts:

"They claim that on Saturday the nineteenth of June, 1926, at about five o'clock in the afternoon, Mrs. Ives received information from Mr. Elliot Farwell as to relations between Mr. Ives and Mrs. Bellamy that affected her so violently and painfully that she thereupon——"

"I can't stand hearing it all over again," remarked the red-headed girl in a small ominous whisper. "I can't stand it, I tell you! If he starts telling us again that Sue Ives went home and called up Stephen Bellamy, I'll stand up and scream so that they'll hear me in Philadelphia. I'll——"

"Look here, you'd better get out of here," said the reporter in tones of unfeigned alarm. "Tell you what you do. You crawl out very quietly to that side door where the fat officer with the sandy moustache is standing. He's a good guy, and you tell him that I told you that he'd let you out before you fainted all over the place. You can sit on the stairs leading to the third floor; I'll get word to you when he's through with the evidence, and you can crawl back the same way."

"All right," said the red-headed girl feebly.

The reporter glanced cautiously about. "It'll help if you can go both ways on four paws; the judge doesn't like to think that he's boring any member of the press, and if he sees one of us escaping, he's liable to call out the machine guns. Take long, deep breaths and pretend that it's day after to-morrow."

The red-headed girl gave him a look of dazed scorn and moved toward the left-hand door at a gait that came as close to being on four paws as was compatible with the dignity of the press. The fat officer gave one alarmed look at her small, wan face and hastily opened the door. She crawled through it, discovered the stairs, mounted them obediently and sank somewhat precipitately to rest on the sixth one from the top.

Down below, she could hear the mob outside of the great centre doors, shuffling and grunting and yapping——Ugh! Ugh! She shuddered and propped up her elbows on her knees and her head on her hands, and closed her eyes and closed her ears and breathed deeply and fervently.

"If ever I go to a murder trial again——What happens to you when you don't sleep for a week?... If ever—I—go——"

Someone was saying, "Hey!" It was a small, freckled boy in a messenger's cap, and he had evidently been saying it for some time, as his voice had a distinctly crescendo quality. He extended one of the familiar telegraph blanks and vanished. The red-headed girl read it solemnly, trying to look very wide awake and intelligent, as is the wont of those abruptly wakened.

The telegram said: "Come home. All is forgiven, and he's through with the evidence. It's going to the jury in a split second. Hurry!"

She hurried. Quite suddenly she felt extraordinarily wide awake and amazingly alert and frantically excited. She was a reporter—she was at a murder trial—they were going to consider the verdict. She flew down the white marble stairs and around the first corner and through the crack of the door proffered by the startled guard. There were wings at her heels and vine leaves in her hair. She felt like a giant refreshed—that was it, a giant....

The reporter eyed her with his mouth open. "Well, for heaven's sake, what's happened to you?"

"Everything's all right, isn't it?" she demanded feverishly. "They won't be out long, will they? There's nothing——" A familiar voice fell ominously on her ears and she jerked incredulous eyes toward the throne of justice. "Oh, he's still talking! You said he was through—you did! You said——"

"I said through with the evidence, and so he is. This is just a back fire. If you'll keep quiet a minute you'll see."

"I wish simply, therefore, to remind you," the weary voice was saying, "that however unusual, arresting and dramatic the circumstances surrounding the testimony of these last two witnesses may have been, you should approach this evidence in precisely the same spirit that you approach all the other evidence that has been placed before you. It should be submitted to exactly the same tests of credibility that you apply to every word that has been uttered before you—no more and no less.

"One more word and I have done. The degrees of murder I have defined for you. You will govern your verdict accordingly. The sentence is not your concern; that lies with the Court. It is your duty, and your sole duty, to decide whether Susan Ives and Stephen Bellamy are either or both of them guilty of the murder of Madeleine Bellamy. I am convinced that you will perform that duty faithfully. Gentlemen, you may consider your verdict."

Slowly and stiffly the twelve men rose to their feet and stood staring about them uncertainly, as though loath to be about their business.

"If you desire further instruction as to any point that is not quite clear to you," said Judge Carver gravely, "I may be reached in my room here. Any of the exhibits that you desire to see will be put at your disposal. You may retire, gentlemen."

They shuffled solemnly out through the little door to the right of the witness, the small, beady-eyed bailiff with the mutton-chop whiskers and the anxious frown trotting close at their heels. The door closed behind them with a gentle, ominous finality, and someone in the courtroom sighed—loudly, uncontrollably—a prophecy of the coming intolerable suspense.

The red-headed girl wrung her hands together in a despairing effort to warm them. Twelve men—twelve ordinary, everyday men, whose faces looked heavy and stupid with strain and fatigue ... She pressed her hands together harder and turned a pale face toward the other door.

Susan Ives and Stephen Bellamy had just reached it; they lingered there for a moment to smile gravely and reassuringly at the hovering Lambert, and then were gone, as quietly as though they were about to walk down the steps to waiting cars instead of to a black hell of uncertainty and suspense.

Those in the courtroom still sat breathlessly silent, held in check by Judge Carver's stern eye. After a moment he, too, rose; for a moment, it seemed that all the room was filled with the rustle of his black silk robes, and then he, too, was gone, with decorum following hard on his heels.

In less than thirty seconds, the quiet, orderly room was transformed into something rather less sedate than the careless excitement of a Saturday-afternoon crowd at a ball park—psychologically they were reduced to shirt sleeves and straw hats tilted well back on their heads. The red-headed girl stared at them with round, appalled eyes.

Just behind her they were forming a pool. Someone with a squeaky voice was betting that they would be back in twenty minutes; someone with an Oxford accent was betting that they'd take two hours; a girl's pleasant tones offered five to one that it would be a hung jury. Large red apples were materializing, the smoke of a hundred cigarettes filled the air, and rumour's voice was loud in the land:

"Listen, did you hear about Melanie Cordier? Someone telephoned that she'd collapsed at the inn in Rosemont and confessed that Platz had done it, and about one o'clock this morning every taxicab in Redfield was skidding around corners to get there first. And she hadn't been there since last Friday, let alone collapsed!"

"Well, you wouldn't get me out of my bed at one in the morning to hear Cal Coolidge say he'd done it."

"Did you hear the row that Irish landlady was setting up about a state witness taking her seat? Oh, boy, what an eye that lady's got! It sure would tame a wildcat!"

"Anyone want to bet ten to one that they'll be out all night?"

The voice of an officer of the court said loudly and authoritatively, "No smoking in here! No smoking, please!"

There was a temporary lull, and a perfunctory and irritable tapping of cigarettes against chair arms. The clock over the courtroom door said four.

"Have some chocolate?" inquired the reporter solicitously. The red-headed girl shuddered. "Well, but, my good child, you haven't had a mouthful of lunch, and if you aren't careful you won't have a mouthful of dinner either. Lord knows how long that crew will be in there."

"How long?" inquired the red-headed girl fiercely. "Why, for heaven's sake, should they be long? Why, for heaven's sake, can't they come out of there now and say, 'Not guilty'?"

"Well, there's a good old-fashioned custom that they're supposed to weigh the evidence; they may be celebrating that."

"What have they to weigh? They heard Mr. Phipps, didn't they?"

"They did indeed. And what they may well spend the next twenty-four hours debating is whether they consider Mr. Phipps a long-suffering martyr or a well-paid liar."

"Oh, go away—go away! I can't bear you!"

"You can't bear me?" inquired the reporter incredulously. "Me?"

"No—yes—never mind. Go away; you say perfectly horrible things."

"Not as horrible as you do," said the reporter. "Can't bear me, indeed! I didn't say that I thought that Phipps was a liar. As a matter of fact, I thought he was as nice a guy as I ever saw in my life, poor devil, even if he did read the *Idylls of the King* aloud.... Can't bear me!"

"I can't bear anything," said the red-headed girl despairingly. "Go away!"

After he had gone, she had a sudden overwhelming impulse to dash after him and beg him to take her with him, anywhere he went—everywhere—always. She was still contemplating the impulse with horrified amazement when the girl from the Louisville paper who sat three seats down from her leaned forward. She was a nice, cynical, sensible-looking girl, but for the moment she was a little pale.

"There's not a possibility that they could return a verdict of guilty, is there?" she inquired in a carefully detached voice.

"Oh, juries!" said the red-headed girl drearily. "They can do anything. They're just plain, average, everyday, walking-around people, and average, everyday people can do anything in the world. That's why we have murders and murder trials."

The girl from the Louisville paper stood up abruptly. "I think I'll get a little air," she said, and added in a somewhat apologetic voice, "It's my first murder trial."

"It's my last," said the red-headed girl grimly.

The officer of the court had disappeared, and all about her there were rising once more the little blue coils of smoke—incense on the altars of relaxation. Why didn't he come back?... The clock over the courtroom door said five.

On the courtroom floor there was a mounting tide of newspapers, telegraph blanks, leaves from notebooks and ruled pads—many nervous hands had made light work, tearing, crumpling, and crushing their destructive way through the implements of their trade. There was an empty pop bottle just by the rail, apple cores and banana skins were everywhere, clouds of smoke, fragments of buns, a high, nervous murmur of voices; a picnic ground on the fifth of July would have presented a more appetising appearance. Over all was a steady roar of voices, and one higher than the rest, lamenting: "Over two hours—that's a hung jury as sure as shooting! I might just as well kiss that ten dollars good-bye here and now. Got a light, Larry?"

The door to the left of the witness box opened abruptly, and for a moment Judge Carver stood framed in it, tall and stern in his black robes. Under his accusing eye, apples and cigarettes were suddenly as unobtrusive as the skin on a chameleon, and voices fell to silence. He stood staring at them fixedly for a moment and then withdrew as abruptly as he had come. While you could have counted ten, silence hung heavy; then once more the smoke and the voices rose and fell.... The clock over the courtroom door said six.

The red-headed girl moved an aimless pencil across an empty pad with unsteady fingers. There were quite a lot of empty seats. What were those twelve men doing now? Weighing the evidence? Well, but how did you weigh evidence? What was important and what wasn't?... And suddenly she was back in the only courtroom that she could remember clearly—the one in Alice in Wonderland, and the King was saying proudly, "Well, that's very important." "Unimportant, Your Majesty means." And she could hear the poor little King trying it over to himself to see which sounded the best. "Important—unimportant—important——" There was the lamp—and the date on the letters—and the note that nobody had found—unimportant—important.... There was a juryman called Bill the Lizard. She remembered that he had dipped his tail in ink and had written down all the hours and dates in the case on his slate, industriously adding them up and reducing the grand total to pounds, shillings, and pence. Perhaps that was the safest way, after all.

June 19, 1926, and May 8, 1916.... A boy came running down the aisle with a basketful of sandwiches and chewing gum; there was another one with pink editions of the evening papers; it was exactly like a ball game or a circus.... Where was he? Wasn't he coming back at all?... Outside the snow was falling; you could see it white against the black windowpanes, and all the lights in the courtroom were blazing.... Well, but where was he?

A voice from somewhere just behind her said ominously, "Can't bear me, can't she? I'll learn her!"

The red-headed girl screwed around in her seat. He was leaning over the back of the chair next to her with a curious expression on his not unagreeable countenance.

The red-headed girl said in a small, abject voice that shocked her profoundly, "Don't go away—don't go away again."

The reporter, looking startlingly pale under the glaring lights, remarked casually, "I don't believe that I'll marry you after all."

The red-headed girl could feel herself go first very white and then very red and then very white again. She could hear her heart pounding just behind her ears. In a voice even more casual than the reporter's she inquired, "After all what?"

"After all your nonsense," said the reporter severely.

The red-headed girl said in a voice so small and abject that it was practically inaudible, "Please do!"

"What are we doing in here?" inquired the reporter in a loud clear voice. "What are we doing in a courtroom at a murder trial, with two hundred and fifty-four people watching us? Where's a beach? Where's an apple orchard? Where's a moonlit garden with a nightingale? You get up and put your things on and come out of this place."

The red-headed girl rose docilely to her feet. After all, what were they doing there? What was a murder trial or verdict or a newspaper story compared to——She halted, riveted with amazement.

Suddenly, mysteriously, incredibly, the courtroom was all in motion. No one had crossed a threshold, no one had raised a voice; but as surely as though they had been tossed out of their seats by some gigantic hand, the crowd was in flight. One stampede toward the door from the occupants of the seats, another stampede from the occupants of the seats toward the door, a hundred voices calling, regardless of law and order.

"Keep that 'phone line open!"

"They're coming!"

"Dorothy! Dorothy!"

"Have Stan take the board!"

"Where's Larry? Larry!"

"Get Red—get Red, for God's sake!"

"That's my chair—snap out of it, will you?"

"Watch for that flash—Bill's going to signal."

"Dorothy!"

"Get to that door!"

And silence as sudden as the tumult. Through the left-hand door were coming two quiet, familiar figures, and through the right-hand door one robed in black. The clock over the courthouse door stood at a quarter to seven.

"Is there an officer at that door?" Judge Carver's voice was harsh with anger. "Officer, take that door. No one out of it or in it until the verdict has been delivered."

Despairing eyes exchanged frantic glances. Well, but what about the last edition? They're holding the presses until seven. What about the last edition? Hurry, hurry!

But the ambassador of the majestic law was quite unhurried. "I have a few words to say to the occupants of this courtroom. If at the conclusion of the verdict there is a demonstration of any kind whatsoever, the offenders will be brought before me and promptly dealt with as being in contempt of court. Officers, hold the doors."

And through another door—the little one behind the seat of justice—twelve tired men were filing, gaunt, solemn eyed, awkward—the farmers, merchants, and salesmen who held in their awkward hands the terrible power of life and death. The red-headed girl clutched the solid, tweed-covered arm beside her as though she were drowning.

There they stood in a neat semicircle under the merciless glare of the lights, their upturned faces white and spent.

"Gentlemen of the jury, have you agreed on a verdict?"

A deep-voiced chorus answered solemnly, "We have."

"Prisoner, look upon the jury. Jury, look upon the prisoners."

Unflinching and inscrutable, the white faces obeyed the grave voice.

"Foreman, how do you find as to Stephen Bellamy, guilty or not guilty?"

"Not guilty."

A tremor went through the court and was stilled.

"How do you find as to Susan Ives?"

"Not guilty."

For a moment no one moved, no one stirred, no one breathed. And then, abruptly, the members of the fourth estate forgot the majesty of law and remembered the majesty of the press. Three minutes to seven—three minutes to make the last edition! The mad rush for the doors was stoutly halted by the zealous guardians, who clung devoutly to their posts, and the air was rent with stentorian shouts: "Sit down there!" "Keep quiet!" "Order! Order!" "Take your hands off of me!"—and the thunder of Judge Carver's gavel.

And caught once more between the thunder of the press and the law, two stood oblivious of it. Stephen Bellamy's haunted face was turned steadfastly toward the little door beyond which lay freedom, but Susan Ives had turned away from it. Her eyes were on a black head bent low in the corner by the window, and at the look in them, so fearless, so valiant, and so eager, the red-headed girl found suddenly that she was weeping, shamelessly and desperately, into something that smelt of tweed—and tobacco—and heaven.... The clock over the door said seven. The Bellamy trial was over.

The judge came into the little room that served him as office in the courthouse with a step lighter than had crossed its threshold for many days. It was a good room; the dark panelling went straight up to the ceiling; there were two wide windows and two deep chairs and a great shining desk piled high with books and papers. Against the walls rose row upon row of warm, pleasant-coloured books, and over the door hung a great engraving of Justice in her flowing robes of white, smiling gravely down at the bandage in her hands that man has seen fit to place over her eyes. Across the room from her, between the two windows, his robes flowing black, sat John Marshall, that great gentleman, his dark eyes eternally fixed on hers, as though they shared some secret understanding.

Judge Carver looked from one to the other a little anxiously as he came in, and they smiled back at him reassuringly. For thirty years the three of them had been old friends.

He crossed to the desk with a suddenly quickened step. The lamps were lighted, and reflected in its top as in a mirror he could see the short, stubby, nut-coloured pipe, the huge brass bowl into which a giant might have spilled his ashes, the capacious box of matches yawning agreeably in his tired face. The black robes were heavy on his shoulders, and he lifted an impatient hand to them, when he paused, arrested by the sight of the central stack of papers.

"Gentlemen of the jury, the long and anxious inquiry in which we have been engaged——"

Now just what was it that he'd said to them about a principal and an accessory before the fact being one and the same in a murder case? Of course, as a practical matter, that was quite accurate. Still—He ran through the papers with skilled fingers—there! "An accessory after the fact is one who——"

There was a knock on the door and he lifted an irritated voice: "Come in!"

The door opened cautiously, and under the smiling Justice in her flowing robes a little boy was standing, freckle-faced, blue-eyed, black-haired, in the rusty green of the messenger's uniform. Behind him the judge could see the worried face of old Martin, the clerk of the court.

"I couldn't do anything with him at all, Your Honour. I told him you were busy, and I told him you were engaged, and I told him you'd given positive orders not to be disturbed, and all he'd say was, 'I swore I'd give it into his hands, and into his hands it goes, if I stay in this place until the moon goes down and the sun comes up.'"

"And that's what I promised," said the small creature at the door in a squeak of terrified obstinacy. "And that's what I'll do. No matter what——"

"All right, all right, put it down there and be off." The judge's voice was not too long-suffering.

"Into his hands is what I said, and into his hands———"

The judge stretched out one fine lean hand with a smile that warmed his cold face like a fire. The other hand went to his pocket. "Here, if you keep on being an honourable nuisance, you may have a career ahead of you. Good-night, Martin; show the young gentleman to the door. If any one else disturbs me to-night, he's fired."

"Oh, by all means, Your Honour. Good-night, Your Honour."

The door closed reverently, and His Honour stood staring absently down at the letter in his hand, the smile still in his eyes. A fat, a plethoric, an apoplectic letter; three red seals on the flap of the envelope flaunted themselves at him importantly. He turned it over carelessly. The clear, delicate, vigorous writing greeted him like a challenge:

> "Judge Carver.
>
> "To be delivered to him personally without fail."

Very impressive! He tore open the sealed flap with irreverent fingers and shook the contents out on to the desk. Good Lord, it was a three-volume novel! Page after page of that fine writing, precise and accurate as print. He lifted it curiously, and something fluttered out and lay staring up at him from the table. A piece of blue paper, flimsy, creased and soiled, the round childish writing sprawled recklessly across its battered surface:

> 10 A. M., June 19th.

> Pat, I'll catch either the eight or eight-thirty bus———

Very slowly, very carefully, he picked it up, the smile dying in his incredulous eyes.

> Pat, I'll catch either the eight or eight-thirty bus. That will get me to the cottage before nine, at the latest. I'll wait there until half past. You can make any excuse that you want to Sue, but get there—and be sure that you bring what you promised. I think you realize as well as I do that there's no use talking any more. We're a long way beyond words, and from now on we'll confine ourselves to deeds. It's absurd to think that Steve will suspect anything. I can fool him absolutely, and once we settle the details to-night, we can get off any moment that we decide on. California! Oh, Pat, I can't wait! And when you realize how happy we're going to be, you won't have any regrets either. You always did say that you wanted me to be happy—remember?

Judge Carver pushed the deep chair closer to the lamp and sat down in it heavily, pulling the closely written pages toward him. He looked old and tired.

"Midnight.

"MY DEAR JUDGE CARVER:

"I am fully aware of the fact that I am doing a cowardly thing in writing you this letter. It is simply an attempt on my part to shift my own burden to another's shoulders, and my shoulders should surely be sufficiently used to burdens by this time. But this one is of so strange, awkward, and terrible a shape that I must get rid of it at any cost to my pride or sense of fair play— or to your peace of mind. If the verdict to-morrow is guilty, of course, I'll not send the letter, but simply turn the facts over to the prosecutor. I am spending to-night writing you this in case it is not guilty.

"It was I who killed Madeleine Bellamy. It seems simply incredible to me that everyone should not have guessed it long before now.

"Kathleen Page, Melanie Cordier, Laura Roberts, Patrick, Sue, I myself—we told you so over and over again. That singularly obnoxious and alert Mr. Farr—is it possible that he has never suspected—not even when I explained to him that at ten o'clock I was in the flower room, washing off my hands? And yet a few minutes later he was asking me if there wasn't a sink in the pantry where my poor Sue might have cleansed her own hands of Mimi Bellamy's blood—and every face in the court was sick with the horror of that thought.

"We told you everything, and no one even listened.

"Who knew about the path across the meadow to the summerhouse? I, not Sue. Who could see the study window clearly from the rose garden? I, not Sue. Who had that hour and a half between 8:30 and ten absolutely alone and unobserved? I, not Sue. Who had every motive that was ascribed to Sue multiplied ten times over? I, who had known poverty beside which Sue's years in New York were a gay adventure; who had not only a child to fight for, but that child's children; who, after a lifetime of grim nightmare, had found paradise; and who saw coming to thrust me out from that paradise not an angel with a flaming sword, but a little empty-headed, empty-hearted chit,

256

cheap, mercenary, and implacable, as only the empty-headed can be.

"I know, Judge Carver, that the burden that I am trying to shift to your shoulders should be heaviest of all with the weight of remorse; and there is in it, I can swear to you, enough remorse to bow stronger shoulders than either yours or mine—but none, none for the death of Mimi Bellamy.

"Remorse for these past weeks has eaten me to the bone—for the shame and terror and peril that I have brought to my children, for the sorrow and menace that I have brought to that gentle soul, Stephen Bellamy—even for the death of poor Elliot Farwell; that was my doing, too, I think. I do not shirk it.

"I am rather an old-fashioned person. I believe in hell, and I believe that I shall probably go there because I killed Mimi Bellamy and because I'm not sorry for it; but the hell that I've been living through every day and every night since she died is not one shadow darker because it was I who gave her the little push that sped her from one world to another.

"When that unpleasant Mr. Farr was invoking the vengeance of heaven and earth on the fiend who had stopped forever the silver music of the dead girl's laughter, I remembered that the last time that she laughed it had been at an old woman on her knees begging for the happiness and safety of two babies—and the world did not seem to me to have lost much when that laughter ceased. That is frightful, isn't it? But that is true.

"I'll try to go back so that you can understand exactly what happened; then you can tell better, perhaps, what I should do and what you should do with me. First of all, I must go very far back, indeed—back thirty years, to a manufacturing town in northern New York.

"Thirty-one years ago last June, my husband left me with the nineteen-year-old daughter of my Norwegian landlady. You couldn't exactly blame him, of course. Trudie was as pretty as the girl on the cover of the most expensive candy box you ever saw, and as unscrupulous as Messalina—and I wasn't either.

"I was much too busy being sick and miserable and cross and sorry for myself to be anything else at all, so he walked off with Trudie and nineteen dollars and fifty cents out of the teapot and left me with a six-weeks-old baby and a gold wedding ring that wasn't exactly gold. And my landlady wouldn't give me even one day's grace rent free, because she was naturally a little put out by her daughter's unceremonious departure, and quite frankly held me to blame for it, as she said a girl who couldn't hold her own man wasn't likely worth her board and keep.

"So, just like the lady in the bad melodramas, I wrapped my baby up in a shawl and started out to find work at the factory. Of course I didn't find it. It was a slack season at the factories, and I looked like a sick little scarecrow, and I hadn't even money for car fare. I spent the first evening of my career as a breadwinner begging for pennies on the more prominent street corners. It's one way to get bread.

"In the next twenty years I tried a great many other ways of getting it, including, on two occasions, stealing it. But that was only the first year; after that we always had bread, though often there wasn't enough of it, and generally it was stale, and frequently there wasn't anything to put on it.

"When people talk about the fear of poverty, I wonder whether they have the remotest idea of what they're talking about. I wasn't rich when I married Dan; I was the daughter of a not oversuccessful lawyer, and I thought that we were quite poor, because often we went through periods where pot roast instead of chicken played a prominent part in the family diet, and my best dress had to be of tarlatan instead of taffeta, and I possessed only two pairs of kid gloves that reached to my elbow, and one that reached to my shoulder.

"I was very, very sorry for myself during those periods, and used to go around with faintly pink eyes and a strong sense of martyrdom. I wasn't at all a noble character. I liked going to cotillions at night and staying in bed in the morning, and wringing terrified proposals from callow young men who were completely undone by the combination of moonlight and mandolin playing. Besides playing the mandolin, I could make two kinds of candy and feather-stitch quite well and dance the lancers better than anyone in town—and I knew most of Lucile by heart. Thus lavishly equipped for the exigencies of holy matrimony, I proceeded to elope with Mr. Daniel Ives.

"I won't bother you much with Dan. He was the leading man in a stock company that came to our town, and three weeks after he saw me sitting worshipping in the front row we decided that life without each other would be an empty farce and shook the dust of that town from our heels forever. It was very, very romantic, indeed, for the first six days—and after that it wasn't so romantic.

"Because I, who could feather-stitch so nicely, was a bad cook and a bad manager and a bad housewife and a bad sport—a bad wife, in short. I wasn't precisely happy, and I thought that it was perfectly safe to be all those things, because it simply never entered my head that one human being could get so tired of another human being that he could quietly walk out and leave her to starve to death. And I was as wrong about that, as I'd been about everything else.

"I'm telling you all this not to excuse myself, but simply to explain, so that you will understand a little, perhaps, what sent my feet hurrying across the meadow path, what brought them back to the flower room at ten o'clock that night. I think that two people went to meet Madeleine Bellamy in the cottage that night—a nice, well-behaved little white-headed lady and the wilful, spoiled, terrified girl that the nice old lady thought that she had killed thirty years ago. It's only fair to you that I should explain that, because of what I'm going to ask you to decide. And it is only fair to myself that I should say this.

"For twenty years I was too cold, too hot, too tired and sick and faint ever to be really comfortable for one moment. And I won't pretend that I looked forward with equanimity to surrendering one single comfort or luxury that had finally come to make life beautiful and gracious. But that wasn't why I killed Madeleine Bellamy. I ask you to believe that.

"The real terror of poverty isn't that we ourselves suffer. It is that we are absolutely and utterly powerless to lift one finger to protect and defend those who are dearest to us in the world. Judge Carver, when Pat was sick when he was a baby I didn't have enough money to get a doctor for him; I didn't have enough money to get medicine. When I went to work I had to leave him with people who were vile and filthy and debased in body and soul, because they were the only people that I could afford to leave him with.

"Once when I came home I couldn't wake him up, and the woman who was with him was terrified into telling me that he'd been crying so dreadfully that she'd given him some stuff that a Hungarian woman on the next floor said was fine for crying babies. I carried him and the bottle with the stuff in it ten blocks to a drug store—and they told me that it had opium in it. She'd given him half the bottle—to my Pat. And another time the woman with him got drunk and——But I can't talk about that, not even to make you understand. He never had any toys in his life but some tin cans and empty spools and pieces of string. He never had anything but me.

"And I swore to myself that as long as he had me he should have everything. I would be beauty to him, and peace and gentleness and graciousness and gaiety and strength. I wasn't beautiful or peaceful or gentle or gracious or gay or strong, but I made myself all those things for him. That isn't vanity—that's the truth. I swore that he should never see me shed one tear, that he should never hear me lift my voice in anger, that he should never see me tremble before anything that fate should hold in store for either of us. He never did—no, truly, he never did. That was all that I could give him, but I did give him that.

"It took me seventeen years to save up enough railway fare to get out of that town. Then I came to Rosemont. A nice woman that I did some sewing for in the town had a sister in Rosemont. She told me that it was a lovely place and that she thought that there was a good opening there for some work, and that her sister was looking for boarders. So I took the few dollars that I'd saved and went, and you know the rest.

"Of course there are some things that you don't know—you don't know how brave and gay and gentle Pat has always been to me; you don't know how happy we all were in the flat in New York, after he married Sue and the babies came. Sue helped me with the housekeeping, and Sue did some secretarial work at the university, and Pat did anything that turned up, and did it splendidly. We always had plenty to eat, and it was really clean and sunny, and we were all perfectly healthy and happy. Only, Sue never did talk about it much, because she is a very reserved child, in any case, and in this case she was afraid that it might seem a reflection on the Thornes that she had to live in a little walk-up flat in the Bronx, with no servants and pretty plain living.

"And Mr. Lambert was nervous about bringing out anything about it in direct examination for fear that in cross-examination Mr. Farr would twist things around to make it look as though Sue had undergone the tortures of the damned. Of course, we didn't have much, but we had enough to make it seem a luxurious and care-free existence in comparison to the one that Pat and I had lived for over fifteen years.

"Those things you don't know—and one other. You don't know Polly and Pete, do you, Judge Carver?

"They are very wonderful children. I suppose that every grandmother thinks that her grandchildren are rather wonderful; but I don't just think it about them; they are. Anyone would tell you that—anyone who had ever seen them. They're the bravest, happiest, strongest little things. You could be with them for weeks and never once hear them cry. Of course, once in a very long while—if you have to scold them, for instance— because Pete is quite sensitive; but then you almost never have to scold them, and when Pete broke his leg last winter and Dr. Chilton set it he said that he had never seen such courage in a child. And when Polly was only two years old, she walked straight out into the ocean up to her chin, and she'd have gone farther still if her father hadn't caught her up. She rides a pony better than any seven-year-old child in Rosemont, too, and she isn't five yet—not until January—and the only time that she ever fell off the pony she never even whimpered—not once.

"They are very beautiful children too. Pete is quite fair and Polly is very dark, but they both have blue eyes and very dark eyelashes. They are so brown, too, and tall. It doesn't seem possible that either of them could ever be sick or unhappy; but still, you have to be careful. Polly has been threatened twice with mastoiditis, and Pete has to have his leg massaged three times a week, because he still limps a little.

"That's why I killed Madeleine Bellamy.

"The first time I realized that there was anything between her and Pat was almost a month before the murder, some time early in May, I think. Sue had been having quite a dinner party, and I'd slipped out to the garden as usual as soon as I could get away. I decided to gather some lilacs, and I came back to the house to get the scissors from the flower room. As I passed the study I saw Pat and Mimi silhouetted against the study window; she was bending over, pretending to look at the ship he was making, but she wasn't looking at it—she was looking at Pat.

"I'd always thought that she was a scatterbrained little goose, and I had never liked her particularly; even in the old days in the village I used to worry about her sometimes. She used too much perfume and too much pink powder, and she had an empty little voice and a horrid, excited little laugh. But I thought that she was good-natured and harmless enough, when I thought about her at all, and I was about to pass on, when she said something that riveted me in my footsteps.

"She said, 'Pat, listen, did you get my note?' He said, 'Yes.' She asked, 'Are you coming?' And he said, 'I don't know. I'm not sure that I can make it.' She said, 'Of course you can make it. We can't talk here. It doesn't take ten minutes to get to the cottage. You've got to make it.' He said, 'All right, I'll be there. Look out; someone's coming.' They both of them turned around, and I could hear him calling to someone in the hall to come in and look at the ship.

"I stood there, leaning my head against the side of the house and feeling icy cold and deathly—deathly sick. It was as though I had heard Dan calling to me across thirty years.

"From that moment until this one I have never known one happy hour, one happy moment, one happy second. I spent my life spying on him—on my Pat—trying to discover how far he had gone, how far he was prepared to go. I never caught them together again, in spite of the fact that I fairly haunted the terrace under the study window, thinking that some afternoon or evening they might return. They never did. Mimi didn't come very often to the house, as a matter of fact.

"But on the evening of the nineteenth of June, at a little after half-past six, someone did come to the study window, who gave me the clew that I had been seeking so long. It was Melanie Cordier, of course. I was just coming back from the garden, where I had been tying up some climbing roses, when I saw her there by the corner near the bookcase. She had a book in her hands—quite a large, thick book in a light tan cover, and she was looking back over her shoulder with a queer, furtive look while she put something in it. She shoved it back onto the shelf and was starting toward the hall, when she drew back suddenly and stood very quiet. I thought: 'There is someone in the hall. When Melanie goes out it will mean that the coast is clear.'

"It wasn't more than a minute later that she left, and I started around to the front of the house to get to the study and see what she had put in that book. I was hurrying so that I almost ran into Elliot Farwell, who was coming down the front steps and not looking any more where he was going than if he had been stone blind. He said, 'Beg pardon and brushed by me without even lowering his eyes to see who it was, and I went on across the hall into the study, thinking that never in my life had I seen a man look so wretchedly and recklessly unhappy.

"No one was in the hall; they were all in the living room, and I could hear them all laughing and talking—and I decided that if I were to find what Melanie had put in the book I'd better do it quickly, as the party might break up at any minute. I had noticed just where the book was—on the third shelf close to the wall—

but there were three volumes just alike, and that halted me for a minute.

"The note was in the second volume that I opened. It was addressed to 'Mr. Patrick Ives. Urgent—Very Urgent.' I stood looking at that 'Urgent—Very Urgent' for a minute, and then I put it in the straw bag that I carry for gardening and went out through the dining room to the pantry to get myself a drink of water, because I felt a little faint.

"No one was in the pantry. I let the water run for a minute so that it would get cold, and then I drank three glasses of it, quite slowly, until my hand stopped shaking and that queer dizzy feeling went away. Then I started back for the hall. I got as far as the dining room, when I saw Pat standing by the desk in the corner.

"There's a screen between the dining-room door and the study, but it doesn't quite cut off the bit near the study window. I could see him perfectly clearly. He had quite a thick little pile of white papers in his hand, and he was counting them. They were long, narrow papers, folded just like the bond that he'd given me for Christmas, a year ago—just exactly like it. And while I was standing there staring at them, Sue called to him from the hall to come out on the porch and see his guests off, and he gave a little start and shoved the papers into the left-hand drawer and went out toward the hall.

"I gave him a few seconds to get to the porch, before I crossed through the study. I was terrified that if he came back and found me there he'd know I had the note and accuse me of it—and I knew that when he did that all the life that I'd died twenty lives to build for us would crumble to pieces at the first word he spoke. I couldn't bear to have Pat know that I suspected how base he was—that I knew that he was Dan all over again—a baser, viler Dan, since Dan had only had me to keep him straight, and Pat had Sue. I felt strong enough and desperate enough to face almost anything in the world except that Pat should know that I had found him out. So I went through the study and the hall and up the stairs to my room in the left wing without one backward look.

"Once in my room, I locked the door and bolted it—and pushed a chair against it, too, to make assurance triply sure. That's the only thing that I did that entire evening that makes me think I must have been a little mad. Still, even a biased observer could hardly regard that as homicidal madness.

"I went over to the chintz wing chair by the window and read the note. The chair was placed so that even in my room I could see the roses in the garden, and a little beyond the garden, the sand pile under the copper beech where the children played. They weren't there now; I'd said good-night to them outside just a minute or so before I finished tying up the roses. I read the note through three times.

"Of course, I completely misread it. I thought that what she was proposing was an elopement with Pat to California. It never once entered my head that she was referring to money that would enable Steve and herself to live a pleasanter life in a pleasanter place, and that her talk of hoodwinking Steve simply meant that she could conceal the source of the money from him.

"If I had realized that, I'd never have lifted my finger to prevent her getting it. I thought she wanted Pat. I'd have given her two hundred thousand dollars to go away and leave him alone. The most ghastly and ironical thing about this whole ironical and ghastly business is that if Mimi Bellamy hadn't been as careless and slip-shod with her use of the word 'we,' as she was with everything else in her life, she would be alive this day under blue skies.

"Of course it was stupid of me, too, and the first time that I read it I was bewildered by the lack of endearments in it. But there was all that about her hardly being able to wait, and how happy they would be; and the note was obviously hastily written—and I had always thought she had no depth of feeling. I suppose that all of us read into a letter much what we expect to find there, and what I expected to find was a twice-told tale. I expected to find that Pat was so mad about this girl that he was willing to wreck not only his own life for her but mine and Sue's and Polly's and Pete's. And I couldn't to save my soul think of a way to stop him.

"I was reading it for the third time when Melanie knocked at the door and announced dinner, and I put it back in my bag and pushed back the chair and unlocked the door and went down.

"When I heard Pat and Melanie and Sue all tell you that dinner was quite as usual that night, I wondered what strange stuff we weak mortals are made of. When I think what Sue was thinking and what Pat was thinking and what I was thinking, and that we could laugh and chat and breathe as usual—no, that doesn't seem humanly possible. Yet that's exactly what we did.

264

"Afterward, when they went into the study to look at the ship, I decided that I might just as well go into the rose garden and finish the work that I'd started out there. I'd noticed some dead wood on two of the plants, so I went to the flower room and got out the little knife that I kept with some other small tools in a drawer there. It's a very good one for either budding or pruning, but I keep it carefully put away for fear that the children might cut their fingers. Then I went out to the garden.

"For a while I didn't try to think at all: I just worked. I saw Miss Page coming back from the sand pile, and a minute or so later Sue came by, running toward the back gate. She called to me that she was going to the movies and that Pat was going to play poker. I was glad that they were not going to be there; that made it easier to think—and to breathe.

"As you know, she returned to the house. I don't believe she was there more than five minutes before she came running by again and disappeared through the back gate. I sat down on the little bench at the end of the rose garden and tried to think.

"I was desperately anxious to keep my head and remain cool and collected, because one thing was perfectly clear. If something wasn't done immediately, it would be too late to do anything. The question was what to do.

"I didn't dare to go to Pat. At bottom, I must be a miserable coward; that was the simple, straightforward, and natural thing to do, and I simply didn't dare to do it. Because I thought that he would refuse me, and that fact I couldn't face. I was the person in all the world who should have had most trust in him, and I didn't trust him at all. I remember that when I lie awake in the night. I didn't trust him.

"I didn't dare to go to Sue, either, because I was afraid that if she knew the truth—or what I was pleased to consider the truth—she would leave him, at any cost to Polly and Peter or herself. I knew that she was possessed of high pride and fine courage; I didn't know that they would be chains to bind her to Pat. I didn't trust her either.

"It wasn't Pat and Sue and Mimi Bellamy that I was looking at, you see. It was Dan and I and the boarding-house keeper's Trudie.

"I sat on the bench in the rose garden and watched the sunlight turning into shadow and felt panic rising about me like a cold wind. I knew that Sue hadn't a cent; her father had left her nothing at all, and she had refused to let Pat settle a cent on her, because she said that she loved to ask him for money.

"And I remembered ... I remembered that Dan had taken nineteen dollars and fifty cents out of the teapot. I remembered that I had learned only a few weeks before that I could only hope at best for months instead of years to live. I remembered that Sue couldn't cook at all, and that it was I who had done up all the children's little dresses in those New York days because she couldn't iron, and made them, because she couldn't sew— and I wouldn't be there. I remembered that the only relation that she had in the world was Douglas Thorne, and that he had four children and a wife who liked jewellery and who didn't like Sue. I remembered that the massage for Pete's knee cost twenty dollars a week, and that when Polly had had trouble with her ear last winter the bill for the nurses and the doctors and the operation had come to seven hundred and fifty dollars. I remembered the way Polly looked on the black pony and Pete's voice singing in the sand pile....

"And then suddenly everything was perfectly clear. Mimi, of course—I'd forgotten her entirely. She was waiting in the gardener's cottage now, probably, and if I went to her there and explained to her all about Polly and Pete, and how frightfully important it was that they should be taken care of until they could take care of themselves, she would realize what she was doing. She was so young and pretty and careless that she probably hadn't ever given them a thought. It wasn't cruelty— it was just a reckless desire to be happy. But once she knew— —I'd tell her all about Pat's ghastly childhood and the nightmare that my own life had been, and I'd implore her to stop and think what she was doing. Once she had stopped—once she had thought—she wouldn't do it, of course. I felt fifty years younger, and absolutely light-headed with relief.

"I looked at my little wrist watch; it said ten minutes to nine. If I waited until nine it would be almost dark, and would still give me plenty of time to catch her before she left. It wouldn't take me more than fifteen minutes to get to the cottage, and I much preferred not to have anyone know what I was planning to do. No one would miss me if I got back by ten; I often sat in the garden until then, and I had a little flashlight in the straw bag that I used at such times, and that would serve my purpose excellently coming home across the meadows.

"I decided not to go back to the house at all, but simply to slip out by the little gate near the sand pile and strike out on the path that cut diagonally across the fields to the Thorne place. There were no houses between us and Orchards, so I would be perfectly safe from observation. By the time I had gathered up my gardening things and looked again at my watch it was a little after nine, and I decided that it wouldn't be safe to wait any longer.

"It was a very pleasant walk across the fields; it was still just light enough to see, and the clover smelled very sweet, and the tree toads were making a comforting little noise, and I walked quite fast, planning just what I would say to Mimi—planning just how reasonable and gentle and persuasive and convincing I was going to be.

"The path comes out at an opening in the hedge to the left of the gardener's cottage. I pushed through it and came up to the front steps; there was a light in the right-hand window. I went straight up the steps. The front door was open a little, and I pushed it open farther and went in. There was a key on the inside of the door. I hesitated for a moment, and then I closed it and turned the key and dropped it into my bag. I was afraid that she might try to leave before I'd finished explaining to her; I didn't want her to do that.

"She heard me then, and called out from the other room, 'For heaven's sake, what's been the matter? I didn't think that you were ever coming.'"

"She had her back turned as I came into the room; she was looking into the mirror over the piano and fluffing out her hair. There was a lamp lit on the piano and it make her hair look like flames—she really was extraordinarily beautiful, if that red-and-white-and-gold-and-blue type appeals to you. Trudie'd had a mouth that curled just that way, and those same ridiculous eyelashes. And then she saw me in the mirror and in three seconds that radiant face turned into a mask of suspicion and cruelty and malice. She whirled around and stood there looking me over from head to foot.

"After a moment she said, 'What are you doing here?

"I said, 'I came about Pat, Madeleine.'

"She said, 'Oh, you did, did you? So that's his game—hiding behind a woman's skirts! Well, you can go home and tell him to come out.'

"I said, 'He doesn't know that I'm here. I found the note.'

"Mimi said, 'They can send you to jail for taking other people's letters. Spying and stealing from your own son! I should think you'd be ashamed. And what good do you think it's going to do you?'

"I came closer to her and said, 'Never mind me, Madeleine, I came here to-night to implore you to leave my son alone.'

"And she laughed at me—she laughed! 'Well, you could have saved yourself the walk. When he gets here, I'll tell him what I think of the two of you.'"

"I said, 'He's not coming. He's playing poker at the Dallases.'

"She went scarlet to her throat with anger, and she called out, 'That's a lie! He's coming and you know it. Will you get out of here?'

"I said, 'Madeleine, listen to me. I swear to you that any happiness you purchase at the price that you're willing to pay for it will rot in your hands, no matter how much you love him.'

"And she laughed! 'Love him? Pat? I don't care two snaps of my fingers for him! But I'm going to get every cent of his that I can put my hands on, and the quicker both of you get that straight, the better it will be for all of us.'

"I said, 'I believe that is the truth, but I never believed that you would dare to say so. You can't—you can't realize what you are doing. You can't purchase your pleasure with the comfort and security and health and joy of two little babies who have never harmed you once in all their lives. You can't!'

"She laughed that wicked, excited little laugh of hers again, and said through her teeth, 'Oh, can't I, though? Now get this straight too: I don't care whether your precious little babies die in a gutter. Now, will you get out?'

"I couldn't breathe. I felt exactly as though I were suffocating, but I said, 'No. I am an old woman, Madeleine, but I will go on my knees to you to beg you not to ruin the lives of those two babies.'

"She said, 'Oh, I'm sick to death of you and your babies and your melodramatics. For the last time, are you going to get out of this house or am I going to have to put you out?'

"She came so close to me that I could smell the horrid perfume she wore—gardenia, I think it was—something close and sweet and hateful. I took a step back and said, 'You wouldn't dare to touch me—you wouldn't dare!'

"And then she did—she gave that dreadful, excited little laugh of hers and put both hands on my shoulders and pushed me, quite hard—so hard that I stumbled and went forward on my knees. I tried to catch myself, and dropped the bag and all the things in it fell out on the carpet. I knelt there staring down at them, with the blood roaring in my head and singing in my ears.

"Judge Carver, what is it in our blood and bones and flesh that rises shrieking its outrage in the weakest and meekest of us at the touch of hands laid violently on our rebellious flesh? I could hear it—I could hear it crying in my ears—and there on the flowered carpet just in reach of my hand something was shining. It was the little knife that I'd been using to cut the dead wood out so that the live roses would grow better. I knelt there staring at it. That story of how all their lives flash by drowning eyes—I always thought that was an old wives' tale—no, that's true, I think. I could see the rose garden with all the green leaves glossy on the big Silver Moon.... I could see Pat and Sue laughing on the terrace, with his arm across her shoulders and the sun in their eyes and the wind in their hair.... I could see the children's blue smocks through the branches of the copper beech.... I stood up with the knife in my hand....

"She screamed only once—not a very loud scream, either, but she caught at the table as she fell, and it made a dreadful crash. I heard someone laugh outside, quite loudly, and I leaned forward and blew out the lamp on the piano. There was someone coming up the front steps; I stood very still. A bell rang far back in the house, and then someone tried the door.

"I thought: 'This is the end—they have known what has happened. If no one answers, they will batter down the door. But not till they batter down the door will I move one hairbreadth from where I stand—and not then.'"

"After a moment I heard the feet going down the steps, then again on the gravel of the main drive, getting fainter and fainter. I waited for a moment longer, because I thought that I heard something moving in the bushes outside the window, but after a minute everything was perfectly still, and I went over to the window and shut it and pulled down the shade.

"I knew that I was in great danger, and that I must think very quickly—and act quickly too. I found the little flashlight almost immediately, and lit it, and pushed down the catch and put it beside me on the floor. I wanted to have both hands free, and I didn't dare to take the time to light the lamp. I was afraid that the person who tried the door would come back. I had realized at once, of course, that if I took the jewels the murder would look like robbery—and I had to make sure that she was dead.

"That took only a minute; the rings came off quite easily, but the catch of the necklace caught, and I had to break the string. I knotted the things all into my handkerchief and put them into the bag, and the trowel and a ball of string that had fallen out, too, and the note, and a little silver box of candy that I kept for the children. There was the key to the front door too. I remembered that I must leave it in the lock as I went out. I used the flashlight to make sure that I wasn't leaving anything, and I was—the knife was still lying there beside her.

"It's curious—of all the things that happened that night, that's the only one that I can't account for. I don't remember how it got there at all—whether I placed it there or whether I dropped it or whether it fell—that's curious, don't you think? Anyhow, I picked it up and wiped it off very carefully on one of her white lace frills and put it back in the bag. And then I tried to get up, but I couldn't. I couldn't move. I knelt there, leaning forward against the cold steel of the little Franklin stove, feeling so mortally, so desperately sick that for a moment I thought I should never move again. It wasn't the blood; it was that perfume, like dead flowers—horribly sweet and strong.... After a minute I got up and went out of the room and out of the house and back across the meadow to the garden gate.

"I stopped only once. I followed the hedge a little way before I came to the path, and I stooped down and dug out two or three trowelfuls of earth close in to the roots and shook the pearls and the rings out of my handkerchief into the hole and covered it up and went on. At first I thought of putting the knife there, too, and then I decided that someone might have noticed it in the drawer and that it would be safer to be put back where it had come from.

"How are they ever able to trace people by the weapons they have used? It seems to me that it should be so simple to hide a little thing no longer than your hand, with all the earth and the waters under the earth to hide it in.

"It was the knife that I was washing in the flower room; it still had one or two little stains near the handle, but there wasn't any blood on my hands at all. I'd been very careful.

"After I'd put everything away I took the note and went upstairs. At first I thought that I'd tear it up, but then I decided that someone might find the scraps, and that the safest thing to do would be to keep it until the next day and burn it. And before the next day I knew that Sue and Stephen had no actual alibi for that night, and so I never burned the note.

"That's all. While I lay there in the dark that night—and every night since—I've tried saying it over and over to myself: 'Murderess—murderess." A black and bloody and dreadful word; does it sound as alien to the ears of all the others whose title it is as it does to mine? Murderess! We should feel differently from the rest of the world once we have earned that dreadful title, should we not? Something sinister, something monstrous and dark should invest us, surely. It seems strange that still we who bear that name should rise to the old familiar sunlight and sleep by the old familiar starlight; that bread should still be good to us, and flowers sweet; that we should say good-morning and good-night in voices that no man shudders to hear. The strangest thing of all is to feel so little strange.

"Judge Carver, I have written to you because I do not know whether any taint of suspicion still clings to any of those who have taken part in this trial. If in your mind there does, I will promptly give myself up to the proper authorities and tell them the essential facts that I have told you.

"But if, in your opinion, suspicion rests on no man or woman, living or dead, I would say only this: I am not afraid to die— indeed, indeed, I am rather anxious to die. Life is no longer very dear to me. Two physicians have told me this last year that I will not live to see another. I can obtain from them a certificate to that effect, if you desire. And I have already sent to my lawyers a sealed envelope containing a full confession, marked, 'To be sent to the authorities in case anyone should be accused of the death of Mrs. Stephen Bellamy, either before or after my death.' I would not have any human being live through such days as these have been—no, not to save my life, or what is dearer to me than my life.

"But, Judge Carver, will the ends of justice be better served if that boy who believes that my only creed is gentleness and kindness and mercy, and who has learned therefore to be merciful and gentle and kind—if that boy learns that now he must call me murderess? If those happy, happy little children who bring every bumped head and cut finger to me to kiss it and make it whole must live to learn to call me murderess?

"I don't want Polly and Pete to know—I don't want them to know—I don't want them to know.

"If you could reach me without touching them I would not ask you to show me mercy. But if no one else need suffer for my silence, I beg of you—I beg you—forget that you are only Justice, and remember to be merciful.

"Margaret Ives."

For a long time the judge sat silent and motionless, staring down at that small mountain of white pages. In his tired face his dark eyes burned, piercing and tireless. Finally they moved, with a curious deliberation, to that other pile of white pages that he had been studying when the messenger boy had come knocking at the door. Yes, there it was:

"An accessory after the fact is one who while not actually participating in the crime, yet in any way helps the murderer to escape trial or conviction, either by concealing him or by assisting him to escape or by destroying material evidence or by any other means whatever. It is a serious crime in itself, but does not make him a principal——"

He sat motionless, his unwavering eyes fixed on the words before him as though he would get them by heart.... After a long moment, he stirred, lifted his head, and drew the little pile of papers that held the life of Patrick Ives's mother toward him.

The blue paper first; the torn scraps settled down on the shining surface as lightly and inconsequently as butterflies. Then the white ones—a little mound of snow-flakes that grew under the quick, sure fingers to a little mountain—higher—higher—blue and white, they were swept into that great brass bowl that had been so conveniently designed for ashes. A match spurted, and little flames leaped gaily, and a small spiral of smoke twisted up toward the white-robed lady above the door. Across the room, between the windows beyond which shone the stars, John Marshall was smiling above the dancing flames—and she smiled back at him, gravely and wisely, as though they shared some secret understanding.

THE END

Made in United States
Troutdale, OR
03/03/2024

18168826R00153